Praise for
and *CATEGORY FIVE*

"*Category Five* packs all of the punch of a full force hurricane. This Mach One thriller deftly pulls the reader to the edge of disaster with heartrending skill . . . Philip Donlay is to aircraft what Tom Clancy is to submarines. If you love the old-style Clancy, you won't put Donlay down."

—**Kathleen Antrim,** Author of No. 1 Best Seller *Capital Offense*

"Superbly written adventure thriller of man vs. nature! A gripping, tension-filled saga that entangles the reader's attention and does not let go."

—**Midwest Book Review**

"Philip Donlay's *Category Five* is a sensational thriller which I couldn't put down."

—**Roger Corman,** acclaimed film producer

"*Category Five* is a great book. The last 100 pages were better than most movies!"

—**Steve Thayer,** *New York Times* bestselling author of *The Weatherman* and *The Wheat Field*

"*Category Five* starts fast and moves like a whirlwind. With realistic characters, a tight plot, compelling science, and over-the-top action, *Category Five* grips you by the throat and doesn't let go."

—**D.P. Lyle, MD,** author of *Murder and Mayhem: A Doctor Answers Medical and Forensic Questions for Mystery Writers* and *Forensics for Dummies*

"Buckle-up and hang on for a great ride! Philip Donlay has crafted a superb adventure that is intense, visually descriptive, and fast paced with no letup in action."

—**Richard Drury,** pilot, author of *My Secret War* and columnist for *Airways Magazine*

"Philip Donlay's *Category Five* is a remarkable debut. It is an exciting read, charged with action, terrific characters, splendid writing, a real adrenaline rush."

—**Pat Frovarp,** *Once Upon A Crime Mystery Books,* Minneapolis, MN

"Donlay has created a compelling, pop-disaster thrill ride."

—**Minneapolis Star Tribnue**

"An excellent debut novel, this combination thriller, action and disaster book has well-developed characters. Mr. Donlay's male lead character, Donovan Nash, is reminiscent of Dirk Pitt. The female lead, Dr. Lauren McKenna, is a meterological scientist. Her job is to oversee the deployment and tracking of a Doppler imager that detects global weather patterns that could affect U.S. military operations overseas. McKenna and her team are trying to leave Bermuda in advance of Hurricane Helena. Nash, who has a history with McKenna, is a pilot who owns Ecowatch, a private rescue operation that's sent to transport the team to safety. When an assassination attempt against McKenna's life fails, Nash must risk his live to save the woman he loves. This book is peppered with scientific details, and the characters will appeal to both men and women."

—**Laurie Trimble,** Special Contributor to *The Dallas Morning News*

CATEGORY FIVE

A NOVEL

Philip S. Donlay

new york

DISTRIBUTED BY PUBLISHERS GROUP WEST

An ibooks, inc. Book.

Distributed by Publishers Group West
1700 Fourth Street, Berkeley, CA 94710

ibooks, inc.
24 West 25th Street
New York, NY 10010

The ibooks World Wide Web address is:
www.ibooks.net

ISBN 1-4165-0487-7
First ibooks printing 2005
10 9 8 7 6 5 4 3 2 1

For my son Patrick

Courage is the price that life exacts for granting peace,
The soul that knows it not, knows no release
from little things;
Knows not the livid loneliness of fear,
Nor mountain heights where bitter joy can hear
the sound of wings.

–Amelia Earhart

ACKNOWLEDGMENTS

This book would not have been possible without the skilled professionals of the National Weather Service and the National Oceanic and Atmospheric Administration. A further thanks to the Defense Intelligence Agency, FlightSafety International, United States Navy and the United States Air Force. I am forever in debt to these talented men and women.

For her wisdom and patience Sheren Frame is without peer. A special thanks also to Nicole Barron, Jonathan Mischkot, Adam Marsh and Emily Burt whose editing skills are second to none. Tom Brandau, Mike McBryde and Bo Lewis for their countless insights and inspiration. To my friends at Harvey's, thank you for the perfect oasis.

A final heartfelt thanks goes to both Rebecca Norgaard and Kimberley Cameron, their steady hands and unwavering encouragement lit the way.

CATEGORY FIVE

CHAPTER ONE

Torrential rain, whipped by gale force winds, lashed at the vehicle. Driven sideways, the deluge pelted the car with sharp, staccato bursts. From the passenger's seat, Dr. Lauren McKenna could feel her apprehension rise. The last reports she'd received indicated that the storm was nearing category two strength. Sustained winds of at least 96 mph would be spinning around the deepening low pressure area. The picturesque island of Bermuda lay directly in the hurricane's path, and time was running out for a smooth departure back to the States.

As she always did, she imagined the storm as it appeared from a satellite. The view from space was always the most breathtaking. She loved the concentric swirls of clouds, the symmetry that finally formed the small eye in the center of the cyclone. In all of her years of tracking hurricanes, she'd never ceased to marvel at nature's largest destructive force.

She was soaked. Her thin cotton blouse clung to her skin and water trickled down her bare legs from waterlogged shorts. Her auburn hair was plastered to her neck. She felt half-naked and more than a little self-conscious. Earlier, she'd caught their driver, Peter, eyeing her, and she'd wanted to cover up. But now, as the storm grew worse, his attention never left the road in front of them. The narrow ribbon of asphalt was visible for only a second after each pass of the wipers. Leaves and branches tumbled across the rain-drenched road, then vanished. She hoped the other car had made it safely to the airport; she'd sent it ahead to get the Air Force plane to wait for her.

Lauren looked anxiously at her watch. It was only ten in the morning, yet the darkness of the storm made it feel like evening. They were cutting it close. If the winds from the hurricane reached a certain level, the plane would leave without them. She'd been warned in her briefing: the Air Force was adamant about not risking damage to one of its aircraft. But the installation of her equipment, then making sure everything was operational, had taken far longer than she'd planned. Her precious experiment was now on a U.S. Navy destroyer headed to intercept the eye of the hurricane. Part of her wanted to be on board when *Jonah* was deployed, but the Defense

Intelligence Agency had vetoed that plan. She'd been ordered back to Washington to begin phase two of the operation.

If everything went as planned, *Jonah*'s Doppler imaging would open up a new dimension in understanding the inner workings of a hurricane. Lauren's primary job within the DIA was to oversee the monitoring and tracking of weather patterns on a global basis. Any meteorological events that could impact military operations were carefully analyzed. From there, her department would disseminate the information to the Pentagon for use all over the world. Eleven days ago, Lauren had begun to run some highly advanced computer simulations on what was then still an unnamed tropical disturbance. Using information on sea temperature, winds aloft, and a dozen other variables, her results had been startling. Lauren's computer models predicted that Hurricane Helena, as it was now named, possessed the ability to develop into what could only be described as a super-hurricane.

It had been a year of drastic weather extremes across North America, from record heat and drought in the southeast to violent thunderstorms that ripped across Canada and the northern United States. Massive squall lines had spawned an unprecedented number of tornadoes—huge F-5 twisters had strewn a trail of death and destruction in Minnesota, Michigan, and southern Canada, places where tornadoes rarely formed.

For the last six months, Lauren had been studying this transformation in the usual weather patterns. To her, it was clear a major climatic shift was well underway, and if she were right about Helena, the worst was yet to come. Lauren knew she was now caught in a mad race to get off Bermuda before the full force of the storm stranded her on the tiny island.

"How much longer until we get to the airport?" Lauren had to raise her voice to be heard above the howling wind.

"Maybe fifteen minutes...maybe more," Peter replied nervously. He didn't look at her. The Mercedes swayed as each burst of wind shook the car, threatening to spin it off the pavement.

Lauren turned to look at her colleague in the back seat. Victor Krueger's eyes were filled with alarm, his face ashen. Both hands were balled up into fists and he leaned against the car door as if ill. He nodded and tried to say something, but his thin features produced only a grimace. Despite her own rising concerns, Lauren smiled to try to encourage him. She had fifteen years' more experience with hurricanes than Victor did. A recent graduate from the Earth Science program at MIT and a new addition to the DIA, Victor was a bright young man full of energy and eagerness. But right this moment she knew he was terrified. He'd become deeply concerned hours ago, as the first angry bands of the storm began to come ashore. Lauren had seen it before—intelligent, rational people, when faced with a hurricane, yielded to something deep within them. Lauren thought of it as an almost primitive, reptilian urge to flee from a great threat. Whatever it was, Victor was in its clutches.

A vicious gust tore at the car. Lauren could feel the tires begin to slide on the saturated road. Just as quickly, Peter slowed and straightened the vehicle, his knuckles white on the steering wheel. Without thinking, Lauren reached down and pulled her seat belt a fraction tighter. Out the side window she could see palm trees as they danced and bent as the force of the storm whipped them into a frenzy. Just beyond, she caught a glimpse of the ocean. The heavy gray clouds blended with the water, making them appear as one. Only the raging whitecaps differentiated sea from sky.

She guessed the gusts were close to 50 mph. She just hoped for everyone's sake that the Air Force jet would still be there. Otherwise, they'd find nothing but an empty ramp. From past experience, she knew every other aircraft had left the storm-swept island hours ago. Her work had come first, but the last thing Lauren wanted to do was ride out the storm on Bermuda.

With a pressing weight, she remembered the promise she'd made to herself and to her daughter. Abigail was staying with Lauren's mother in Baltimore. It'd been the first time she'd left her daughter for more than just a day. Lauren remembered how painful it had been to kiss her little girl goodbye. Only days earlier, Abigail had taken her first tentative steps. Lauren welled up with emotion at the memory: chubby legs teetering back and forth, the look of determination on Abigail's face as she moved unsteadily toward Lauren's waiting arms.

So much had happened since Lauren had shown her devastating hurricane prognosis to the others in her department, then finally to her boss, Director Reynolds. Her actions had set off a chain reaction within the DIA, and propelled her to try to launch *Jonah* nearly a month ahead of schedule. It seemed as if the storm had taken over her life; Helena was now her second child—a fast developing one that held the possibility of growing into a lady with unimaginable fury. At this moment, feeling the first sting from the approaching hurricane, Lauren felt like she was a million miles away from home...and Abigail.

Peter tried to brake as the road curved sharply. He swore as he pumped the pedal repeatedly. Lauren's attention was instantly drawn to him. A huge gust of wind blasted them as he fought for control of the vehicle. Lauren could feel the car begin to slide. She leaned away from the door as they began to skid toward the trees that lined the road. Peter over-controlled, his hands spinning the wheel while he desperately jammed on the brakes. The car fishtailed, then abruptly whipped end for end. Horror gripped Lauren as the vehicle catapulted off the pavement.

She braced herself. The car picked up speed and plummeted down the steep embankment. Someone's scream dissolved in the sharp crack of exploding glass. Thrown against her shoulder harness, Lauren was jerked side to side as they careened into the first tree, then the second. Metal crumpled against the force of the impact. The car buckled and flipped upside down, sliding down the incline on its roof. Lauren covered her face with a forearm as the windshield caved in, showering her with glass and mud. The sound of screeching metal assaulted her ears. In the next instant, the car slammed into the bottom of the culvert and came to a violent stop. The air was forced from her lungs as something pushed her from behind and pinned her hard against the leather dashboard.

Dazed, Lauren used her free hand to clear the mud from her mouth and nose. She struggled to pull in a breath, but couldn't. Terrified she was going to suffocate, she could only struggle in silence. Her head swam as she finally managed a tiny breath, then another. She swallowed and choked on a mixture of water and dirt. Slowly, she was able to open each eye—they fluttered and filled with tears as she carefully wiped away the debris.

Lauren felt as if she were still spinning and it took her a moment to get her bearings. Slowly, she understood that the car was resting upside down under a canopy of trees. Hanging from her seat, Lauren could feel the shoulder harness as it dug hard into her skin. The dashboard was wedged firmly against her chest. She cried out in alarm as she discovered she could barely move her legs. The floor of the culvert was only a foot from her head. She tried to turn and find her companions, but one arm was wedged behind her, the other trapped near her face. She managed a quick glimpse before the pain forced her head forward. But in that instant, she saw that Peter had been killed. Jutting out from his throat were the remains of one of the windshield wipers; it had snapped free and plunged like a missile into the vulnerable flesh. Her stomach lurched at the grisly sight. She swallowed and fought the urge to vomit. Lauren tried bravely to hold on to what little composure she had left. The seat where Victor had been was empty, the door ripped from its hinges.

To her right, almost outside her field of vision, she saw something move. Painfully, she turned, trying to see what it was. A moment later she saw it again, black boots...Someone was walking near the car.

"HELP ME! I'M IN HERE!" Lauren screamed with relief. Barely ten feet away, she knew whoever was out there would be able to hear her cries.

"HELP ME. I'M TRAPPED!" Lauren couldn't understand why the person hadn't rushed to her. Was it Victor...Why didn't he respond?

"PLEASE HELP ME!" she cried out again. "VICTOR, IS THAT YOU? Help me get out of here."

She looked each way as far as she could, but the boots were nowhere to be seen. A feeling of doom seeped into her consciousness. She prayed that whoever it was would come back and pry her free of her prison. But after several agonizing minutes, all she could hear was the relentless howl of the storm.

"PLEASE GET ME OUT OF HERE!" Lauren's voice was shrill, on the edge of complete panic.

Rain pelted the ground around her. She felt utterly alone. Whoever had been outside the car had vanished. She threw herself back and forth, trying to kick her legs, use them for leverage—anything to free herself. But she was stuck. Regardless of what she did, she remained trapped upside down in the wreckage of the car. Her throat tightened as she thought of Abigail. If she died, her daughter would be too young to have any memory of her. All of her hopes and dreams for Abigail's life would vanish. Desperate, Lauren knew she was on the verge of losing everything. She forced herself to take several deep breaths; she needed to try to calm down. If her scientific training had taught her anything, it was to try to stay objective and rational.

Lauren cocked her head as a different noise began to register. Her heart soared—it had to be someone coming to rescue her. She strained to look out the smashed window, the sound coming closer. A new and more pressing fear overwhelmed her as she discovered the source of the commotion. She did have company; water was beginning to flow toward her. The ground had soaked up all the rain it could, and now the runoff was cascading down to the bottom of the culvert. With her head only inches from the soil, Lauren knew it wouldn't take the water very long to pool and fill the space inside the car.

Lauren struggled once again to free herself, but each movement was met with resistance. Twisting and turning, she became angry. The thought of dying in the ugly brown water set her brain on fire. All of the things she wanted to accomplish flashed before her. The mistakes of the last two years reared their ugly head and pummeled her. She saw her daughter, those beautiful blue eyes full of warmth and love. They were the same eyes of Abigail's father, a man her little girl had never met. Lauren choked back a sob that threatened to completely unhinge her. The water splashed and gurgled as it picked up momentum. Seconds later it touched the top of her head. Lauren screamed against the wind and thrashed in vain at the forces holding her prisoner.

CHAPTER TWO

Donovan Nash looked at his watch, then out at the low gray clouds that swept over the Bermuda airport. The rain was racing sideways in billowing sheets. He swore under his breath...they were late. He'd been pacing back and forth in the lobby of Operations. He paused to look out the window. Thirty yards out on the tarmac sat the aircraft he'd just landed. It was the only airplane on the empty desolate field. The highly modified Gulfstream IV SP glistened in the rain—bold blue and gray stripes ran the length of the white fuselage, then swept up the tail, ending with the "Eco-Watch" name proudly emblazoned around the symbol of the globe. On the nose, *Spirit of da Vinci* was neatly printed below the cockpit. Funded by a private foundation, Eco-Watch was one of the premier nonprofit scientific groups in the world. In the eight years since its inception, Eco-Watch had grown from humble beginnings to become one of the leading research organizations in existence. Both of Eco-Watch's specialty aircraft were easily booked two years in advance. The primary focus was hurricane and typhoon study, meteorological events that presented the greatest threat to the world's population. But the overall mission statement was to study any atmospheric condition, from polar weather formations, to holes in the ozone layer, to El Niño. Whatever science needed to find, Eco-Watch would find a way to make it possible.

A few hours ago, Donovan had gotten a frantic call. A key group of scientists was stranded in Bermuda. The Air Force jet that had been scheduled to make the pickup had mechanical problems and canceled. The fact that the call had come from the Pentagon had been unusual, but the government was just one of the many organizations that contracted Eco-Watch's services. During the Atlantic hurricane season, Eco-Watch was on constant alert and often flew missions to support the hurricane hunter flights operated by the Air Force. Just as well, thought Donovan as he studied the sky. The storm had picked up strength in the last hour or so; he doubted the Air Force would have stuck around this long.

Donovan chose to operate under the title of Director of Aircraft Operations—very few people knew that he'd founded Eco-Watch. It took him out of the spotlight and gave him far more freedom than he'd have had otherwise. The last thing he ever wanted to do was get stuck behind a desk. Plain and simple, he loved to fly and did so at every opportunity. As one of the front-line pilots, he enjoyed a camaraderie and closeness with his people he'd never have sitting in an office. He looked at his watch again, then at the water streaming off the roof. These people were cutting it close. Donovan had more leeway than the military, and there was still time left before the full force of Helena was forecast to hit Bermuda.

The plate glass rattled and a low howl resonated above the sound of the rain. Donovan shifted his gaze to his reflection. He'd just turned forty-five years old, though he knew he was still as lean and muscular as he was ten years ago. Genetics had been kind to him. He stood six-foot two, yet had to do very little to maintain his ideal weight. But there were other subtle changes that hadn't escaped him. The lines around his blue eyes were getting more pronounced, as was the gray that had begun to appear at his temples. His strong angular features seemed to have softened. Most men approaching middle age might groan inwardly at the changes, but Donovan welcomed them. Anything that distanced him from the past was welcome.

"They're here. They're coming through the gate now," a voice called across the room from behind the counter. "They'll drive right out to the plane."

"Thanks." Donovan breathed a sigh of relief. They could be airborne in fifteen minutes, home to Eco-Watch's hangar at Dulles airport in Washington within two hours. He started for the door, then stopped.

"Hey. What's the wind right now?"

The station manager looked at the instruments. "It's showing 030 degrees at 25 knots, gusting to 40. I guess I don't need to tell you the barometer is dropping fast."

Donovan smiled. "I think I figured that part out already. Good luck and thanks for all your help." It was no use to try to stay dry. Donovan bolted out of the office and with his head down against the stinging rain, ran toward the waiting jet.

A cream-colored Toyota Land Cruiser pulled onto the ramp, then slowed. They'd been told to expect a military airplane, and Donovan guessed the driver must be unsure of where to go. He waved it toward the Gulfstream. The headlights flashed in acknowledgment, and the four-wheel-drive Toyota quickly covered the distance to the waiting Eco-Watch jet.

The doors of the Land Cruiser burst open, and a large man eased himself down to the ground. Donovan dispensed with any formalities and headed to the rear of the vehicle. He was certain they'd have luggage and equipment and he wanted to get everything loaded as fast as possible. The occupant quickly joined him there.

"I'm Dr. Carl Simmons." The huge man extended a beefy hand. "We were expecting an Air Force jet."

"I'm Captain Nash." Donovan shook Simmons' hand. Simmons was a hulk of a man, huge jowls hiding any inkling that he had a neck. His small eyes looked out of scale on his massive face. Donovan wasn't used to looking up at very many people, but Simmons towered a good four inches above him. "Change of plans. Get on board and I'll start bringing the luggage up."

"The others aren't here yet, are they?" Dr. Simmons asked as he lifted two of the heaviest cases.

"What others?" Donovan snapped his head toward Simmons. Any hope for a quick departure had vanished.

"They're in another car. I left before them to try to get here in time. We can't leave without them."

"We will if I say so," Donovan said, bristling at Simmons' overbearing tone.

"You are going to wait, aren't you?" Dr. Simmons turned his head as a gust of wind and rain peppered them.

Donovan nodded. "I'll wait as long as I can. Now please, get on board while I stow this stuff."

With help from the driver, Donovan hoisted the last of the bags up into the rear cargo compartment. Once everything was aboard, Donovan turned to him.

"Dr. Simmons said there was another car. Any idea how far behind they were?"

"I shouldn't think very far," the driver shouted above the wind. "But conditions are getting worse. They should be here any time."

"Does the other car have a radio?"

The driver shook his head.

"Can you sit tight for a minute? If we get stranded, we might need your help." Donovan could feel the first prickle that something wasn't quite right, like a splinter lodged under his skin. It was a feeling he'd learned never to ignore.

"They paid me for all day," the driver replied. "I'll wait in the car."

Donovan hurried to the stairs that led up into the Gulfstream. He took the steps two at a time, then ducked through the door into the airplane. He pulled the vinyl curtain back over the entrance to try to keep the rain out. Nicolas Kosta, a new Eco-Watch pilot who was along as part of his orientation, eagerly handed him a towel. Nicolas was a study in contrasts. Still in his late twenties, he sported a shaved head and black wire frame glasses. His wide brown eyes and thick eyebrows dominated his narrow face. One moment he seemed twenty-seven, the next he came across as being someone much older.

"We ready to go?" Nicolas asked.

Donovan shook his head. "There's another car. It should be here any moment. Where's Michael? Is he up front?"

"Yes sir," Nicolas reported. "Strapped in, ready to get us out of here."

Donovan nodded. Michael Ross was his closest friend, and a senior captain at Eco-Watch. He and Michael had flown together for years. Donovan knew him well enough to know he probably had a finger poised on the start button. Being caught on the ground with a hurricane sweeping in from the ocean was the last thing either of them wanted.

"Nicolas." Donovan saw the young man stiffen. He wished Nicolas would relax. He was a solid pilot and hard worker. He'd been through the grueling interview process and had the job. "Get Dr. Simmons settled. He seems a little wound up. I'll be in the cockpit. Be ready to leave on my signal."

"Yes sir."

Donovan pulled the towel around his neck and made his way through the narrow passageway to the cockpit. He felt the usual satisfaction at how well his hand-picked crew did their jobs. Eco-Watch, under Donovan's guidance, was a tight-knit group of professionals, at times more of an extended family than a business. He had nearly forty people under his direct supervision, a mixture of pilots, mechanics, engineers, and support staff. Donovan prided himself on knowing each one as more than just an employee. He felt confident that Nicolas could handle things in the back, and that Michael would have everything prepared up front. He opened the door and was greeted by a rush of cool, conditioned air—a sharp contrast to the clinging oppressive atmosphere being pumped northward by the hurricane.

Michael Ross looked up from the chart he was studying. Intelligent blue eyes stood out from a handsome tanned face. At thirty-seven years old, he possessed an irresistible combination of good looks and natural charm. His closely cropped blonde hair and muscular build made him appear as if he'd just stepped off of a Southern California beach.

"About time. Are we finally ready to get the hell out of here?"

"No. We're waiting on one more group," Donovan said. "They should be here shortly."

"Oh, perfect. They can't all ride in the same car?"

Donovan shrugged, then used the end of the towel to wipe his forehead.

"You look a little damp. Is it raining outside or something?" Michael flashed a wry grin in Donovan's direction.

"A little drizzle. Nothing too bad." Donovan matched his friend's tone. Michael's sarcasm was legendary, and constant as the rising sun. Donovan's trained eyes darted around the cockpit. He could see Michael had everything ready to go. The driving storm buffeted the airplane and sheets of rain blurred the view out the Gulfstream's windows.

"What's the wind doing now?" Donovan asked, a crease forming on his forehead as he felt the heavy Gulfstream shudder in the gale.

"Let me check." Michael picked up the microphone. "Bermuda tower. This is Eco-Watch 02. Say the wind, please."

"Wind is 030 degrees at 25 knots with peak gusts to 43 knots."

"Roger, we copy." Michael looked up at Donovan. "It's increased a little from when we landed. But nothing too bad yet. The tower told me that if the wind reached sixty knots they'd have to evacuate the cab and we'd be on our own."

"Hopefully, we'll be long gone before it gets that strong."

"How long we going to give the other car? I'd sure hate to be sitting here when Helena rolls in from the Atlantic."

"Captain?"

Donovan turned at the sound of the voice. He found Dr. Simmons inching his bulk forward.

"Yes?"

"I'm starting to get worried. I would have thought they'd have been here by now. Dr. McKenna was deeply concerned about making this flight before the storm stranded us. All the work we've done here needs to be monitored from Washington."

"Dr. Lauren McKenna?" Donovan felt the air rush from his lungs; his stomach lurched as if he'd just been punched. His face flushed and chills rose from the flesh of his arms.

"Well, yes. She's the project manager," Simmons explained.

Donovan tried to collect himself. Dr. Simmons' worried expression cut through him like a knife.

"Give me the portable VHF radio."

"What are you doing?" Michael eyed him warily as he reached for the small hand-held aviation transmitter and gave it to him.

"I'm going to find her," Donovan said, quietly. He ignored the look of concern etched on Michael's face.

"I'll try to stay in contact with you on 122.8." Donovan checked that the radio's battery was fully charged. "If the wind gets anywhere close to fifty knots you and Nicolas get the *da Vinci* out of Bermuda. I'll ride the storm out here." Donovan knew his friend was getting ready to try to talk him out of this.

"Are you sure?"

Donovan's eyes met Michael's. "That's an order."

They both knew Donovan's painful history with Lauren McKenna. Michael had been with him through the difficult weeks after she'd left—his friend had stayed close, tried to help however he could. It was something Donovan would always be thankful for. It'd been over a year since she'd gone—but in so many ways it seemed like only yesterday. His conflicted emotions gnawed at him. It was a familiar feeling.

"I'll be fine. Just don't put the plane at risk."

"Donovan, I'm serious. Why don't you let me go?" Michael started to get up out of the seat. "I'll find her. You take care of these people."

Donovan shook his head. "Sorry, Michael. But I'm pulling rank on this one. Monitor 122.8. We'll try to stay in touch."

Without waiting for a reply, or having to look again into Michael's disapproving eyes, Donovan pushed past Dr. Simmons and bounded down the air-stairs to the waiting Land Cruiser. Oblivious to the rain, he hurried to the passenger door and hoisted himself inside the Toyota.

"Let's go!" he snapped. "Back the way you came. We need to find the other car—and hurry. We're running out of time."

Donovan buckled his seat belt as the driver nodded. The Toyota lurched forward and headed toward the gate that led out of the airport.

"My name is Ian," the driver said in a clipped British accent. He put out his hand as he braked hard and waited for the gate to open.

"I'm Donovan." He returned the firm handshake. Donovan felt a small measure of relief that Ian's sense of urgency seemed to match his own. He saw the look of determination on his ebony face.

"What kind of car are we looking for?" Donovan asked.

"It's a white Mercedes sedan." The gate inched back just enough for them to pass and Ian gunned the Toyota through the narrow opening out onto the empty road. "It has a government seal painted on the side."

As they sped away from the airport, Donovan wasn't sure what he dreaded most: that something terrible had happened to Lauren, or how he would feel when he was face to face with her.

Donovan stiffened as they rounded a curve and Ian stepped hard on the gas pedal. Ahead of them was the causeway that stretched across Castle Harbour. He'd been over the bridge many times, but never when such big waves were breaking against the pylons. Geysers of water exploded into the air where they were ripped apart by the raging wind. Donovan could feel his leg muscles tighten at the sight. Each large swell dashed rhythmically against the concrete, leaving a frothy wake on the road itself. Ian held the Land Cruiser steady as they plowed through the axle-deep water. Donovan felt his skin turn warm and clammy. He wanted to close his eyes as the water arched toward them and broke over the Land Cruiser. Donovan held his breath. His heart palpitated in his chest—the pounding moving up through his neck and finally hammering at his temples, threatening to crush him as each wave reared up and splashed against the metal of the Toyota. He took his eyes from the waves and looked up at the clouds. Donovan tried to reason with his demons. In his mind the wild ocean had become a living, breathing entity—a forbidding creature that would, on a whim, turn deadly and murderous. From first-hand experience, Donovan knew what a cold, calculating killer it could be. Once upon a time, the sea had taken everything from him.

Donovan sat frozen, unable to stop the barrage of memories. With vivid clarity, he could picture the sudden early morning storm: the deafening thunder and horizontal rain, mountainous waves that had built relentlessly, finally capsizing and smashing his family's chartered schooner. He'd been fourteen years old, and in the chaos of the storm, he'd been thrown overboard, flung helplessly into the giant waves of the southern Pacific Ocean. It was the day he'd become an orphan.

"Man, I've never seen the harbour looking quite like this." Ian held the wheel steady as they pushed across the bridge. "I'd say she's a bit riled up."

Water crashed into the side of the Toyota. Donovan tried to control his breathing. It was as if the sea were attempting to reach in and snatch him from the vehicle. He clenched his teeth, trying to convince himself the weight of the Land Cruiser was stronger than the waves. Donovan knew that if he were somehow washed into the ocean it would surely kill him. The sea had been waiting over thirty years for a second chance.

"Whoa." Ian turned the Land Cruiser hard into a big wave. The vehicle skidded on the blacktop.

They were almost across. Donovan let out a breath of thanks as they once again crossed over onto solid land. It had been years since he'd been threatened by such close proximity to an angry ocean. He tried to blot out the image of how awful it would be if he were once again adrift in such a sea. Ian slowed as they veered right. Donovan noticed a sign; they'd just turned onto Blue Hole Road. He thought of the return trip he'd have to endure to get back to the plane and wished desperately that there were another way to the airport.

"You really going to fly in this?" Ian peered up at the tumbling mass of clouds racing past just above the terrain.

"It's not that bad." Donovan swallowed hard. Flying was far easier than what he'd just gone through. Trying to recover from crossing the causeway, Donovan pulled the portable radio from his belt and switched it on. He waited a moment until the numbers were visible on the display. He verified it was set to 122.8, then held it to his mouth.

"Eco-Watch 02, this is Donovan. Radio check."

"Loud and clear." Michael's voice came through the small speaker.

"Roger. I'll keep the frequency open. If you need to get out of here let me know."

"So far so good. Just find them and get back."

"Will do." Donovan couldn't miss the note of concern in Michael's voice. He turned to Ian.

"Is there any chance they would have taken another route?"

"Haven't driven in Bermuda very often, have you? There's usually only one way to get anywhere. I know the driver; Peter's an old pub mate of mine. I can guarantee you he came this way."

Donovan silently urged Ian to drive faster. He could feel his patience begin to chafe and dwindle. Lauren could be in trouble. It was as if a small voice inside of him was screaming at them to hurry.

"Oh, shit." Ian slowed quickly and maneuvered the Toyota around a large branch that had fallen across the road. "The wind is getting a bit dodgy up here on the hill."

Donovan could see they were gaining elevation as they drove west. It was growing even darker to the southeast. The bulging gray clouds looked close enough to touch as rain hurtled out of the sky with a vengeance. Since they'd left the airport, Donovan hadn't seen a single sign of life: houses and businesses were boarded up; there'd been no other traffic on the road. Donovan rubbed his temples. That he was searching the island for Lauren seemed somehow abstract, and yet at the same time, his pulse raced with both anticipation and fear.

They came around a sharp turn, Ian slowing the Land Cruiser as the tires skidded and slipped on the soaked pavement. He straightened the Toyota and continued up the hill.

"Ian! Go back!" Donovan twisted in his seat. He wasn't sure what he'd seen, but something had registered.

"What was it?" Ian brought the Toyota to a stop. He shifted into reverse, switched on the emergency flashers and carefully began to back up.

"Right here. Stop the car. See those two trees? They're broken in the wrong direction against the storm."

Donovan jumped out into the stinging rain. He ran as fast as he could to the edge of the pavement. Seconds later, he could see the rear end of a white sedan at the bottom of the culvert. It was lying on its roof, the metal along the side dented and scraped. Without hesitation, he jumped down the muddy ravine. He slid, arms outstretched, trying to keep his balance on the slick ground. His momentum quickly carried him down to the wrecked Mercedes. Donovan was unable to stop his forward motion. He twisted and went down hard as he slammed into the fender. Oblivious to the pain, he pulled himself up on his knees and staggered forward to get to the passenger compartment. As he neared the front door he saw a hand—it was the slender shape of a woman's. There was also a bracelet—a handmade, braided gold original. Donovan had bought the bracelet for Lauren in London. Terrified, Donovan grabbed her wrist as he sank to mid-calf in a watery quagmire. He pulled the limp arm, but found he couldn't move her out of the car. A frantic inspection told him that she was wedged in by the wreckage. Terror welled up in his throat as he caught a glimpse of auburn hair floating in the muddy water.

"Oh God. Lauren, hang on!" Donovan couldn't erase the image of his own mother's hand as she slipped beneath the water for the last time. He'd been frozen, unable to help her—the same paralysis threatened to seize him at the sight of Lauren.

"Donovan! Catch!" Ian yelled from the top of the hill. He threw down a wire cable from the Toyota's bumper-mounted winch.

His trance broken by Ian's words, Donovan released Lauren's lifeless hand and was on his feet. The cable had tangled and only come half-way down the slope. Donovan scrambled up the treacherous hillside. Driven by the fear that he could already be too late, he dove for the heavy hook. His hand closed around the cold metal and he slid back down toward the car. Working as fast as he could, urging himself to go even faster, Donovan looped the cable around the rear axle and secured the hook. His hand came away covered with a thick, reddish liquid. For an instant he feared it was blood, then recognized it as brake fluid.

"Pull!" Donovan screamed and gave Ian a thumbs up as he staggered away from the Mercedes. He tried to position himself to get to Lauren in a hurry when the car was clear of the water. The slack in the cable vanished. Donovan could hear metal begin to bend as pressure was put on the axle. He took heavy gulps of air. "Please hurry," he whispered to himself. Donovan felt like every one of his nerve endings was on fire as the Mercedes started to budge. His muscles were taut, ready to spring into action. With agonizing slowness, the Mercedes began to inch up the hill.

"Faster!" Donovan yelled, but he knew Ian was doing the best he could. As the car moved another foot, Donovan charged to the passenger side door. He reached in and found Lauren's hand. He pressed his fingers into her wrist searching for a pulse, he found none. He held her tight as the powerful winch began to overpower the suction holding the car. Water began to pour from the seams as the winch pulled the vehicle to higher ground. Donovan held Lauren's lifeless hand until he could finally begin to see her face; first her chin, then her blue lips, finally her nose and closed eyes.

"Stop!" Donovan yelled. Without hesitation, Donovan reached in and slid his fingers into her mouth. It felt free of debris. Crouched awkwardly on his knees, Donovan leaned in and put his mouth over hers and began forcing air into her lungs. With his powerful right hand, he pushed on her breastbone, urging her heart to beat. Her face was slack and gray. Donovan wasn't religious, but he was cognizant of a barrage of prayers going skyward...pleading for God to let her live. Tears burned his eyes as he blew his life-giving air into her mouth. To his left he saw Ian's hands reach in and grasp her wrist, checking for a pulse.

"Nothing yet," Ian said, gravely. "Keep going man! Don't stop."

Donovan focused on each breath. He willed her to open her eyes. He desperately wished there was a way to inject his life force into her. He held her head in his hands and fixed his gaze on her closed eyes.

"Lauren!" he shouted, not sure if he was more angry or afraid. "Stay with me, Lauren. Don't give up!" Donovan forced more air into her lungs. It was nothing at first, but he thought he felt her mouth quiver. He took a fresh breath and again put his mouth to hers, pushing his oxygen deep into her lungs.

Lauren twisted her head and gagged. Brown water spewed out of her mouth and nose. She turned away and coughed, her breath coming in raspy gulps.

Donovan felt his eyes fill with tears. He tried to support her head with his hands but she turned away. He didn't think he'd ever been so happy to see her green eyes as when she finally opened them.

"Lauren. Can you hear me? Are you hurt?" Donovan could see her try to focus on him. He watched as Lauren seemed to fight through the fog that clouded her brain.

"Donovan?"

"I'm here." A tidal wave of relief swept over Donovan. There was blood on her face from a small cut. He thought of any one of a hundred things that might have precluded him from getting to her in time. The reality of how close it'd been sent an uneasy chill to the pit of his stomach.

"I think I'm still stuck," she said, weakly.

"We'll take care of that in a minute," Ian announced, standing.

"How many others were with you in the car?" Donovan pressed. Besides Lauren, the Mercedes contained only one person...still pinned behind the steering wheel was the driver, obviously dead. Donovan felt a stab of remorse; he knew it was Ian's friend.

"There were three of us all together." Lauren turned to Peter, still strapped into the car next to her. She bit her lip and turned back to Donovan. "Victor. I think he survived. I saw his feet before..."

"I think he's over there," Ian said, quietly. He touched Donovan on the shoulder and pointed to a body lying a dozen feet away. From the angle of the head, it was clear the man had suffered a broken neck.

"Let's get you out of there." Donovan gently squeezed her shoulder. He stood up and looked around for something to pry with.

"Why don't you unhook the cable," Ian managed to say, his face filled with remorse at the sight of the carnage. "We can use the winch to get her free."

Donovan took his eyes from Lauren and looked at the seat, studying how it was wedged in relation to the surrounding metal.

"It's worth a try," Donovan replied. "But please, let up on the slack slowly, we don't want the damn thing to slide back down into the water."

"I understand." Ian began the arduous climb up the rain-washed hill. He turned and waved when he was in position.

Using hand signals, Donovan carefully instructed Ian to let up on the tension of the winch. He was relieved the Mercedes remained stationary. Quickly, Donovan unhooked the cable from the axle. He was about to move away when something caught his eye. Washed clean by the rain, he could see the brake line—and the sharp cut in the shiny black material. He frowned as he processed the implications.

"You still doing okay?" he asked, leaning down and searching for the best place to secure the hook.

"I think so," Lauren answered, her voice stronger. "I don't think I'm hurt. Just get me out of here."

Donovan pulled on the hook to test if he had it secured. "Here we go." Donovan watched as Ian pulled the slack out of the cable. With a loud popping noise the seat broke loose. Donovan quickly slid Lauren from the damaged car and fell backward. Relieved that she was free, he held Lauren protectively in his arms.

"Let's move it, folks!" Ian yelled and waved from the top of the hill. "I think this bloody storm's getting worse. Unhook the cable."

"We have to get you to the hospital." Donovan jumped to his feet. "Can you get up?"

"I'm fine. Nothing seems to be broken, just bumps and bruises." Lauren tested her limbs and touched the cut over her eye. It was still bleeding.

"Let's go. We need to hurry." Donovan stood and held his hand out toward her.

"Oh my God!" Lauren covered her mouth at the sight of Victor's body. Lauren's eyes shot to his feet and saw the tan deck shoes. It hadn't been Victor who was outside the car after all. She turned to say something to Donovan, but hesitated.

"He went quick." Donovan still had his hand outstretched.

"Wait. I have to find my computer." Lauren pulled her eyes from the gruesome sight of Victor's corpse.

"We don't have time." Donovan said, his words punctuated by the sound of thunder as it echoed in the distance.

"It's right here," Lauren pointed. "All of my work is stored inside."

Donovan waited impatiently as she knelt down and snatched the bag. With a splash, her smashed laptop spilled out of a rip in the canvas and dropped to the ground. Donovan could see her computer was destroyed, a jumble of wires and circuit boards exposed to the elements.

"Oh no." Lauren hung her head and collected the pieces.

"We've got to go." Donovan took her by the arm and with strong measured strides negotiated the steep incline up to the road. He was breathing heavily as they reached the Toyota. Ian was still reeling in the cable to the winch. On the hilltop, the wind ripped at their soaked clothes. A steady roar came from the wildly swaying trees.

Lauren took a measured look at the sky. "The storm is coming much faster than we thought."

"How bad is it going to get?"

"I hope I'm wrong, but this one could be one of the worst ever."

Donovan saw the matter-of-fact expression on Lauren's face, the rain running off her furrowed brow as she looked skyward. He felt the chilling effect of her words. She was rarely wrong when it came to her work. Donovan thought of Michael and the others back at the airport.

"Why are you in Bermuda?" Lauren lowered her head and looked at him. "There's supposed to be an Air Force jet to fly us out."

"They couldn't make it. Michael and I got the call this morning, so we flew over to pick you up. As far as I know he's still waiting for us." Donovan hoped this stroke of luck wasn't lost on Lauren. The Air Force wouldn't have come looking for her.

"Michael and the airplane are still on the island?"

"I'm not sure." Donovan shrugged. He knew he'd been out of radio contact for quite a while. "Michael may have been forced to leave by now."

"Climb in," Donovan said, opening the rear door for her. "We need to get out of here as fast as we can."

Lauren nodded. She strapped in and set what was left of her destroyed computer on the seat next to her.

Donovan could see Ian struggling with the winch. He looked past the Toyota and could see the cable stretched taut; it had caught on something while Ian was pulling it up.

"What's wrong?"

"It's almost loose," Ian replied. "I'll have it up in a jiffy."

Donovan heard the whine of the winch above the storm. The cable buffeted against the strain.

"Ian, no!" Donovan shouted into the teeth of the wind.

With a sound like a rifle shot, the hook broke free...a giant steel bullwhip arcing through the air toward the Toyota. Donovan threw himself to the ground just as the cable sliced through the fender above his head. He rolled over and covered himself as it coiled and fell on top of him. Above the wail of the hurricane, Donovan heard Ian scream in agony.

Donovan threw off the cable and jumped to his feet. Ian lay writhing on the ground, both hands covering his bloody left shin.

Ian looked up at Donovan, then at his leg. "How bloody stupid!" He grimaced at the pain.

"Oh no!" Lauren had heard the cable rip into the car and had jumped out into the storm. She knelt down beside Ian, his splintered shin bone visible as the rain washed away the blood.

"We've got to get you to the hospital." Donovan turned his eyes from Ian's broken leg, the white bone a sharp contrast as it jutted from the dark skin. Any hope of making it back to Michael and the *da Vinci* had just been lost. But Ian came first. Without him Donovan knew he would have never found Lauren.

"Let's get him in the back of the car." Lauren jumped to her feet. "I'll get the door."

"Hang on. I've got a better idea." Donovan hurried to the front seat and grabbed the portable radio. He keyed the microphone and went back to where Lauren was waiting with Ian.

"Michael, this is Donovan. You still there?"

"Just barely. Where are you? I've been trying to call."

"It's been a little crazy. We found Lauren and she's okay, but we need an ambulance. Call the tower, see if they can use a land line to get someone out here."

"Give me your exact location."

Donovan was buoyed by the fact that, as usual, Michael never missed a beat, though it came as a mild surprise that he was still on the ground.

"Hang on a second." Donovan turned to Ian.

"We're on Harrington Sound Road. About a quarter mile west of Shark Hole," Ian managed between clenched teeth. "They'll know where I'm talking about."

Donovan relayed the information.

"Good plan." Ian tried to smile. "Now just leave me here and you two try to make your plane."

"Nonsense," Lauren said immediately. "We're going to wait until someone arrives. Do you want us to try to get you into the car and out of the rain?"

"I appreciate the thought. But I think I'd rather only get up once." Ian kept his hands gripped tightly around his leg. As if giving in to the pain, he rested his head on the wet asphalt.

Donovan could see Ian's breathing was shallow and rapid. He was going into shock. He caught the worried look on Lauren's face. No doubt she'd reached the same conclusion.

"Donovan, this is Michael."

"Are they sending someone?" Donovan asked.

"I'm told there's an emergency vehicle only a couple of minutes away. You should have company real quick. Now tell me what happened, and are you headed back here anytime soon?"

Donovan could tell from the strain in Michael's voice that it was time to fly the *da Vinci* out of Bermuda.

"We're both fine; it's Ian who's hurt. Lauren and I are going to stay here until someone shows up, then we're on our way. My guess is we're only about fifteen minutes from the airport. If you can wait, that's great. If not, come back and get us when you can. But don't risk the airplane."

"I understand," Michael replied. "We'll try to sit tight, but I'd suggest you keep the sightseeing to a minimum."

"Yeah, we'll do that. I'll keep you posted. Donovan out." He went back and tucked the radio back inside the Toyota. He felt a knot begin to form in his stomach. He'd just lost the man who was going to get them back across the causeway. The simple fifteen-minute drive loomed large as Donovan pictured the crashing waves. Just as he was closing the door, a police car rounded the corner, its blue flashing lights ablaze. Relieved they'd responded so fast, Donovan looked at his watch and noted the time. He slammed the door and met the officer as he was getting out of the car.

"We have a man down." Donovan pointed at Ian. "Plus, there's a wrecked car down the hill. The driver, Peter I think is his name, plus an American scientist were killed."

"What on earth happened up here?" The policeman knelt down and looked at Ian.

Ian looked up, and with a flash of recognition addressed the policeman by name. "Davie, I'll explain everything later. These people are with the United States government. They have a jet waiting at the airport. Let them go before this bloody storm gets any worse."

The officer eyed the rain-drenched group cautiously.

"For Christ's sake," Ian urged. "It's who I've been working with for the past two days. Top notch folks, they're scientists."

"Wait one moment. Don't anyone leave." The officer jumped up and went back to his police car.

"I'm going to reel in the rest of this cable." Donovan quickly figured out the winch. "Lauren, can you help me make sure it doesn't get tangled up again?" Donovan knew at some point, Michael was going to have to leave. He just hoped that he and Lauren were on board when he did. With Lauren's help, he quickly secured the cable, then crouched down next to Ian.

"You hanging in there?"

Ian nodded. "You'll be out of here in a minute. Davie's a good man. He'll find out in short order how important the doctor is—that she needs to get off the island as soon as possible."

"Before we go, I want to thank you for everything." Donovan gripped Ian's shoulder and made a mental note to see to it that every one of Ian's medical expenses were covered by Eco-Watch.

"Buy me a pint next time you're out this way."

"You can count on it. One other thing," Donovan leaned closer. He didn't want Lauren to overhear him. "I think the Mercedes has a cut brake line. Make sure someone gives that car a good going over after we leave. I'll be in touch."

Ian nodded, but there was no hiding the look of bewilderment and concern in his eyes.

The policeman hurried out of his car. In his hand he had several highway flares.

"I've got it from here. The ambulance will be here shortly. You're free to go."

"Thank you." Donovan hesitated as he climbed into the front seat of the Land Cruiser. All he could think about was the causeway. His mouth was suddenly bone dry. Lauren slid in beside him and fastened her seat belt. Donovan took a deep breath and put the Toyota in gear. Without taking his eyes from the road, he reached for the radio.

"Michael. We're on our way."

CHAPTER THREE

"You'd better hurry." Michael's concerned voice sounded over the radio. "The wind just spiked up over 50 knots. It's getting a little ugly here in paradise. The controller just gave us permission to leave at our own discretion. Seems they're getting ready to evacuate the tower."

"Oh, great." Donovan handed the radio to Lauren. He needed both hands on the wheel as he punched the gas pedal and accelerated the Land Cruiser down the narrow asphalt road.

Lauren studied Donovan. Her conflicted feelings shifted into high gear. She couldn't help but wonder if greater forces were at work here, if he'd been thrust back into her life for a reason. She could clearly remember pleading with the heavens to let her make things right before she died. But now, seated next to him, it all became very complicated again. With Donovan's attention riveted to the road, she let her eyes drink him in. He looked thinner, leaner than before. His hair was shorter, and there was more gray at the temples. She watched as his biceps flexed, fighting the Toyota through each turn. It took her a moment, but she noticed that he was working his jaw muscles and—despite the low light—Donovan was squinting as if he were in pain.

"Are you okay?" Lauren wondered if he'd injured himself and hadn't said anything. Donovan was perhaps the bravest and most capable man she'd ever met. But right now, something was terribly wrong. She knew him well enough to know he was in distress.

"We may have a little problem up ahead."

"What?" Lauren turned to look out the windshield, not knowing what to expect.

"Around the next curve is the causeway across the harbor. It was nearly covered with water when we left the airport. My guess is it's a lot worse now."

"Donovan." The radio burst to life. "It's Michael. How much longer? I'm getting ready to start the engines. It's getting pretty bad. If you're going home with me you'd better get here quick."

"Damn it!" Donovan kept his eyes on the road. "Tell him we're almost there."

Lauren keyed the radio. "Michael. It's Lauren. Donovan says we're almost there."

"Lauren!" Michael's surprise could be heard over the frequency. "We've got the Gulfstream's weather-radar pointed at the storm. There are some big thunderstorms coming in fast. Tell Donovan if we don't take off in the next ten minutes we may be stuck here."

"We understand." As Lauren looked at Donovan, she could see the color had left his face. She turned her attention out the windshield and knew why. The narrow bridge was nearly covered with angry water. She remembered his recurring nightmares, how he'd wake up trembling and gasping in the darkness. She recalled the horrible events he'd endured as a boy. He'd finally told her about the gigantic waves, the boat that had sunk. Before he was rescued, Donovan was adrift in a typhoon for almost two days. He hadn't gone into much detail, but she had no doubt that he'd been horribly traumatized by the ordeal. And now, right in front of them, was his worst nightmare.

Donovan slammed on the brakes and they skidded to a stop.

Lauren could see a vein in his neck pounding wildly. He lowered his head and fought to breathe. "I can drive if you want." Lauren's heart went out to him. She reached across and put her hand on his shoulder.

"Give me a second." Donovan squeezed his eyes shut as if trying to blot out the images in his head.

"Take your time." Lauren slid her hand down and put it inside his. She squeezed it, trying to give him strength. "I know how hard this is. If we miss the plane it's okay. It's not your fault. We can go back and ride out the storm in Hamilton." Lauren was surprised to feel a hint of pleasure at the thought of being marooned in Bermuda with him.

"Donovan! Where are you? It's time," Michael reported. "I've got to get this plane out of here!"

"What shall I tell him?" Lauren fingered the transmit button.

Donovan pulled his seat belt tighter, his voice full of uncertainty. "Tell him to taxi out. We'll try to get there before he leaves."

Lauren repeated the instructions. She saw Donovan's blue eyes narrow at the wave-tossed road. He put both hands on the wheel and gunned the engine. The Land Cruiser leapt toward the narrow bridge. She held on as the Toyota hit the first wave. Silently, she urged Donovan onward as he battled the effects of the wind and water. He made the necessary corrections instantaneously. Water crashed and exploded over the road. The sound of the roaring waves filled the interior of the vehicle. Lauren could see the death-grip he had on the steering wheel; his heaving chest told her he was hyperventilating. She knew he was caught somewhere between this bridge and a raging ocean over thirty years ago. Images of a fourteen-year-old boy and a sinking boat filled her head. She felt helpless to do anything for him as the car plowed into the turbid water, hesitated, then shot forward as it broke free.

"We're going to make it!" Lauren shouted in encouragement. She could see his legs shudder and shake from the strain. Without thinking, she keyed the microphone on the radio.

"Michael! We're crossing the bridge. Are you still there?"

"I'm taxiing out to the end of runway 12. We haven't got any time left. The radar shows nothing but solid red echoes...the worst of the thunderstorms will be here in minutes. We have to be airborne before then."

Lauren felt Donovan put his foot down hard on the accelerator. The Toyota groaned as a wave slammed into the side and threatened to fish-tail them. She knew it wouldn't take much to fling them over the low railing. Lauren had nearly drowned once today—she prayed it wouldn't happen twice. The wheel jerked in Donovan's hands as another wall of water broke over the Land Cruiser. They were driving blind, the frantic windshield wipers momentarily useless. She felt an impact, and heard the sound of screeching metal as the Toyota sideswiped the railing.

"I can see the end!" Lauren called out above the roar of the wind and waves. "Keep going. We're almost across!"

Donovan guided the Toyota as straight as he could. In a rush of inertia the Land Cruiser shrugged off the last wave and burst into the clear.

"We made it!" Lauren shouted in triumph. "There's still time."

Donovan shifted out of low gear and mashed the gas pedal. They careened around a corner, his foot touching the brake to keep the speeding Land Cruiser on the road.

Through a gap in a line of buildings, Lauren caught sight of the Gulfstream as it moved away. "I see them!"

"Get down, Lauren. We're not stopping!" Donovan pointed the Toyota at the chain link fence.

She slid down in her seat and braced herself. He gripped the wheel and winced as they plowed into the gate. The Land Cruiser jumped and bucked as it mowed down the metal. The windshield cracked but held. Lauren raised her head and saw that a half mile down the deserted airport the Gulfstream had taken the runway. The water behind the jet was whipped into a frenzy as Michael increased the thrust on the *da Vinci*.

"TELL HIM WE'RE HERE!" Donovan shouted.

Lauren already had the radio to her mouth. "MICHAEL! WE'RE COMING UP FAST ON YOUR RIGHT. WAIT!"

In an instant, Lauren saw the plume behind the airplane vanish as Michael pulled the power back.

"LET'S MOVE IT, FOLKS," Michael urged over the radio.

Donovan spun the Toyota around the wind-buffeted plane. He slammed on the brakes and switched off the ignition.

As Lauren gathered her computer, someone was already lowering the stairs on the jet. Donovan reached across the seat to help, then they both jumped from the Toyota and ran for the plane. Moments later, winded and soaked, they were inside the *da Vinci*.

"I've got the door!" Nicolas yelled and stepped aside so Donovan could take his rightful place up in the cockpit.

Donovan nodded and quickly made his way forward. He burst onto the flight deck. He expected an irreverent remark from Michael, or at least something sarcastic, but what he found was a look of concern mixed with relief.

"You okay?" Michael asked.

"Yeah. Thanks for waiting." Donovan strapped in and adjusted his seat. He heard Nicolas secure the cabin door behind him. The light on the panel winked out. They were ready to go.

"I want full left aileron," Michael ordered. "This could get interesting."

Donovan did as instructed. His eyes swept the instrument panel. The six large CRT screens glowed brightly. The weather radar showed a solid line of red and yellow precipitation echoes directly off the end of the runway. The airspeed indicator was jumping back and forth, meaning the wind was pushing almost sixty knots. Donovan's confidence in Michael was total. A former Naval aviator, Michael was a natural pilot, probably the best he'd ever seen.

"I'm ready when you are."

"Here we go." Michael stood on the brakes and pushed the two throttles up to the stops. Behind them, mounted high on the aft fuselage, the two Rolls Royce Tay engines spooled up and strained against the airframe. When they reached maximum thrust, Michael released the brakes. The *da Vinci* leapt forward into the fury of the approaching hurricane.

"80 KNOTS!" Donovan called out. He could feel Michael countering the cross-wind, the powerful windshield wipers battling the deluge of rain as they picked up speed.

"OH, SHIT!" Michael cried out.

Donovan stiffened. Dead ahead, blown by the storm, three 55-gallon drums were being rolled and tumbled across the runway. Donovan sat helpless. There was no way they were going to miss them.

"I've got it!" Michael grabbed the controls and hauled back.

"We're only at 100 knots!" Donovan shouted. He knew they needed another 30 knots to get airborne. He tensed and waited for the sensation of the landing gear crashing into the barrels. He could see Michael battle the controls as he yanked the Gulfstream off the ground. The jet responded as it shuddered into the sky. Donovan knew they couldn't have missed the barrels by more than a few inches. In a heartbeat, the momentary lift was depleted and the *da Vinci* thudded heavily back onto the pavement. Michael released the back-pressure on the controls and struggled to keep the airplane on the runway as they continued to accelerate.

"V1." Donovan called out the takeoff safety speed. "Rotate!"

Once again, Michael pulled back on the controls. This time the Gulfstream broke free of the earth and clawed steeply into the turbulent sky.

"Gear up." Michael held on as the airplane slugged its way through the low clouds. "We can't go straight ahead. I've got to start a turn to the northeast."

Thrown around in the small cockpit by massive jolts of turbulence, Donovan forced his hand to the gear lever. The rain was deafening as it vaporized on the nose of the jet. He could see Michael trying to counter the heavy wind shear as the airplane climbed into the conflicting rivers of air. Up and down drafts tossed them savagely in the sky. Donovan watched as huge sheets of static electricity blew from the airframe. He took a quick look out the side window. The wing of the G-IV was flexing up and down as they plowed through the storm.

"Should I be talking to anyone?" Donovan turned to Michael, the microphone in his right hand.

"Maybe the man who built these things." Michael said between clenched teeth.

Donovan kept his eyes glued to the instruments. Michael had the Gulfstream banked hard, turning as fast as he could. The worst of the weather was quickly falling away behind them. The turbulence began to let up as well as the rain.

"Bermuda said to contact New York Oceanic directly," Michael explained. "The frequency is already set. Surprisingly, seems like we're the only airplane in the area. Go figure."

Donovan made eye contact with Michael, happy the sarcasm had returned. A look of guarded triumph was etched on Michael's face. Donovan knew he and Michael felt the same sense of relief. Unspoken words passed between the two close friends. They both knew they'd avoided disaster by only inches. Later, over drinks, Donovan knew they'd laugh at how close it had been, toast their continued good luck, then add this to their list of harrowing flights. Donovan gave Michael a nod that he understood their shared thoughts. Then he raised the microphone and called Air Traffic Control.

"New York. Eco-Watch 02 is airborne off of Bermuda. We're climbing on course, out of twelve thousand feet going to flight level 230."

"Roger Eco-Watch 02. You're the only airplane in my airspace. You're cleared to climb to flight level 410. In fact, you're cleared direct to Dulles. Report level at 410."

Donovan read back the clearance, then sat back in his seat. Michael had the *da Vinci* climbing like a rocket. The powerful jet hurtled upward toward the promise of clear sky above the hurricane. He thought of Ian. He hoped the brave driver had made it to the hospital. He wondered about the severed brake line and the two dead men. But most of all, his thoughts were fixed thirty feet behind him...on Lauren.

CHAPTER FOUR

The sleek Gulfstream burst free from the last tendrils of the storm into the stark blue sky at 35,000 feet. As far as Donovan could see, a carpet of white clouds marked the upper reaches of Hurricane Helena.

"Gotta love that sight," Michael remarked as he slid on his dark glasses. He adjusted the autopilot's rate of climb. All the aircraft systems were working perfectly.

"Yeah, feels good," Donovan said absently, his attention focused on the time remaining until they touched down back at Dulles.

"Why don't you send Nicolas up? I'm thinking you might like to dry off." Michael looked at Donovan over the top of his sunglasses. "Then... I don't know. You could go back and visit with our passengers or something?"

"I'm fine." Donovan stopped what he was doing and looked across the cockpit. "So she's back there. Nothing's changed."

"Nothing except you," Michael challenged. "I saw the expression on your face when you charged out of here to go find her. I hardly think you'd have gone off like you did if it had been Dr. Simmons who was missing."

Donovan knew Michael was right. But at this very moment he had no idea what he felt. Seeing Lauren had affected him on so many levels. He wasn't sure if he was elated, angry, or simply frustrated that it all might mean nothing at all. He'd saved her, and that remained the most important aspect of the day. The fact she'd nearly died was like a bad dream he couldn't shake. He thought of the brake line—and couldn't help but wonder if the accident had somehow been orchestrated. And if so, by whom? But there weren't any answers here in the cockpit. Michael was right. He needed to get up and go to the back. He unfastened his harness.

"I'm going."

"It's about time," Michael said, without looking up.

"I'll be back in a little while," Donovan replied, defensively.

"I hope not. For over a year you've wanted nothing more than to talk to Lauren. This is your chance; now go. Send Nicolas up. He deserves a little time in the cockpit. Talk to her. She's more important than sitting there on your ass playing copilot."

"You better be right. If not, I'll be back shortly, and we can discuss your poor judgment all the way back to Dulles." Donovan slipped out of his seat and quietly left the cockpit. He made his way down the narrow aisle and paused to survey the interior. Instead of a luxurious corporate layout with plush seats and a stateroom, the Eco-Watch jet was a flying scientific platform. The austere cabin had four research stations on each side of the aisle. In the rear of the jet were the racks that housed the computers and data collection equipment. The beauty of the aircraft was that, within a short time, different probes and sensors could be installed, set up, and run. The *da Vinci* was the perfect airborne platform for the host of scientific endeavors in which Eco-Watch was involved. Back at Dulles, the *Spirit of Galileo,* a sister ship, sat in the hangar, undergoing a hurried conversion to support a high-altitude research mission. Each year, different universities and other worthy groups were given access to the aircraft. It was Donovan's ongoing vision that one day there might be a global fleet of Eco-Watch aircraft. But despite Eco-Watch's deep-pocketed supporters, each Gulfstream cost almost fifty million dollars. He would have to be patient, which wasn't his strong suit.

Donovan stood in the semi-darkened passageway. He could see Lauren seated at one of the stations. She had a blanket pulled up over her shoulders. She looked small and vulnerable, though Donovan knew she was anything but. The cut on her forehead had been bandaged. She'd pulled her wet hair away from her face. He was caught off-guard by how beautiful she looked. His thoughts fell back in time to a moment not unlike this one...when they'd flown their first hurricane-hunting mission together.

They'd met before a series of reconnaissance flights. Donovan didn't believe in love at first sight, but since the moment he laid eyes on Lauren his life had never been the same. He'd first seen her at a pre-flight briefing, and he'd been totally wrecked by her startling green eyes, her delicate features. He remembered sitting transfixed at the way her face magically lit up when she smiled. She was tall, five foot nine, graceful and athletic. Donovan had been mesmerized by the way she moved. Each insignificant gesture, from brushing her mid-length auburn hair behind her ear, to walking across the room, seemed charged with sexual energy. She was all business as she addressed the team and discussed what she expected from the Eco-Watch flight crew. Donovan was captivated by her intellect, her command and poise as she spoke. After three days of flying sorties out of Miami, he couldn't stand it any longer. He'd asked her out to dinner and to his surprise she'd accepted. In a short time he'd learned that she was an only child, born in Baltimore and now living in Virginia. Her father had been career Navy and they'd moved all over the world as she grew up. She was eight years younger than he, had done her undergraduate studies at Princeton, then earned her master's and a Ph.D. in earth science from MIT. Three magical evenings later, it felt as if they'd known each other for years. After dinner, they'd walked to the beach, and he'd leaned in and kissed her. Later that evening, she'd come to his hotel room and they'd made love.

That night marked the beginning of the best year of his life. For nearly twelve months, they'd traveled, laughed, grown close in a very short time. It was perfect. Donovan could feel all of the barriers he'd carefully constructed slowly begin to peel away. Lauren was a remarkable woman... right up until the day she'd left.

He'd returned from a flight and she'd met him at the hangar. He could still picture her standing next to his old Range Rover. She'd worn a light blue sundress, her hair tumbling down around her shoulders. She seemed to him the most beautiful woman in the world, and his heart soared. He took her in his arms and hugged her, but when he went to kiss her, she turned and accepted it on her cheek. It was then that he saw her eyes brimming with tears. In a blur of anger and pain Lauren demanded to know who Elizabeth was...was she the blond woman she'd seen him with? Tears trickled down her face as she stood defiantly, waiting for his answer.

Donovan lowered his head—he couldn't believe his two worlds had overlapped. He knew instantly what Lauren was talking about...what she'd somehow seen. The last thing he'd ever do was be unfaithful, but there was no way he could explain. The blond was Stephanie VanGelder, the niece of the man who'd raised him. She was someone he'd grown up with; Stephanie was like a sister to him. He also couldn't tell her about Elizabeth. That name was one of the few links with the man he used to be. Donovan's carefully crafted existence hinged on his silence. With tears streaming down her face, Lauren waited for the answers he couldn't give. She shook her head, then whispered quietly to him. She explained that she didn't want him ever to try to find her. Then she said goodbye. Donovan heard the unbearable words as if they had been spoken down a long tunnel. She'd been so direct and succinct. He'd been caught completely off guard. All he could do was stand there, his life shattered, as she got into her car and left.

Devastated, and despite what she'd asked, he'd tried to find her. But she'd moved, left her job...and vanished.

Donovan remained motionless, caught up in his powerful memories, until Dr. Simmons began a small round of applause. Lauren looked up and smiled in recognition of Donovan's actions. Embarrassed at the attention, Donovan nodded, then moved back through the cabin.

"Well done, Captain." Dr. Simmons extended his hand. "Not only for saving Dr. McKenna, but getting us off the island."

"You're welcome." Donovan lowered his head. From past experience he instinctively hated being the center of attention. Lauren looked up and their eyes met briefly. She nodded her approval at Dr. Simmons words.

"It was a group effort," Donovan added. "I'm glad it all worked out. I am sorry about Victor, though. There wasn't anything we could do for him."

At the mention of Victor, everyone became silent.

"Can I get anyone anything?" Donovan said after an appropriate interval.

"I could use a slug of bourbon." Dr. Simmons studied his hand as if to see if it were still shaking.

"Sorry, we don't have any alcohol on board," Donovan explained, then added, "Though that directive might come under review."

"What would you like me to do, sir?" Nicolas got to his feet and eyed the cockpit door.

Donovan couldn't take his eyes from Lauren. "Why don't you go up and keep Michael out of trouble? I'm going to stay back here for a while."

"Yes sir. There are some dry clothes in the back if you want to change." Nicolas sidestepped Donovan and hurried forward.

Donovan took a deep breath and made his way to Lauren. Her face broke out in a gentle smile; her eyes found his. He stood next to her and could see she was tinkering with her shattered computer. He couldn't believe she could have lost a fellow scientist, nearly drowned, and could now fuss with a computer that had obviously been destroyed. All he found in her magical green eyes were more questions.

Lauren looked up, waiting for him to speak.

"I don't think your computer is going to make it." Donovan didn't know what else to say. His mind was a blur of images. A million questions flew through his mind and he discarded every one of them. He eyed the lavatory at the rear of the plane and considered the promise of dry clothes.

"I know," Lauren replied, and pushed the pieces away from her.

"Well...I was just taking a break, thought I'd change into some dry clothes. I'm glad you're okay." The tension between them had just gone off the chart. It felt like the temperature in the cabin had suddenly risen twenty degrees. He mentally cursed himself as he walked away from her. It served him right, he decided. Nothing more had happened today than running into an ex-girlfriend. Furious with himself for expecting more, he grabbed the spare flight suit and stormed into the lavatory.

Lauren leaned back against the seat and felt the first waver of emotions. She didn't know what to do. She fought for control, staunchly refusing to unravel in the back of Donovan's jet. Yet the guilt and remorse cascaded down and threatened to shatter her resolve. If she knew the right thing to do, she'd do it in a heartbeat. But she'd left him for valid reasons. Despite how wonderful he was on the surface, there were things about Donovan Nash that she couldn't accept. He possessed a mysterious side she could never quite pin down. It was almost as if he were two different people. She thought back to the day she'd overheard the ominous message on his answering machine. Donovan had been in the kitchen. He must have thought she was out of earshot. Lauren had distinctly heard a woman's voice, calling to confirm a day, a flight number, and a time for Donovan to meet Elizabeth. She was arriving at Dulles International Airport. As if to confirm her worst fear, Donovan had quickly erased the message. More than anything, Lauren had wanted to block out what she'd heard, but couldn't. The next day, she'd driven to the airport at the appropriate time. She'd spotted his Range Rover and waited. Across the parking lot, she finally saw Donovan—walking hand in hand with a beautiful blonde. The woman was pressed close to him, her face beaming. Lauren couldn't miss the unmistakable flash of a wedding ring on her hand.

The drive back to Washington had been a blur of tears and anger. When she'd confronted him later, his face had drained of color. His shocked look told her everything she'd needed to know. It was obvious he'd been caught cheating on her. She knew in that instant that she could never stay with him. She'd chastised herself over and over for missing the obvious clues. The fact that they never went out much, or spent any time with his friends. How much he'd resisted any of her attempts to get him to attend public functions. His sterile apartment, which she'd chalked up to his being a bachelor, was obviously a safe house for his extramarital affairs. She'd fallen for a married man and hadn't seen it coming until it was too late.

She'd already endured the first month of their breakup when she discovered that she was pregnant. More than anything she wanted the baby, but she didn't want Donovan. It was an easy decision; the last thing she wanted was to break up his marriage. As she'd told herself a thousand times since then, she'd done the right thing. But if that were the case, why was her heart telling her something different right now?

Lauren heard the door to the lavatory open. She felt Donovan's presence as he came up behind her.

"Donovan?" She hesitated as he stopped and turned. She could see the flash of annoyance that crossed his face.

"Yes?" he managed politely, waiting impatiently for her to speak.

Lauren hadn't expected him to act so distant. His blue eyes were cold and forbidding.

"I did want to thank you for everything you did today. You and Michael were wonderful." She bit her lip as his expression remained icy.

"Just doing my job," he said flatly, then turned to go.

As he walked the dozen steps to the flight deck, she wanted to call out to him. The silence between them threatened to choke her. Without looking back he opened the cockpit door, slipped inside, and carefully shut her out.

Lauren felt her eyes well with the first hint of tears. She lowered her head and tried to erase the scornful look Donovan had given her. She wasn't sure what had set him off. What did he want from her? Whatever it was, Lauren was positive he'd be even angrier to discover he had a daughter. Lauren knew in her heart that what she had to tell him wasn't what he wanted to hear.

She thought of Abigail and absently fingered her smashed computer, glad she'd had the presence of mind to grab her laptop from the wreckage. Lauren sniffed as she fought her emotions.

At least she'd get a new computer, one without Cheerios stuffed into the printer port 'compliments of Abigail.' Lauren shook her head and smiled weakly at the memory. She turned the computer over to see her daughter's handiwork. The smile vanished at the sight of the perfectly clean holes.

Lauren studied the printer connection. There was no way the Cheerios had magically removed themselves; Abigail had packed them hopelessly deep. Lauren hadn't had time to have it repaired before she'd left. The first pinpricks of suspicion began to creep to the surface: this wasn't her computer. It was in her computer bag. It was the same make and model. But it wasn't hers—it couldn't be. The image of the black boots flooded into her brain. Had someone swapped laptops? If she'd died back in the culvert, no one would have known. The implications rocked her as she mentally went through the classified information stored in her hard drive. Schematics of highly classified, miniature radar components were at the top of the list. The Pentagon had allowed her access to the systems for her hurricane research. She understood fully how guarded they were about the data; it was straight out of the latest high-tech missile guidance platforms.

Lauren rubbed her arms at a sudden chill. She remembered her detailed orientation at the Defense Intelligence Agency. Her first week at DIA had focused on security. She glanced at the closed door that led to the cockpit. Last winter another breach of security had taken place in Russia...and it, too, revolved around an Eco-Watch jet that Donovan Nash was piloting.

CHAPTER FIVE

The wheels of the Gulfstream kissed the concrete. Donovan ignored the sun-drenched September day, relieved to finally be home. After his disastrous journey to the cabin to try to talk with Lauren, he had returned to the cockpit. Michael had been supportive, but finally Donovan had withdrawn and became lost in his thoughts, and he and Michael had flown the last hour in silence.

Donovan finished the appropriate after-landing checks. Eco-Watch's facility was tucked into the far northwest corner of the sprawling Dulles International Airport. The large complex housed not only the two Gulfstreams, but also a Bell 206 helicopter. The structure was comprised of a two-story office suite as well as a large maintenance area that wrapped around two sides of the main hangar. The facility had been modernized in the last two years. There was now room for a total of four Gulfstreams and the expected increase in staff. As always, they'd radioed ahead. The ground crew would be standing by to receive them.

"Wonder who that is?" Michael remarked as their hangar came into view.

Donovan saw the same helicopter Michael did. It didn't look familiar. As they made the final turn into the ramp, the large blades on the mysterious helicopter swung into motion. Just to the side of the helicopter sat a U.S. Customs vehicle. It was standard procedure for Customs to meet any international flights.

"My guess is it's here for our passengers." Donovan studied the helicopter. "They're sure gearing up for a quick departure."

"You get the feeling that this mission is a little different from most? Usually the scientists aren't treated like VIPs."

Donovan agreed. He also knew the last minute call to retrieve Lauren and her team had come from the Pentagon. It was all very strange. As Michael swung the big jet around on the tarmac, Donovan scribbled down the registration number of the helicopter. Moments later, they shut down the two engines and Michael threw off his harness.

"I'll get everyone off." Michael slid out of the seat.

Donovan nodded at his friend—Michael had read his mind. All he wanted at this point was for

Lauren to simply walk off the airplane and vanish. It was what she was good at. He continued securing the airplane, carefully going through each item on the lengthy checklist. Donovan tried to put her out of his thoughts as he waited for everyone to deplane. Somewhere in the back of his mind, Donovan wondered where she was going, who was waiting for her arrival. It was a lonely thought that there wasn't anyone waiting for him. As he gathered up a three-ring notebook to log the flight time for the trip, he heard the cockpit door slowly open. Donovan didn't look up as he continued to write, but in his peripheral vision he could see Lauren's legs as she stood in the doorway. The silence was threatening to suffocate him. What was she waiting for? He finished writing and looked up, ready to face her, but she was gone.

Donovan leaned over and watched as she hurried across the tarmac to the Customs official. The agent waved her through and she went immediately to the helicopter. Donovan watched as she stopped and glanced up at the Gulfstream. He could see her clearly in the afternoon sunlight; his shoulders slumped at how beautiful she was. She offered him a sad smile and a hesitant wave, then ducked down and boarded the chopper. Moments later the helicopter lifted off and turned east. As the noise from the beating rotor slowly subsided, Donovan knew that as quickly as he'd found her, she'd vanished once again.

He shook off the weight of his sorrow, and walked out of the cockpit and down the airstairs. Aware that Michael was waiting for him, Donovan went in his direction.

"Sorry, buddy." Michael offered a halfhearted smile.

Donovan nodded. A silent moment passed between the two friends.

"Hey, you want to come over for dinner?" Michael changed the subject. "Susan and the kids would love to see you. We were going to cook out tonight, nothing fancy."

Donovan shook his head. He was tempted—Susan and Michael's two young sons were the nearest thing to family Donovan had left. Patrick and Billy were a source of great joy. Billy, the youngest, was a hockey star. Though only ten years old, he was a force to be reckoned with on the ice. Patrick, the oldest, was truly a gifted athlete. He excelled at every sport, but his first love was baseball. Over the years, Donovan had spent more than a few pleasurable Saturday afternoons in the bleachers, rooting for Patrick's team. He loved Michael's family dearly, but tonight he felt like being alone.

"Or, I could call Susan." Michael shifted his tone and gave Donovan a sly wink. "Tell her you and I are going out to get blind drunk. We did have a hell of a day."

Donovan smiled at his friend, thankful for the concern. "I appreciate the invitation, but I'm fine. I have some work to finish here, then I'm going home. But I'll take a rain check on dinner."

"Whatever you want." Michael fell in step beside Donovan as they walked toward the offices. "But you got to admit, the idea of going out drinking wasn't bad. It is a Saturday night, and as you well know, there is an age-old tradition of intrepid aviators reveling until the wee hours. It's more than a birthright, it's a grave responsibility."

Donovan was forced to smile at the seriousness of the declaration. Michael's credo was always to leave them laughing. In the eight years they'd been flying together, he and Michael had closed their share of bars. The memories of their exploits were like a treasured family photo album.

"I think we've upheld that tradition a time or two."

"We are perhaps the best that ever lived," Michael replied quickly, his seriousness reaching a comical level. "But we can't afford to lose our edge. All around us are up and coming young pilots, looking to unseat the kings. It's one of the penalties of our immense talent."

"You go on home." Donovan tried to smile one more time. "Give Susan and the kids a hug for me. I'll see you bright and early Monday. Enjoy what's left of the weekend."

"Call if you change your mind about dinner." Michael hesitated a moment. "Or if you need anything—the door is always open."

"I know, and I appreciate it. See you Monday."

The ground crew had just finished easing the *da Vinci* into its space next to the *Galileo*. Across the polished floor of the immaculate hangar, Donovan spied the man he was looking for. Frank Moretti headed up the maintenance section of Eco-Watch. Frank was always in motion, a nervously energetic Italian. He stood no more than five foot five, his thin, wiry frame capped by a bald head, though Frank combed a section of hair from left to right in a feeble effort to disguise the obvious. A toothpick always protruded from the side of his narrow mouth, bobbing up and down as he spoke. What Frank lacked in physical presence, he more than made up for with his keen mechanical eye. Donovan had hired him away from a long career at Gulfstream Aerospace. He hadn't come cheap, but when it came to the two modified G-IVs tucked in the hangar, Donovan was convinced there wasn't a man alive who knew more about them than Frank. Each and every one of the Eco-Watch pilots trusted the man with his life.

"Frank," Donovan called out as he walked closer. "You got a minute?"

Frank looked up from a table. He'd been studying a set of blueprints.

"What's up?" A frown flashed across his already stern face. "You didn't hurt my airplane, did you?"

"No, we didn't hurt your plane. But I do need a favor." Donovan wasn't going to be the one to tell Frank about the empty drums in Bermuda, or how close they'd come to hitting them.

"Sure." Frank took a handkerchief out of his pocket and wiped his forehead. The afternoon sun was beginning to shine into the hangar. It was getting even warmer.

"That helicopter that met us. Any idea who it belonged to?"

Frank shook his head. "Not a clue. But you want me to find out, right?"

"Only if you have the time. I'd also love to know where they were going." Donovan was counting on Frank's intimate knowledge of the area's aviation community to pay off once again.

"I'll see what I can do," Frank replied, with a slight glimmer in his eye. "It was a new machine. A Bell 427. It has Pratt and Whitney turbines. I believe their tech rep owes me. Did you by chance catch the registration number?"

Donovan knew he was probably being played. "It was N37808." He had no doubt that Frank already knew the number, and that he'd also seen Lauren get into the helicopter. One of the drawbacks of working with an intimate group was what Donovan described as 'the small town effect'; everyone seemed to know what everyone else was doing. Despite his best intentions, his past relationship with Lauren probably wasn't a secret.

"Got it," Frank nodded.

"Is everything going to be ready for Monday?" Donovan wanted to change the subject. He was also curious about the status of the *Galileo.* He and Michael were scheduled out early Monday morning for a high-altitude hurricane reconnaissance flight.

"Yeah. We're almost there." Frank gestured at the blueprints. "Though I'm convinced the wiring diagram for the new antenna array was drawn by chipmunks. But we'll figure it out."

"Like you always do." Donovan glanced at his watch. He had no idea what he was going to do with what remained of his day. A part of him knew if he stopped moving, the weight of seeing Lauren would crash down around him.

"See you Monday." Donovan knew he should let Frank get back to work.

"I'll be here." Frank nodded.

Donovan took the back stairs up to his office. It was quiet. All the doors down the carpeted hall were closed. He let himself in, switched on the light, and gently barricaded himself from the world. He opened the small refrigerator and took out a bottle of water. Unscrewing the plastic cap, he sent it flying across the room, where it bounced off the wall and rattled into the wastebasket. He ignored his desk and sat down on the sofa that lined one wall. He grabbed the remote control for the television and turned it over and over in his hand, debating whether to switch on the set or not. On the shelves he saw his books and the Gulfstream models. There were photographs on each wall, pictures of people and places. His favorite was a shot taken of every Eco-Watch employee gathered around both airplanes on the ramp. It was the day they'd taken delivery of the *da Vinci.* The excitement in the air had been electric. Donovan let his gaze wander to the photographs of him and Michael, a collage of memories taken all over the globe.

There were also several pictures of oceangoing ships. A small but growing section of Eco-Watch was the marine unit. The foundation had recently allocated funds to expand into the oceanic research arena. There were three ships now, two based in Norfolk, Virginia, the other operating out of Hawaii. Like their aviation counterparts, they roamed the planet gathering data in the name of environmental science. Donovan stood back. The informal gallery represented eight years' worth of Eco-Watch missions. He and his people had been to virtually every corner of the globe.

His eyes darted to the bottom left drawer of his credenza. Inside was a photograph of Lauren. In his mind's eye, he could visualize the snapshot. They'd been on vacation in San Francisco. She'd looked radiant that day, her face a mix of seduction and serenity. Her hair had been tousled by the wind, the sunset filtering through the strands. The picture had given her an angelic quality, almost otherworldly. He knew he should have gotten rid of it long ago, but could never quite bring himself to toss it in the trash.

Donovan thought back to the day's events in Bermuda. His internal battle with the bridge still haunted him. At one point in his life he'd loved the ocean, been at home in and under the water. He had been a strong swimmer and fearless diver. But that person was gone now, swept away by a vengeful sea. What remained was a man terrified at the prospect of being in the water. He'd buried his fear for years, tried to blot out the root cause. But today had dredged it all up. Donovan felt the anguish begin to build. He briefly wondered how long a man could keep losing little pieces of himself and still survive.

At war with his emotions, Donovan reached for the remote control and commanded the television to life. He tuned the set to the Weather Channel, then took a long pull from his water, the lump in his throat seeming to wash away as he focused on a satellite shot of the Atlantic Ocean. He was amazed at how far Helena had traveled since they'd left this morning for Bermuda. The mass of clouds was churning northeast. The time-lapsed images from space easily showed the rotation around the eye. He imagined Bermuda must be getting hammered. Donovan toggled the volume until the meteorologist's voice could be heard.

"The National Weather Service has upgraded Helena to a category three hurricane. Peak winds near the eye wall have been recorded at 115 miles per hour. The eye is now located 79 miles southwest of Bermuda and the storm is moving northwesterly at eleven knots. We'll be right back with the latest projections of Helena's expected track. All of you living on the East Coast stay tuned as we continue to follow Helena's movement."

Donovan flipped the channel. He knew there was no way they could project if and when Helena might make landfall. Donovan silenced the set. Still feeling wrung out, he went to his desk and sat down. It was as he'd left it earlier. There was a pile of paperwork he knew he should do, but he swept it aside. Instead, he opened the bottom drawer and found the picture of Lauren.

The voice of reason urging him to let her go, he instead drank in the warmth of her smile. He looked into her eyes and relived all the reasons he'd lost her. If he were simply Donovan Nash, Director of Eco-Watch, they'd still be together. He'd lost her because of who he really was. It was the most indefensible reason of all.

Donovan slid the photo back into the drawer. He took a deep breath to try to quiet himself. He'd failed today on so many levels, first with the raging sea, then in his attempts to reach out to Lauren. He knew in his heart that anything he might say and do at this point was probably a waste of effort. She was lost to him forever. His controlled and calculated life had cost him the woman he loved.

CHAPTER SIX

"I've explained this to you a dozen times—Donovan Nash's boots were a different style from the ones I saw." Lauren was growing tired of this game. For the last half hour they'd simply been asking her the same questions again and again. Each barrage focused in on Donovan.

"Dr. McKenna. You were upside down in a wrecked car in the middle of a hurricane. I find it difficult to believe that you could be aware of different styles of footwear."

Lauren ground her teeth. The helicopter had whisked them directly from Dulles to DIA headquarters. She'd barely had time to change clothes, then call and check in with her mother before being called in to this debriefing. She had a million things to do and these guys were starting to irritate her.

"I'm a woman. I notice things like that," she remarked coolly. "Look. If Donovan Nash wanted to steal my computer, why did he save my life? It would have been far easier for him to let me drown."

"Dr. McKenna. What is your relationship with Mr. Nash?"

"He's a friend." Lauren wished her feelings were as simple as her words.

"You are aware of a previous investigation centered around Mr. Nash?"

Lauren nodded that she was.

"Have you ever passed sensitive documents to Mr. Nash?"

Lauren glared at the agent who had asked the question. "That is perhaps the most ridiculous thing I've ever heard. You may have a security leak, but it isn't me and I doubt very much if Donovan is involved either."

"Would you please answer the question?"

"I've never passed sensitive information to anyone."

The door to the room opened. Lauren looked up to see her boss, Deputy Director Calvin Reynolds. Tall and thin, Calvin always made an entrance. He was in his late fifties and had been with the DIA almost thirty years. Round wire-frame glasses were perched on his hawkish nose. Each strand of his thinning gray hair was carefully combed straight back. As he did almost every day, Calvin wore suspenders. Today they were red, and matched his perfectly knotted tie. Lauren prayed that this was her chance to escape the interrogation.

"If you're about finished here," Reynolds announced, "I need Dr. McKenna."

Lauren didn't wait for a reply. She stood and glared at the two men. "Yes. We're done." She turned toward Calvin and mouthed a silent thank you.

Reynolds held the door open for her to pass, then addressed the investigators. "I've just received a message from the Navy. Dr. Kenneth Browning is missing. He was last seen about to board the USS *Thorn*. Now he's vanished. They suspect he was swept overboard as they steamed toward the eye of the hurricane. One dead, another missing. I'd like some answers, gentlemen."

Standing in the hall, Lauren could clearly hear the news of Kenneth's disappearance. He'd been her right hand man on the project and she'd last seen him this morning in Bermuda. Lauren remembered the awkward hug he'd given her before they'd parted company. She could easily picture him waving goodbye. It was just before she and Victor had made their mad dash for the airport. Her knees felt weak and unsteady as she processed the fact that he, too, could be dead.

Calvin turned to Lauren and said quietly, "I'm sorry about Kenneth. But with so much happening right now, I don't have time to sugar-coat every new development. This entire project is going to hell...and me with it."

Lauren was still in shock. Of all her people, Kenneth was by far the nicest and least deserving of an untimely death.

"But enough of my problems." Calvin tried to force a smile. "They're getting ready to deploy *Jonah.* Let's get down there and see if something good has come out of all this."

Lauren nodded and fell in step beside Calvin. She could feel the adrenaline begin to pump. *Jonah* was her brainchild: a state-of-the-art advancement in hurricane research.

"I hope the Navy can launch it without Kenneth," Lauren worried out loud. "That was why he went out on the ship. After all of his design work on the flight envelope and propulsion systems, he really felt he was needed when they reached Helena's eye."

"We've established a direct link with the destroyer USS *Thorn.* You're going to be in charge of the deployment from here. I don't need to remind you how much we need this experiment to work."

"It'll work," Lauren said, convincingly. "We're going to have an around-the-clock, real-time view of Helena and how she's behaving."

They reached the metal door of the operations room and Calvin stopped. "Helena is now a category three storm. Do you still think she could go to a category five?"

Lauren looked directly into Calvin's eyes. "It's not a matter of if—but when."

Calvin nodded and blew out a quiet breath. "Then let's get *Jonah* airborne. If what you say is true, we're going to need all the hard evidence we can acquire before we sound the alarm and evacuate all of our resources in Helena's path."

Calvin swiped his ID card through the slot and entered his code. The sound of the lock echoed through the hall. Lauren entered into her arena: computers, satellites, and the realm of global weather patterns. She hurried to her section and sat down before an array of large, high-definition television screens. This was the most complex system of computers and communications equipment money could buy. Using her password, Lauren quickly linked up through the DMSP-3 satellite. The Defense Meteorology Support Program, or DMSP, was a series of military dedicated weather satellites. Her primary role within the DIA was to monitor the earth for weather patterns that might affect ongoing military operations. A few keystrokes later, and the main screen produced a clear image of the fantail of the USS *Thorn.* In the background she could see the partially inflated *Jonah.*

"This is Dr. McKenna. Who am I speaking to?"

"Dr. McKenna. This is Lt. Joseph Herrera. Can you hear me okay?"

"I read you five by five, Lt. Herrera." Lauren was relieved the link was of such high quality. She could see every detail of the operation. "How did *Jonah* ride out the passage through the storm? Were there any problems?"

"No problems." Herrera paused. "I gather you know about Dr. Browning?"

"Yes, I know," Lauren said quietly. She felt a growing sadness fighting to be heard. She pictured Kenneth, his crooked grin and sheepish smile. His little habit of clicking the mechanism on his pen when he was nervous or deep in thought. But most of all she remembered how passionate he was about the *Jonah* project. He was the one who had come up with the name, comparing the eye of a hurricane to the belly of a giant whale.

"Dr. McKenna...are you still there?"

"Yes. Let's get started." Lauren cleared her throat. "First, I need to know the current weather at your location. Specifically, how much wind is going over the stern of the ship?"

"As you know, it's very calm here in the eye. We're making nine knots, which is the amount of wind over the fantail."

"Perfect. Now I need you to double check that the support wires aren't tangled and that the lines will uncoil as we inflate the airship."

"Already done."

"Good. Now, the bottles of hydrogen are numbered as to which specific compartment inside the balloon's envelope we fill first. Do you have Kenneth's—Dr. Browning's checklist with you?"

"Yes."

"I'm going to do one last integrity check from here. Stand by."

Lauren took her eyes from the screen. The eye wall of the hurricane was clearly visible behind the ship. The vertical mass of churning clouds triggered another burst of adrenaline. This is what Lauren lived for; trying to understand these storms seemed to be in her blood. She quickly activated *Jonah*'s onboard computer and let it run a self-diagnostic test. The small high-speed computer was at the heart of everything *Jonah* could do. Once the airship was inflated, it would quickly ascend within the eye of Helena.

Lauren was proud of what she'd been able to construct. Inside the unmanned airship sat a miniaturized Doppler radar array. Current Doppler radar units were huge and ungainly. The most portable of them could only be situated on the beds of large trucks, or mounted inside a dome on a four-engine transport plane. Lauren had been able to take tiny components from the radar systems used in guided missiles and adapt them for her lightweight airborne radar. *Jonah* could be maneuvered inside the eye via satellite commands and, for seven days, give them an actual radar signature of the eye wall. All of the data was relayed back through the DMSP satellites to this room. Singularly, or in conjunction with research flights run by NOAA—the National Oceanographic and Atmospheric Administration—her system would usher in a new era of real-time storm data.

"Okay, Lt. Herrera. We're good at this end. Let's get *Jonah* in the air."

"Yes, ma'am."

Thrilled, as if watching a new life being born, Lauren sat and watched as the silver envelope began to inflate. It rose into the air, steadied by the control lines. The airship was powered by two electric ducted-fan propellers. A generator inside provided the power for the radar and the engines. Weight had been critical, so Lauren had used highly flammable hydrogen as the gas to float *Jonah*. As the stored fuel was depleted, the balloon would become lighter. Then they could simply switch over and use the hydrogen as the fuel source for the generator. It solved many of her problems. Like a butterfly emerging from a cocoon, *Jonah* filled and rose majestically above the ship.

Lauren typed commands to the propulsion system and watched as each of the propellers jumped to life.

"I'll make one complete sweep of the radar before we cut it loose," she said to Herrera. She powered up the array and waited for a computer display to her left to show her the Doppler radar image. On cue, a red band began to form on the black screen. Excited beyond belief, Lauren watched as *Jonah* began to transmit data. She studied the return and her smile turned into a frown. She quickly adjusted the parameters. The images switched from red to purple. In less than a minute, the screen showed an angry magenta ring around the ship. It was as if she'd been able to

X-ray the engine of the storm. Helena was growing more powerful.

"Lt. Herrera. Release the balloon!" Lauren watched as the cables broke away and *Jonah* sailed skyward behind the ship. The internal Global Positioning System would take over and keep *Jonah* centered perfectly in the eye.

"It's away!" Herrera reported.

"Thank you so much." Lauren felt a mixture of relief and urgency. "Lt. Herrera. I'd suggest you inform the captain his best way out of the eye is to turn to the southwest. The hurricane is building rapidly. I'm going to try to send this data to the bridge. It might prove to be useful."

Lauren looked over at Brent Whitaker, the DIA communications specialist sitting next to her. He reminded her of an actor on one of her mother's television programs. Brent had a dark complexion and a full head of tousled black hair. The only thing that spoiled his movie star looks was a slight potbelly and a scraggly goatee. Lauren knew he'd recently transferred from another project to assist with *Jonah*. She'd been impressed with his work, and how quickly he'd melded with their small group. Brent nodded that he could facilitate the transfer.

"Thanks, Dr. McKenna. Glad we could help," Herrera said quickly; then the transmission was severed.

Lauren stood from the console and marveled at the pictures being sent back from *Jonah*. Her thoughts went out to the men aboard the destroyer. She hoped they could safely navigate their way back out of the storm.

"Let's go to my office," Calvin whispered so only Lauren could hear. "We need to talk."

Lauren was reluctant to leave, but she knew from the tone of Calvin's voice what he wanted to say must be important. All of the information from *Jonah* would be recorded by a round-the-clock team of meteorologists. Her job had been to design it and get it operational. Others would mind the store while she finished up her Bermuda report, then somehow found time to rest. In her brief conversation with her mother, she'd heard Abigail in the background. Despite her triumph with *Jonah*, she could feel her fatigue beginning to drag her down. All she wanted was to go home and be with her daughter.

Calvin Reynolds breezed past his assistant. "Unless God or the president calls, I don't want to be disturbed."

"Yes, sir," the assistant replied, as if it were a typical request.

Calvin went into his spacious office and gestured for Lauren to take a seat across from his desk. Then he closed the door behind them.

Lauren took a seat, eyeing the more comfortable wingback chairs behind her. It was where she and Calvin usually conducted their meetings. Apparently his intention was to be more formal. She waited patiently as he quickly sifted through his message slips. He glanced at one sheet of paper on his desk, then laid it aside.

"First, I'd like to say how impressed I am with *Jonah*. From what little I just witnessed, it would appear that we're on the right track. Nice job."

Lauren nodded and waited for the other shoe to drop. Calvin was nothing if not a bureaucrat. His highly political job demanded a constant level of maneuvering. They'd known each other for years, from her days at MIT. He'd tried to recruit her back then on behalf of the Defense Intelligence Agency, but she'd declined. Then, right after she'd left Donovan, she sought him out. Calvin cleared the usual red tape, and within days Lauren held a position as a senior member of the DIA's meteorological forecast team. The information she and her staff gathered was disseminated to every branch of the military, as well as to the Central Intelligence Agency and the National Security Agency. Meteorology often played a role in the government's intelligence-gathering capability, as well as in ongoing military operations.

"I've just received some more disturbing news." Calvin scratched his nearly bald head, careful not to disturb what little hair he had. "Kenneth Browning's body was just discovered in Bermuda. He was murdered."

"Oh no." Lauren shook her head in disbelief.

"This business about someone swapping computers is, frankly, mind-boggling. What at first appeared to be an accident is now shaping up to be a full-fledged attempt at stealing classified information."

"Did they find my computer...with Kenneth, I mean?" Lauren sniffed as she fought her tears.

"No. We think whoever killed Kenneth has your laptop. Everyone else in your department is accounted for, which makes this person or persons from an outside agency. I don't need to remind you of the magnitude of this breach."

"Do you really think people would kill to get their hands on what I had in my computer?"

"You only have to pick up a newspaper to understand how many Third World countries might have biological or even nuclear weapons, but no way to deliver them accurately. The contents of your laptop would go a long way in solving their problems."

"I'm sorry. I think like a scientist, not a soldier. You're right. We took those radar components right out of the front-line missile inventory. It was the only way to solve our weight problems on *Jonah.*"

"Internal Investigations has already keyed in on Donovan Nash. Give it to me straight, Lauren. What do you think happened out there?"

"I think the person who was at the accident site took my computer, then replaced it with a destroyed one of the same type. I highly doubt that Donovan Nash was the one who did it."

"Why?" Calvin said quickly.

"Because had I died, it would have taken days to discover that it wasn't my computer at the accident site."

Calvin nodded. "So you don't think there's any tie-in with today's events and the fact that, eleven months ago, Donovan Nash landed a plane full of classified communications equipment on Russian soil?"

"I do not," Lauren said flatly. "If there had been any proof of Donovan's wrongdoing, EcoWatch would have been shut down. Am I right?"

"Probably," Calvin said. "But in light of what happened in Bermuda...all bets are off. This second incident is too strong to ignore."

"I'll agree there's a coincidence. But in my opinion it ends there."

Calvin lifted a sheet of paper from his desk. "This is the preliminary examination of the computer you gave us. A secret internal code that identifies each DIA computer is missing—as in not installed. The computer is definitely a decoy. Despite the condition of the case, they lifted two sets of fingerprints—yours and Mr. Nash's. The hard drive is scrambled gibberish. It's believed to have been intentionally sabotaged to make it appear that all of your data was lost." He let the report fall back to his desk.

"Donovan did touch the computer, right before we boarded the plane. It would follow that his prints would be on it."

"I'll buy that. Now back to the question at hand. I'm concerned that this mysterious person was at the scene so fast. You said it was only a matter of minutes? How could someone engineer this theft if they didn't know the car was going to crash?"

Lauren felt the blood drain from her face. If what Calvin was saying were true, then the accident was rigged and someone had tried to kill her. Her eyes grew wide as she looked across at him.

"I think you survived an attempt on your life," Calvin said solemnly. "The same person or persons also killed Kenneth."

"My guess is whoever took the computer is still on Bermuda."

"I think they'd have to be." Calvin said, getting out of his chair. He began to pace. "You were the last plane out, and leaving on a ship would be improbable given the storm. But they could have downloaded the information and e-mailed it anywhere in the world by now," Calvin said, a tinge of hopelessness in his voice.

"They'd have to get into it first. Bypass all the passwords and safeties. I think that would take them awhile."

"True." Calvin pondered her words. "All we can do is alert the Bermuda authorities and have some field people on the first plane to Bermuda. I'll need your help in determining when that might be."

"Of course." Lauren had no idea what was going through his mind. Could he really shut down all avenues of escape from Bermuda? A slight chill came over her as she decided she didn't really want to know what all Calvin or the U.S. government could or couldn't do.

"That's all for now. Go get some rest. You must be exhausted."

Lauren nodded. "I'll plot a window for you to fly to Bermuda. Though I don't think it'll be for at least the next eighteen to twenty-four hours."

"I'll be waiting for the information." Calvin's eyes darted around his office until he found what he was looking for. "Before I forget, they sent you up a new computer. You'll have to reset all the passwords and protocols. The note here says that they've already loaded in the links to *Jonah.*"

"Oh, good." Lauren slipped the laptop from its case; it was exactly the same make and model as the one she'd had. It wouldn't take her long to get it up and running.

"Be alert for any signs that someone has tampered with your data. It might be the first sign that they've gained access to the system."

"Trust me. I'll give everything a good look... and thanks." Lauren gathered her new computer and left Calvin's office. She hoped she didn't look as bad as she felt. Everything that had happened was swirling around in her head.

"There you are." Simmons hurried to catch up with Lauren. He was breathing hard when he reached her.

"Carl, what is it?" Lauren wondered if something had happened to *Jonah*.

"I just heard," he lowered his voice. "They say Kenneth is dead."

Lauren nodded.

"I can't believe all of this is happening." Carl took a quick look up and down the hallway. "I've also noticed a lot of different people around. I have a feeling they're from the investigations side of things. Is something going on I should know about?"

"I don't know." Lauren couldn't discuss what she knew with anyone.

"I'm just worried about you," Carl said sincerely. "You've been through a lot."

"Thank you." Lauren understood Carl's concern. Since they'd begun working together, she'd had no greater champion of her and her work than Carl. It was as if he'd designated himself her mentor and protector.

"If there's anything I can do," Carl said, looking into Lauren's eyes, "you know where to find me."

"I appreciate your concern. But I'm fine." Lauren needed to get to her mother's house. The thought of seeing Abigail swept some of her burden away. Kids were wonderful in that respect. They don't care if mommy was almost killed, that people mommy knew were dead. They just wanted mom. Lauren missed her little girl so much it was almost a tangible pain.

"If I hear anything I'll let you know," Carl offered.

"I'll do the same," Lauren said as she began to walk away. She hurried to her office, grabbed her things, and headed out of the building. As she pulled out into traffic she wondered if she were being followed. There were a dozen cars behind her on the busy road. Would Calvin do that to her? If not Calvin, then perhaps the two men who had interrogated her? She wondered if their orders were to spy on her, or protect her? Either way, the implications were unsettling. She caught herself looking for Donovan's Range Rover. Was it possible she could be wrong...was he somehow involved in all of this?

The glare from the sun forced Donovan to put on his dark glasses. The asphalt parking lot shimmered in the heat. He'd finally been forced to escape the confines of his office; it had begun to feel like a prison. He opened the door of his ten-year-old Range Rover. It was like an oven inside and the rush of hot air caused him to step backward. He reached in and touched the leather seat with his hand. It felt safe. The cell phone clipped to his belt sprang to life, the shrill bell almost drowned out by a Boeing 747 that was climbing out overhead. Donovan swept the phone to his ear, sliding into the Range Rover so that he could hear.

"Hello."

"Is this Mr. Donovan Nash?"

"Yes. Who is this?" He didn't recognize the caller.

"This is Guardian Security. We have an alarm reported at 22332 Oatlands Road in Loudoun County."

"Get the police out there. Tell them I'm on my way!" Donovan ignored the heat and immediately cranked the ignition.

A moment later he whipped out of the Eco-Watch facility and roared down the access road. He blew through a stop sign, the tires squealing as he took the first turn. The property on Oatlands Road outside Washington, D.C. had belonged to his mother. He didn't live there, but the estate was one of the most important things in his life. It was why, years ago, he'd had a sophisticated security system installed. The thought of thieves or vandals inside the house left a bitter taste in his mouth as he jumped onto Route 28 and accelerated south.

Donovan merged onto Route 50. As he'd hoped, the traffic was light. On the four-lane road headed west, his speed crept up near 80 mph. Keeping one eye on the road, he found his cell phone and dialed information.

"I need the number for the Loudoun County Sheriff's office."

"Would you like me to connect you?" The operator offered.

"Yes!" Donovan urged as he swerved and passed a truck on the right.

"Loudoun County Sheriff's office."

"This is Donovan Nash. I understand there is an alarm sounding at 22332 Oatlands Road. Can you tell me if there's a unit headed out there?"

"I'm sorry. I can't give that information out over the phone."

"I'm the caretaker of that property." Donovan was careful not to reveal to her that he was actually the owner. Through a maze of trusts and corporations, his connection was carefully hidden and he wanted it to stay that way. "Please check your security file. My name is on the list."

"I just did, Mr. Nash. Can you tell me your Social Security number?"

Donovan rattled it off and waited for the dispatcher to respond.

"Yes, Mr. Nash. There is a car on scene. They have someone in custody."

"I'll be there in ten minutes." Donovan crossed Highway 15 and headed toward the small town of Aldie.

"I'll alert the officer on scene that you're on your way."

"Thank you." Donovan severed the connection, relieved that whoever set off the alarm had been caught. He ground his teeth as he was forced to slow within the Aldie city limits. The collection of antique shops, furniture stores, and historic buildings was usually a source of interest, but Donovan ignored them as he pressed down the narrow street. He saw Dwight's General Store ahead on the left, and as always, smoke poured from the outside barbecue pit. Just beyond was his first chance to get off the main road. He braked hard and threw the Range Rover around the tight turn, then gunned the engine and climbed the steep hill. A cloud of dust billowed behind him as he raced the last mile down the unpaved road.

Donovan slowed as he approached the estate. He could see a police car past the low rock wall. Usually, he made this drive slowly, pulling into the property filled with a quiet, reverent mood. The massive stone house had been in his family for almost a hundred years. As he covered the last fifty yards he could see the officer standing next to the car, the silhouette of someone's head visible in the back seat.

Donovan waved at the deputy, shut off the engine, and jumped out of the Range Rover.

"Mr. Nash?" the deputy asked, his hand resting on the butt of his revolver.

"That's me." Donovan slowed his mad rush. "I called dispatch."

"Can I please see some identification?"

Donovan handed over his driver's license, then peeked into the back seat of the sheriff's car. He was met with the startling dark eyes of a young woman. She wore jeans and a white tee shirt. Her short black hair framed a face more cute than beautiful. He couldn't imagine she was a day over twenty-five.

"Thank you, Mr. Nash. Just needed to check."

"Where did you find her? Was she in the house?" He glared at the young suspect.

"Please step this way." The deputy gestured as they moved out of earshot from the young woman.

"I found her outside in the backyard. Claims she was lost and had car trouble. She came to the house to find help."

"Did you find her car?"

"Yeah. It's about a quarter of a mile up the road. It wouldn't start. I also ran a check on her. She's clean."

"You think she's telling the truth?" Donovan felt relieved, yet still slightly wary.

"I think so. Maybe you should check out the house and make sure?"

"What's her name?" Donovan dug in his pocket for the keys.

"Erin Walker."

The name didn't ring any bells. "I'll be right back." Donovan looked over the deputy's shoulder at Erin. Her wide eyes seemed filled with fear and uncertainty.

Donovan walked around the side of the house. She'd been caught out back; it seemed as good a place as any to start his inspection. From the top of the hill, the view to the east always brought a wealth of childhood memories. The huge oak tree where a tire swing used to be, the lake he swam in every afternoon, visible at the foot of the rise. The property covered almost 200 acres and it had been his kingdom as a young boy. If he closed his eyes he could almost hear his mother calling to him from the kitchen.

He checked the windows—they all seemed to be intact. He examined the back door and it looked fine also. The alarm system could be tripped by applying a slight force to either a window or a doorknob. It was the perfect system for a rural address. He unlocked the door and slipped inside. The wood floor creaked under his feet. He stood and ran his eyes over each detail of the room. Roughhewn beams soared overhead and sunlight filtered through the interior, giving the room almost a cathedral feeling. Donovan breathed in the rustic aroma of the old house. It'd been weeks since he'd had the time to come for a visit. He strode to a cabinet and deactivated the main alarm. A quick inquiry indicated the back door sensor had been tripped. He quickly went room to room until finally he began to relax. It seemed everything was as it should be. He left the house and trotted to the detached garage. It was also made of stone, a smaller version of the main house. The doors and windows were locked tight. It looked as if Erin Walker's story might be legitimate. Donovan was about to head back to the front of the house when an odd flash caught his eye. He crossed the lawn and knelt under a bush. A metallic object lay on its side, partially hidden under the shrub. Donovan reached in and pulled it out. It was a 35mm Nikon. He turned it over in his hand. There were twenty pictures already exposed. He worked quickly, using a small stick to depress the rewind button. The camera whirred in his hand as the film was pulled back into the canister. He popped open the case and stashed the cartridge in his pocket. He put the camera back where he found it, then went to join Erin Walker and the deputy.

"Everything looks fine," Donovan called out as he neared the police car.

"I'm glad." The deputy had his handkerchief out and was wiping his neck against the oppressive heat. "Do you want to press trespassing charges?"

"I don't think that'll be necessary." Donovan looked at Erin again for any clue to who she might really be. She seemed to be trying to manufacture a look of embarrassment, but now Donovan didn't buy it. They briefly made eye contact. He felt himself being studied the way a predator might eye its quarry. For that instant, she seemed older and maybe even a little dangerous. Donovan was mildly intrigued by the perception. Not only did he have the upper hand, but whoever Erin Walker was—she was way out of her league.

"Okay, then." The deputy shifted his belt and leaned forward to shake Donovan's hand. "I'll take her to town and she can arrange to have her car towed."

Donovan returned the handshake. "Thanks for all your help." He took one more glance at Erin, who had yet to utter a word.

As soon as the squad car drove out of view, Donovan went to the garage and unlocked the door. He found the tool he was looking for and went back out to the Range Rover. He drove down the road to Erin's car. The white Honda Accord was parked on the shoulder. He eased the Range Rover behind her car, then looked up and down the road—it was deserted. As casually as if he were taking a walk, he crossed to the Honda. There were no stickers or identifying marks on the windshield. It had been awhile, but Donovan expertly worked the thin metal tool down into the door. Seconds later, the lock was open. Oblivious to the heat, he made a quick but methodical search of her car. As he suspected, it was virtually devoid of personal effects. He leaned down and popped both the hood and the trunk. He went to the front of the car first and lifted the hood. It didn't take him long to spot the problem. All four leads to the spark plugs had been pulled back far enough to sever the connection. Donovan smiled. It was an old trick. Until Erin pushed them back in, the car wouldn't have a prayer of starting. Her ruse had easily fooled the deputy.

He closed the hood and went around to the trunk, where his exploration became slightly more fruitful.

The camera bag was partially hidden under a blanket. He pulled it out and discovered an assortment of filters and telephoto lenses. He knew it was expensive equipment. Whoever Erin was, surveillance seemed to be her immediate mission. Donovan also found another camera body, a Nikon identical to the one he'd found at his house. He helped himself to a roll of film from the dozen or so stashed in the bag, then put everything back where he found it. Before backing away, he memorized her Virginia plate number.

Back at the house, Donovan pulled the Range Rover into the spacious garage. He closed the door and stepped out onto the polished floor. He lovingly placed his hand on the canvas cover draped over his Porsche. The wonderfully overpowered Carrera GT convertible was almost as much fun as the Gulfstream. He left the garage and went straight for Erin's camera. He loaded the new roll of film, then fired off twenty shots into the palm of his hand. Once he was finished, he positioned the camera exactly where he'd found it. He smiled as he tried to picture Erin's expression when she developed the film.

Donovan went into the house and pulled a cold beer from the refrigerator. He put the cold glass to his forehead; the heat inside the house was oppressive. He took a long drink from the bottle and the icy fluid roared down his parched throat. He let out an audible sigh as he headed upstairs. It wouldn't take him long to prepare for Erin's return.

Donovan sipped the last of his beer. He decided against another and sat back in his chair. The house and garage were all closed up. Donovan sat in the third-story window with his own camera resting on his lap. He'd not only be able to observe her, but also to photograph her. With his connections, he'd be able to find out exactly who she was. But right now, the last thing he wanted was to confront her and tip her off. It was in his best interest to let her feel as if she had the upper hand. Donovan knew she was a professional of some sort, though not a very good one—she'd been caught. But she was up to something. Donovan felt the roll of film in his pocket. As soon as Erin came and went, he'd use the small darkroom to develop the photographs.

Donovan didn't have to wait long. He leaned forward and found his target through the viewfinder as a car pulled up and stopped next to Erin's Honda. He saw her jump out of the passenger's seat and run to her car. Through the 300mm lens he fired off a rapid succession of shots. As expected, she hurriedly fixed the spark plug wires, then waved at the other car. Donovan never saw the driver, but did get the license plate. Erin slid behind the wheel and started the motor. Moments later, the Honda disappeared. Donovan moved quickly to the other side of the house. Within seconds, he could see Erin running from her car to where she'd left her camera. Donovan zoomed in on her face; he wanted a good shot. He watched as she crouched down and grabbed her Nikon. Without pausing to inspect it, she dashed back toward the Honda.

Once she was gone, Donovan walked downstairs, grabbed another beer, then made his way down to the darkroom. Thankfully, it was somewhat cooler in the basement, though Donovan quickly forgot about the heat as he went to work. It took him awhile, but finally he ran Erin's developed film under the cool water in the sink. From there, he carefully hung the negatives to dry. Tilting his head to the side, he began inspecting the images. His fear grew as he went from one shot to the next and studied each exposure. Donovan easily recognized what Erin Walker had photographed. Out behind the house, down a gentle hill, was the family cemetery. The names on the stones had been captured perfectly. Erin Walker may not have her pictures, but she'd seen the markers—which now made her the most dangerous person in Donovan's life.

Donovan left the darkroom and went outside, feeling numb as he tried to understand how Erin had not only discovered the house, but knew enough to find the graves and shoot pictures. He looked to the west. The sun was just settling over the Blue Ridge mountains, the sky turning from blue to orange. Crickets and locusts had already begun their nightly chorus. Donovan could hear the deep voice of the bullfrogs from the lake.

He walked down the brick walkway that led to an open area bordered on one side by an ancient sycamore tree. A fruit bat swooped low overhead, then turned and was gone. He knew he couldn't stay, so he stood outside the low wooden railing that surrounded the family cemetery. He looked at the two markers that were closest to the gate. In the gathering darkness he looked upon the finely chiseled marble: Robert D. Huntington, 1931-1968. Next to it was his mother's stone: Elizabeth K. Huntington, 1936-1968. Despite the years, the memory of his dead parents was still a dull ache. His father's tomb was empty; they'd never found his body after the boat sank. After years of debating, Donovan had finally made the decision to bring his mother's remains back home to Virginia. He'd resisted for the longest time, thinking somehow that she belonged on the small island in the Pacific, near his father, close to the sea and the man she'd loved.

Donovan lowered his head, forever haunted by the sound of his mother's cries for help, the sound of the wind and waves before she went under for the last time, her hand reaching for help before it slipped beneath the water. Frozen by fear, Donovan had clung desperately to a section of wood, paralyzed, unable to help. He knew he'd only been a boy at the time, but he never forgave himself. Now, whoever Erin Walker was, she'd connected him with the house and the graves of his parents and grandparents. It wouldn't take her long to figure out the links between his parents' graves and the vast fortune of Huntington Oil. From there it would be a quick jump to tie him to his past—as the sole heir to billions of dollars.

Behind his parents' markers was another collection of headstones. One in particular would send Erin down a road that could destroy everything he'd worked so hard to build. It was the grave of his great-grandfather, whose name he'd taken: Donovan Nash.

Donovan turned away as thoughts of Lauren came crashing down on him. He lowered his head at the sudden weight. Deep down, he knew seeing her today had only served to reopen the old wounds. Yesterday, his world seemed safe and protected, but right now he knew it was unraveling at both ends. He knew he still loved her... and despite his considerable resources and abilities, there wasn't a single thing he could do to change the way things were.

CHAPTER SEVEN

Lauren abruptly opened her eyes and her dream vanished into the quiet darkness of the bedroom. Momentarily confused, she struggled to understand what had awakened her from her deep sleep. She finally saw her mother peeking through the door.

"Lauren, honey. Are you awake? There's a phone call for you. They said it's urgent."

"I'll be right there, Mom." Lauren threw back the sheet and pulled on her thin cotton dressing gown. A quick glance at the clock told her it was five-thirty in the morning. The sleep she'd hoped to get had just been cut drastically. She cinched the belt around her waist and quickly went downstairs. She saw the worried look on her mother's face as she put the phone to her ear.

"This is Dr. McKenna."

"Lauren. It's Calvin. Sorry to wake you, but there have been some developments."

"What's happened?" Lauren ran her hand through her hair. Her fatigue evaporated at the tone of Calvin's voice.

"It's Helena. The barometric pressure is going through the floor. The latest information from *Jonah* is telling us that we've gone from category three to category five in near record time. There is a NOAA hurricane hunter aircraft on its way to verify our readings."

"What's the pressure now?" Lauren closed her eyes and squeezed the bridge of her nose. "We've seen explosive deepening before. How sharp was the drop?"

"All of the readouts have been e-mailed to you. But the latest barometric pressure is 27.10 inches."

Lauren felt her empty stomach churn. The drop was staggering.

"How fast is she moving?" Lauren caught her mother's eye, then pointed at the coffee pot. She mouthed a thank you as her mom understood.

"About the same. Between eleven and twelve knots, on the same track as before. She's not making any definitive moves yet."

"She might not." Lauren pictured the location of the high-pressure ridge that was behind the long heat wave beating down on the Southeast and Mid-Atlantic states. As long as that dome stayed where it was, Helena wouldn't have any choice but to run directly at the Baltimore-New York City corridor.

"Why don't you look at the data the lab sent you, then come on in. I know it's Sunday and you must still be exhausted. But I've already gotten a call from the Pentagon. Everyone is starting to get a little edgy."

"I'll be there as soon as I can." Lauren began to inhale the aroma from the coffee maker. She knew she'd need more than a few cups to get her through the morning.

"See you then."

Lauren hung up the phone and began to organize her thoughts.

"Trouble?" her mother asked, softly.

"The hurricane." Lauren tried to smile. Her mother had been a saint since Abigail had been born and most recently with the deployment of *Jonah.* More than anything, Lauren wished the three of them could spend the entire day together. She imagined her mother could use a break and Lauren needed a respite from Helena and the DIA.

"I need to go get on the computer. Can I talk you into bringing me a cup of coffee when it's ready?"

"Of course."

Lauren quickly padded up the carpeted stairs and tip-toed into Abigail's room. Her daughter was sound asleep. Lauren breathed in the scent of Abigail's things: the baby powder, the fresh sheets. She leaned down and adjusted Abigail's blanket, then stood and marveled as her baby slowly breathed in and out. Lauren was filled with love as she reached down and lightly touched Abigail's tiny face.

"Is she still asleep?" her mother whispered from the hall.

Lauren nodded and quietly backed away. Hopefully, Abigail would sleep another two hours or so.

"Here's your coffee."

"Thanks, Mom." Lauren took the warm mug and saw a questioning look on her mother's face. They'd talked last night after she'd gotten home. Lauren had left out the part about nearly being killed, but she did confess she'd seen Donovan.

"I'm sorry, but I have to go to the office today," Lauren apologized.

"We'll be fine. Don't worry about a thing." Her mother hesitated. "How are you doing this morning?"

"I'm okay. Just a little tired." Lauren knew it wasn't the answer her mother was looking for.

"Are things a little clearer?"

"Mom," Lauren exhaled. "Nothing's changed. I know you and I disagree about Donovan. But it's just the way it has to be."

"I understand. I just thought—"

"I don't want to argue this morning," Lauren cut her off. "I have a ton of things to do and I need to be out the door in a little over an hour. This hurricane is going to be the death of me before it's all over. Can we just not talk about Donovan?"

Lauren saw the hurt in her mother's eyes and a twinge of guilt jabbed her heart. For the most part Lauren and her mother were best friends, especially since her father had passed away, but at times she could be so stubborn. Coffee in hand, Lauren swept into the study and switched on her new laptop. Lauren sipped her coffee, more interested in the caffeine than the taste. Moments later, she was looking at the first page of readouts. Her brow furrowed as she studied the latest Atlantic Sea State Analysis. The infrared satellite clearly showed Helena's position and width. Lauren was both horrified and fascinated as she processed the information. Helena was now positioned 110 miles northwest of Bermuda. Lauren made a mental note to tell Calvin that it would be another ten hours, minimum, before he could send a plane to Bermuda. She thought of the men aboard the USS *Thorn.* She could only imagine what their journey out of the eye must have been like.

The next image was from the DMPS satellite. With its microwave imager she was able to filter out the overriding cirrus clouds and examine the underlying convective cloud structure. The thunderstorms around the eye were sharp and defined. She knew she was looking at the massive engine of the storm. The formation of such a distinct pattern of cumulonimbus clouds told her that Helena was very much alive and well.

Next, Lauren scanned a dozen other pages of data, from steering winds to the high and low altitude prognostic charts. She shook her head when she saw the sea surface temperature readings. A hurricane needed heat to stay alive, and from what she was reading, Helena would soon be able to suck up the tepid water from the ongoing heat wave. A category five hurricane that made its way into the bath-water temperature ocean off the east coast would only have one option—to grow bigger and even more deadly.

Lauren rubbed her temples. She clicked back to her own computer model she'd used to develop her initial scenario for Helena. She shook her head as she studied the comparison. Helena was more intense, earlier, than even Lauren had predicted.

She leaned back in her chair and put both hands around her coffee mug. She thought back to her theoretical physics class at MIT. In meteorological circles, there was an operating theory that a super hurricane, or hypercane as they were called, could form in the Atlantic Ocean. Winds of up to 300 mph could rage around the eye. Storm debris and vapor would be thrown as high as twenty miles above the earth. If such a hypercane made landfall, a storm surge with waves as high as 100 feet would obliterate any coastline. Lauren felt a shiver run down her neck. She logged off and went toward the bathroom. She needed to get to her lab and communicate with *Jonah*.

Lauren was halfway down the hall when she heard Abigail softly cooing in her crib. She went in and found her daughter wide awake, smiling up at her.

"Hello, honey." Lauren reached down and picked her up. She kissed the warm skin of Abigail's cheek. Her daughter let out a peal of laughter, then pulled Lauren's hair.

"Oh, she's awake." Lauren's mother breezed into the room. "Here, let me take her. She probably needs to be changed."

"I can do it." Lauren turned to her mother and held Abigail close.

"Mother. I need you to do something."

"Of course. What is it?"

"I think it would be best for you to take Abigail and get out of Baltimore. Maybe go visit Aunt Paula in Chicago. I don't care where you go, but you have to leave town."

"Lauren. Are you serious? Is it the hurricane?"

"Yes," Lauren said quietly, gently kissing Abigail on the neck. "Don't worry about what it costs, I'll cover all the expenses. But I want you and Abigail away from the East Coast."

"If you really think we should..."

Lauren nodded. "Oh, and one more thing. Don't tell anyone. If you can get a flight this evening I'll take you to the airport. I have to be at work early on Monday, so tonight might work better. Maybe you could check with the airlines later? I'll call you when I can, and we can coordinate."

"Mama!" Abigail threw up her hands and squirmed with obvious excitement at being near her mother.

"Well, good morning, my little angel." Lauren smiled at her daughter. She decided she could be a few minutes later than she'd planned. "Would you like for Mommy to change you and get you breakfast?"

Donovan had been lying in bed, wide awake, when the phone rang. He'd spent an awful night, plagued by one bad dream after another. As he'd tossed and turned, he'd been trapped; waves of reporters thundered toward him. He'd been unable to escape the mob as they clamored to reach him. He'd awakened, bathed in sweat, a death grip on the mattress. He reached over to the bedside table and snatched the instrument with one hand.

"Hello."

"Good morning, Donovan. It's William."

Donovan sat up in bed, instantly concerned. It was unlike his friend to call so early in the morning, especially on a Sunday. To the rest of the world, William VanGelder was the chairman of the board of Eco-Watch. But to Donovan, William was his oldest and most trusted advisor. A mentor, who over the years since his parents died, had guided and directed him with the unwavering devotion of a father. William was the one person on the face of the earth who was aware of all of the intricacies of Donovan's other life.

"What's up?" Donovan answered, a worried tone in his voice. "I was going to call you later."

"We have a problem. I'll have coffee and Danish waiting for you when you get here."

"Give me an hour." Donovan threw his legs out of the bed as he hung up the phone. He and William never spoke of anything specific on the phone. It was a lesson William had taught him years ago. Donovan scratched his chest and tried to imagine what had happened that would prompt such an early meeting. A flurry of issues flew through his mind, none of them good. With a frown on his face, Donovan headed for the bathroom.

The needle spray from the shower washed away any lingering remnants of his troubled night's sleep. Donovan stretched his sore muscles under the hot water, knowing the stiffness was from pulling Lauren from the car.

Donovan dried off, decided not to shave, then threw on some khaki slacks and a knit golf shirt. He went down the stairs of his Centreville townhouse and grabbed a bottle of orange juice from the refrigerator. He picked up the pictures he'd developed the night before and headed for the garage.

Quickly, he armed the security system and slid into the Range Rover. He carefully backed out onto the quiet cul-de-sac. He came and went at so many odd hours he barely knew any of his neighbors. The small collection of town homes was close to the airport and served his day-to-day needs perfectly. It was a comfortable area, yet not ostentatious enough to draw any attention to himself. It fit his lifestyle and salary from Eco-Watch perfectly.

In the humid air, the morning sun was a blood-red disk. Donovan slid on his dark glasses, nudged the air conditioner up a notch, and headed for Fairfax.

As he drove, Donovan kept trying to figure out how Erin Walker had found him. Could she be with the government? If she were with the FBI she wasn't very good—or it could be her ineptness was simply an act. The questions whirled in his head. Part of the puzzle seemed to go back eleven months ago, to the only time he'd received any unwanted attention. It had all taken place last winter—after his and Michael's very public experience in Russia. It seemed to be an issue that wouldn't die. He'd hoped it was all behind him, but the more he thought about it, the more he believed it had resurfaced yet again. Donovan thought back to that cold November day.

He and Michael had been cruising at 41,000 feet. In the back of the *Galileo* was a group of scientists from NASA. Their mission was to study and chart the roaring high altitude winds that swept out of Siberia and formed the North American winter weather patterns. The flight was routine and monotonous. Donovan had sat quietly, sipping a cup of coffee. Below them, the clouds boiled from a Siberian storm as it raced eastward toward the Aleutian Islands, ultimately to impact the weather in Western Canada, then across the United States.

"I'm picking up a faint distress call on the UHF radio." Michael sat up straight in his seat and gave Donovan a look of alarm. "Switch over; see what you make of this."

The distorted words came through Donovan's headset. Most of it was garbled, or foreign. But he heard a Mayday at the beginning of each broadcast. He scanned the angry clouds beneath them. His stomach tightened and he felt his muscles automatically tense at the thought of someone in the water. From experience, he knew what the storm was doing to the Arctic Ocean, some eight miles below them.

"Call them. See if they can read us." Donovan waited as Michael did as instructed.

"Nothing." Michael shook his head.

"Did you get any kind of position?" Donovan asked quickly.

"What I hear is mostly static." Michael adjusted the volume. "I can make out the Mayday. I think maybe they're also saying the name of a ship. The voice is heavily accented, Russian I'd bet, but the Mayday is definitely English."

Donovan keyed the intercom to the cabin area and spoke quickly to James Holland, the lead scientist in the back of the plane. He and James had known each other for years, had flown dozens of mission together.

"James. We're picking up a distress call on the UHF radio. Tune in 243.00. Any way you can get it on tape?"

"Stand by."

Donovan and Michael exchanged concerned looks while they listened to frantic calls from an unknown voice.

"We've got it," James reported. "Tapes rolling. We all agree it's Russian."

"Michael. Talk to air traffic control, see if there's any other aircraft in the area. Find out if any surface ships are responding."

Donovan kept thinking that there had to be a way to make sure the people in peril were being heard. "James, can you figure out a way to relay this distress call to someone who can translate it?"

"I'm already working on that. We're establishing a data link with Elmendorf Air Force Base in Anchorage. With any luck we should have some results momentarily."

"Donovan." Michael turned in his seat. "Air traffic control says this is the first they've heard of a distress call. We're pretty far north of the commercial tracks. The closest plane is an Air Force C-5 Galaxy. But they're almost 200 miles south of us."

"I want to talk to the C-5 pilots." Donovan's heart began to pound in his chest. The mere thought of people in the water always brought on a private horror.

"You're dialed in. Their call sign is Reach 321."

Donovan nodded and keyed the microphone. "Reach 321, this is Eco-Watch 01. How do you read?"

"Loud and clear, Eco-Watch. What can we do for you?" The slight southern drawl filled the headset.

"We're a research flight about 200 miles north of your position. We're hearing a faint distress signal on UHF. Frequency 243.00. Can you tell me if you're receiving the same call?"

"We'll get right back to you on that."

Donovan waited impatiently for the reply. He knew that each tick of the clock was precious; every minute in the water was like an hour in hell. He tried to keep his breathing slow and steady, despite his urgent thoughts screaming at him to hurry and do something—anything—to help those people.

"That's negative on the distress call," Reach 321 finally reported. "We don't hear a thing."

"Okay. Thanks." Donovan turned to Michael. "My thinking is the Mayday is coming from farther north, or else the C-5 would have picked it up, too."

"I agree. Let's go." Michael keyed the microphone to advise air traffic control of their heading change.

Donovan reached up and spun the autopilot control knob. The *Galileo* responded immediately and banked toward the new heading.

"Talk to me, James. Tell me what we have." Donovan needed more information.

"Hang on a second; we're still putting this together."

"You've got the airplane, Michael. I'm going back."

Donovan threw off his harness and quickly swung out of the seat. He slid through the narrow cockpit door and hurried aft toward James' position. He could see the scientist's shiny bald head above the console. Half-moon reading glasses were positioned midway down his nose. He was writing furiously.

"Have you got it?"

James looked up and nodded. "Elmendorf just sent us the translation. "It's a Russian Akula class nuclear submarine, the *Drakon.* They carry a crew of seventy-three. They've had a fire on board and they're taking on water. They have no idea of their position."

Donovan leaned on the steel frame supporting the equipment. "Can we somehow find out their last known position? Maybe we can make an educated guess where they might be."

"Elmendorf is trying to contact the Russian Navy, and they've also talked to the Coast Guard. There aren't any other ships in the area due to the storm. They have no idea where to even start looking," James replied, frustration rising in his voice. "As far as anyone knows, we're the only ones who've heard the SOS."

Donovan looked into the expectant eyes of James and the two other scientists, then at the onboard equipment that stretched the length of the cabin.

"James. You said they're on fire?"

"That's what the translator at Elmendorf said. What are you thinking?"

"I'm wondering if it might be possible to use some of this high-priced hardware and get an infrared image from a satellite. Could we find a burning submarine in the middle of all this cold water?"

James' eyes lit up and he instantly began to type commands to the computer.

Though calm and collected on the surface, inside, Donovan was anything but. He wasn't afraid for himself or his crew. They were warm and dry, miles above the waves. He knew there was no safer place than in the ruggedly built Gulfstream. But the thought of sailors aboard a burning, sinking vessel pulled at him from a very private part of himself.

"I think I might have something!" James cried out triumphantly. "Right here. This is from NOAA-12. It's just a small dot really. I've enhanced it as much as I can. At first I thought it could be just a glitch, a ghost image—we get those from time to time during enhancement. But then I checked the same area from NOAA-14. Presto! The image is in the same place. I think this tiny speck is the sub, and the streak you can see is smoke."

It had taken Donovan only a second to process the infrared image himself.

"Get me the latitude and longitude. Tell Elmendorf what we've found, and inform them we're going to assist. Find out how long until rescue elements can get there."

"Will do," James replied, quickly.

Donovan turned to head back to the cockpit, a million things going through his mind. How badly was the sub damaged? Were there men in the water?

"Any changes?" Donovan asked as he took his seat.

"None. Hang on. I'm getting some coordinates from James." Michael carefully wrote the numbers on his chart, then looked up at Donovan. "This is where they are?"

"It's a Russian submarine. They're on fire and taking on water. We're the only ones who've heard the distress call."

"I'll read. You type," Michael replied, solemnly. He paused until Donovan's fingers were poised on the keyboard to the Flight Management System.

Donovan began to enter the crucial information. Once they loaded the information in the computers, they'd be able to lock in and fly directly to the crippled sub. He had carefully selected each number, then waited for Michael to verify the data.

"Couple it up. Let's see how far we have to go." Michael waited for the information to appear on the screen.

Donovan activated the new entry. In an instant, the FMS displayed the direct course to the sub. His earlier hunch had been correct; the distress call had come from the north.

"Bingo! They're 240 nautical miles dead ahead." Michael began comparing the electronic data against his chart.

"Tell air traffic control what we're doing and where we're going." Donovan adjusted the heading slightly to counter the powerful winds at 41,000 feet. "We'll also need clearance to descend down to a thousand feet when we get closer."

Michael looked up from his map. "We're going to be well inside Russian airspace when we reach the sub. Mind telling me what you plan on doing when we get there?"

"We've got," Donovan gestured to the FMS, "twenty-two minutes to figure that out."

"And less than ten minutes to spend overhead." Michael, too, surveyed the data. "Otherwise, we don't have enough fuel to get back to Anchorage."

"We're going to need more time," Donovan said, grimly. "Run some numbers and see how long we can stay with the sub and still make Cold Bay, or maybe King Salmon."

Michael nodded. He keyed the microphone and quickly arranged the clearance that Donovan wanted. When he gave the controller the coordinates of the distress call, the calm voice warned him about operations within Russian-controlled airspace.

"They've cleared us as requested. We can descend at our discretion. Oh, and by the way, they warned us about playing too close to the Russians."

Donovan smiled. The airspace violation was the least of their problems. He knew as well as Michael that if the Russians managed to get a fighter in the air, it was doubtful they'd be able to find a lone civilian Gulfstream in the middle of an Arctic storm.

"Okay. Let's go over a few things. Then you'll have some work to do in the back of the plane before we start down." Together, he and Michael quickly discussed their fuel situation and tried to plan some contingencies. Once that was finished, they went over a hastily laid plan to save the Russian sailors. Michael shot out of his seat once they'd covered everything. Donovan sat alone with his thoughts. He watched as the Gulfstream hurtled through the frigid air to the tiny pinpoint of ocean where people might be dying.

Thankfully it didn't take long for Michael to brief James and the others. They in turn prepared the equipment. Donovan had the cockpit situated when Michael returned.

"You ready?" Donovan asked as Michael readied himself for the descent.

"Any time you are." Michael cinched up his harness, then tested the straps to make sure they were tight. "I'm thinking this might get a little bumpy. What do you think?"

Donovan shot his friend a quick glance. Michael's sarcasm, honed by years of practice, was always a source of comfort. "Somewhere between a big thunderstorm and a hurricane."

"Oh, is that all? I was afraid it might be worse ...somewhere between a tornado and one of your landings."

"Call the *Drakon* one more time." Donovan was glad Michael seemed loose and relaxed. "See if you can let them know we're coming."

"Russian submarine *Drakon*. This is Eco-Watch 01. How do you read?" The only reply was more static. "*Drakon*. This is Eco-watch 01. Our ETA to your position is twelve minutes. Please respond."

"They'll see us soon enough," Donovan finally offered. He didn't want to think of all the reasons why radio contact had been lost. Conversation in the cockpit went silent as the blue sky evaporated and the Gulfstream knifed into the clouds. Donovan let the autopilot guide the plane flawlessly through the upper reaches of the atmosphere. Each minute put them deeper into the storm. Heavy turbulence began to toss the *Galileo* around the sky. Ice lashed at the exposed metal on the wings and tail.

"All the anti-ice systems on?" Donovan asked, his eyes glued to the instrument panel.

"Yeah," Michael replied as he looked out the side window. "There's no ice on the wings."

The Gulfstream shuddered as it shed huge waves of turbulence. The up and down drafts pummeled the *Galileo* as they descended lower into the storm. Donovan and Michael both pictured the fast-approaching water. The sunlight gradually dissolved into a dirty diffused gray.

"2,500 feet," Michael reported evenly as the radar altimeter came to life.

Donovan had been ready for the call. The radar altimeter was the most important system in the cockpit right now. It gave them a direct distance to the surface of the water. It would be the one instrument that would keep them from joining the Russians in the ocean.

"2,000 feet."

"How far to the sub?" Donovan clicked off the autopilot and took over manual control of the Gulfstream. The airplane came alive in his hands. He felt each jolt as it resonated through the airframe.

"Ten miles. We'll be there in four minutes."

Donovan nodded. He tried to prepare himself for what the ocean might look like. A submarine was a very small target; only the conning tower would stick up from the waves. He hoped there was still some smoke; it would make it far easier to locate them. If only they could break out of the weather. If they didn't have visual conditions at 500 feet, Donovan would have no choice but to abort the descent.

"1,500 feet. I've got water straight down!" Michael called out. "We're almost through."

Donovan looked outside just as the Gulfstream thundered out from the bottom of the overcast. He added power and leveled the *Galileo* safely between the clouds and grayish-green water. Immediately, he began to sweep the horizon. The wave-tossed ocean was filled with car-sized chunks of ice.

"How far?" Donovan asked

"Less than five miles. They could be anywhere. It's going to be dark soon, too."

A tiny flash caught Donovan's eye. Then another.

"There!" Donovan banked the *Galileo* into a steep turn. "I've got them!" A wave of relief swept over him. Less than two miles off the left wing, two flares drifted through the murky sky. He dropped the G-IV down to 200 feet and slowed. There was no sub to be seen. He shook his head as he realized it must have slipped beneath the waves. As they passed overhead, Donovan was horrified to see two dirty yellow rafts. Both had been flipped over, and men wearing survival suits were in the water. Some clung to the capsized rafts, others were adrift in the twenty-foot waves. Donovan rocked the wings back and forth to assure the sailors they'd been spotted.

"Holy shit!" Michael exclaimed. "The submarine is gone."

"Are we depressurized?" Donovan flew past the survivors and set up for another pass.

"Yeah." Michael checked to make sure there wasn't any differential pressure remaining in the cabin.

"Tell them to get ready in back."

Donovan leveled the plane and counted in his head. He planned the next turn to put them back over the same spot in the ocean.

"Donovan, Michael...this is James. The door won't open. It's stuck!"

Donovan shot Michael an alarmed look. Above all, they needed to open the rear baggage door.

"I'm on it," Michael said without hesitation, and began to unfasten his harness. "I bet it's frozen from all the moisture."

"Hurry," Donovan urged needlessly; he knew Michael was well aware of their rapidly deteriorating fuel situation.

"I'll be on the intercom shortly." Michael jumped out of his seat and scrambled out of the cockpit.

Donovan was alone once again. He banked the Gulfstream and headed back toward the survivors of the *Drakon*.

"Donovan, you read me?"

"I hear you, Michael. Did you get it open?"

"No. It's stuck big time. I've beat on it as much as I dared. It's frozen solid. There's no way we're going to be able to toss out one of our rafts. It was a great idea. At least they have the coordinates. James said he's already sent them to Elmendorf."

Donovan's shoulders slumped. If they could somehow get one of the rafts in the water, then rescue elements could easily home in on the built-in emergency transmitter. He knew it would take time for a ship to reach this area. The men in the water would drift with the storm. An accurate way to home in on them was critical. He cursed to himself as he flew over the survivors. He could see the desperate sailors wave as the *Galileo* flashed past at 200 knots.

"Hang on. James and I are going to try something else," Michael called out excitedly.

Donovan began the long count in his head again as he flew the Gulfstream away from the Russians. He tried not to look at the fuel gauges.

"Okay. It's open partway!" Michael reported. "I think it's enough. Give me two minutes to rig up the static line."

"Get ready to drop on my command." Donovan had every intention to fly right on the deck and release the raft. The line Michael had rigged would inflate the raft after it had cleared the door. The raft should inflate and land softly on the water. The emergency transmitter would start working immediately, and most importantly, it would stay with the men in the water.

"We're ready when you are," Michael finally reported.

Donovan lined the jet up with one of the yellow rafts. He pulled back on the power and allowed the Gulfstream to descend closer to the wind-swept waves. He had no choice but to guess the correct trajectory. The men in the water loomed large in front of the jet. Donovan held it as steady as he could.

"Now!" he shouted into the microphone.

"Raft away!"

Donovan added power and banked hard. The G-IV came around fast. Donovan caught sight of the yellow bundle as it impacted the dark water. The white splash subsided and Donovan realized that it hadn't inflated. The fully packed raft hit the water and vanished. The emergency transmitter was silently sinking to the bottom.

"Damn it! Michael, it didn't inflate. What happened?"

"The line snapped before it pulled the lanyard. It's the slipstream. We're too fast."

"Use the other raft," Donovan said.

"It's our last one. Are you sure?"

"We'll keep it—if you really think we'd have a prayer of ditching in this water, then being able to actually climb in the thing and survive."

"Good point. Let me rig a better system back here. Can you drop the gear and flaps? Slow us up as much as possible?"

"You got it." Donovan blew out a deep breath. He knew they were going to be critical on fuel. Hopefully they'd be able to climb up high and use the jetstream to get every mile out of what they had left.

"Okay. We're ready again. If this doesn't work, I'll jump out there and pull the damn thing myself."

Donovan knew such a declaration meant it was going to work. Michael was one of the most resourceful men he'd ever met. In a flurry of motion, Donovan lowered the flaps and landing gear. The *Galileo* slowed dramatically and he added power to compensate for the immense drag. Their rate of fuel burn went even higher. Donovan banked the G-IV around for their final run. Whether this attempt worked or not, they'd have no choice but to leave and head for the safety of Alaska.

Dead ahead he could see the sailors in the icy water. He hoped their survival suits were as good as the ones the U.S. Navy used. They were designed to ward off hypothermia in the frigid ocean. Donovan could easily put himself in their place. He knew they were helpless to do anything but try to keep their heads above water as the waves swept them up one side and dropped them down the backside. A roller coaster designed in hell itself.

Donovan had the Gulfstream slowed as much as he dared. The Russians faces were turned upward as he guided the G-IV directly overhead.

"Now, Michael!" Donovan held his breath and hoped the raft was inflating as it fell to the water.

"It worked!" Michael cried out through the intercom. "It's floating, just as pretty as you please."

Donovan banked hard to the left. Just as Michael promised, he saw their raft join the others. Moments later, through his headset, he heard the distinct signal of the emergency locator transmitter as it began to broadcast. Rescue vessels would now be able to home in on the men.

Donovan then raised the flaps and gear and began a slow climb to the east. Michael would join him shortly for the flight back to Alaska.

"Skipper," Michael uttered over the intercom. "We have a little problem. The door jumped out of its tracks. It's wedged into the frame and won't close."

Donovan grimaced at the words. If they couldn't close the door, they wouldn't be able to pressurize the airplane.

"Is it permanent? Or can you do something?"

"I think it's going to stay this way. James and I have both tried to pry it loose. But it's not moving. I may have used a little too much force when I opened the damn thing."

"I'd have done the same thing." Donovan knew he would have done whatever it took to get the door open and the raft into the water. "I think you should get back up here. This throws a little wrinkle in our plans."

"I'm on my way."

Donovan leveled off underneath the overcast and slowed down. He frowned as he studied their fuel situation. Without the ability to pressurize they couldn't climb to a fuel-efficient high altitude. Their situation had just gone from serious to critical. In a burst of understanding, Donovan made a wide turn to the west. Alaska was now out of the question. The Russian coast was their only hope of finding dry land.

"God, it's cold out there." Michael slid into the cockpit, blowing into his cupped hands. He quickly took his seat and surveyed the instruments. A moment later, he shot Donovan a startled look. He cocked his head as he grasped the plan.

"It's all we have," Donovan said as he shrugged. "I've never been to Russia. Have you?"

"Uh, yeah. Go there all the time," Michael quipped. "Any idea where in Russia we're headed?"

"I thought I'd leave you something to do." Donovan squinted at the dull light from the setting sun.

Michael grabbed the charts and began the process of finding an airport close enough for them to land. "I just hope we don't get our hands slapped for taking a plane full of sophisticated computers and technology into Russia. I seem to remember a memo to that effect once upon a time."

"I wrote that memo. You actually read it? I'm impressed." Donovan knew Michael had a huge aversion to paperwork. But he also remembered the meeting he had with the head of the National Security Agency. The nature of their high-tech mission put them in a classified materials status.

"It was an accident," Michael replied as he quickly calculated a rough distance on the chart. "I thought it was a party invitation."

"James, you still there?" Donovan transmitted.

"Yeah, I'm here."

"We're going to have to land this thing on Russian soil. I suggest you throw out anything you don't want to end up in the Kremlin. But leave the satellite up-link array as it is. It's our only way to reach the outside world."

"Are you sure?" James replied. "It's on the list of equipment to destroy."

"I'll take full responsibility," Donovan said quietly.

"Turn twenty degrees to the left," Michael reported. "I'm going to load the coordinates for the nearest landfall. I'm thinking we should get over land as quickly as we can. Seems our life rafts fell out of the plane."

"You did good work back there." Donovan turned to the new heading.

"I just hope we helped those poor souls." Michael shot Donovan a sideways glance. "I also hope the Russians take that into consideration when they impound our plane and put us in jail. I seem to have forgotten to get a Russian visa or any landing permits before we left."

"We'll be fine." Donovan scanned the distant horizon, then looked at their fuel status. He hoped he was correct.

"Okay." Michael looked up from the FMS. "Our new destination is Beringovskij. Since our database excludes Russia, it's the best I could do. Hopefully they have an airport, and the weather isn't too ugly. But most of all I hope they have some vodka. I think I might want a drink when we get on the ground."

Donovan gave Michael a quick smile. "First round is on me. Now that we have a destination in mind, I think we should use the link with Elmendorf to let everyone know what we're doing. Maybe they can run some interference for us?"

"I like that plan. In the meantime, maybe you can practice your Russian and start looking for MIGs." Michael switched to the cabin intercom and began to explain to the men in back what was needed.

A long twenty minutes passed before the rugged coast of eastern Russia came into view. They'd done everything they could think of to prepare themselves for their unannounced arrival. Elmendorf had promised to try to reach the Russians. They were able to confirm that Beringovskij did have an airport, though the condition and facilities were suspect. Donovan continued to fly below the overcast. More than anything he wished they'd have at least spotted one ship headed out toward the crew of the submarine. But the ocean was as empty as the sky.

"Jesus, it's getting dark, but I think I can see some smoke or something off to the right." Michael pointed just off the nose. "On the other side of that hill. Can you see it?"

"I'm going to slow down and go right at the town. Hopefully we'll see the airport." Donovan's attention was glued to their fuel status as he nudged the Gulfstream into a gentle turn. They could only stay in the air for another fifteen minutes at the most.

"Don't fly low enough for them to shoot at us," Michael joked. "I hate it when people shoot at me."

Slowly, the gray town came into view. Smoke rose from the stacks of a factory at the water's edge. Beyond the port, apartment buildings and small houses lined the roads until civilization gradually ended. The outskirts of town were only black rocks and snow. In the haze from Beringovskij, Donovan's eyes traced the route of what looked to be a dirt road. As he'd hoped, it led to the airport. The single runway appeared to be carved out of the forbidding landscape. There was one solitary building and no airplanes to be seen. The runway itself looked less than a mile long. The width was a mystery as only the center portion was free of snow. A tattered windsock told him which direction to land. It was going to be a tight fit for the *Galileo*.

"Oh, man," Michael whistled softly, as they flew over the town. "Is there still time to go back out to sea and ditch?"

"It's not much, is it? I hope they have jet fuel, or this might be home for a while."

"All of a sudden, Anchorage in November doesn't seem so bad," Michael said wistfully.

"I'm going to circle around and enter on a left downwind. The wind is favoring the north runway. The plan is to plunk this thing down on the end—then try to get it stopped. I don't think the runway is much more than 5,000 feet long." Donovan banked the airplane around the desolate airfield and began to configure the *Galileo* for landing. Michael finished the checklists as they rolled out on final approach. Donovan held the G-IV steady in the brisk wind. The runway looked even shorter than before. He nailed the exact speed they needed. The airplane was set up perfectly. The massive main gear touched down on the rough asphalt. Donovan mashed the brakes. He sensed the airplane settle as the spoilers flew up on each wing. He pulled hard on the thrust-reverse levers. The sound of the engines flooded the cockpit. He felt the anti-skid working through his feet as he kept the jet on the center of the runway. The end was coming fast...It was going to be close.

"80 knots," Michael called out. "Don't let up!"

Donovan pushed hard against the brakes; he didn't dare release any of the pressure. The entire airframe shuddered as it rolled down the uneven runway. The roar from the reverse thrust reached a crescendo. The energy from the landing slowly diminished as they neared a giant snowbank at the far end of the runway. Donovan brought the Gulfstream to a complete stop. Only a hundred feet remained, just enough room to turn around.

"Nice job." Michael turned to Donovan. "I wonder what else we can do for fun today?"

"We may just be getting started." Donovan wheeled the airplane around to taxi to the ramp.

"Why don't you be in charge of dinner reservations? I'm in the mood for someplace with atmosphere. A well-stocked wine cellar would be a plus."

Donovan nodded. "Sure thing. I'll see what I can do."

The ramp looked deserted. Donovan maneuvered the jet to one corner and set the brakes. They started the Auxiliary Power Unit. The APU was a small turbine engine in the tail that powered the electric and bleed-air systems. Until the remaining jet fuel ran out, they'd at least have lights and heat.

Donovan felt drained. He took his hands and feet off the controls. He wasn't surprised they felt weak. He forced himself up out of the seat and followed Michael to the back of the plane. Being on Russian soil was a complete wild card. They hadn't talked with anyone, and they didn't have any kind of a clearance. He wondered if they'd been tracked by Russian radar. Donovan's overriding concern at this point was to keep the airplane from being confiscated and gutted. He knew he was taking a risk by not destroying the satellite up-link. If worse came to worst, he'd do whatever it took to keep it out of Russian hands, even if it meant destroying the fifty million dollar airplane—and their only way out.

After they waited nearly twenty minutes in the Russian twilight, a truck finally labored down the road headed in their direction. Donovan and Michael gave each other pensive looks as the vehicle parked in front of the Gulfstream. Six Russian soldiers armed with automatic weapons piled out and took up positions around the airplane. A solitary figure then waved and walked up the stairs.

"Hello," he said, his expression as cold as the Russian air.

Surprised that the stranger spoke English, both Donovan and Michael returned the greeting and invited him into the warmth of the Gulfstream.

"You are Eco-Watch?"

Donovan nodded and motioned again for the Russian to come aboard.

"You are welcome here," he said in halting, barely understandable English. A smile finally appeared on his leathery face.

"We had an emergency." Donovan guessed the man was a civilian dignitary of some kind. He wore no military markings.

The man nodded each time Donovan spoke, his wide smile adding to Donovan's confusion. After nearly fifteen minutes, Donovan and his crew finally understood that word had been forwarded to make him and his Eco-Watch team as comfortable as possible. Further discussions assured Donovan that his airplane was safe and someone was coming to help.

It took nearly two hours, but Donovan was driven into the city and allowed to talk on the telephone with a ranking official from the closest military base. He learned that the beacon he'd dropped was being homed in on, and the survivors of the Russian submarine were in the process of being rescued. Special clearance was also being sent to Elmendorf Air Force Base in Alaska to allow a C-130 cargo plane with mechanics and fuel to land and assist the stranded Gulfstream. But since the C-130 wouldn't be ready to leave until the next day, Donovan and his crew were encouraged to enjoy the hospitality of Beringovskij.

Another hour passed as Donovan went back out and helped his team secure the *Galileo.* It started to snow as they huddled in the truck and bounced their way back into town. The driver dropped them in front of a plain brick building. The team hurried inside and was delighted to discover it was a hotel.

Once the first bottle of vodka was presented, and a round of toasts were offered by their Russian hosts, the night began to lose its clarity. After the third bottle was emptied amid the cheers of both American and Russian drinkers, another bottle materialized and the party continued into the wee hours of the dark Russian night.

The next day, feeling chewed up and spit out from their night of drinking with the Russians, Donovan and Michael were driven out to meet the Air Force C-130. Moving slowly, Donovan stayed with one group of airmen as they began transferring fuel from the transport plane to the Gulfstream. Michael, equally in pain, supervised the mechanics who repaired the cargo door. Within five hours they were ready to depart. Donovan gathered up his team and after many bear hugs and salutes from their new Russian friends, finally took the runway and departed for the long flight to Anchorage. Two days later, they arrived back in Washington D.C. to discover they were international heroes. The media machine was in full gear and clamored all over them to interview the daring pilots who'd rescued the stricken submariners. For Donovan, a man who more than anything wanted to avoid the spotlight, it was a nightmare.

Donovan looked up, mildly surprised to find himself turning off Prosperity Road and weaving the Range Rover down the tree-lined street that led to William's estate. He'd been lost in the memories of Russia.

Hidden behind mature oaks, a forest of dogwoods and manicured gardens, William's twenty-room colonial house was barely visible. Donovan slowed, but before he could stop and push the button, the iron gate swung open. He drove through and negotiated the brick-covered driveway that rose to the arched entrance.

Donovan smiled when he saw William standing in the doorway, his tall wiry frame topped with a thick shock of white hair. His fierce, dark eyes were surrounded by wrinkles and the inevitable lines of time. Intimidating to most, Donovan knew them as a source of great warmth. In the public arena, the seventy-two year-old man always cast an imposing presence. He was widely regarded as one of the elite, a major player in a city filled with powerful people. William's career had spanned nearly fifty years, and in that time he not only sat on the board of Huntington Oil, but he'd also been an economic and foreign policy advisor to every administration since Eisenhower. Once named a diplomat-at-large by the State Department, he'd spanned the globe "pissing out fires" as William jokingly put it. Even today, William easily had the ear of any sitting president, as well as the chairmen of a dozen Fortune 100 companies. Donovan had no idea how many corporate directorships the elder statesmen held, or exactly how far his sphere of influence stretched. But William VanGelder was easily one of the most connected men in America. He'd been Donovan's father's best friend—they'd gone to Dartmouth together—and in the years that followed, William was considered a member of the family. It had been William who had rushed to the Pacific after Donovan was orphaned. With the love and dedication of a parent, William became his legal guardian. Donovan loved him like a father.

"As usual, right on time." William opened the door as Donovan came closer.

Donovan stepped into the house and the two men shook hands, then embraced. William lived alone. His wife had died years ago and the statesman had never remarried. Donovan always felt as though this house and this man represented home for him. At some point over the years, William had begun to call him son. It somehow made them both feel closer. Donovan didn't know what he'd do if he ever lost William.

"Good to see you." Donovan stood back and smiled. "Did your staff run away again?"

William chuckled at the old joke. "I gave them the weekend off. We'll have to fend for ourselves. I've got breakfast ready in the study."

Donovan fell in step beside him as they walked down the wide hallway to the south wing of the house. The carpets and paintings were like old friends. The ornate woodwork and massive chandeliers seemed to sparkle as if welcoming him home. Donovan felt a security with William he rarely found with anyone else.

"Here, sit." William gestured toward two rich leather chairs situated in a corner of the large room. Bookcases filled two walls, and opposite them was a gallery of photographs that showed William in the presence of a veritable Who's Who of American industry and politics. As always, Donovan's eyes went to the picture of his parents. It was taken in Venice when he was a boy. His mother and father, forever young and in love. On a nearby table sat a silver carafe of coffee, two cups, and a small platter filled with Danish.

Donovan filled both cups, handed one to William, then sat down in the soft chair. He waited until William added cream and sugar to his coffee, then slowly stirred the mixture. Donovan was patient. William was a man who always carefully crafted what he was going to say.

"I received some disturbing news this morning." William softly placed his spoon on the saucer and took a measured sip. "I understand there was some unpleasantness in Bermuda yesterday?"

Donovan nodded, "There was an automobile accident. Two people were killed. I arrived in time to keep it from being three."

"The third being Lauren?" William looked directly at Donovan.

"Yes." Donovan lowered his eyes. "I had no idea she was in the group we were asked to pick up. They were late and I went off to find her. The car went down an embankment and she was trapped inside. There was also a man named Ian; he was injured. I'm going to have Eco-Watch pay for his medical bills."

"Of course." William paused. "Are you okay?"

Donovan knew the question was intended to probe at several different levels. Virtually nothing occurred in Donovan's life without William's knowledge. William represented the only person Donovan could truly talk with at times. William had been there from the very beginning of his relationship with Lauren.

"I'm fine," Donovan lied.

"I'm glad to hear that," William nodded, but an expression of concern came over his face. "The information I was given indicated that some sort of computer theft took place. The authorities have made you their prime suspect."

"What? Her computer was destroyed." Donovan's mind whirled from the implications.

"I'm only relaying what I've been told. Unfortunately, it's going to be an issue we need to deal with."

"I will tell you, I don't think the car wreck was an accident. I saw one of the brake lines. It looked to me like it had been cut."

"Right now the DIA is in an uproar. Seems they also have a murdered scientist who was supposed to leave Bermuda aboard a Navy ship."

"Lauren works for the DIA?"

William nodded. "It was news to me, too. She's been working on some cutting-edge technology to measure hurricane intensity. I don't know much beyond that."

"That would explain why she was in Bermuda."

"As you know, the DIA will try to throw a net around anyone they think is involved. Including you and Eco-Watch." William sighed. "The fact of the matter is that they still haven't forgotten that you flew an airplane full of the latest satellite communication technology into Russia. Of course, that, in and of itself, wasn't the end of the world. But, here you are again at the scene of another incident. In their eyes, you and Eco-Watch are the common denominator."

"I had a bad feeling the Russian thing hadn't died. You and I both know I'm not involved in any of this. It's purely circumstantial. I guess it doesn't matter that we helped save thirty-seven Russian sailors, the *Galileo* was never tampered with, and once we were fueled, we flew back to Alaska. Case closed."

"Obviously they couldn't find a direct connection, but the case definitely hasn't been closed."

Donovan clenched his teeth and nodded. He felt his world begin to close in on him. He unconsciously made a fist. Of all the things he'd fight to protect, Eco-Watch was at the top of the list.

"There's something else I need to show you. I don't know yet if it's related, but it couldn't have come at a worse time."

Donovan took the folder that William handed him. He opened it and pulled out the contents. Clipped to the first page was a passport-sized picture of Erin Walker.

"How do you know about her?" Donovan, startled, looked up at his mentor. "She's why I was going to call you today. I met her yesterday afternoon. She was snooping around mother's house."

"That doesn't come as much of a surprise, I'm afraid. Just read." William gestured for Donovan to continue.

Donovan scanned the first page. It consisted of a short biography. Erin Walker lived in Arlington, was twenty-seven years old, unmarried, and a graduate of Georgetown's School of Journalism. She was currently employed by the *Washington Post* as an investigative reporter, though she'd worked there less than a year. She'd grown up in Boston, raised by a middle class couple. Donovan flipped the sheet over. Page two was a photo of him at the house in Aldie. The next showed him driving his Porsche. Obviously, someone had been following him. He could tell the grainy photographs had been shot with a telephoto lens. The next picture was of his townhouse, followed by a photo of Lauren.

"She took these?" Donovan couldn't take his eyes from the pages. He felt the little hairs on the back of his neck stand up. Someone had managed to make copies of Erin's files. Donovan glanced up and gave William a questioning look.

"I know. It's not something I do very often, but sometimes it's a necessity. Keep going and you'll know why I had this woman investigated."

Donovan turned to the next document and was horrified to find a copy of a DIA report. It had CLASSIFIED stamped at the top. Quickly, Donovan scanned each paragraph. He and Eco-Watch were named as possible security risks. It outlined his rescue mission to Russia. He saw not only his name, but Michael's as well. It was almost more than he could bear. It was bad enough that the DIA was trying to link him to their problem, but Eco-Watch and Michael as well?

"How can she have all of this? I mean, I can understand she followed me, though I always thought I was being careful. But this report from the DIA?"

"I'm not sure. But it was obviously leaked to her, since there's no other way for her to have those files. You said you met her last night?"

"Yes. She set off the alarms at the country house. By accident, I came across her camera and confiscated the film. I developed it last night and discovered pictures of the grave-markers in the cemetery. I managed to get a picture of a license plate, someone who picked her up. It would be nice to know who else is involved."

"If she's seen the cemetery, it's only a matter of time before she figures out you're not who the world thinks you are." William slowly shook his head, a look of regret filling his eyes.

Donovan looked down at the report in his hands. "Is this all of it? Or is there more? How much does she know?"

"You can read the rest at your leisure. The crux of the matter right now is that she has more questions than answers. But she's looking for a conspiracy. She thinks Eco-Watch could be a front for clandestine government operations. Then she goes on to theorize that you might be selling top secret information—hence your big house in the country and a half-million-dollar sports car."

"She what?" Donovan slapped the papers down on his lap. "Who does this woman think she is?"

"As I said, the timing is unfortunate. If she's tied you to the house and has seen you in your car, the logical question she must be asking is how you afford such luxuries."

"We both know it's not what it appears to be."

"If she has a source inside the DIA, then it's only a matter of time before she finds out about what happened in Bermuda. As we speak, I can assure you the DIA and the FBI are starting a full investigation of you and Eco-Watch."

Donovan's temples throbbed.

"We need to stop her," William said solemnly.

"I can't believe this is happening," Donovan said, reeling at the implications. "This could be the end of everything I've worked so hard to build. In one fell swoop it will not only destroy the life I've tried to have, but Eco-Watch could also cease to exist. I can't let it happen."

"What would you like me to do?"

"Nothing." Donovan looked down at the dossier. "I think I need to read the rest of this."

William nodded as he rose. "I should also add that what you have there is only a small part of what Ms. Walker possesses. My source was, shall we say, interrupted as he was obtaining this for us."

"I just can't believe she's doing this. I mean, what would prompt her to start looking into my life? As far as anyone is concerned, I'm a nobody. There's got to be a reason for her to go to all this trouble."

"When you discover her motivation, you'll know how to deal with her."

"How much time do you think I have?" Donovan knew that discovery meant an instant change in his life. Relationships would shift overnight. It would destroy everything.

"I have no idea. Maybe a week? Hopefully we can find out more before we have to make any major decisions."

"I can't imagine anything worse than this. After all we've done, to be found out by a single reporter."

"I'd like to tell you something." William leaned forward and put his hand on Donovan's forearm. "You haven't had an easy life, son, and I can't begin to tell you how proud I am of all you've accomplished...But I always feared that this day would come. My only surprise is that you managed to stay hidden for so long."

"I still might pull it off." Donovan knew the words sounded hollow.

"If anyone can, it's you." William gave Donovan's arm a squeeze of encouragement. "Whatever happens, you know I'll do everything I can. I'm here for you always."

"I know." Donovan put a hand over William's. "I'll live. All I ask is that if I have to leave EcoWatch, you'll do everything you can to make sure it survives. It represents the best thing I've ever done."

"You have my word. I'll leave you alone so you can read." William started to leave, then stopped and turned. "Are you sure this wouldn't be the time to explain everything to Lauren? It might be useful."

"I can't," Donovan said honestly.

"Costa Rica was a long time ago."

Donovan crumbled a little inside at William's words. "It doesn't feel that way at times. I can still see Meredith as if it were yesterday."

"I won't even pretend to understand how you must feel. I loved Meredith, too. But life does go on, son. You survived the loss of Meredith. You grieved as any man would. Years later you met Lauren and she fell in love with you...and you her."

"Then she left," Donovan remarked quickly. "Let's not forget that part."

William reached for the door to the study. "Don't forget the reason she left."

William's soft-spoken words were like a blow to his stomach. Donovan inwardly sank at the memory. Lauren had confronted him just after he'd finally brought his mother's remains to rest in the family cemetery. There was no way he could include Lauren in the process. It would have created far too many problems. It had been a difficult and emotional time for him as he stood at the plot and buried her once again. There had been only three other people at the tiny ceremony. A minister, William, and William's niece Stephanie. She lived in Europe, and had flown back for the memorial. He could still remember his shock and fear as Lauren had asked him pointblank about the blond. He had no response; he'd been caught off guard at a time when his defenses were down. He wouldn't lie to her, yet he couldn't tell the truth. He'd stood there mute as he ran through a full range of emotions. He couldn't explain that Stephanie was a friend, that Elizabeth was his mother. It would have led to his having to tell Lauren everything, something he wasn't prepared to do. He could still see Lauren's wounded expression. Her eyes were full of anger and betrayal, condemnation he did...and didn't deserve.

"Am I not right?" William challenged quietly.

"Yes and no." Donovan sighed. "But right now I have far bigger problems than my relationship with Lauren."

"Yes you do. All I'm suggesting is that if everything is going to be made public, she might appreciate it coming from you, instead of reading about it in the newspaper. There might be some tactical value in your being the messenger."

"I'll keep that in mind." Donovan watched as the only link with his other life let himself out of the room. Alone in the study, Donovan took a moment to collect himself. He looked down at the picture of Erin Walker. Her eyes were pretty, as was her smile, but to Donovan she represented a threat to everything he held sacred. If she divulged who he was the world would once again make him its focal point. It wouldn't take her long to start unraveling the mystery. The disturbing thought hurtled him back in time, seventeen years ago, to when Robert Huntington became Donovan Nash.

Donovan lowered his head as the inevitable images began to assail him. Meredith Barnes had been a wild card from the very beginning. He could still remember her unruly mane of curly red hair, freckled face, and startling green eyes. She was a smallish woman with a fiery Irish temperament and deep-felt passions. Meredith always said her mission in life was a simple one—to educate and perhaps save mankind from itself. An environmental activist, Meredith cut a wide swath wherever she went. What with her rallying cries in defense of the Brazilian rain forests, against over-fishing the oceans, and man's irresponsible use of chemicals, Meredith Barnes was a force to be reckoned with. Her tireless dedication and energy made her the key spokesperson for the environmental movement the world over.

Meredith had been invited to be the keynote speaker at a conference in San Jose, Costa Rica. The political summit of Third World environmentalists promised to be a landmark gathering. Meredith had orchestrated a historic assemblage of people who could help preserve the valuable forests in Central and South America. The night before they'd left, Donovan had asked her to marry him, and she'd said yes. Deliriously happy, they both knew they were destined to spend their lives together.

As they'd flown to Costa Rica, they'd laughed at their rocky beginning and marveled at how intertwined they'd become since then. They'd met after a private fund-raiser, one of the many social outings Donovan attended. He'd donated money to her cause and was about to leave for the evening when she'd cornered him. In what he learned later was typical Meredith style, she tore up his check and threw the pieces defiantly up in the air. She demanded to know how, as the heir to the Huntington Oil fortune, he could sleep at night. She stood on her tip-toes and poked him in the chest as she rattled off a dozen ways his multinational company was polluting the earth. At that moment, Meredith was the last person he thought he would have fallen in love with.

The confrontation with her caused him to take a hard look at how Huntington Oil did business. With her as a sounding board, Huntington Oil adopted a series of measures that turned the company into a model for eco-friendly industries worldwide. In the process, he and Meredith had slowly fallen in love.

The Costa Rican conference represented a huge opportunity to bring environmental issues to the world stage. Donovan, as one of the richest men in the world, and Meredith, one of the world's most loved champions for ecology, brought a storm of media attention to the conference. Donovan had rented a villa in the hills above San Jose, to provide them with an oasis of calm away from the chaos of the conference itself. It was a decision that had haunted Donovan for the last eighteen years.

They'd left the security of the conference and were headed to the villa. The initial reception had gone well and he and Meredith were reveling in their early success. As the car wound through the narrow streets, they were unaware that they were being followed. In the blink of an eye, a car blocked their path and hooded gunmen leaped out and surrounded them. Their driver was killed instantly in a hail of bullets. Donovan was slammed in the face with the butt of a rifle. His last image of Meredith was of her kicking and screaming as she was dragged from the back seat.

The next three weeks were a living nightmare. The media turned into a feeding frenzy focused on Meredith's kidnapping. Members of the summit fled to their home countries. Overnight the conference dissolved into mayhem as the ransom demands made the papers. Caught between the posturing governments of both Costa Rica and the United States, Donovan desperately tried to pay the ten million dollar ransom—but the bureaucrats blocked his efforts. Frantic, Donovan used his own people to try to contact the terrorists. He arranged to pay them the money, but only after he talked to Meredith, for proof that she was still alive. The phone call had come in the middle of the night. Meredith's weak voice reached out to him in the darkness. In a rush of words, she begged him not to give in to their demands for money, for it would only serve to fuel the enemies of her work. As the phone was yanked from her hand, he heard her cry out that she loved him, then the line went dead. The next day her lifeless body was found in a muddy field. She was twenty-eight when her life ended.

Devastated with grief, he'd taken Meredith's body home to California. What he would never have expected was the angry reception he received. Environmentalists were outraged that billionaire Robert Huntington had allowed their matriarch to be killed. Rumors surfaced that he'd had her killed to stop her assault on the industrialized countries. The media picked up on the story and he was vilified on a global level. So quick and complete was his guilt in the public's eye—the protesters so angry—he'd been unable to attend Meredith's funeral. Despite a press release about his efforts to save her, it only took days before he went from being one of the cultural elite to one of the most despised men in the world. Meredith was a beacon of light for millions of people and he'd let her die.

Ultimately, Meredith's death forced Donovan to retreat to his one true sanctuary, his mother's house in Virginia. He could clearly remember fighting the pain of losing Meredith, the helplessness of having his life so tragically altered. Then there were the death threats against him, as well as against his friends and colleagues. There was a call to boycott Huntington Oil. In the end, he'd finally decided drastic times called for drastic measures. Robert Huntington would die. He, along with all of his money, would cease to exist. It only took him and William a few weeks to arrange the details.

He'd left Reno, Nevada in a Beechcraft King Air, one of several airplanes he owned and regularly piloted himself. He'd been careful to make sure there were witnesses who saw him climb aboard the plane that evening. As darkness fell, he flew westward on the normal flight plan toward Monterey. At the prearranged time, with the airplane on autopilot, he left the cockpit and moved to the back of the plane. As the seconds ticked off his watch he said a quiet goodbye to his life as Robert Huntington. At the exact moment he'd calculated, he pushed through the exit and parachuted into the night sky. He watched as the strobe lights on his airplane faded in the distance. The King Air had enough fuel to fly several hundred miles out to sea before its engines quit. As planned, he landed just south of Modesto in a plowed field. Once he'd wrapped up the parachute, he contacted William on a small two-way radio. Half an hour later William picked him up and they drove away.

The next morning in a hotel room in Oakland, he and William watched on television as the floating debris from his King Air was discovered in the Pacific Ocean. The media confirmed that billionaire Robert Huntington had perished. Speculation flew as to whether the crash was an accident, a murder, or perhaps even a suicide. So ready to embrace his death, the media never stopped to consider that he might actually be alive. Huntington Oil released a statement confirming the passing of its beloved chairman and quickly named a successor from the board of directors.

That evening, well disguised and armed with a fake passport, he and William boarded a privately chartered jet for Europe.

At the end of several months, his cosmetic surgery scars had healed. Twenty pounds lighter and sporting a full beard, he left Switzerland. From the ashes of his old life rose a new man. With a flawless set of documents and a well-thought-out history, Donovan Nash began his new life. He and William had liquidated his public assets, disguised his fortune in a myriad of trusts and foreign institutions. For nearly a decade, he bounced around between continents. He rediscovered his love of flying, and worked as a pilot in Asia, Europe, and Africa. He used his money and skills to make relief flights into war or famine-plagued areas. Though no one was looking for a dead man, he was always careful never to reveal his previous life to those around him. It had taken years, but Donovan finally came across the idea that would fully embody his and Meredith's shared dream. Using part of his vast fortune, he established the foundation that funded Eco-Watch. Now on a truly global scale he was making a difference. He liked to think Meredith would have been proud of him.

Donovan blinked back the tears. The memory of Meredith represented a longing he would carry forever. He'd been twenty-seven when she died. He was now forty-five. Up until a few months ago, not one in a thousand people in the country had ever heard of Eco-Watch. Donovan was convinced that Erin had started her investigation after the events in Russia. With the dossier in hand, he went in search of William.

"William?" Donovan called out through the silent house.

"I'm out here."

Donovan went through a set of French doors onto the patio. William was sitting in the shade with the Sunday paper. Donovan smiled; it was a ritual the two of them developed years ago. They would talk for hours about whatever events were occurring: the victories and defeats in the arena of business and politics, the failings and triumphs of individuals and governments. It was one of the many ways by which William had educated Donovan in the ways of the world.

"Finished?" William lowered the paper.

"I have two questions."

"I'll answer if I can."

"How did you find out she was investigating me?"

"She asked for an appointment with the head of the Phoenix Foundation. No doubt to try to discover who exactly was funding Eco-Watch." William smiled. "I arranged for that meeting to take place, at which time our investigation of her began."

"Where can I find her right now?"

William nodded as if expecting the question. "I made the call a few minutes ago. She's at her apartment."

"What did you tell her?" Donovan couldn't believe William had contacted her.

"Relax. She thinks she's going to have brunch with someone from the foundation. Someone who wants to talk off the record. It wasn't much of a lie, was it?"

Donovan nodded; the old man was still as shrewd as they came. The Phoenix Foundation was the primary financial body behind Eco-Watch, as well as a dozen other philanthropic endeavors.

Each year the foundation gave away millions of dollars of Donovan's money. He and William both sat on the board.

"No. I guess that's not stretching the truth much."

"I'd love to see the look on her face when you show up. Should be an interesting meeting." William turned the page of the newspaper. "I suggest you go shave and make yourself presentable. You need to be at the Westfields Conference Center in two hours."

The hotel was only minutes from his townhouse. Donovan knew he had plenty of time to go home and get ready.

"I'd almost consider trying to buy her off," Donovan thought out loud. "But I don't think she's the type."

"Neither do I, or I would have made that overture. But you need to be careful. She already thinks you're a dangerous man, so be careful you don't give her any ammunition. I think the key is to convince her she is entirely wrong about you, that she'll become the laughing-stock of Washington journalism if she publishes."

"I already thought of that tactic. What if it doesn't work?"

"You could always seduce her," William said, nonchalantly.

"What on earth would make you say that?" Donovan heard the words, but couldn't believe William had said them.

"Go with your strengths, son. She doesn't know you've read some of her notes, only that you found her camera. Tell her you could still have her arrested for trespassing, but that you're more intrigued than angry. It's an opportunity that's already in place."

Donovan shook his head, though he had to admit that William made a good case for a more subtle approach. He remembered the old saying about keeping your friends close, but your enemies closer.

"She's fascinated with you, or she wouldn't have gotten this far with her investigation. My guess is this young woman can't help but wonder what makes a man like you tick. It would be far easier to show her she's wrong about you than to try to tell her. Besides, she is rather fetching."

"You're the ladies man, not me." Donovan was always amazed at the caliber of women seen on William's arm at various Washington social and political events. "We both know you could sell ashes to the devil. Plus, your life is far more interesting than mine."

William grinned at the remark.

"We'll see what happens. I think it's going to be one of those last minute, go-with-my-gut-calls."

"You do that very well," William said, quietly. "It's why there are thirty-seven Russian men still alive to be husbands and fathers. Not to mention Lauren, and all the other people you've helped in your life. If you really stop and think about it, this Walker girl is really no match for you."

Donovan didn't really need the pep talk. But considering that his carefully orchestrated life might be unraveling in the next few hours, he soaked up the words.

CHAPTER EIGHT

Lauren rubbed her tired eyes. For the last three hours she'd been at her lab, sitting in front of the computer screens, working with *Jonah* and a National Oceanic and Atmospheric Administration reconnaissance flight. The NOAA aircraft had been making runs into Helena, flying precise paths in relation to *Jonah*. Using perspectives from the two Doppler systems, Lauren and NOAA had painted the first 3-D picture of the inner workings of a category five hurricane.

The turbulence had driven the four-engine P-3 farther and farther out from the eye. They were now at the outer reaches of *Jonah*'s range. But the results so far had been staggering. Helena was rapidly becoming the most powerful hurricane of the last decade. Her sustained winds were building upward of 195 mph. The pressure was so low that tons of seawater were being lifted as the ocean bowed up within the eye.

Lauren was still haunted by the reports from the USS *Thorn.* The 563-foot warship had been severely battered as it traversed its way out of the storm. Reinforced armor plated metal had torn and buckled under the force of eighty-foot waves. Major sections of the ship's superstructure had been pounded, then ripped away. Lauren knew that a cubic yard of water weighed 1,700 pounds. In the guise of a hurtling wave, the physics surrounding its destructive properties were astounding. The destroyer was now out of harm's way, limping southwest towards the Naval base at Norfolk, Virginia. Lauren lowered her head at the thought of the nine men reported lost at sea.

"I'll take over if you want." Dr. Simmons eased his girth into a seat next to Lauren. "You look shot. Let me finish this up for you."

"Thanks." Usually Lauren hated relinquishing her seat on the front lines, but she felt totally drained. Her earlier conversation with Calvin had done nothing to settle her frayed nerves. They were still waiting for the weather to allow a flight into Bermuda. The only good news was that due to the hurricane, most of the communications on the island were down. Whoever had her laptop, even if they'd hacked their way inside, hadn't been able to do anything with the information. If events went as planned, Calvin's security team would be able to get to Bermuda and find those responsible before there was any real damage done. She'd wanted so much to ask about Donovan's involvement, but she couldn't. She wanted to believe he was innocent...but a small nagging voice kept asking, could she be wrong?

Lauren's mother and Abigail weighed heavily on her thoughts also. She knew they were packing, getting ready to leave town. There was a flight out of Baltimore first thing in the morning. It would be Abigail's first airplane ride, and Lauren wouldn't be there for her. The thought of missing any small first in her daughter's life caused a sharp pang of guilt.

"Dr. McKenna." Brent Whitaker leaned in close. "Here are the early statistical-dynamic observations. We're loading them into the computer right now. You should have access to them in a few minutes."

Lauren stepped over and took the printout from his outstretched hand. "Thank you." She'd look it over when she went back to her office.

"Oh, and Doctor?" Brent swiveled in his chair and took off his glasses. "I just wanted—needed to ask you something."

"Yes?"

"Is there anything that's going to slow this hurricane down? Am I missing something here?"

"No, you're not missing anything. Unless we have a major shift in the steering currents controlling Helena, she's coming ashore."

"That's what I thought. I've been keeping an eye on them, but they're staying the same. As far as I can see, there's nothing on the horizon that's going to turn or dissipate this thing."

"It's still a hurricane." Lauren knew she was trying to sound optimistic, despite the reality of the situation. "And it's still far out to sea. An awful lot can happen."

"I know. It's just that I've never really been in the path. I've studied a lot of weather, but from in here it all seems abstract."

"Maybe you should put in a bid for some field work. It always helps to have some hands-on experience in the real world."

"I've been trying," Brent sighed.

"You want me to put a word in for you?"

"I'd appreciate that more than you could imagine."

Lauren gave the young man a look of encouragement as she walked away. With Victor dead, she could use a new assistant. She made a mental note to ask Calvin about him.

She slipped out of the lab and went straight to the ladies' room. Relieved it was empty, she leaned forward and studied her reflection in the mirror. As she suspected, her red-tinged eyes had the hint of dark circles under them. She pulled a few rogue strands of hair back over her ear and straightened her blouse in the waistband of her slacks. Lauren washed her hands, then smoothed out her lab coat as best she could. It was then she looked down and saw the report that Brent had handed her. The data jumped off the page—

no wonder Brent had been so concerned. She quickly headed for her office. She hadn't gotten halfway there when her pager hummed at her waist. She stopped and read the message. It was from Calvin. He'd obviously called her at the lab and her office. His patience must be growing thin for him to beep her in the building. Moments later, she reached the door that led into Calvin's office.

"Go right in, Dr. McKenna." His assistant motioned toward Calvin's door.

"Thank you." Lauren knocked lightly and walked in. "You were looking for me?"

Calvin was on the phone. He pointed at a chair and continued his conversation. "Yes, sir. I'm well aware of what that costs. I think it's far too early to make that determination. Mr. Secretary, my expert just walked in. I'm going to put you on speaker."

Lauren knew she was going to be put on the spot. She sat up and again scanned the papers she had in her hand. Brent had unknowingly handed her the exact information she needed. Helena had somehow compacted herself, and in the process grown stronger. It was something no scientist had ever seen. This storm was now operating outside the realm of known hurricane behavior.

Calvin pushed a button on his phone.

"Mr. Secretary, I have Dr. Lauren McKenna with me. She's our leading scientist in the atmospheric forecasting unit."

"Hello, Dr. McKenna. Morris Bradshaw here. I'm familiar with some of your work. Very impressive. Very forward thinking."

"Why thank you, Secretary Bradshaw." Lauren had never spoken with the Secretary of Defense before. It was he to whom the DIA ultimately answered.

"Why don't you ask Dr. McKenna what you just asked me?" Calvin nodded in Lauren's direction. "I'm sure she can shed more light on the problem than I can."

"I'll cut right to the chase, Dr. McKenna. This hurricane, how big is it going to get? And when and where is it going to make landfall?"

Lauren was scanning the latest information as he asked the questions. She knew her answer would shape the military's emergency contingency plans. It was the National Weather Service's job to coordinate with civil disaster preparedness teams. They were the people who issued the warnings and evacuation notices. Her job was to make sure the people and assets of the armed forces were fully aware of any meteorological events that might impact their operations.

"Mr. Secretary, at this point it's a little too early to be specific. The storm is still almost three days from landfall. But the geographic area I'm concerned with would be from Washington D.C. all the way north to Rhode Island. We could see catastrophic winds and ocean conditions between those two points. Once the storm moves ashore, there's the risk of tornadic activity and flooding rain for several hundred miles inland. All military assets in that corridor, in my opinion, are at risk."

"Jesus! You're serious?"

"Yes, Mr. Secretary. I think we're going to see one of the strongest storms in history come ashore in the next seventy-two hours. It's a very compact, but violent hurricane at this moment. We in atmospheric research have never seen a storm of this magnitude. And frankly, I don't see anything that's going to slow it down."

"Is Washington, D.C. itself at risk?"

"Not in a strategic sense. We could see some flooding from the storm surge and damage from high winds. But as I'm sure you know, hurricanes quickly lose their energy once they pass over land. Washington is just far enough inland, and in this case, just far enough south to miss the full fury of Helena."

"What about Baltimore, Philadelphia, and New York?"

"They are at risk. But I'm especially concerned about New York City. If Helena were to come ashore at that precise spot, we'd have an unimaginable disaster on our hands."

"Dr. McKenna, could you please elaborate?"

"If Helena does what I think she'll do, we could have a seventy-five to ninety-foot storm surge wash directly up both the Hudson and East rivers. Everything below the sixth floor in Manhattan will be underwater. Older buildings will simply collapse. Subways would be flooded; the city will stop functioning for weeks or months. We're looking at the possibility of 300 plus mile-per-hour winds. The low-lying areas of Long Island, into New Jersey, could be scrubbed clean. I won't even try to predict the loss of life and property, sir."

"Holy mother of God. Calvin. Is this right? Could this happen?"

Calvin looked directly at the phone. "If it's what Dr. McKenna says, then I believe it."

"Okay. Here's what I'm going to need from your end. I want hourly reports on this hurricane. I'm going to brief the Cabinet and the Joint Chiefs. Any change in the status of this storm and I want to know about it immediately. Calvin, make sure Dr. McKenna has my direct number. Good news or bad, I want it as quickly as you find anything out. Am I clear on this point?"

"Yes, Mr. Secretary."

"I'll expect to hear from you soon."

Lauren looked at Calvin as the line went dead.

"I know I might have put you on the spot, Lauren." Calvin scratched his nose as he searched for the words he was looking for. "I was only asking for an update. Couldn't you have sugar-coated it a little?"

"I did," Lauren replied evenly. "I'll need to go crunch some numbers. The good news is with *Jonah* we're receiving more data than ever before. This is going to be the most well-documented hurricane in history. Of all the storms I've ever studied, this is the one that we need to understand. The bad news is I don't think this is a freak hurricane. I have a bad feeling that we're seeing a marked shift in the global weather patterns...and super-hurricanes are one of the byproducts."

"I hope you're wrong." Calvin absently tapped his pencil on his desk.

"Me, too." Lauren paused. "I'm having my mother take Abigail and leave Baltimore. They're going to Chicago."

"You are?" A look of alarm came over him. "You really think this is going to be a catastrophe?"

"Of the highest order. As hard as I search for any hint that Helena is weakening, or turning—all I find is the opposite."

"Keep me posted." Calvin jotted down a number from memory. "Here's Bradshaw's direct line. I'd appreciate it if any communication came through me first. But if that's not possible, don't hesitate to call him yourself. Our first priority is to keep the Pentagon up to date."

"I'll either be in my office or the lab." Lauren stood to go. She hesitated for a moment. "Any word on the investigation?"

"I'm not at liberty to discuss it at this time."

Lauren nodded and let herself out of Calvin's office and headed for her own. The sudden shift in his behavior had been obvious, but Lauren had no idea what it meant. She wondered if she herself were under investigation. If there weren't a category five hurricane coming their way, would she be on suspension? A hundred questions flew through her mind as she walked into her office and settled behind her desk. As Brent had promised, the latest data had been downloaded. She logged on and began to sift through the information. The DIA's new weather-dedicated computer was a marvel of speed and efficiency. It processed data at a rate of 3.2 trillion instructions per second, almost thirty times faster than the computer it replaced. With the click of a mouse, Lauren was looking at the latest Doppler images from both *Jonah* and the NOAA P-3. As before, the high-reflectivity of Helena's eye wall was astounding. Monstrous up and down drafts were at work, both feeding and releasing the tremendous energy of the storm.

She scanned the constant readouts from *Jonah.* The barometric pressure was now down to 26.82 inches. As she clicked back out to the view from the DMSP satellite, she was struck once again by the organized beauty of Helena. With her knowledge of the existing winds and surrounding atmospheric conditions, she could see Helena squeeze in between the high pressure area stalled over Georgia, and a weaker high pressure dome over Nova Scotia. Lauren quickly began to augment the image. First, she added the steering winds. The west to east jet stream was still in place. Acting like wind over a chimney, it allowed Helena to continue to grow. After adjusting for a new set of sea-surface temperature values, Lauren clicked the mouse and sat back while the computer calculated new track information. Moments later, the information blinked to life on her screen. Lauren bit her lip and moved closer. It was the worst of all possibilities. The computer showed the mass of churning clouds continuing to build in strength. There was a slight northerly correction to her current track, but not enough to swing it out into the North Atlantic. Lauren rubbed her arms at a sudden chill, though she didn't know if it was from the air-conditioning or the information staring back at her. She pulled her lab coat tight...in seventy-two hours Helena would come ashore at New York City. Only by then it would be so powerful, it would be as if a 100 mile wide, F-4 tornado hit the city. While a typical tornado only lasted a few minutes, Helena's winds would lash at the city for hours. To make matters worse, Helena would arrive at the same time as high tide, with storm surge and wave heights as high as 100 feet. Her dire predictions to Secretary Bradshaw had been on the conservative side. She knew the National Weather Service was looking at basically the same information. The warnings would be going out; people all up and down the East Coast would be alerted. Lauren shook her head in despair. Helena wasn't something you could prepare for—the destruction promised to be of a magnitude no one had ever experienced.

Donovan Nash made a quick drive through the parking lot and spotted Erin's white Honda. He looked around to make sure he wasn't being observed, then jumped out and affixed a small object underneath her car. It only took him a moment. Relieved no one had spotted him, he drove directly to the main entrance.

After collecting the ticket from the valet, Donovan entered the high-ceilinged lobby. The tile floor reflected the huge chandelier that hung overhead. There were dozens of people conversing in small groups, the murmur of their conversations echoing around the large room. Donovan scanned the lobby looking for Erin. He finally spotted her. She was seated in a high-backed chair, staring directly at him. There was a panicked look on her face. Donovan wondered briefly if she were going to bolt. She wore a navy blue dress, a simple necklace flashing from her neck. The contrast from yesterday to today wasn't lost on Donovan. Erin Walker looked far more sophisticated and mature this morning than she did sitting in the back of a sheriff's car. He wondered if she'd developed her film yet. Had she figured out he'd taken her film, or did she think her camera had malfunctioned? As he neared, he could see her worried eyes dart from side to side, as if she were trying to decide which way she could run. Donovan closed in on her.

"Good morning, Ms. Walker," Donovan said, trying not to sound threatening. "Nice to see you again."

"Hello, Mr. Nash." Erin squirmed ever so slightly in her chair.

"Did you figure out what was wrong with your car?" As Donovan hovered over her, he could see a vein in her wrist pumping furiously.

"Yes. Thank you. It was something with the spark plugs. I didn't really understand the whole mechanical explanation. But it works now, which is all I care about."

"That's good to hear," Donovan said, sweetly. "They really do have an excellent Sunday brunch here. Do you come here often?"

"This is my first time." Erin glanced over Donovan's shoulder. "I'm actually meeting with someone."

"Oh really?" Donovan feigned surprise. "Business or pleasure?"

"That's none of your business, Mr. Nash." Erin smiled, but the tone of her voice was serious.

Donovan unbuttoned his blazer and sat down in a chair across from hers. He could see in her eyes that her stress level had just gone higher. He smiled at her as he formed his words.

"You can call me Donovan. You know, I was hoping I would run into you again. I wanted to apologize about yesterday. I'd had a hard day, then when I received the call from the sheriff, well, it was kind of the straw that broke the camel's back. You weren't doing anything wrong and I'm sorry you were treated like a criminal."

"Thank you," Erin said, warily.

"I'm the caretaker of the estate and I fear I was a little overprotective. The owners are out of the country a great deal and it's my responsibility to keep an eye on the place. My worst fear is that something happens when they're away."

"I understand." Erin's eyes narrowed. "Who does live there? It's a beautiful house."

"It's a long story." As Donovan had hoped, her curiosity was beginning to replace her apprehension. "I work for a research organization. It's funded by various grants and foundations. The owners of the house are among those kind enough to donate money to our work. What do you do?"

"I'm a student," Erin lied. "I'm working on my MBA at Georgetown."

"Good for you," Donovan remarked, being as charming as he dared. He could almost hear the gears in her head trying to weigh the advantage of continuing the conversation with him or waiting for her source from the foundation.

"Well, I'm glad we ran into each other. I'd ask you to join me for brunch but perhaps another time?" He acted as if he were getting ready to leave.

"Mr. Nash—I mean Donovan." Erin hesitated, then looked down at her watch. "I was supposed to meet someone here for business, but they're late."

"Oh?" Donovan settled back in his chair, a twinkle coming to his eye. "Would it be improper for me to suggest that we maybe go somewhere else? I've always found that if you get stood up, it increases your bargaining power later."

A wry smile came to Erin's mouth. "I like that idea. Is there another restaurant close by?"

Donovan thought back to William's sage words of advice. Erin was more than eager to get close to the man she was investigating. He wondered how far this exchange could go.

"It's not as nice as this. But there's a Marriott not far from here. The food is decent."

"Let me leave a note. Then we can go." Erin stood and smoothed her dress. Donovan rose also and ushered her toward the front desk.

"Did you valet park?" Donovan asked. "I can have them bring both of our cars up. You can follow me over."

Erin slipped the ticket out of her purse and handed it over. Donovan took it and headed out into the bright morning sun. He wondered what was running through Erin's mind. Did she really think their meeting was random? He rehearsed in his mind what he would and wouldn't divulge. The important thing was to find out as much about her motivation as he could. As Donovan waited for their cars to be brought up, one thought did occur to him. What if Erin were far more intelligent than she initially seemed? It would make her considerably more dangerous than he'd first thought.

"Okay. I'm ready." Erin joined him under the covered entrance.

"The cars should be up shortly," Donovan said, then smiled. "I must say, you look nicer today than you did yesterday sitting in a police car."

"God, I hope so," Erin laughed easily, stepping a fraction closer to him. "So are you a pilot? Was that a flight suit you had on yesterday?"

"Yeah. I'd just landed when the call came in. That was part of my crummy day. I'd just flown in from Bermuda."

"Really?" Erin frowned as if trying to put two and two together. "Isn't that where the hurricane is?"

Donovan nodded and watched her expression closely. "It's what I do. I fly for an organization called Eco-Watch. I doubt if you've heard of us."

Erin cocked her head. "It sounds vaguely familiar. Wasn't there something in the news awhile back about them?"

"Yeah. It's ancient history now. So, what brought you out to the country anyway?"

"I was out shopping for antiques. I'd never been out to Aldie before. I live in Arlington and I don't get out of the city very often. I was trying to take a scenic route back home when my car died."

Donovan nodded as if interested. But she'd told her first truth; he knew she did actually live in Arlington. The valet brought up the Range Rover; another followed shortly with her Honda.

"Follow me." Donovan smiled as he walked her to her car. He knew this was going to be an interesting test of wills.

As they pulled out of the hotel drive, Donovan took out his cell phone and dialed William. He held his arm close; he didn't want Erin to realize he was on the phone.

"It's me," Donovan said quickly when the phone was picked up. "I'm with her now; we're going for brunch."

"Nicely done," William replied. "I'm glad you called. I've just received some new information."

"What now?"

"The license plate you had me run. The car that dropped off your visitor last night. It belongs to a photographer with the *Washington Post*."

"Figures." Donovan looked in his rearview mirror; Erin was four car-lengths behind. "We've probably seen some of his work."

"That would be my guess. Be careful."

"Do me a favor. Can you give me a call in forty-five minutes or so? Nothing important, but I might want an excuse to leave."

"No problem. When should we arrange to meet again?"

"I'm not sure. I'll touch base with you later today. I have to fly in the morning. I'd say tomorrow afternoon at the latest."

"Very well. Good luck."

"Thanks." Donovan disconnected the call, then looked back at Erin. He wondered how many people were involved in her investigation. Did he have a prayer of trying to keep a lid on her story? Or was it already too late?

They pulled into the parking lot of the Marriott. Donovan was counting on it not to be very crowded. Tourist season was wrapping up and the business travelers would be in short supply on a Sunday morning. Erin pulled up next to him. Donovan came around and opened the door for her.

"Thank you." Erin stood and looked around her. "I didn't know this place was here."

"It's kind of tucked in behind the trees." Donovan gestured toward the door. He walked beside her and caught the aroma of her perfume, which was stronger than before. They walked in and made their way to the restaurant. In a matter of moments they were seated at a table next to the window, well away from any other patrons.

"The air conditioning feels good," Erin remarked. "I can't believe the heat this summer. It's the worst I've ever seen."

"The hurricane should at least bring us some rain." Donovan hated that they were talking about the weather. He felt as if he'd lost some of the momentum he'd gained.

"You know," Erin continued, "it occurred to me as we drove over here. I don't really know very much about you."

Donovan held her gaze. She was a good liar. He couldn't see any sign of weakness in her brown eyes.

"I had the same thought. Here I am sitting with a known criminal. I hope I'm safe."

Erin laughed. "I'm not a criminal. Besides, I doubt if someone like you has much to fear."

"Someone like me?" Donovan asked, innocently. He studied her face, the way her short hair made the line from her ear down her neck look sleek and inviting. Her smile was infectious, two small dimples forming when she laughed.

"I do have a confession to make." Erin lowered her eyes as the waitress came and filled their coffee cups.

Donovan waited until the waitress left two menus and walked away.

"You were about to make a confession," Donovan prodded, thinking this should prove interesting.

"I do remember you now. From the newspaper. Weren't you the one who saved all those Russian sailors? Last winter, after their submarine sank or something?"

Donovan nodded. "Yes, that's me. But like I said earlier, it's ancient history."

"You're a brave man." Erin reached into her purse, then leaned forward and placed both hands on the table. "Not many people would have done something like that."

"I was in the right place at the right time. Plus I had a lot of help." Donovan caught something different in her eyes. Was it respect, fear, or something else?

"What do you do when you're not flying all over the world rescuing people?"

"Mostly paperwork," Donovan countered. His internal alarms had just gone off. He'd watched as Erin had reached into her purse then positioned the small leather bag differently on her chair. If he were a gambling man, he'd bet that she'd just switched on a tape recorder.

"No, really," Erin said, smiling. "What does Donovan Nash do for fun?"

"Well, let's see." Donovan clasped his hands together and looked straight at her. "It might be easier to tell you what I don't do. I don't allow my charming brunch companion to record our conversation. I thought reporters were supposed to ask permission if they were going to use a tape recorder. Now please put it on the table and turn it off."

Erin's eyes narrowed as she returned his gaze. "I have no idea what you're talking about."

"You don't want to go to jail, do you?" Donovan took a sip from his cup, his eyes never leaving hers.

"Is that a threat?"

"It's a fact of life, I'm afraid. After you left yesterday, I found a few articles missing. At first I thought they might have been misplaced. But as I searched later, I couldn't find them. I do hope you're getting all of this on tape. If the police were to search your car I'm afraid they'd find the stolen items in the trunk."

"You bastard." Erin hesitated, then reached into her bag, switched off the miniature recorder, and laid it on the table.

"Thank you." Donovan picked it up and set it carefully off to the side. "Now tell me, Erin, were you surprised when your pictures didn't turn out?"

"What do you want from me?" Erin's eyes burned with anger and fear. "This wasn't a chance meeting, was it? You set this up, didn't you?"

Donovan shrugged. "It doesn't matter. What does matter is why you were snooping around shooting pictures of my friend's house."

"Look. What I told you was true. My car broke down and I went up to the house for help. It's as simple as that. Now, if you'll excuse me I've had enough of this harassment."

"I'm calling 911," Donovan said smoothly, making no move to block her exit.

Erin froze as Donovan picked up his cell phone.

"You're setting me up," Erin hissed. Her face had gone red with anger.

"How does it feel?"

"I have no idea what you're talking about."

"I think we'll get along far better if we both drop all the pretense. I found your camera and took the film. I replaced it, then shot a few pictures of the palm of my hand, but you already know that part. I also waited for you to come back and retrieve the Nikon. I enjoyed the part where it took you all of seven seconds to fix your car. The guy who brought you back out to the estate works for the *Post*. Now I'd suggest we both start over from the beginning."

Erin glared at him. "I'm a writer. I'm doing a story on Eco-Watch."

Donovan silently applauded her determination. As she stared at him with her angry eyes, he could almost hear the gears in her head trying to decide how much to reveal.

"How's it going?" Donovan replied, dryly. "You know, in the past when people have done a story about us, they come visit the facility, meet the people. We're more than happy to assist any legitimate writer."

"What's your point?"

"I'd suggest you keep talking. We both know it's not that simple." Donovan's finger lightly traced the buttons on his phone.

"Look." Erin sighed heavily, her eyes darting anxiously around the room. "I started working on a story about you, no big deal. You're a celebrity, right?"

Donovan shrugged.

"I'm just doing my job. If you want to know any more than that, you can buy a copy of the paper."

Donovan's expression never changed. He turned and looked out the window, then casually punched the send button on his cell phone.

"No, wait!"

Donovan lowered his hand and turned toward her. Even though his bluff was weak, it seemed to be working. Right now he wanted as much information as he could get. This might be his only chance to try to stop her.

"Go on." Donovan gestured with the phone in his hand. "The truth this time."

"I live and breathe the truth, Mr. Nash. Or shall I call you Robert Huntington?"

The words were like a giant vise that reached out and tightened around his chest. It had been nearly two decades since he'd heard another person call him by that name.

"Excuse me?" Donovan tilted his head as if he'd missed what she'd said.

Erin leaned forward. "I was up all night on the computer, but I finally figured it out. Donovan Nash is actually the late billionaire Robert Huntington. It's all so clear now. Your car, your house in the country...you're him."

Donovan stared at her. He wished he could say something that would wipe the superior grin off of her face. She'd said what he feared most and was now gloating in her revelation.

"I can tell by your expression that I'm right," Erin said, triumphantly. "It's hard to believe I'm sitting across the table from *the* Robert Huntington.

"That's pretty far-fetched." Donovan was having trouble getting a full breath. The tables had just turned and he felt powerless. Images of the press flew through his mind—the hordes of jackal-minded men and women clamoring outside his house in Los Angeles after Meredith was murdered. His carefully orchestrated "normal" life was going to end. He didn't know what he felt most, sadness or anger.

"You can stop acting like you don't know what I'm talking about. Or maybe I can refresh your memory? Let's see...where should I start? You graduated magna cum laude from your father's alma mater of Dartmouth. A double major in business and economics—plus I believe you're also fluent in both French and Spanish. From there you went to England and attended Oxford University, where you earned another degree in international business strategies. Once you took the helm of Huntington Oil you were easily one of the top ten richest men in America. Shall I continue?"

Donovan sat motionless as the memories washed over him.

"I found pictures of you back then. The number of magazine covers you graced is quite impressive. It was years ago, and the face is somewhat different, but I'm guessing you had plastic surgery. Your eyes are the same; you have the same build. You're him. Your body was never recovered. The entire plane crash scenario was just a ploy."

Donovan took a measured sip of his coffee.

"Why?" Erin prodded. "You had everything. Why vanish?"

"Why do you think?" he said finally, knowing the pain and anguish were visible in his eyes. He saw Erin recoil at the change in his demeanor. "Why does everyone think that being rich erases all of life's pain? If you've done your research, then you know about Meredith Barnes."

"I'm not the enemy." Erin leaned back and lowered her eyes. "I'm a reporter who uncovered the story of the year. Of course I know about Meredith Barnes—who doesn't? But that's not the story...you are."

"No matter the cost?" Donovan felt all of his buried hatred toward the media come to the surface. "Even if you destroy something worthwhile in the process?"

"The truth is the truth." Erin looked him in the eye. "I don't play God, Mr. Nash. It's not my call."

Donovan knew he'd lost. Erin had something of immense value and nothing he could say or do would change her mind. He thought of her notes, the espionage charges, the leaked DIA report. It occurred to him that her discovery of Robert Huntington would erase all of that. Eco-Watch could go on as before. If he managed this correctly, then perhaps he would be the only victim.

"I can only guess what you are thinking," Erin continued to press. "Please don't try to change my mind. I can assure you, it'll be a waste of time."

"I'm aware of that. If you'd wanted money you'd have asked by now. I know all about people going to extreme lengths to take money from those who they think have too much."

"I just want the story. Nothing else."

"You've never lost a loved one, have you?"

Erin lowered her head. "I'm sorry for your loss. But it doesn't change anything."

Donovan nodded."Okay. Here's where I make you a deal."

"I've been waiting for this part," Erin replied.

"I'll give you the story. You can have an exclusive."

"What's the catch?"

"You have to give me some time to get my affairs in order. There are things I need to do, people I need to talk to before all of this comes out."

"What assurances do I have that you won't release the story to someone else, steal my thunder?"

"That's what's important to you, isn't it? Your thunder? The fact that you'll make the front page."

"Up to now, I haven't made it out of the Arts and Leisure section. I'm good at what I do and this will go a long way toward proving that to everyone."

"You have my word," Donovan said simply. His mind was still working on a way to minimize the damage this woman was about to inflict.

"Not good enough." Erin shook her head.

"It'll have to be." Donovan gave her a piercing stare. "My cooperation doesn't come without a price, Ms. Walker. What I want from you is the identity of the person who leaked you the classified DIA documents. We both know that neither myself nor Eco-Watch is in the business of espionage."

Erin swallowed hard at his demand; her eyes grew large.

"You're a dangerous man," she said finally. "I can only guess you've somehow seen my notes."

"I have my sources also, but I'm not unreasonable," he countered, feeling he'd scored a minor victory. "Don't you agree I'm probably not someone who needs to steal and sell classified data?"

"Perhaps not. I'll have to think about it."

"You do that." Donovan pulled out a business card and jotted down the number of his cell phone. "Here's how you can reach me. We can start working on this the minute you agree to help me."

"If you have as much to lose as you claim...a girl might wonder if she's safe." Erin took the card from his outstretched hand. "Am I?"

"Perfectly," Donovan promised. "I wouldn't have bothered to talk to you if that weren't the case. I think you know by now, I'm in the business of helping people, not hurting them."

"I had to ask." Erin looked slightly embarrassed as well as relieved. "There are a lot of strange things going on in Washington."

"I won't say it's been enjoyable." Donovan's voice was filled with a strange detachment.

Erin picked up her tape recorder and stood to leave. "I'll be in touch. But we do have a deal, right? You won't leak this story to anyone else?"

"Only if you help me."

"I think I can arrange that." Erin slung her purse over her shoulder.

Donovan felt hollow, but managed a nod.

"There's really nothing in the trunk of my car, is there?" She cocked her head as if finally understanding.

He shook his head. "I'll be waiting for your call."

Donovan watched as the Honda sped out of the parking lot. He left some bills on the table and went outside. He started the Range Rover and waited for the air conditioning to make the interior livable. With the push of a button, he dialed William.

"It's me again. Our date was cut short. She just left."

"Did it go well?"

"No. She knows everything. How are things at your end?"

"I think we made some progress. I'll know within the hour. Did she get our little gift?"

"Yes." Donovan knew he was referring to the tracking device he'd put under her rear wheel well.

"Good. Now go relax, play golf. Do something except worry about what's going to happen. I think we've accomplished a great deal this morning."

"I'll talk to you later." Donovan felt a rush of warmth for his oldest friend. "And thank you for everything."

"It's my pleasure. Take care of yourself."

Donovan hung up the phone. He felt both drained and vulnerable. The last twenty-four hours had been an emotional roller coaster. For the time being, everything was out of his hands. He thought of Lauren. What would she make of all of this? Was William right? Should he tell her everything—before she read about him in the newspaper? Feeling dejected, Donovan put the Range Rover into gear and headed away from the hotel. He wasn't sure where he was going, only that he needed to be in motion.

CHAPTER NINE

Lauren made her way down the hallway. Since it was Sunday, the entire floor was nearly deserted. Most of the people were in the lab watching Helena's progress. In the last two hours the hurricane had intensified as it rotated toward the coast. Lauren finally had to leave, feeling the walls starting to close in. Her head throbbed from too many hours staring at computer monitors. She needed to find something to take or her headache would linger all day. As more data had come in, Lauren had the overwhelming impression she was watching a slow-motion train wreck. Even if Helena started to dissipate right at that moment, it would still impact the U.S. as a devastating storm—and everything she'd seen told her Helena was only growing stronger.

Lauren went into her office and sat wearily at her desk. She looked in her purse for some aspirin but found none. Irritated, she quickly scoured the contents of her desk and again came up empty. She slammed the last drawer shut in frustration. She leaned back and kneaded the knotted muscles in her neck. A memory of Donovan's back rubs jumped into her consciousness. She closed her eyes and wished the uninvited images of him would stop. She thought of the research flight scheduled for early in the morning. Under any other circumstances she wouldn't go, but being two people short, it was now a necessity. She wondered if Donovan would be flying the mission, or if he'd pass.

The phone on her desk erupted. Lauren jumped at the intrusion and quickly snatched the receiver before it could ring again.

"Dr. McKenna."

"Lauren. Calvin here. Can you please come to my office?"

"On my way." Lauren quietly replaced the phone. She swung out of her chair and headed down the hall.

"Doctor." Brent called out from the door of the lab as Lauren hurried past. He had a clipboard in his hand.

"Yes?" She stopped and looked in his direction.

"We were just looking for you. The director wants you."

"I'm on my way."

Brent jogged to where she stood. "Here's the latest track printout from *Jonah.* The steering winds have definitely accelerated. She's picked up two knots."

"Can I have that?" Lauren took the clipboard and scanned the data. She looked into Brent's eager face. She knew he was trying very hard to please her. She remembered her promise to recommend him for field duty.

"Pretty amazing, isn't it?"

"Yes it is. Thanks. I really need to go. I'll be back in the lab as soon as I'm finished with Calvin." She noticed him eyeing her figure.

"I'll be at my station monitoring the storm." Brent lowered his eyes to the floor.

Lauren turned away from him and smiled. She wondered if Brent were trying to impress her to get out of the lab, or if there were another, more *personal* reason for his eagerness to please. The thought was both flattering and beyond contemplation. He was a nice kid, but nearly a decade younger. Still, it was nice to be noticed; thought of as a woman instead of just another lab coat. The thoughts vanished as she hurried into Calvin's office.

"Close the door." Calvin looked up as she arrived.

Lauren swung the heavy door until it latched. She turned and found him getting out from behind his desk. He was headed for the leather chairs, his signal that this was going to be a more relaxed dialogue instead of an official conversation. He waited until she'd settled, then sat down himself.

"What a morning! I've been on the phone non-stop since we last spoke. Capitol Hill and the Pentagon are pretty riled up about this storm. They've corroborated your estimates with the National Weather Service and NOAA, as well as with NASA. Hell, I think they'd bring in the local weather man from Channel Five if they thought they could gain some insight."

"I just told them what I thought."

"I understand, and you did a good job. The information from *Jonah* is proving to be the most real-time asset we have right now in predicting the hurricane. Which makes us the lead agency as far as the White House is concerned."

"The White House?" Lauren asked, not sure what Calvin was building up to.

"The last call I fielded was from Drew Montori. Do you know who he is?"

Lauren nodded. He was the president's Chief of Staff. Everything that reached the Oval Office first went through Montori.

"He was fully briefed on the situation and had just spoken with the director of the Federal Emergency Management Agency. He gave me some numbers."

"Damage assessment?" Lauren ventured.

Calvin nodded as he slid his glasses on, then looked down at his hastily scribbled notes.

"Up until now, Hurricane Andrew has been the costliest disaster in U.S. history. Something like twenty billion dollars, almost a quarter million people left homeless. He gave me those numbers as a reference. Helena, if it comes ashore where you estimated—and by the way, everyone else's calculations seem to be more or less in line with yours... Anyway, if Helena does what we think she'll do, the Eastern Seaboard from the tip of Long Island down to Atlantic City will be totally destroyed. As you said, New York City will cease to function. Even being conservative, they think damage will easily run into the trillions of dollars. Loss of life will be somewhere in the neighborhood of 10,000 to 15,000 people."

Lauren nodded in agreement at the grim projections.

"Millions will lose their homes and livelihoods. The White House says the long-term economic damage would be off the chart. This disaster is being compared with a nuclear detonation over New York City. In their words, it's unacceptable."

"Tell them to get used to it. Helena is coming," Lauren said, forcefully. She held up the clipboard Brent had given her. "And faster than we thought."

He nodded and removed his glasses. He fidgeted in his seat.

"What's up, Calvin?" Lauren asked, quietly. She'd known him a long time and only on rare occasions had she seen him stall.

"Your security clearance has just been upgraded. What I have to tell you is for your ears only. It will not, I repeat, *not* be shared with anyone. Do I make myself clear?"

"Yes." Lauren ignored the small chill that ran up and down her spine.

"There's something the Pentagon and the White House are considering. Seems a few years back, a bright young graduate student at MIT proposed a bold plan to alter the size and energy of a hurricane."

Lauren physically jumped in her seat. With a sinking feeling, she knew Calvin was talking about her.

"You remember, I take it?"

"Calvin." Lauren's body went numb. "I wrote that paper as a joke. I was sick and tired of studying hurricanes. I'd had it up to my eyeballs about their formation and structure. One night, I decided to just blow the damn thing up. I did it as a lark. My professor got a kick out of it and it was over. It was never intended to leave the classroom!"

"He got a kick out of it, all right. He forwarded it to the Pentagon. The operation is called 'Thor's Hammer'."

"Oh no." Lauren heard her voice waver. "They can't. It's not a reality; it's a joke. I used all sorts of imaginary principles, starting with a bomb big enough to have an effect. This is crazy!"

"According to what Montori told me, a lot of people have honed your theory over the years.

They're convinced your original concept still holds up. The detonation of a high-yield nuclear device in the eye of a hurricane will alter the dynamics to the point the storm begins to fall in on itself."

"Calvin." Lauren leaned forward and used her hands for emphasis. "It would take a nuclear bomb in the 100-125 megaton class to even put a dent in Helena."

"It's being transported from storage to an Air Force base in Texas as we speak. It's 115 megatons. They're modifying a B-1 bomber to carry the device."

Lauren jumped to her feet. "Never in my wildest dreams did I intend for my stupid little paper to become someone's plan!"

"From what I've been told, it's a brilliant theory."

Lauren's hands went to her temples as she processed the information. She began to pace back and forth behind her chair. "Calvin, the bomb that destroyed Hiroshima was a measly fifteen kilotons. You're telling me that they have a device eight-thousand times bigger lying around to use on Helena?"

"It was built years ago...for this purpose. They wanted to use it on Andrew, but as that storm formed over the Caribbean, they couldn't get a clean shot before it hit Florida. Helena is out over the open Atlantic. It's the perfect opportunity, as outlined in your original hypothesis."

"Oh, screw my hypothesis!" Lauren stopped pacing and steadied herself. "I'm sorry, Calvin, but my God! I feel like someone read my diary and plastered it up on a billboard. We can't go around and nuke every bit of bad weather we find on the planet. This is the most irresponsible act I've ever heard of. Helena is already a product of our own doing. I truly believe that we're moving toward a major climatic shift due to a dozen factors, not the least of which is global warming. Have they learned nothing from witnessing our past errors?"

"You're preaching to the choir, Lauren." Calvin removed his glasses and inspected them against the light. "Forget for a moment that this was your brainchild. I can tell you that you will in no way be named as the author of the plan. I saw to that. But our—my question to you is...will it work?"

Lauren studied Calvin. He was dead serious. Any moral reservations she might have were insignificant. At that moment she knew that the government, despite any of her reservations, was going to try to blow up Helena. She took a deep breath, put both hands on the back of the chair, and tried to collect her thoughts. Slowly, she weighed her objections against the devastation of New York City, against the horrific damage estimates she'd heard.

"They have their experts," Lauren said, softly. "Ask them."

"I'm asking you." Calvin finished cleaning his wire-rim glasses and slid them onto his nose.

"Why?" Lauren knew Calvin was fishing.

"They have the device. You have the knowledge of hurricanes. Plus, we have *Jonah*. The exact placement and altitude of the air-burst within the storm is still being debated."

"You're kidding me." Lauren cocked her head and despite her anger she could feel the scientist in her begin to take over. Analytical thought began to override her emotional reluctance. The physics of both the hurricane and the detonation began to race through her mind.

"They'll be delivering the weapon from very high altitude," Calvin continued. "The B-1 bomber will need some base line upper wind information to place the device exactly where it needs to be. That's where you come in. You and *Jonah*."

"How 'clean' is this bomb?" Lauren asked, wanting to delay her participation. Part of her wanted to put as much distance from the operation as she could. But, another part of her wondered if they would get it right if she didn't help.

"It's a hydrogen bomb, of course. It's ninety-seven percent fusion. I'm told what little radiation there is will be sent high into the stratosphere."

Lauren nodded in agreement. "At least they got that part right."

"Would you please sit down and discuss this rationally?" Calvin gestured toward a chair. "I know you're not thrilled with this; I'm not sure

I am either. But it's what we're faced with. I'm asking for your help. You, as a professional."

"I'd feel better if you made it an order," Lauren remarked, anger and exasperation in her voice.

"Fine. It's an order."

Lauren nodded. The small victory helped soothe her conflicted emotions. She continued to pace, far too agitated to sit still.

"My original theory speculated that the device be detonated near the strongest point of the eye wall. In Helena, as with most hurricanes in this hemisphere, the southeastern quadrant of the rotating storm is the most intense. You don't want to allow the bomb to actually enter the storm itself. The up and down drafts will disrupt the trajectory. It's important to maintain the drop in the relative calm of the eye itself."

"Go on." Calvin began taking notes.

"The initial blast will reach a temperature close to a million degrees centigrade, which is 10,000 times hotter than the surface of the sun. Everything it touches will be instantly vaporized in the expanding high-pressure gas bubble. As you know, the internal mechanism of a hurricane is relatively fragile, a delicate balance of temperature, winds, and pressure. The shock wave from the explosion expands outward at 100 times the speed of sound. The engine, or eye wall of the hurricane, is gone in the blink of an eye. The severe low pressure is replaced with what we call an over-pressure event. It becomes a storm without a way to build or even sustain itself. In layman's terms, we're gutting Helena. In a flash of energy and light, Helena will die and all that will remain will be a disintegrating tropical storm mass.

"So you have no doubt it will work?" Calvin stopped writing and looked up. "This bomb is big enough to gut the storm."

"I have lots of doubts. It will definitely alter Helena as we know it. But there is another danger. One I didn't include in my paper."

Calvin looked at her expectantly.

"Imagine this." Lauren hesitated as she tried to recall the details. "As the bomb detonates, tons of water vapor will be pulled up into the gigantic mushroom cloud. Keep in mind, this bomb is twice as big as any ever set off. The surrounding water has been superheated from the fireball. If the force of the initial shock wave isn't powerful enough to eliminate the rotation of the hurricane, then what we could create is a smaller, more intense storm center than we had before."

Calvin furrowed his brow.

Using her hands, Lauren continued: "Picture a mushroom cloud, except it's spinning. The heated water is now doing what it was doing before, except the ocean is near boiling. That energy could re-form into an incredibly intense storm. Smaller, yet its power could be off the scale. It could create some kind of mutant event. A hybrid storm—part hurricane, part tornado. It could have winds over 500 mph."

"No one said a thing about this possibility." Calvin shook his head in dismay. "What are the odds we could be jumping from the frying pan into the fire?"

Lauren shrugged, "Maybe fifteen to twenty percent. No one really knows."

"God damn it!" Calvin pulled himself up out of the chair and walked to his desk.

Lauren watched as he tossed his pen down and glared at the phone. She wondered what was going through his mind. It surprised her that no one had mentioned the potentially negative side effect of the operation.

"I'm going to pass along what you've told me," Calvin said wearily. "But to tell you the truth, I don't think it will make much of a difference. The key question here is the exact detonation point within the storm. That's what they want from us."

"I don't know," Lauren said, honestly. "It will all depend on the data we receive from *Jonah,* as well as information about the high altitude winds. If we could determine both within a few hours of when they want to set it off, it'll give us the best chance to get it right."

Calvin nodded. "They've set 250 miles as the minimum distance from the coast. How soon will Helena reach that point?"

Lauren picked a number off the top of her head. "I'd say sometime tomorrow, maybe around noon or so."

"You're scheduled to go out on the Eco-Watch jet tomorrow, right?"

"Yes. We're going to test some equipment that should allow us to interface high altitude information from the Gulfstream with data from *Jonah*. But with the same information, it would be easy for us to calculate the exact drop coordinates."

"Can you do that without any of your team being aware of what you're doing? We don't want anyone to know about this until afterward."

"What about the rest of the world? We aren't going to start a war by setting off an H-bomb, are we?"

"No. The president has spoken with the other nuclear-capable countries. To be honest, everyone is just as curious as we are if this will work."

"My God. What have I done?"

"It's not you, Lauren; someone else would have thought of this at some point. Focus on the devastation Helena is going to inflict on New York City. I'm told the emergency management teams are having trouble getting people to evacuate the shore areas. Millions of New Yorkers refuse to believe this storm will harm them. It's going to be a slaughter."

Lauren felt defeated. She'd read countless papers on the psychological impact impending weather phenomena had on people. Denial was still the major reason people were killed in the path of severe weather. The section of the coast that was most vulnerable was an area that rarely saw deadly storms. The denial factor would be especially high. The loss of life could indeed be staggering.

"I want you to take the rest of the day off. It's important for you to be sharp in the morning. Who among your staff will be going with you?"

"I think Dr. Simmons and I could handle all the telemetry readings."

"I'd like you to take Brent Whitaker. He's as good with the computer models as anyone. It might be good to have him along."

"Fine. He's been wanting some field duty."

"Inform them. I'm going to double check with Eco-Watch that the equipment is ready to go. What time do you want to be airborne?"

"Make it an 0830 takeoff. We can get our readings and get out of there. I'd like to be back here before they do it...I want to watch it in real time from here in the lab."

"Consider it done." Calvin moved to escort Lauren to the door. "Now get some rest."

Lauren nodded.

"Now go—and not a word to anyone about what we discussed. Try to relax. If I need you I'll reach you on your cell phone. Otherwise, I don't want to hear from you until we're linked up in the morning from the Eco-Watch plane."

Lauren nodded and let herself out of the room. She resisted the temptation to slip into the control room and look at Helena. Instead, she went to her office and collected her things. She quickly called

Carl and Brent to tell them about tomorrow's mission. Once she was finished she left the building. To the meteorologist in her, the muggy air outside spoke volumes about the coming storm—a storm that one way or the other was going to rewrite the history books. She tried to push her own historical footnote from her mind. What she really wanted right now was to go home.

As Lauren negotiated the heavy traffic on I-95, she couldn't shake the odd sensation of knowing that Helena would cease to exist tomorrow, or at least cease as they knew it. Lauren was so engrossed in her thoughts that she was mildly surprised at how quick the drive home had been. She pulled up in her driveway and shut off the car. It wasn't until she'd opened the door and slid out into the muggy afternoon that she realized another car had pulled up behind hers.

Terrified, Lauren instantly thought of the attempt on her life in Bermuda. She thought about bolting for the safety of the house, but instead froze, not wanting to lead anyone to where her mother and Abigail waited. Lauren held her breath as a young woman got out and walked toward her.

"Excuse me."

"Who are you?" Lauren challenged.

"I didn't mean to startle you. My name is Erin Walker. I'm a writer for *The Washington Post.* I wonder if I might have a few words with you?"

Lauren eyed the woman. She didn't appear threatening.

"Please," Erin continued. "It will only take a few minutes of your time."

"I don't have anything to say to you." Lauren reached into her purse for her phone. She quickly scrolled down until she found the number for Calvin's direct line. She positioned her finger on the send button. If she needed help, Calvin would be her best hope.

"Oh, but I think you do."

"Any inquiries from the press need to be approved through my office," Lauren turned as if to dismiss the reporter.

"I'm not writing about the DIA," Erin said quietly. "I'm writing about Donovan Nash."

Lauren froze. How did this woman connect her to Donovan? How did she find out where she lived? She thought of Abigail inside the house. The last thing she wanted was for Donovan to read in the newspaper that he was a father. Lauren turned to face her questioner.

"I have no idea what it is you're after. But I only know Mr. Nash professionally."

"Look," Erin let out a breath. "I'm doing a story about Donovan Nash the person. Not the man behind Eco-Watch. I know you were involved with him. Now, I can write about the relationship with your help...or I can do it without. Your choice. But I'd think you'd want to make sure your voice was heard."

Lauren's heart pounded in her chest. "I'm sorry, but you're wasting your time. I've never been involved with Mr. Nash. Now I'd appreciate it if you'd leave."

"Are you sure that's the position you want to take?"

"There isn't any other position. You're chasing ghosts."

"Interesting choice of words."

Lauren had no idea what the woman's cryptic response meant.

"Here's my business card," Erin continued. "I can't tell you everything I know right now. But in a few days when you read about Mr. Nash in the *Post*—you may want to call me. We can sit down and talk then."

Lauren took the card, surprised at the confidence in the reporter's tone. She watched as the woman strode back to her car.

"I'll be expecting your call," Erin called over her shoulder.

Lauren looked down at the card, then at her phone. She pushed the button, and moments later Calvin answered.

CHAPTER TEN

Donovan eased the gearshift smoothly into second, then released the clutch on the speeding Porsche. The transmission whined and the low-slung sports car slowed magnificently. Feeling the warm wind through his hair, Donovan touched the gas pedal and moved with the car through the sharp corner. The stereo belted out the loud driving guitar of Jimi Hendrix. He gunned the engine, absorbed with the sheer power of the 5.5 liter, ten-cylinder motor. Finally, he tapped the brake and fishtailed the last thirty feet to the driveway of his estate. With a final flurry, he accelerated down the long driveway and finished with a tire squealing half turn to a stop. He switched off the ignition and noticed William's Jaguar parked near the garage.

Donovan pulled himself out of the car and hurried to the house to find William. He called out, but there wasn't any response. From the kitchen window, he spotted the immaculately dressed older man down near the cemetery. William's head was bowed, and in his hand was a large bouquet of flowers.

Donovan quietly walked out the back door and went to join his friend. It had been a long time since they'd both been here together. It brought back the memories of his mother's funeral. Then his thoughts drifted to the day he'd asked William to help him cease being Robert Huntington. It somehow seemed fitting they were here together again, eighteen years later, as all of their work was crashing down around them.

Donovan approached, making sure he made enough noise to alert William of his presence, since he didn't want to startle him. William turned and looked as he came closer. Donovan could see tears in his eyes.

"I thought you'd be out here," William said, his voice cracking with emotion. "It's been far too long since I came to pay my respects."

"The flowers look nice." Donovan could see that William had laid bouquets on both his mother's and his father's graves.

"You know," William mused out loud, "I remember the first time your father invited me out here. It was in the early '50s, '52 I think."

"It must have been beautiful then. I'm afraid I haven't kept up Mom's gardens like she would have," Donovan said, with a small measure of guilt. "She really knew how to brighten up a house."

"Yes, she did."

"We gave it a good go, didn't we?"

"I'm sorry I didn't catch this sooner. We might have been able to stop this reporter."

"It's okay." Donovan patted William on the back and pulled away. "I made a deal with her. I'm going to give her the exclusive story. In return, she's going to help us find the person who is pointing at Eco-Watch as the source of the DIA leaks. It's a fair trade. Eco-Watch survives. I think Michael will make a great Director of Operations, don't you? I've also been giving a great deal of thought about what you said about Lauren. Maybe it *is* time to talk to her...explain everything."

"Oh, son..." William cast his eyes downward, reaching into his inside coat pocket. "I'm afraid I have bad news."

"What? Nothing's happened to Michael or Lauren, has it?" Donovan's eyes grew wide.

William shook his head and handed Donovan an envelope.

"Is this from the tail we have on Erin?"

"Yes. After Erin left you, she went straight home. A short time later she left again."

Donovan slid a finger against the seal and pulled out a photo. He felt as if he'd been struck with a wrecking ball. Lauren was standing and talking with Erin.

"I'm told the meeting only lasted a few minutes and the exchange seemed to be somewhat combative in nature. We of course have no way of knowing what was said. Erin went home afterwards and to my knowledge is still there."

Donovan couldn't believe Erin's source was Lauren. The betrayal was too huge to grasp: the woman he loved had reached out and destroyed him once again. Donovan lowered his head. No wonder she wouldn't talk to him yesterday on the plane. He'd saved her life and she was stabbing him—and Eco-Watch—in the back. Donovan let the photo drop from his hand.

"I'm sorry, son."

"Me, too."

"I think maybe a drink is in order."

Donovan looked at William. It seemed like there should be a thousand things to say, to do. But he felt immobilized with the certain knowledge that the death of Donovan Nash was going to be slow and painful.

"How could she?" Donovan lowered his head. "I just want to get this over with. How much legal trouble do you think there'll be? I did crash a plane. Faked my own death. I've got to think some district attorney somewhere will want to try to make a name for himself."

"Leave that to me. I'll make it as painless as possible. We'll issue a statement when the news breaks. My guess is the statute of limitations is in play here. In no time at all you'll be free to do whatever you wish."

"Thanks." Donovan stood straight and fought to gather his emotions. He swayed like he'd been punched. "I will take you up on that drink. You still have any of those Cuban cigars left? The ones I brought you last month?"

"Of course," William nodded. "I always carry a few in the car. Would you like me to get them?"

"Let me. You're in charge of the drinks. I need to put the Porsche away, then I think I'd really enjoy a good smoke out on the patio."

William cupped his hands together. "Wonderful idea. What would you like?"

"Maybe a hemlock, straight up."

"I was thinking about something a touch more soothing," William replied, calmly. "Maybe some cognac? Or a dry martini?"

Donovan felt an inkling of relief at their exchange. It was like a breath of normalcy in the middle of his own personal tempest.

"I'll have a cognac. I think there's an unopened bottle in the cabinet above the bar."

"I'll find it and meet you out back." William started to go, then turned and tossed his keys to Donovan. "The cigars are inside the glove box; you'll see the small humidor. There should be a lighter also."

"Got it." As Donovan walked to the car, he noticed the clouds had thickened; a light breeze blew from the northeast. It occurred to him that he hadn't watched a single weather report all day. There seemed to be an urgency in the atmosphere, as if charged with a forbidding energy. He stopped and studied the sky. The birds were flitting anxiously from tree to tree. He knew they could also feel the coming storm.

Donovan stored and covered the Porsche. He checked the doors, even though he knew Helena was poised to strike far to the north. Northern Virginia could see some heavy wind and rain. He went to William's car and retrieved the humidor. Walking back to the main house he thought of the connection between Erin Walker and the storm brewing unseen in the distance. Two destructive entities were at work, and each was going to leave a trail of destruction and pain in its path.

Donovan settled into a wooden chair and handed a cigar to William. He saw that his friend had taken off his jacket. He was seated in his vest and tie, as casual as he ever got.

"Here you are." William traded Donovan a snifter for a cigar.

"Thank you." Donovan swirled the dark amber liquid in the glass, then breathed in the heady aroma of the Cuban tobacco.

"I had a thought." William unfolded a small penknife and began to carefully cut the end from the cigar. "It might be a good idea if you could persuade Ms. Walker not to reveal the existence of this place. If you're careful, you might be able to preserve it as your refuge. I hate to think of this serenity spoiled by those who would try to gain access."

"I'd already thought about that." Donovan took the knife from William. "I'm not sure I'm going to stay in the area. It might be time to leave."

"Europe, Africa, Australia? Like you did once before?" William blew out a slender plume of smoke. "You always end up back in Virginia. Why leave?"

"I know," Donovan agreed, but he knew it wasn't that simple. His thoughts zeroed in on Lauren, the image of her with Erin.

"I'd like to drink to the fervent hope that I never again witness the expression that's on your face right now." William tipped his glass in Donovan's direction.

"I'm sorry." Donovan halfheartedly returned the toast. "I feel so unsettled. It's like I have all this energy, yet I can't do a damn thing. Events are happening all around me and all I can do is stand and watch. It's what I tried so hard to escape after Meredith was killed. I feel like a deer caught in headlights, and there are cars coming in both directions."

"I know." William took a sip of his cognac. "At the risk of sounding maudlin, I would like to say that you were right about Lauren. I was wrong. I've been trying to nudge you back in her direction for months. I'm sorry."

The wind freshened in Donovan's face, the dry leaves in the oak tree above them rustling in the breeze. It was a welcome sensation, and signaled the first impulse from Helena. By this time tomorrow, it would be pouring rain.

"What do you say we take a walk down by the lake?" William suggested. "I always enjoy the smell of the water. If I sit here, this cognac will go straight to my head."

Donovan stood and waited while William slipped on his coat and buttoned the front. Cigars and drinks in hand, they took their time walking side by side down the winding path that led to the lake. The sun was setting and the air felt heavy from the weight of the clouds. As they stood at the edge of the water, Donovan couldn't help but think of his childhood. His father had been away a great deal of the time, running Huntington Oil. He and his mother divided their time among several of the family's homes. The coasts of Maine, Florida, and California were different stops as the seasons changed. There had been tutors, nannies, private airplanes, and limousines—all the accouterments that vast wealth provided. But each summer he always looked forward to their time spent here. His mother's fervent intent was to have a small part of his childhood resemble hers. He'd skinny dip in the lake and spend hours in the woods catching turtles and snakes. One of the groundskeepers had taught him to fish and built him the tire swing. These memories represented his most treasured moments as a child. Donovan felt comforted by them. They somehow served as a measurement with which to help him gain perspective. He wondered if this had been William's intention in taking this walk. His friend's shrewdness was almost uncanny at times. Donovan wondered if their long silence was in deference to the expected mood this place would invoke. Donovan finished the last of his cognac. His cigar had long gone out.

"Thank you, William," Donovan said at last. "It's getting late. I think we should head back. Tomorrow is going to be a difficult day."

"You'll handle it well," William said reverently nodding. "You always do."

CHAPTER ELEVEN

The morning sky was filled with slate gray clouds. Donovan, as he always did, studied them as he made the drive to work. For a large portion of the night he had been unable to sleep. The few fitful hours he had managed were filled with images of both Lauren and Meredith. Over the years, Meredith had grown larger in death than she'd ever been in life. A martyr for environmentalists, documentaries had been made about her remarkable life and untimely death. In each perspective, he'd been portrayed as the self-serving, uncaring billionaire who had refused to pay the ransom. Public opinion of him had probably changed very little in the last eighteen years. He tried to imagine what he would do when he was thrust back into the public eye once again—into the life he'd tried so hard to escape.

In the wee hours, unable to sleep, he'd switched on the television and followed Helena's progress. The storm was still situated far out to sea, but according to the local news stations, her effects were already being felt up and down the coast. Hurricane warnings had been posted. All along the East Coast, people were boarding up their homes; cars were jammed on little-used evacuation routes. There was chaos as people fled. Gas stations were sold out, supermarkets and hardware shelves stripped bare of essential items. Violence had erupted, and looting had already begun. Donovan knew from experience that the panicked atmosphere would only grow worse as Helena charged in from the open ocean.

He had mixed emotions about today's flight. On the one hand, he couldn't wait to see a hurricane with the size and fury of Helena. Yet he knew he'd be flying with Lauren in the back of the Gulfstream. He sighed. At least the lines had been drawn. She'd used her position to damage and discredit Eco-Watch. In his mind it was easily the worst transgression she could have orchestrated. He'd debated about whether or not to say something to her, but each time he imagined the scenario he found himself growing angry. It was still beyond his comprehension that she could have wounded him in such a way. He'd finally decided the best plan was to ignore her. He wanted to take the flight and the only way to get through the day would be to focus on his job, his life with

Eco-Watch. For all he knew it could very well be his last mission as Donovan Nash.

He eased the Range Rover into his reserved parking place and shut off the engine. He saw Michael's car, as well as those of the rest of the morning staff. With the weight of the world pressing down on him, Donovan grabbed his flight bag and headed to the front door. He pushed open the glass doors that led into the lobby. He went to the small kitchen and poured himself a cup of coffee, then walked down to the doors that led to the hangar. Inside the well-lit space, he could see both the *da Vinci* and the *Galileo*. He spotted Michael and Lauren talking near the nose of the *Galileo*. She looked relaxed, wearing khaki pants, sneakers and a dark green tee shirt. Her hair was tied back in a small ponytail. She held a clipboard, her eyes sparkling as she smiled and put her hand on Michael's shoulder.

"Hey, Skipper, good morning."

Donovan turned and found Randy Kordek walking toward him. His boyish features and crew cut made him look like he was no more than twenty years old. But in reality, Randy was thirty, a highly experienced pilot with almost three thousand hours in the Gulfstream. Randy was the third crew member for this morning's flight. Because of the range and endurance of the Gulfstream, they sometimes flew with a third fully-qualified pilot. It gave all of them a break on some of the eight- to ten-hour missions.

"Hello, Randy," Donovan replied. "Did we get the mission profile from the science team yet?"

"Yeah. I think Dr. McKenna gave it to Michael. You want me to go find out?"

Donovan checked his watch. "I'd appreciate it. Can you bring it up to my office? I have some other things I need to do before they pull the airplane out."

"Sure thing." Randy paused. "You ever seen a hurricane like this one? I heard even NOAA suspended their flights into the storm after one of their planes sustained some damage."

"I heard that, too." Donovan knew that the NOAA flights were usually into the heart of the storm, at altitudes of less than fifteen thousand feet. He couldn't begin to imagine the fury of the storm down low.

"It's the biggest storm I've seen." Donovan moved aside so Randy could slip past into the hangar. "I'll be upstairs getting the weather. Bring me the route so I can file a flight plan."

"Will do."

Donovan retreated to his office. He tossed his bag onto the couch and settled behind his desk. With the touch of a button, his computer sprang to life and he began to access the aviation weather. He sipped his coffee as he studied the latest satellite image of Helena. She was almost 250 miles across, but he could easily spot their destination. The eye was a small dark circle positioned in the center of the stark white clouds. He clicked on another page and committed the high altitude wind patterns to memory. He also retrieved the latest surface observations from Dulles, Washington National, and Baltimore airports. He expanded his search and printed out the forecasts. His last jump was to the Doppler radar composite. Only fifty miles off the coast, the first yellow and green images of the coming thunderstorms could be seen. They were scattered enough at this point not to give rise to much concern. But if this mission lasted more than six hours, the heavier bands behind might become an issue. Donovan shrugged. If they had to, they could fly south to get out of Helena's reach. He made a mental note to fill the Gulfstream with every last drop of fuel she'd carry. He was waiting for the last page of the weather to be spit from the printer when he heard a small knock at the door. He turned, expecting to find Randy with the profile. Instead, Lauren was standing there, an expectant look on her face.

"May I come in?"

Donovan nodded.

"Randy said you wanted the mission profile." Lauren walked toward him and pulled a sheet of paper from her clipboard. "It's pretty straightforward."

Donovan took the paper and tried to focus on the criss-crossing flight path. It was simple. They'd be flying a standard bracketing maneuver. It would give them the most accurate sampling of the hurricane's steering winds.

"Are you okay?" Lauren knew it shouldn't take him more than five seconds to understand the data, yet he seemed to be giving it his undivided attention.

"I'm fine," Donovan said without looking up. Under the desk, his legs were wire taut. Out of his peripheral vision he could see her hip slide slightly to one side as she shifted her weight. He wished she would take the hint and leave. It seemed impossible that this was the same woman he'd once loved.

"I've been thinking. After everything that happened on Saturday..." Lauren hesitated, losing her nerve to reach out to him. "I was hoping we could—"

"Could what?" Donovan looked up from his desk. He could see the surprise and confusion in her eyes.

"I don't know." Lauren seemed to struggle to find the right words. "After the other day, we didn't even say goodbye. It's bothered me all weekend."

"You said goodbye over a year ago." He thought of the picture of her in his drawer, then the photo with Erin.

Her shoulders slumped at his words. She'd never heard him sound so bitter and wounded.

"But that's water under the bridge, as they say." Donovan shuffled the papers in front of him. He found a paper clip and methodically fastened them together.

"So there's no room left to even talk?"

"I'm talked out. But I can tell you one thing," Donovan's anger rose, "if I wanted to hurt you, I'd have done it directly. I would never have gone behind your back to discredit you."

"What are you talking about?"

"Let's drop the pretense. I know what you've been doing. I know about the leaks to the press."

"I have no idea what you're referring to." Lauren unconsciously stepped back; the anger coming from Donovan filled the room.

Donovan placed both hands on his desk as if steadying himself. "I know you're the one who has been discrediting Eco-Watch...What I don't know is why. What would make you try to destroy everything I've worked so hard to build?"

"Donovan. You're the last person I'd want to hurt. And you know there's no one who believes in Eco-Watch more than I do. Now please tell me what you think I did!"

"Look." Donovan sighed as he stood. He regretted bringing it up. Obviously, she would deny her part until hell froze over. "This isn't the time or place to discuss this. We both have important jobs to do today."

"Are you proposing we sit down and talk later? A real conversation, as opposed to what we're having right now?"

Donovan wondered what Lauren was after. He was about to explain that a meeting was the last thing he wanted, when he caught something in her eyes. Was it a flicker of hope?

"Mr. Donovan Nash?"

Donovan looked past Lauren as a male voice called out his name from the doorway. Two men in suits breezed into the room. They both flashed official IDs as they moved closer.

"What can I help you with?" Donovan looked at their badges; they were DIA.

"I'm Special Agent Dixon. This is my partner, Special Agent Hollingsworth. We need you to come with us."

"Why?" Donovan shot them a guarded look, then glared at Lauren. He knew she had to be behind this intrusion.

"We need to ask you some questions. Now if you'll please come with us."

Lauren turned to the men. "Mr. Nash is required to assist the DIA on a very important mission this morning. I'm sure whatever you need to do can wait until later."

"I'm sorry, Dr. McKenna," Dixon shot back. "But my orders are to bring Mr. Nash with us back to DIA headquarters."

"This is bullshit!" Her temper began to rise. "No one is going anywhere until I speak with Director Reynolds." Lauren pulled out her cell phone and began to dial.

"Mr. Nash." Hollingsworth stepped closer, pulling his coat aside to display his weapon. "Please keep your hands where I can see them."

"Calvin! It's Lauren." She turned away from the men. "I'm at the Eco-Watch hangar. Two men just showed up here. They're DIA. As I speak, they're trying to take Donovan into custody. Need I remind you it would be nice if we could make our flight this morning!"

Donovan stood and watched as Lauren listened to whomever she had on the other end of the line. She turned and glared at the two men. Donovan couldn't miss the semi-smug expressions on the faces of the DIA agents. He had a sinking feeling that Lauren wasn't going to win.

"We'll talk later." Lauren angrily snapped the phone shut and turned to look at Donovan.

"I'm sorry." She lowered her eyes. "There's nothing I can do."

"It's okay." Donovan felt an odd rush of affection for her sweep over him. In the face of everything he knew, her concern and anger seemed genuine. But it didn't make any sense.

"This is such a mess." Lauren moved closer. "I don't know what to say. I think this is absurd."

"That's enough, Dr. McKenna," Dixon warned as he slid between them. "He'll get his chance to explain."

Donovan saw the expression of alarm on Lauren's face. He was completely confused. Why was she trying to protect him now, after all she'd done to precipitate these events?

"Pat him down," Dixon ordered.

Donovan stood motionless as Hollingsworth frisked him. He locked eyes with Lauren. She was clearly horrified.

"He's clean. You want me to cuff him?"

"That's up to you, Mr. Nash," Dixon said, carefully. "Will you come on your own accord? Not make any trouble?"

"If I were going to make trouble, you'd have seen it by now," Donovan replied, still conflicted over Lauren's words and actions.

"Okay. Let's go." Dixon nodded at his partner and stood aside to escort Donovan out of the office.

"Lauren," Donovan called out over his shoulder. "Tell Michael what's going on. He and Randy can fly the trip, but it's important for him to call William. He needs to be informed. Michael has the number."

Lauren nodded. "I'm sorry. I'll find you as soon as I get back."

Donovan was thankful that the lobby was vacant as they left the building. He was put into the back seat of a waiting government car. As they drove away, Donovan turned and looked back. Lauren stood at the window of his office, her hand covering her mouth. Somewhere, deep inside, he knew that her reaction wasn't rehearsed—she was truly in shock at his being taken. All of a sudden, everything seemed completely out of sync. He'd accused her of leaking information and she'd acted as if he were speaking gibberish. Her guilt was further diminished by her actions when the DIA showed up. Either Lauren was a far better liar and actress than he ever dreamed, or he and William were wrong about a great many things. Donovan didn't know exactly what was waiting for him at DIA headquarters. Hopefully, once William threw his formidable powers into the loop, his arrest would be short-lived. Donovan took a long look at the facility. The *Galileo* was being pulled out onto the ramp. The people about to climb on board were who he lived for. He knew he would miss them far more than he could imagine. He thought he'd have one last day of flying before he became Robert Huntington once again. But as they sped through the gloomy morning toward the District, he knew it wasn't to be.

Michael!" Lauren called out the second she burst onto the hangar floor. She quickly covered the distance to where he stood.

"What's up?"

"Donovan was just arrested! Two DIA agents took him away."

"They took Donovan?"

Lauren could see a look of suspicion on Michael's face. "He said for you and Randy to take the trip, but he wanted you to call William VanGelder."

"Did they say where they were taking him?"

"To DIA headquarters at Bolling Air Force Base."

"Oh, perfect." Michael leaned closer. "You're with the DIA, right?"

Lauren nodded and braced herself. The furious look in Michael's eyes spoke volumes. She knew Michael was a force to be reckoned with when he was angry.

"Then you call your bosses and tell them I'm not flying until they bring Donovan back." Michael's face was a picture of defiance. "Fix it or this airplane stays parked."

"It's not that simple." Lauren tried to keep her voice calm. She didn't want to fight with Michael.

"I don't know how to make this any more simple. No Donovan...no flight."

"If there were ever a mission we needed to make, it's this one. Donovan wanted you and Randy to take it."

"Give me a break!" Michael ran his hand back through his hair. "Your people come in, arrest the Director of Operations, who is also my friend. Then you want me to play nice and take the flight! I think that's pretty ballsy, Lauren."

"I'm sorry, Michael. I can't explain everything to you right now, but you'll understand later."

"Make me understand right now," Michael challenged, barely concealing a look of contempt.

Lauren averted her gaze from Michael's withering stare. It occurred to her that outside of her own team of scientists, she probably didn't have a friend in the entire building.

"You stay here." Michael stormed off toward operations. "I'm going to get to the bottom of this!"

Lauren stood in the middle of the hangar. Hopefully, after Michael made his phone calls, he'd calm down. She felt momentarily lost. To the east, Helena was tracking straight for New York. To the west, an Air Force B-1 bomber was loaded with a hydrogen bomb, ready to try to obliterate Helena. Lauren felt caught in the middle, squeezed by two forces she couldn't stop. She checked her watch, thankful that her mother and Abigail would be well on their way to Chicago by now. She'd dropped them off at the Baltimore airport early this morning for their flight. But for everything else to work as planned, she and her team needed to be off the ground in the next twenty minutes.

She couldn't help but think of Donovan. Calvin's words replayed over and over in her mind. He'd said they'd uncovered some new evidence, that they were questioning the reporter who'd visited her yesterday. But how could they think Donovan was still involved? Lauren felt her anger and frustration begin to well up inside of her. What had set Donovan off this morning? What information did he think she'd leaked? She tried to filter out his words and focus on his emotions. She'd never seen him so wounded and deflated...and the worst part was it was from something he thought she'd done. The part she did understand was the dramatic shift she'd seen in his demeanor as the agents were taking him away. Lauren knew she might be grasping at straws, but despite his angry words, she knew the caring look in his eyes wasn't her imagination.

"Damn it!" Lauren swore under her breath. She turned and looked at the *Galileo,* her team already aboard, waiting for her to start running the equipment checklists. She glanced in the other direction, at the door Michael had disappeared through. Finally, more pissed-off than anything else, Lauren headed across the hangar floor to find Michael.

She saw him through a glass section in the door. He had a phone to his ear. She pushed through the door into the office, then stood motionless as she heard the tone of his voice.

"Yes, sir. I understand, sir." Michael didn't look up at her entrance. He turned his back and glanced at his watch. "We can be airborne in fifteen minutes. Yes, sir. I'll do everything I can."

Lauren stood silently as he lightly replaced the receiver. When he turned, the expression on his face was full of confusion.

"Okay. You win." Michael's words were full of angry reluctance.

"It wasn't a contest," Lauren said. "I wish I could tell you how important this mission is, Michael. But I can't. You'll understand before the day is over. I tried to get them to leave Donovan alone, but something bad has happened. I'm worried about him."

"Me too." Michael's voice softened. "I was just ordered to take this flight. I'm to do anything the DIA asks. William told me to cooperate fully, and make no statements regarding Donovan."

"Oh no." Lauren's hand flew to her mouth. The one time she'd met the chairman of Eco-Watch, she'd sensed Donovan had no bigger champion than William VanGelder. The two men seemed to have Eco-Watch's pursuits as their mutual ambition.

"Did he say anything else?"

"Only that he'd handle Donovan's problems, and for us to get into the air and complete the mission."

"Then that's what we should do. The sooner we get going the faster we can get back."

"You know what this is all about, don't you?" Michael's eyes narrowed and he stared directly at Lauren. "What happened in Bermuda?"

"I can't talk about that." Lauren changed the subject. "Here's the weather Donovan pulled up, plus the flight profile. My people will be ready to go when you are."

"Fine." Michael angrily snatched the papers from her hand. "My guess is when all the smoke clears, you'll be at the heart of Donovan's problems. It seems to be a particular talent of yours."

Lauren whirled around and stormed out into the hangar. Michael's words stung, but she refused to allow him to make her the whipping boy for Donovan's plight. Her emotions collided once again. In her heart she wanted to believe Donovan was innocent; he wasn't the kind of man to steal anything, let alone DIA secrets. Lauren wiped away the trace of a tear. Right now all she wanted was to get this flight over with.

She hurried to the Gulfstream, climbed the stairs, and went to join her team in the cabin.

"I'm all booted up and ready, Dr. McKenna." Carl Simmons looked up from his console. His jowls quivered as he spoke. The humidity had already produced damp stains on his shirt.

"Good." Lauren looked at the station across the aisle. She could see Brent was already strapped into his seat, pecking away furiously at his keyboard. A look of total concentration was etched on his young features.

"Brent. How are you doing?" Lauren asked as she moved to her position directly behind Simmons.

"I'm getting there. I keep losing the link with the DMSP-3 satellite. I wanted to get an early readout from *Jonah,* but right now I can't."

"We've run into that before," Lauren explained. "I think it has to do with the position of the antenna on the airplane, or to all the other antenna arrays on the airport. It will clear up as soon as we lift off."

"Oh," Brent leaned back, a sheepish look on his face. "That makes sense. I guess I'll take a little break then. I was sure hoping it wasn't me doing something dumb."

"Just relax." Lauren tried to smile at the young man. "There's not much to do until we get close to the eye."

"I still can't believe you volunteered for this flight," Simmons said as he shook his head at Brent. "Do you have any idea how mind numbingly boring these can be?"

Lauren tuned out their exchange. She sat down and switched on her equipment. No one on board knew the real intent of their mission. It wouldn't be until much later that they would realize they were collecting targeting information for the largest hydrogen bomb detonation in history. Once they were orbiting high above Helena's eye, Lauren would be able to sift through both the onboard data and the readouts from *Jonah.* From that, she would calculate a point in space that would, she hoped, deliver a killing blow to Helena.

One by one, Lauren ran through each system, checking integrity and continuity. Satisfied that everything was working properly, she sat back and looked out the large oval window. She saw that they'd just disconnected the fuel hose from the airplane. It wouldn't be long until they started to taxi. She looked off into the distance at the low gray sky; a few drops of rain had streaked the thick acrylic window. If operation Thor's Hammer didn't work, there was no telling what they might create. Her thoughts shifted to Donovan, wondering what was happening to him. A steady stream of scenarios played through her mind and none of them bode well for the two of them. She feared he might be lost to her forever.

"Everyone strap in," Michael called out as the heavy door swung upward into place. "Check your intercoms. We're getting out of here."

Lauren slid the small headset over her ear and found the push-to-talk button. She and her team established that they were connected. Michael checked in from the cockpit. His cold, sterile manner wasn't lost on Lauren. He used the station numbers instead of their names. Behind her, she heard the low rumble as each of the big engines was started. She tried to relax as they began to taxi.

A sharp ring sounded from her briefcase. Lauren immediately chastised herself for not switching off her cell phone when she'd entered the Gulfstream. In one swift motion she brought the instrument to her ear.

"Lauren. I'm so glad I caught you."

"Mother," Lauren said, sitting up straight in her chair, "where are you?"

"Oh honey. This has been a nightmare. We're in Newark, New Jersey. Our flight out of Baltimore was canceled. They promised me if I wanted to connect through Newark, Abigail and I could get to Chicago only forty-five minutes late. But we missed our connection. Now they don't know when the next flight will be."

Lauren heard Abigail's little voice in the background. Newark was only a few feet above sea level. If Helena wasn't stopped, she'd easily wipe the airport from the map.

"Mother, I'm in the Eco-Watch airplane. I'm not sure how long we'll have this connection. Get on a flight. Any flight...I don't care where you go, but get away from the coast."

"I'm trying. But the gate agent told me they've got delay problems all through the system. I'm sure it'll be fine. They wouldn't leave us here with the storm coming."

Lauren put her head back against the headrest. Her mother was being naïve. Lauren felt the self-recrimination coming in waves. She hadn't been there to help them check in. Instead, she'd dropped them at the Baltimore airport and sped off. The guilt welled up inside and threatened to choke her.

"Mother! We're about to take off. I'm going to lose the connection. Please...do whatever it takes to get out of there."

"I'll try."

Moments later, they took the runway and Lauren was pushed back into her seat as the Gulfstream accelerated down the runway. They lifted off and began a steep climb, followed by a sweeping turn to the left.

"Mother. Can you hear me?" Lauren listened for an answer, but was met with only silence.

"Hello?" Lauren pulled the phone from her ear and saw that the signal had been lost. Her arm went limp and dropped into her lap. She suddenly wanted to be anywhere but headed out toward Helena. She should be on her way to Chicago with her mother and Abigail. She wouldn't have allowed them to go to Newark. This was all her fault.

Lauren tried to collect herself. If the next few hours went as planned, there wouldn't be a hurricane anymore. Problem solved. But if they created something else, something more deadly ...she pictured the intense, high-speed, hyper-cyclone she'd described to Calvin. Then she would have had a hand in killing not only thousands of people, but maybe her own mother and daughter.

"Hey, Doctor," Simmons transmitted through the intercom system. "You looking at what I'm looking at?"

Brent turned around to look at her. His expression of excitement had vanished, replaced with a look of profound disbelief. Lauren glanced at her computer monitor as it began to fill with images. Her eyes jumped to the barometric pressure in Helena's eye. It read 25.38 inches of mercury. It was the lowest pressure ever recorded. Helena had found a way to grow in the few hours since they'd last looked at the data. Straight in Helena's path, the temperature of the ocean would steadily rise. The heat would be used to power the ferocious engine of Helena's eye. She could intensify even more in her last remaining hours. Lauren wondered if anything on earth could stop such a powerful force.

"I see it," Lauren replied. "Let's break into our specific areas. I'll monitor *Jonah.* Brent, you keep an eye on each one of the communication interfaces. It's critical we keep these wheels greased and the information headed to the lab. Carl, you're in charge of collecting the upper wind data when we get closer. I want a detailed analysis starting at fifty miles from the eye."

"Yes, ma'am." Brent turned in his seat.

"Lauren," Simmons interjected. "It'll be awhile before we get there; do you mind if I connect to the mainframe? I'd like to plug this new data into our running model."

"Sure, have at it." Lauren wished she could tell him not to bother with the time-consuming work, but she couldn't.

"Gives me something to do on the way out," Carl replied.

Lauren nodded absently and tried to focus on the task at hand. She knew she had to stop this hurricane. She began to click from one display to another as she continued to study the incoming data. Helena had far outstripped the minimum winds for a category five hurricane. Right this moment, spinning around the eye were winds in excess of 285 miles per hour. Lauren had no way to measure the height of the waves, but they had to be tremendous. She put the satellite image into motion and watched, transfixed, at the violent rotation around the eye. She could tell from the scale that the tiny hole of placid air in the center of the storm was no more than fifteen to eighteen miles across. She expected that as the storm grew stronger, the eye could shrink by half. With a click of the mouse, she went back to the live Doppler image from *Jonah*. The intensity of the eye wall was beyond anything she'd ever seen. The mass of churning echoes spoke volumes about Helena's fury. As she manually pivoted *Jonah* around 360 degrees, she cautiously noted that the greatest concentration of convective activity was along the southeastern quadrant. She didn't expect that to change much in the next several hours. The bomb would have to be detonated in that area of the eye. The next, and more tricky of the calculations, would be to predict an altitude that would produce the maximum effect. She switched the image back again to the view from space. The curvature of the earth was clearly visible. She pondered the fact that if Mother Nature could produce a storm like this...she could also create a bigger one. The changing global climate would ensure that this same set of conditions could exist again. There wasn't a city in the world that could withstand this kind of force. Lauren processed the numbers as they flashed on her screen. Right now, Helena was more tornado than hurricane—a two-hundred-mile-wide tornado. But instead of passing in a matter of seconds, as a true tornado would, Helena would be far more leisurely, taking hours as she ensured complete destruction of anything in her path.

Lauren looked out at the clouds as they broke into the clear morning sky. She couldn't shake the sick feeling in her stomach about her mother and daughter. What was happening? Her mother didn't have a cell phone, or Lauren would be trying to reach her on *Galileo*'s satellite phone. Perhaps she could relay a message through Calvin. Maybe he could find out if they were going to make it out of Newark.

Abruptly, her thoughts shifted to Donovan. She couldn't shake the look on his face, the betrayal in his eyes. What in the world had spawned such a total reversal from Saturday? Waves of regret washed over her as she thought of all the times she'd almost called him, the nights when she wanted nothing more than to go to him. Now he was in trouble, and he'd accused her of something she knew nothing about.

"Dr. McKenna," Carl's voice sounded through her headset. "Lauren...we're coming up on the first dropsonde point."

"So soon?" Lauren leaned forward as she checked the time. She chastised herself for letting her thoughts distract her. Their scientific work began in earnest once the first of many dropsondes were released from the Gulfstream. Suspended from a small parachute, the instruments in the dropsondes would relay barometric pressure, temperature, and wind flow. They would also measure the dew point and the GPS Doppler frequency shifts, which in turn would give Lauren the best information about the horizontal and vertical wind components. The data would then be forwarded back to DIA for further analysis. In the end, the crew of the B-1 bomber would have what they needed to deliver their package.

"We're still fifteen minutes from the eye," Carl reported. "But I'm going to start my telemetry readings."

Lauren's eyes danced around her instruments. They were level at 45,000 feet. The clouds seemed to boil just beneath them. She guessed the tops were around 43,000 feet or so, far higher than most hurricanes.

"Something is happening to *Jonah,*" Carl announced as he began furiously to type on his keyboard.

Lauren's practiced eye scanned her computer screen looking for the cause of the problem.

"I've lost *Jonah.*" Carl held his hands out in disbelief.

"Don't move, Carl!" Brent threatened. "Raise your hands and put them behind your head."

Startled, Lauren looked up to see that Brent had a gun pointed at Carl.

"Stay where you are, Lauren." Brent moved from behind his console.

"Brent, what's the meaning of all this?" Lauren's eyes went from the gun to the determined expression on Brent's face. "What are you doing?"

"Carl just shut down *Jonah.* I watched him send the commands."

Lauren looked at Carl. "Did you?"

"I didn't do anything!"

"I'm with Internal Investigations." Brent kept the gun trained on Carl's chest. "I've been monitoring your actions since we left Dulles. I saw what you did, Carl. Now I need you to move slowly away from the console."

"Do it, Carl." Lauren felt her anger began to rise. She knew him well enough to believe the flushed look on his face was one of guilt.

"Fine!" Carl pulled his girth up from his chair. "But you're both wrong! I wasn't doing anything I wasn't supposed to!"

"Move down the aisle toward the rear of the plane." Brent gestured with his pistol. "Lauren, I want you to try to retrace his steps on the computer. Back up anything you find."

Lauren nodded as she unfastened her seat belt. Her mind was racing. She couldn't even begin to process the implications if Brent's allegations were true. All she wanted at this point was to get *Jonah* back up and running. Everything depended on that information.

"Now, Carl. Move it!" Brent stepped back to make more room in the aisle.

Lauren stepped quickly to the vacated position and began to type commands into Carl's computer. Before she could pull up the first page, she caught a sudden movement out of the corner of her eye. With more speed than she would have thought possible, Carl lunged at Brent, a beefy hand locked over the pistol. Lauren shot from her chair and raced forward. She knew she had no chance of helping Brent fight Carl.

Lauren yanked open the cockpit door. "I need help!"

"What the—" Michael snapped his head around at the sudden intrusion.

"Carl disabled *Jonah*! He attacked Brent! Hurry!"

"Go!" Michael barked at Randy, even though the copilot was already half out of his seat.

Lauren was about to lead Randy to the back of the plane when a hand reached out and grabbed her arm. She was held firmly in place as Randy raced past her.

"Stay here." Michael ordered. "What the hell is going on?"

Lauren looked past Michael. In the distance she could make out a slight depression in the blanket of clouds. It was her first glimpse of Helena's eye.

"Lauren, I want some answers!"

"Carl attacked Brent." Lauren broke her gaze with Helena and looked at Michael. "We think he sent some unauthorized commands to *Jonah*. Brent is with Internal Investigations. He tried to arrest Carl...then there was a fight."

"I'm turning this thing around." Michael shook his head. "This mission is over!"

Lauren was about to try to convince him otherwise when a sharp report sounded from the back of the plane. Michael grabbed for the controls at the same time a larger explosion rocked the *Galileo*. Lauren heard herself scream as she was thrown up against the side wall. Outside, the horizon tilted crazily as Michael fought for control of the jet. In front of her, a dozen red lights flashed on the panel, and the sound from a warning horn filled her ears. Her fear rose as the jet raised up on one wing. She was suddenly terrified they were going to flip upside down.

"GET IN THE SEAT! PUT YOUR OXYGEN MASK ON!" Michael yelled above the warning horn, both hands on the controls trying to control the wildly unstable Gulfstream.

Lauren did as she was told. The cockpit masks were the same as the ones in the back. Her initial training in the aircraft came back to her as she slid the mask over her head. She winced as the seal bit hard into her skin. Michael had brought the Gulfstream back from the brink; the wings were almost level again. She watched as his hands flew around the cockpit. First, he slipped on his own mask, then reached up and silenced the warning horn. Without hesitation, his hands brought back the right throttle. Lauren could read a series of warnings illuminated on the center cathode-ray tube. From the cryptic abbreviations, she saw they were losing cabin pressure. The air in the cockpit had turned ice cold and her eyes were suddenly assaulted by the bone-dry air. She sat helpless and watched in horror as more lights came to life: a fire in the right engine, low oil pressure, low hydraulic pressure. Michael reached out and pulled a red handle next to her knee, and twisted the lever.

They'd descended out of 45,000 feet. She could see Michael's jaw working; his finger was mashed on the push-to-talk switch on the controls. Lauren could see the whites of his knuckles as he held the Gulfstream against invisible forces. Lauren looked to her right and found Randy's headset. She slipped it on and heard an air traffic controller's urgent words.

"Eco-Watch 01. This is New York Center. We copy your Mayday. You're cleared to do anything you need to do. There are no other airplanes in my airspace."

"The fire is out. I'm pretty sure we've had an uncontained turbine failure," Michael replied calmly. "We're through 44,000 feet and descending."

Lauren's eyes grew large as she looked down at the churning mass of clouds beneath them. With each passing second, they were drawing closer.

"Roger, Eco-Watch 01. New York Center clears you to descend at your discretion. Keep us advised of your intentions. When you can, we need number of souls on board and fuel remaining."

Lauren looked at the control wheel. There was a button marked ICS—she knew it was for the intercom system. She pushed the switch.

"Michael, can you hear me?"

"Yes." Michael nodded and turned toward her. "Get your seat belt fastened!"

"What about Randy?"

"If he were coming back, he'd have been here by now. Buckle up!"

Lauren reacted numbly as Michael's statement soaked in. What was going on in the back of the plane? Were Randy, Brent, and Carl still alive? Lauren shook off her grisly thoughts as she pulled the straps tight around her hips. She saw the swirling tops of Helena reaching up for them.

"Michael, we can't go into the hurricane. We have to level off!" Lauren's eyes grew wide with fear at the thought of the jet descending into the teeth of the violent storm.

"We don't have a choice!" Michael pulled his own harness tighter. "We've had some kind of catastrophic failure of the right engine. This plane won't stay up here on only one engine. We're losing cabin pressure. Somewhere back there, the pressure vessel has ruptured. If I don't get us down we'll all die when the oxygen runs out."

Lauren scanned the horizon. She was disoriented. A quick look at the compass told her they were now headed south. She stretched, trying desperately to look out Michael's side window.

"What is it?" Michael asked.

"Where's the eye? We can descend into the eye of the hurricane. The air is relatively calm. If we go into the storm itself I don't think the airplane will stay in one piece. As of yesterday, even the NOAA planes suspended their operations. The last Hurricane Hunter flight reported turbulence of almost 5 Gs as they tried to get out of the storm. Can we take that kind of punishment?"

"Not even close." Michael gently banked the airplane back to the north. "I can see the depression of the eye, but we're not going to get in clean. We're going to have to penetrate the clouds and come in from the side."

"Oh my God." Lauren remembered the last image she'd seen from *Jonah,* the vivid echoes of the towering thunderstorms. "I have to get to the back. I think I can get us a better picture of the storm from there."

"You can't," Michael said, quickly. "Nothing back there is working. When we're down to one generator, all the scientific equipment shuts down automatically. It's designed to protect the essential aircraft systems."

"Michael," Lauren said, suddenly. "Can I link up with DIA headquarters from up here?"

"I'm not sure what's working and what's not. You're best bet is the satellite phone. What have you got in mind?"

"If I can talk to them, they might be able to help thread us through the worst of the weather."

"Do it!" Michael ordered. He reached up and adjusted the *Galileo*'s weather radar.

Lauren reached for the phone, thankful she had a dial tone. She quickly dialed a number from memory. She brushed Michael's hand from the radar controls. She could work the radar just as easily as he could and it would allow him to concentrate on flying the crippled jet. She adjusted the tilt on the Honeywell radar mounted in the nose of the *Galileo.* The screen lit up with angry bands of precipitation echoes. The radar was working, but it was primitive compared to the resources at the DIA. If she worked this right, they could use the Doppler from *Jonah* and infrared images from the DMSP-3 satellite to weave their way to the safety of the eye.

"I think we should turn to the left. We need to avoid this cluster of thunderstorms." Lauren pointed at their radar screen.

"I'm trying." Michael replied.

Lauren urged someone to pick up the phone. She could picture the scene in her lab at DIA headquarters. Steven Hughes would be the specialist on duty. Steven was the definition of nervous energy. He'd be studying Helena, constantly running his hands back through his thinning brown hair. At his side would be a huge plastic cup. Lauren had given up trying to keep track of how much Dr. Pepper Steven drank in one day. But Steven was bright, and would instantly know what they needed.

"Hello! Steven?" Lauren demanded the instant the phone was answered. The world outside went gray as the Gulfstream plummeted into the clouds. The first tremor of rough air rocked the airframe.

"Yeah. Who's this?"

"Steven. It's Lauren McKenna. We have an emergency. Listen carefully; I only have time to say this once. I'm in the Eco-Watch jet. We've had an engine failure, and we're descending into the hurricane. We have to try to make it to the eye. I need your help!"

"Oh, Christ! I'm right here at the primary station. Give me your position."

Lauren was buoyed by the fact that Steven had instantly grasped the situation, but she wasn't sure exactly where they were.

"Never mind," Steven said. "I just found your heat signature on the infrared satellite picture. Hang on while I pull up an overlay. Give me your heading and altitude."

"We're through 40,300." Lauren's eyes darted around the panel. "We're on a north heading."

"Okay. Got you. Turn left, twenty degrees. You're going to need that heading for the next eleven miles."

Lauren relayed the information to Michael, who quickly turned the Gulfstream to the new heading.

"Okay, Dr. McKenna. This could get a little ugly. For some reason we've lost contact with *Jonah,* but I think I can do this with the satellite image. Have you ever worked one of those mazes where the key is to get from point A to point B without touching any of the lines?"

Lauren knew exactly what he was talking about. "Yes," she replied.

"I'm pretty good at those. This is going to be a three dimensional version of the same game. In eight miles, I'm going to want a hard thirty degree turn to the left."

"Then what?" Lauren asked. The Gulfstream's radar showed only varying shades of red and purple.

"I got to tell you, this really sucks," Michael added as he fought the turbulence.

"They say be ready for a hard turn to the left." Lauren was amazed at how calm Michael was. "It'll be a thirty degree turn."

"This thing is flying like a tank," Michael remarked. "I have a bad feeling the tail was damaged when the engine let go."

"Donovan always told me this airplane was the best flying machine ever built." Lauren leaned forward until she made eye contact with Michael. "Was he telling me the truth?"

"Yes." Michael nodded and gave her a wink. "She'll get us where we need to go."

"Start the turn...Now!" Steven ordered. "Once you roll out, you'll have a narrow corridor for almost thirty miles. After that, we're going to have to punch through a narrow band of thunderstorms. If you can stay above 35,000 feet, you should miss the worst of it."

"We're at 34,000 feet right now," Lauren reported.

"I'm doing the best I can, Dr. McKenna," Steven said evenly. "You should see the ugly weather you're missing. By the way, I sent out the call. In a few minutes the entire place is going to know you need help. I suspect Calvin should be here anytime now. You're doing great."

"Thanks." Lauren held on tight as the Gulfstream plowed into an area of turbulence. The airplane rose, then slammed down hard. Michael battled the forces as a loud blast of precipitation pelted the windscreen. A queasy sensation rocked Lauren's stomach; it was the first grip of real sustained fear she'd felt. She couldn't help but wonder what it would feel like if the airplane came apart. An icy shiver raised the flesh on her skin. Even if they made it to the eye...then what? Would they just circle until the sky turned as bright as the sun and they were vaporized by the bomb? Did they even have enough fuel to wait out the blast, or would they die in the water? Lauren gripped the seat and tried to keep the phone to her ear as the jet was battered by another wave of turbulence. For the second time in three days, Lauren wondered if she'd live to see her daughter again.

Donovan was in a nearly colorless room. White walls, no windows. A solid black table sat between him and special agent Dixon. The questioning, so far, had been civil and polite.

"Mr. Nash." Dixon rubbed his chin as he thought. "Who did you give Dr. McKenna's computer to once you'd made the swap?"

Donovan looked puzzled.

"We know about you and Kenneth Browning," Dixon said as a matter of fact.

"I have no idea what you're talking about. Who is Kenneth Browning?"

"One of the people you killed in Bermuda." Dixon leaned back as if he'd just moved a crucial chess piece into position.

"I didn't kill anyone. Has it occurred to you that I wasn't even scheduled to be in Bermuda? Do your notes explain that I was home when the call came to make the trip?"

The look of superiority was instantly erased from Dixon's face.

"You know what?" Donovan hoped he could deliver a verbal blow that would end this once and for all. "I would think your people could have put the pieces together a little better. How could I have organized anything in Bermuda when it was a scheduled Air Force trip? They had a mechanical problem and I went in their place. Explain how I engineered all this when I wasn't supposed to be there?"

"You tell me." Dixon regained a trace of his smirk.

"It's because I didn't. I couldn't have."

Dixon's smirk evaporated. "I think you swapped the computer, then saved Dr. McKenna to throw us off the track."

"You're fishing." Donovan sat back and folded his arms in front of him. "But I can't imagine it would take very much to throw you off track."

"Let's go back eleven months to your unscheduled trip to Alaska."

"Now you're asking if I arranged for a Russian submarine to catch fire, so I could save half their crew, then divert to Russian soil?"

"You know what I mean," Dixon said, angrily.

"No, I don't know what you mean. Can you hear yourself? Do you even listen to your own questions? They don't make any sense at all." Donovan was beginning to get a bad feeling that this was just the first part in an interrogation that was designed to go on for many more hours.

"Let's go back and review certain events in Russia. Why didn't you jettison all of the classified equipment before landing on Russian soil?"

Donovan was about to answer when the door behind Dixon flew open. A man barged into the room and looked straight at Donovan. He was nattily dressed with suspenders and slicked back hair.

"Nash. You're with me!"

Donovan didn't think twice. This was his chance to escape.

"Director Reynolds." Dixon quickly got to his feet. "I was just getting started here."

"No. You're just finishing. I want Mr. Nash in my office. Mr. Nash, follow me."

Donovan didn't bother to look at Dixon as he breezed into the hallway. "You're the person Lauren called this morning, aren't you?"

"Don't say a thing until we're in my office," Calvin said, abruptly. He stayed two steps ahead of Donovan as he strode down the corridor.

Donovan wasn't sure what was going on, but Director Reynolds was obviously far higher up the food chain than agent Dixon. Was this the DIA's version of good cop, bad cop? Though he decided it might be more like dumb cop, smart cop. Donovan wished he could make one phone call and at least let William know where he was.

"In here." Calvin pointed at an open door. He moved aside and let Donovan go in front of him. "Take a seat in my office; I'll be right there."

Donovan walked past the secretary's desk and into the moderately sized room. Out the rain-streaked window, he could see the Potomac River, and just beyond was Washington National Airport.

"Donovan?"

He turned and found Erin Walker seated in a chair. Her arms were folded defensively in front of her. There was an unsettled, almost frightened expression on her face.

"I trust you two know each other." Calvin blew into the room and allowed the door to slam behind him.

"We've met." Donovan stood where he was, not at all sure where this was going.

"Have a seat next to Ms. Walker." Calvin threw a folder down on his desk, then turned to face them, putting his weight against the edge of his desk.

Donovan settled into the chair and folded his hands in his lap. He hated the feeling of being surrounded by government officials. It brought back an avalanche of unwanted images from Costa Rica—helpless feelings, as politically-blinded men grappled with Meredith's kidnapping.

"I'm not a very happy man this morning. I've got a big problem, and you two seem to be in the middle of it." Reynolds cleared his throat, then fixed his angry eyes on Donovan. "Mr. Nash. You've been at the heart of an investigation we've had underway for almost eleven months. Your presence in Bermuda set off a chain of events that made it necessary to bring you in for questioning. I'm certain you're aware of our concerns."

Donovan nodded. He'd seen his wallet, cell phone, and key ring on Reynolds' desk. Next to him, Erin was sitting rigid in her seat. Her unblinking eyes were fixed on Reynolds. He wondered what she'd told him.

"Why is Ms. Walker here?" Donovan asked.

"We connected her to a member of our staff. We searched her apartment this morning and found photographs and files pertaining to both Eco-Watch and to the DIA. The last thing that's going to happen is for this investigation to be played out in the *Washington Post* before I can deal with it internally."

A phone rang behind Reynolds. He ignored it.

"My story has nothing to do with anything concerning you," Erin protested weakly.

"What I want right now, from both of you, is total cooperation. You each seem to have pieces of this puzzle and you're not leaving until I know everything." Reynolds turned around, visibly annoyed at the ringing phone. He picked up the offending cell phone and tossed it to Donovan.

"Answer that damn thing!" Reynolds snapped. "It's been going off all morning."

"Hello." Donovan had caught it cleanly.

"Where in the hell are you!" William's relief was clearly evident.

"I'm sitting in DIA headquarters. I'm with Director Reynolds."

"There's a problem. It's the *Galileo.* Michael's in trouble."

A jolt of fear shot through Donovan. "What happened?"

"The FAA called Eco-Watch. They in turn called me. Michael is out over the hurricane and he's had an engine failure."

"Oh, God, no." Besides Michael and the others...Lauren was on the flight.

"I'll be there as fast as I can."

"You're not going anywhere!" Reynolds barked. "Now get off the phone."

"William," Donovan exhaled heavily, "Director Reynolds says I can't leave. Do whatever you have to do to fix this. Anything."

"Give me five minutes," William said, then hung up.

"Now as I was saying." Reynolds acted as if he were collecting his thoughts. "As far as I'm concerned, you two are in substantial trouble."

"Director Reynolds." Donovan gathered himself up and stood. "As much as I'd love to stand here and debate what is obviously an internal DIA problem, I can't. I'm leaving. An Eco-Watch plane is in trouble. We both have people aboard who need our help."

"What kind of trouble?" Reynolds' tone softened.

"All I know is what I've just told you. I don't have any more information than that, which is why I have to go."

"I don't know what you think you can do, but you're not leaving."

"Look. I've had about enough of your political posturing." Donovan fought his rising emotions. He had to get out of here. He leveled an icy glare at Reynolds. "I've done nothing and I doubt if Ms. Walker has done anything either. Charge us or let us go."

"Excuse me. Director?" The door had opened and Reynolds's secretary had stuck her head into the room.

"I said I didn't want to be disturbed!"

"You have a priority-one call from the White House," she said, and immediately shrunk from the doorway.

Reynolds turned and snatched the phone from its cradle. "Director Reynolds. Of course I'll hold." Reynolds stared wide-eyed at Donovan. "Yes, Mr. President."

Donovan turned and gave Erin a reassuring nod. He knew this call was William's doing.

"Yes, sir, he's with me now. I understand. I'll do everything I can, sir. Thank you, sir."

Reynolds reverently replaced the phone and rubbed his eyes with both hands.

Donovan reached to help Erin to her feet. Reynolds had just gotten an earful from the President of the United States. It would take him a second to recover.

"Let's go," he whispered. Erin took his hand when the secretary opened the door again.

"There's an emergency in Operations! They need you right away, sir!"

"Nash, you're free to go. So are you, Ms. Walker."

"I'll want a helicopter ready as quickly as possible." Donovan turned to the secretary. "Do you know if the emergency is regarding an Eco-Watch flight?"

"Yes. They're talking to them right now."

"May I come with you?" Donovan looked expectantly at Reynolds. He knew the answer would be yes.

"Follow me." Reynolds nodded and handed Donovan his wallet and keys.

Donovan's heart was pounding as Reynolds led them to a heavy metal door posted with a dozen security warnings. Someone threw it open as they approached. Within seconds, Donovan was standing behind a console with a large screen in front of him. It took him a moment to understand what he was looking at. To his left, a man seated directly in front of the composite image began to speak.

"Okay, now. You're about to make another turn. This one is going to be to the right. Let's make it fifteen degrees. You'll be on that heading for ten miles. This is going to be the first area of weather you're going to penetrate. It's a narrow band, only six miles across. Hopefully, it won't be too bad."

"We understand," Lauren's voice came from an overhead speaker. "Just tell us when to start the turn."

A knot formed in Donovan's stomach. Where were Michael and Randy? Why was Lauren relaying information? Donovan could tell from the sound of her voice that she had her oxygen mask on. He focused on the screen until he found the tiny infrared image that was the *Galileo.* It was surrounded by massive thunderstorms. He could see the course the Gulfstream was trying to fly.

"I need to know what in the hell is going on!" Reynolds bellowed as he squinted at the screen.

"We're trying to thread them through the storms to get to the safety of the eye," Steven said without looking up. "They've lost an engine and also their pressurization."

"How far have they descended?" Donovan leaned forward and put a hand on the back of Steven's chair. "Have they said anything about injuries?"

"At last report, they were down below 30,000 feet. I have no idea about the people on board. Dr. McKenna called us directly on this line."

"Can I talk to them? I'm with Eco-Watch," Donovan said.

Steven turned to look at Reynolds, who nodded.

"Here you go." Steven handed him a telephone handset. "You're on speaker, and they need to turn in a minute and a half."

"Lauren." Donovan's throat threatened to close off. "Lauren, it's Donovan. Are you all right?"

"Donovan! So far we're fine. But the airplane is really messed up."

Donovan winced at the fear in Lauren's voice. "Can I talk to Michael?"

"Hang on," Lauren replied.

Donovan watched the second hand creep around a large chronograph across the room. He felt as if events were hurtling past at an incredible rate, but the slowly dragging clock told him otherwise.

"It won't work," Lauren reported. "To talk on the phone, I have to pull my oxygen mask out from my face a little bit. It takes two hands and he's busy flying."

"Are all the instruments working?"

"Michael says yes. But he wants you to know he thinks the controls are damaged."

"They need to get ready to turn," Steven interrupted. "It's going to be a fifteen degree turn to the right."

"Lauren, get ready to turn."

"Now!" Steven pointed at Donovan.

"Tell Michael, fifteen to the right. And hold on." Donovan looked on as the small ghostly image on the screen began to turn toward a solid band of echoes.

"We're turning," Lauren replied.

Donovan watched as the Gulfstream penetrated the line. He held his breath and prayed they'd make it through.

"It's getting rough!" Lauren transmitted. "Oh my God!"

Donovan grimaced. He knew firsthand what it was like to fly into a thunderstorm. It was one of the most terrifying things a pilot could experience. He pictured Michael at the controls and knew that if any pilot could get it done, it was Michael. Erin moved closer. Donovan glanced over and saw that her face had gone shock white.

"Thirty more seconds," Steven reported.

"Lauren," Donovan urged. "You're almost through."

All ears were on the speaker, which remained silent. "Lauren. Can you hear me?" Donovan stared helplessly at the screen. He had no idea how accurate the satellite image was. If the Gulfstream broke apart, how long would it take to register on the monitor?

"I show they're through," Steven said, calmly. "They'll have a bit of breathing room before the next line."

"Donovan, are you still there?" Lauren's shaken voice came over the speaker.

"I'm here. Is everything okay?"

"That was pretty bad. Michael doesn't know how much more of that the airplane can take. How close are we to the eye?"

"They'll have one more area to get through." Steven used the tip of his pen to show Donovan the intended path on the screen. "Right now we're going to work them around the storm this way and all that will be left are these thunderstorms. Then they'll be in the clear."

Donovan looked at the last area Steven had referred to...It was part of the eye wall. His heart sank at the sight. "Lauren, you only have one more section of the storm to get through. It's going to be rough. How high are you right now?"

"We've managed to level off at 27,000 feet."

Donovan nodded—27,000 feet was the maximum single engine service ceiling of the Gulfstream. He knew Michael would have the jet slowed to ride out the turbulence. It was Michael's report of control damage that worried Donovan the most. A perfectly good Gulfstream would probably stay in one piece through the eye wall, but a damaged one might be nothing better than a crap-shoot. A wave of guilt came over Donovan. He was supposed to be flying the Gulfstream. It should be him up there with Michael and Lauren. If he lost them, they'd be added to the list of people in his life who had died. Donovan shook himself free of the unthinkable. He turned to Steven.

"How long do you think it'll be before they make it into the eye?"

"Hard to say." Steven rubbed his eyes. "The bands of weather keep shifting."

"Donovan, it's Michael. I have a few seconds here to talk."

"Go ahead." Relief swept over Donovan at the sound of his friend's voice.

"This airplane is pretty screwed up. Is there any way those techno-wizards down there can use their satellite to zoom in, tell me what I'm dealing with, such as how much damage there is to the plane?"

"I've got a better idea," Donovan said, quickly. "I'll be there in the *da Vinci* as fast as I can. You've got a lot of fuel. Let's do this right. Do you have any idea what happened?"

"Yeah. Lauren came up to tell us there was a fight going on in the back. Randy went to help. I think I heard a gunshot right before the number two engine came apart."

Donovan leveled a withering glare at Reynolds.

"And just for the record," Michael continued. "This hurricane is starting to piss me off."

Donovan was glad Michael could still make a joke. "I'm on my way. Listen for us on the Eco-Watch frequency. Donovan out."

"Where's that helicopter?" Donovan spun towards Reynolds. "I need it five minutes ago. You and I will talk about this later."

"Someone take him to the helicopter pad!" Reynolds raised his voice.

Donovan turned to Steven. "How can you and I stay in touch?"

"You can use satellite phone, HF, or VHF. Take your pick." Steven scribbled the numbers on a pad of paper and handed it over.

"Your helicopter is waiting." A young woman put down a phone and moved to escort Donovan out of the room.

"I'm going with you," Erin said, her tone leaving no room for argument. "You promised me an exclusive."

"Come on." Donovan let it look like this was her victory, but he had no intention of letting her out of his sight. "But you're my assistant first, reporter second. Nothing leaks about this until it's over. You got that?"

Erin nodded as they blew out of the room and hurried to the waiting helicopter. As they ran, Donovan pulled out his cell phone and hit the speed-dial for Eco-Watch.

"Operations, this is Peggy."

"Peggy, it's Donovan." He was relieved it was her; Peggy had been with Eco-Watch longer than any of the other dispatchers. She was intelligent and deadly efficient.

"Oh thank God! We've been trying to find you. Michael's in trouble."

"I know. I just spoke with him. Have Frank get the *da Vinci* ready to fly, and find someone to go with me. I'll be there in ten minutes."

"Frank already has the airplane on the ramp; he's just finished fueling. Nicolas should be here any minute. I know he's new, but he's the closest. We'll be ready to roll when you get here. I've already filed the flight plan and air traffic control knows to give you priority handling."

"Good work, Peggy." Donovan followed Erin through a door that led outside. In the distance he could see the same helicopter that Lauren had gotten on the other morning. Its rotors were turning.

"Are Michael and Randy okay?" Peggy asked.

"Michael is...I don't know about Randy. See you in a few minutes."

"Please hurry," was all Peggy said before she hung up.

CHAPTER TWELVE

"He's on his way." Michael handed the phone back to Lauren and again put both hands on the controls. "Once we get safely into the eye, I'm going to need you to get to the back and find out what the hell happened."

"Donovan's coming?" Lauren took the phone from him.

"Yeah. He's going to use the other plane and fly out here. He'll be able to check out the damage to our plane. If I'm thinking what he's thinking—once we know what we're dealing with, he can lead us out of here."

Lauren nodded. It sounded feasible. The Gulfstream rocked in the light turbulence as sheets of precipitation were slung at the windshield. Outside, the opaque gray nothingness of the storm began to close in on her. She turned around and looked back. She could barely see the right wing-tip. The levels of darkness came and went. She knew they were playing a deadly game of cat and mouse inside the worst hurricane ever recorded. Helena had tried to kill her once already; Lauren couldn't help but wonder if she'd succeed this time. Lauren almost pictured Helena as a living, breathing entity. She wondered if, in some supernatural way, Helena knew that Lauren was out to kill her, destroy her before she could make landfall. As if to answer Lauren's question, another series of violent jolts battered the airplane.

"Jesus!" Michael battled to keep the airplane steady. "Ask them what in the hell is going on."

"Steven, it's getting rougher. Can you get us out of this?"

"I'm trying. The storm is shifting. Three minutes ago you had a clear path. Now it's closing in." Lauren was thrust against her harness. She felt the sting of the straps as they dug into her hips and shoulders. The world outside turned darker; torrents of water lashed at them. She was having trouble holding the phone to her ear.

"This is turning into a mess," Steven said anxiously. "You need to make a ninety degree turn to the right. Everything's closing in. You have to turn. There's no other way. It's the shortest distance to the eye."

"Turn ninety degrees to the right!" Lauren quickly relayed to Michael. "We're closed off. We have to make a run for the eye, NOW!" Lauren had to shout against the noise of the rain. She could see the determination in Michael's eyes as he fought against vicious up and down drafts to turn the plane. The tail slewed back and forth as Helena's sheering winds tore at them from both sides. Lauren looked at the onboard radar. It was useless. A barrier of water kept the signals from spreading outward. Nothing beyond their nose was registering.

Lauren cringed as the turbulence worsened. Despite the seat belt pulled hard across her lap, she came up off the seat, only to be pressed down hard moments later. She could hardly focus on the instrument panel. She had no idea how Michael could fly the plane.

"How much further?" Lauren screamed into the phone, but her plea was met with silence.

"Steven! How much further?" She had a bad feeling that the severity of the storm had broken up the digital satellite signal. If she ever talked to Steven again it would be because they'd survived and made it to the eye.

"Lauren!" Michael managed to transmit. "I need your help. Put your hand on the left throttle. I need both hands to fly!"

Lauren did as she was told. The throttle felt foreign in her hand.

"Pull it back three inches!" Michael ordered as the airspeed built rapidly in the maelstrom.

Lauren pulled it back. The dials on the instrument panel moved counterclockwise.

"Get ready to push it all the way forward to the stops."

The airplane vibrated and groaned as they flew into even heavier rain.

"Push it now. Fast!"

Michael's calm, yet firm voice sounded in Lauren's headset. Without hesitation, she jammed the lever forward. The Gulfstream lurched forward and flew out of the grip of the massive downdraft.

"Perfect. Now ease it back one inch."

Lauren's arm trembled as she tried to measure the exact position Michael wanted. "Like that?"

"Yes. But be ready. We're not finished yet."

Lauren nodded. Even though the air in the cockpit was icy cold, a sticky heat spread over her body. The warm flush of fear swept through her.

"Ease it back just a little. Half an inch."

Lauren battled her fear and moved the throttle as instructed.

"OH! SHIT!" Michael yelled. "All the way forward!"

Lauren couldn't move. The bottom felt like it had dropped out from under them. Her hand had been flung from the throttle. Against the negative G-forces, Lauren forced her hand downward to grip the cold, black throttle. She slammed it all the way to the stops and held it there. She whispered a small prayer for Michael, then herself.

"Get ready to pull it back!" Michael yelled.

Lauren knew they were caught in the massive up- and down-drafts near the eye wall. Back at her lab, she'd marveled at its sheer force, but now she and Michael were inside, fighting for their lives. The darkness deepened as they plummeted downward toward the ocean. Lauren was forced down into her seat. Her outstretched arm felt as if 100-pound weights had suddenly been attached. She held on to the throttle for dear life.

"Pull it back halfway!"

Lauren fought the G-forces. The skin on her face was being pulled down, and her head grew heavy. She eased the throttle back, but felt like she'd gone too far. Trying to concentrate, she adjusted it forward. She glanced at Michael. He nodded as his eyes swept the panel. A quick look at the altimeter showed them being swept upward through 30,000 feet.

Like a six-mile-high roller-coaster ride, Lauren's stomach lurched as they reached the apex. She could sense the change in gravity. Her insides fluttered as Michael banked the airplane hard to the right.

"One more time. Push it all the way forward." Michael's authoritative voice sounded through the intercom. Just as Lauren was about to ease the throttle forward, a bright light caught her in the eyes. It forced her to turn her head. She blinked against the harsh brightness and looked up. Above them, she found a small circle of blue sky.

"We made it!" Michael reached across and gave her hand a squeeze, then took the throttle and pulled it all the way back. "Hang on. I'm going to dive this thing down so we can breathe without our masks."

A wave of relief washed over her battered body. Despite the harness, she'd been thrown around the cockpit like a rag doll. With a mixture of terror and wonder, she scanned their surroundings. Far above them, the sun hung perfectly in a clear sky. Majestic streaks of light raced to the ocean below. Stretched out on either side of them was the eye wall, a violent churning mass of greenish-black clouds. Somehow, they'd managed to come from hell itself and make it into Helena's inner sanctum.

Lauren looked down. She was still gripping the satellite phone in her right hand. As if suspended in some slow motion loop of time, she raised it to her ear.

"Hello. Is anyone there?"

"Dr. McKenna! You made it!" Steven's voice was filled with relief.

"We're in the eye. Michael has us descending to a lower altitude." Lauren was exhausted; her legs began to tremble.

"Perfect," Steven replied. "Be advised, *Jonah* is at your twelve o'clock position and five miles. The last information we had was it was hovering at 3,000 feet."

Lauren turned to Michael. "*Jonah*'s in front of us, they think it's floating at 3,000 feet. Let's don't run over it."

Michael raised up and peered out the front of the Gulfstream. "I'm going to level off at 10,000 feet; it'll save us a little fuel. Once I do, you need to get to the back."

Lauren nodded that she understood. Neither of them knew what had happened to the rest of the crew. She spoke to Steven. "We're going to stop at 10,000 feet." She hesitated, then added, "How far is the eye from the coast?"

"Uh, stand by."

Lauren waited. She could picture him calculating the distance. She doubted he was aware of how critical her question really was.

"The eye is now 330 nautical miles from landfall."

"How fast is it moving?"

"Last reading was fifteen knots. She's picked up a little more speed in the last two hours."

Lauren did the math in her head. In five hours, the eye would make its way to the minimum distance for the detonation—with them circling helplessly inside.

Lauren glanced at Michael. "How much fuel do we have left?"

"I'm not sure yet." Michael glanced at the Flight Management System. "On one engine, down at 10,000 feet, I'm guessing we'll have five, five and a half hours. That's if we haven't sprung a leak somewhere."

Lauren took a deep breath to calm herself. If they couldn't find a way out of the hurricane, they could all measure the remainder of their lives against the coming nuclear detonation.

"Ahhh," Michael groaned as he pulled off his oxygen mask. He rubbed the red compression lines on his face. "It's safe to breathe normally. God, it feels good to get that thing off."

Lauren followed suit and removed hers. The sensation of breathing normally was wonderful.

"Okay." Michael found his sunglasses and slid them on. "I've got everything under control here. Go to the back—but be careful. I'm hoping the loss of pressurization knocked everyone out."

Lauren handed him the phone and began to unfasten her seat belt. "This is Steven. He's the one who threaded us through the worst of it."

"Got it." Michael gave her a weak smile. "And by the way. You were pretty amazing back there. I don't think we would've survived if you hadn't made that phone call."

Lauren reached over and kissed him on the cheek. She knew from Donovan what a skilled pilot Michael was. She was betting he had far more to do with their being alive than she did.

"I'll be back as soon as I can." Lauren slipped out of the cockpit. She steeled herself against what she might find once she was in back.

After the bright sunlight in the cockpit, she had to stop until her eyes adjusted to the dim light in the cabin. Slowly, she began to comprehend the violence that had been inflicted on the jet. The narrow aisle was strewn with computer equipment and other debris. Part of the insulated headliner had broken loose and was hanging from the ceiling. There were exposed wires dangling from above. She was suddenly thankful that there wasn't any electrical power back here. Lauren quickly made her way aft. She pushed aside the last section of insulation. Carl was sitting slack-jawed in a seat, his arms limp at his side. His chest was moving in and out. Lauren turned to find Brent and Randy.

"Dr. McKenna! Back here. I need some help."

Lauren turned and saw Brent leaning over a body on the floor. She knew it had to be Randy. She carefully stepped over a bundle of wires that stretched across the aisle and went to them.

"Is he..?" Lauren knelt over Randy's inert body.

"I don't know." Brent had pulled off Randy's mask, then leaned forward to check the pilot's respiration.

Lauren looked up at the wrecked computer rack. There were dozens of small holes in the side of the plane. Sunlight streamed in through the ruptured pressure vessel.

"At least he's breathing." Brent looked toward the front of the plane. "Did you check Carl?"

"Yes. He's unconscious but alive. Are you hurt?" Lauren turned to Brent, thankful that at least one of her team was alive and talking.

"I'm fine. Are you okay?"

"Uh-oh." Lauren pointed at the sight of blood starting to creep out from under Randy's body.

"Oh shit!" Brent gathered himself and used his strength to gently lift Randy onto his side. "Can you see where he's bleeding?"

"It's his shoulder." Lauren wiped away the worst of the blood. She found the small puncture through a rip in his flight suit.

"He had his back to the engine when the gun went off. Then there was a bigger explosion. I managed to get to him and secure a mask so he could breathe. Then I sat here and tried to hold him steady. I was strapped in, but he was thrown all over the place after we went into the storm."

"Stay here. There's a first-aid kit in the front of the plane. I'll be right back." Lauren hurried as fast as she could to retrieve the kit. As she passed Carl, she noticed his eyes fluttering. He was starting to come around.

"He's starting to wake up!" Lauren yelled back toward Brent.

"Leave him to me."

Lauren ran and pulled the white and red metal box from its mounting. She was five steps from the cockpit. It only took her a second to stick her head through the door.

"Michael." She hesitated until he turned towards her. "Randy's hurt. He's bleeding, but still alive. Brent seems to have everything under control. But I did see a bunch of holes in the side of the airplane."

"I'm not surprised," Michael said, nodding. "Was that a gunshot we heard?"

"Yes. The bullet went into the engine."

"That's just great." Michael shook his head in disgust. "I'm guessing the entire turbine section of the engine came apart. I've lost the connection with the DIA. I think the satellite must be blocked by the storm."

"I'll be back up to help as soon as I can. My guess is they'll try to re-task the satellite. It can take awhile so we'll have to keep trying."

"As soon as you can, I need you to give both wings a careful check for fuel leaks."

Lauren held up the first-aid kit. "I'll do that right after we take care of Randy."

Michael nodded. "Don't let me keep you."

"Any word from Donovan?" Lauren asked.

"Nothing yet." Michael shook his head. "But I'd sure hate to be in his way right about now."

Donovan felt the reassuring thump as the landing gear swung up into the belly of the *da Vinci.* Only 200 feet above the ground, he banked the Gulfstream sharply to the east, and watched as the Dulles terminal building flashed beneath them. He ignored the standard airspace speed limits and allowed the powerful jet to accelerate to 300 knots.

Nicolas sat beside him in the copilot's seat, an Eco-Watch cap pulled down low over his shaved head. He instantly carried out each of Donovan's commands. Strapped in the jump-seat, Frank Moretti had his toothpick working feverishly in his mouth. Donovan knew the chief of maintenance hated to fly, yet Frank hadn't said a word as he'd climbed aboard. The ground vanished as they hurtled into the clouds. Donovan ignored the light turbulence as they thundered eastward.

"Any word yet?" Donovan asked, refusing to pull the power back on the twin Rolls Royce engines. A feeling of dread had been lodged in his chest since the DIA chopper had lifted off. It had only taken them minutes to cover the distance from the District to the waiting Eco-Watch Gulfstream. Nicolas and Frank had the airplane ready and they'd bolted off the ground in record time. Sitting alone in the back of the speeding jet was Erin. He'd offered to leave her behind, but she'd staunchly refused. Donovan hadn't had time to argue with her. At least he didn't have to worry about what she was up to. For all intents and purposes, she was in his protective custody.

"Nothing yet." Frank had the satellite phone receiver to his ear, getting updates from DIA headquarters.

Nicolas subtly pointed to the overheated engines. The Turbine Gas Temperature gauges were bouncing near the red line.

"I see it." Donovan knew Nicolas was just doing his job. "They'll live."

"Just so you know." Nicolas nodded, then turned to Frank. "Can you get us the latest latitude and longitude of the eye? I need to plug it into the FMS."

"It's now..." Frank paused as he listened. "North 36 25.4. West 069 04.0."

"Got it." Nicolas expertly typed on the small keypad, then turned to Donovan. "There's the new course, sir. We're 369 nautical miles away. At this speed we'll be there in less than forty-five minutes."

"Thanks." Donovan banked the Gulfstream to the new heading. He prayed Michael had enough airplane left to get the damaged jet into the eye of the hurricane. Michael was as good as they came, but structural damage was something that could reach out and kill even the best pilot.

"THEY MADE IT!" Frank cried out. "THEY'RE IN THE EYE!"

A fraction of tension left Donovan's body. Against improbable odds, Michael had somehow made it to relative safety. Donovan's emotions threatened to push to the surface. A lump formed in his throat and his eyes burned with relief.

"Frank, find out how high the hurricane goes. We're going to have to drop in through the roof of the storm. The more we know, the faster we'll get there."

Donovan listened as Frank followed his orders. He knew from Frank that Michael had filled the Gulfstream with fuel before they'd left this morning. The more fuel, the more time they had to find a solution.

"I can't raise Michael yet," Nicolas reported. "I'll try again in five minutes after we're higher."

"DIA says the last reports from Michael were that he had to go to 45,000 to clear the tops."

Donovan gave Nicolas a sideways glance.

"Washington Center," Nicolas transmitted to air traffic control. "Eco-Watch 02 requests flight level 450."

"Roger Eco-Watch 02. You're cleared to flight level 450 and you're free to navigate at will."

"Roger, Washington," Nicolas replied. "We'd like the hand-off to New York as soon as possible. Do you know if they're talking to Eco-Watch 01?"

"I'll have that hand-off in about six minutes. As far as I know, they've lost radio contact with 01."

"Roger," Nicolas said.

Donovan looked over at the other two men in the cockpit. He knew they shared his same thoughts. Each of them would do whatever it took to bring the *Galileo* home.

"You've got the plane, Nicolas." Donovan threw off his harness. "I'm going to the back for a little bit. Let me know if anything changes."

Donovan squeezed past Frank and made his way to where Erin sat. She was sitting at one of the scientific workstations, looking out the window at the gray emptiness. She turned and looked up at him. He saw the concern in her eyes.

"Did we hear yet?" she asked, anxiously.

Donovan nodded. "They made it to the eye."

"Oh, thank God." Erin quickly crossed herself. "I've been sitting back here terrified that we'd turn around, that if the plane slowed down it would mean they didn't survive."

"I know the feeling." Donovan sat down at the station across from her. "I need to ask you something."

"What?" Erin replied cautiously; her guard went up.

"How much did you tell the DIA this morning?" He looked at her with a serious expression. "How much do they know?"

"You mean about you? Our secret?"

Donovan nodded.

"Nothing. We had a deal, remember?"

"So no one at the DIA knows much more than they did yesterday?"

"No."

"Is Lauren McKenna the person who's been passing you information?" Donovan needed to hear it from Erin firsthand.

Erin's eyes fluttered as she shook her head. "No. Not at all. Why would you think that?"

"But..." At this moment, Donovan wasn't sure of anything. "You visited her yesterday."

"So what?" Erin replied, cautiously. "How do you know about that?"

"Never mind. So it's not Lauren who gave you the classified files?"

Erin shook her head.

"Why did you go see her?"

"Insurance. I wasn't sure I could trust you—I was trying to hedge my bets. If you bailed on me, I was still going to write my story and I asked her for her cooperation."

"What did she say?"

"She told me to get lost."

"I told you we had a deal." Donovan glared at her, then reached up and snatched the satellite phone mounted on the wall. It worked on a separate line from the one in the cockpit. Quickly, he secured a connection. The phone was answered on the first ring.

"William, it's me."

"Good to hear your voice, son. Where are you?"

"I'm in the *da Vinci*. We're headed out to rendezvous with Michael. What do you have from that end?"

"Nothing that you don't know. I'm headed out to the airport shortly. I can't sit here and wait. I'll feel better if I can be right there in Operations."

"I understand. We'll be in constant contact with Peggy. I could use a favor, though."

"Name it."

"Can you talk to the Navy, or the Coast Guard? Find out how long it would take a ship to reach the eye...if they even can? If Michael has to ditch."

"Understood." William's voice grew quieter. "I had to tell the President who you really are this morning. It was the only way to make him understand you'd be an unlikely spy. He promised me he'd run some damage control. But we probably owe him."

Donovan felt a small smile come to his lips. William had done what it took to get the job done.

"The good part," William continued, "is right now, I've got his full attention. Which under the circumstances, might be advantageous."

"You got me out of there, that's what mattered most." Donovan saw they'd broken free of the murky gray clouds. The *da Vinci* climbed high into the rarefied atmosphere.

"I'll find out about the Navy. I should be at Eco-Watch in less than twenty minutes."

"I'll talk to you then."

"Donovan," William paused as he formed the words. "Do whatever it takes to save them."

"I will." Donovan hung up, then looked across the aisle at Erin. "Looks like you'll get two exclusives in one week. One about me, the other about this. Lucky girl."

"When it rains it pours." Erin brushed her hair away from her eyes. "Now can you tell me exactly what we're going to do—when we get where we're going?"

"The first thing is to get up close and personal with the other airplane. We need to see exactly how much damage they have to the airframe. Frank used to be an engineer with the company that builds these airplanes. He'll be able to give us his expert opinion as to how much punishment they can take."

"You mean to fly back out the way they came?"

Donovan nodded. "Hopefully, we'll be able to lead the way, test the water so to speak. If we can find a soft spot in the hurricane, we might be to able ease them out of the storm."

"And if that won't work, your friend is checking with the Navy?"

"Worst scenario is they have to ditch," Donovan answered, grimly. "They'll have to ride out the storm in the water, at least until we can get some rescue elements in there to pick them up."

"But either way you think you can save them?"

"Nothing is a given," Donovan said, bluntly.

"What are you saying? That we could all die trying to save the other plane?"

"It's a possibility." Donovan leveled his gaze at her. "You volunteered, remember?"

Erin eyed him cautiously. A look of resignation came over her face as she nodded.

"You of all people should understand the lengths I'm willing to go to save the people I care about." Donovan leaned across to get her undivided attention, to hear the intensity in his voice. "After all I've lost in my life. My parents...Meredith. Do you think I'd be able to fly off and leave Michael and the others to die?"

"That's not what I was saying," Erin stuttered.

"I hope when you write your story you'll talk about what a slow death survivors can go through. The empty nights when you plead with the heavens to take you, too, followed by waves of guilt and despair. Dying is the easy part—it's surviving that's the real trick."

Erin shrunk in the face of Donovan's barrage.

"Everyone dear to me is on the other airplane. It's a matter of loyalty...and love. Put that in your story. Those people are worth more to me than all the money in the universe."

"Donovan!" Frank yelled from the cockpit. "We have Michael on the radio!"

"You love her, don't you?" Erin said before he'd taken two steps.

Donovan kept walking. Erin wouldn't understand, even if he tried to explain. It was about more than Lauren. It was about Michael, Randy, and the others who'd entrusted Eco-Watch with their safety. In ten years they'd not had a single fatality. Donovan wasn't about to start now.

"We've got him on the VHF." Frank turned as Donovan came barreling into the cockpit.

"Good work," Donovan said, then strapped in and reached for his headset. He saw from the FMS that they had a tremendous tailwind. They were only thirteen minutes from the eye.

"Michael," Donovan transmitted the instant he was settled. "It's Donovan. How you doing?"

"I'm not sure yet. Lauren is still in the back. I'm told Randy is hurt, though I don't know how badly. This airplane is pretty screwed up. The controls are a little stiff and I keep feeling a vibration in the elevator. Other than that, I'm having a pretty good day."

"How much fuel do you have left? Frank wants to know if there's anything wrong with the airplane besides the controls." Donovan had a million questions, but he needed to understand the essentials first.

"Frank's with you?" Michael asked, cautiously. "I know I'm screwed if you got him up in an airplane."

"Frank says he only comes on the important flights," Donovan replied, dryly. "Now, how much fuel do you have left?"

"On one engine, I'm showing I have four hours and eleven minutes until dry tanks. But I haven't had a chance to check for any fuel leaks. As for the rest of the plane, I still have all my instruments up front and everything reads fine. Lauren did tell me we have a bunch of holes in the fuselage, hence the loss of pressurization. Ask Frank if this thing is still under warranty."

"Don't worry about it. We'll buy another one." Donovan was encouraged by Michael's usual flippant mood.

"Where are you guys?"

"We're at 45,000 feet, about ten minutes out. We'll be coming in over the top of the storm. Once we get to the eye, we'll come down and take a look."

"We'll be here," Michael replied.

"How much oxygen do you have left?" Donovan was mentally working on a plan. "If you climbed back up as high as you could go...how long could you stay there?"

"I've already given that some thought. Lauren and I used the masks for quite a while before we could start down. I'm showing about half of our supply left. That would get us a little ways. I have no idea about the status of the bottles in the cabin. Lauren will have to check that for me. But we do have the two portable bottles, which might give us another fifteen, twenty minutes."

"Okay. It's just a thought." Donovan felt his idea dissolve. With such a depleted system, they would be hard-pressed to stay up as long as it would take to get over the worst of the weather.

"Can I ask how far away the nearest ship might be?" Michael ventured.

"I'm working on that," Donovan replied. "With the storm it's not like there's much to pick from."

"Anything would be better than trying to make this airplane float. I'm not sure, but I think it'd make a lousy boat. Plus, we don't have any oars."

For the first time, Donovan could feel the stress in Michael's voice. He looked at both Nicolas and Frank. From their expressions they'd heard it also.

"If we knew more about the holes in the pressure vessel," Frank was thinking out loud, "we might be able to plug them up enough to hold pressure in the cabin."

"Good thought." Donovan turned to the former engineer, "How high could a stripped Gulfstream climb?"

"You mean if they threw out all the equipment, everything that wasn't welded down? Interesting...Let me think about that for a minute."

"I can feel the wheels turning from here," Michael transmitted. "Care to fill me in?"

"Frank's working on a few things. We'll know more when we can look at your airplane."

"I can see the eye." Nicolas pointed just off the nose. "Jesus, it's not very big."

Donovan looked up and saw the indention in the sea of clouds. Nicolas was right; it was far smaller than others he'd seen.

"Michael. We see the eye. We're about to start down. Are you still at 10,000 feet?"

"Yeah. I'll stay here. I'm making left turns to stay in the clear air. The airplane turns better in that direction. You'll see me. We're the only airplane in the pattern."

"Hang in there, buddy. We're almost there." Donovan grabbed a handful of throttles and began to ease the *da Vinci* from its high altitude perch. Nicolas adjusted the tilt on their weather radar. Below them, wound tightly around the eye, were the rings of violent weather. The Gulfstream shuddered as they closed the distance with the thin wisps of vapor that marked the upper reaches of Helena. As if hurling over a huge crater, the sky beneath them opened up. Donovan clicked off the autopilot and banked the Gulfstream hard to the left, while pulling the speed brake handle. On the sleek wings, panels were forced out into the slipstream. Responding to Donovan's sure hand, the *da Vinci* began to spiral downward into what looked for all the world like a huge hole.

"My God!" Nicolas remarked nervously as they screamed down from the heavens. "I've never seen anything like this."

"This is what you guys do for a living?" Frank replied, his hands gripping the edge of his seat. The toothpick had gone motionless as he peered out the windshield.

"This is a once-in-a-lifetime deal, I can assure you." Donovan gently increased their bank angle to keep them in the eye. "I want all eyes peeled for Michael's airplane. I'm going to level off at 12,000 feet until we find him. The last thing we need is to have a mid-air collision."

"Sounds like a plan." Nicolas raised his seat to get a better glimpse out the front of the plane. "I just can't get over how narrow this shaft is. It's like flying down a gopher hole."

"I see them!" Frank pointed from between the two pilots. "Down low at ten o'clock."

Donovan squinted and moved his head back and forth until he spotted the white speck. He carefully adjusted their descent angle to be able to come down behind the *Galileo*.

"We've got you in sight." Donovan radioed to Michael. "What's your speed?"

"I'm back to 200 knots. What do you need?"

"That's fine." Donovan raised the nose to start bleeding off the excess speed. The throttles were back at idle. They were still 10,000 feet above Michael.

"Hang on," Donovan muttered as he threw the jet into a tighter turn. He continued to bring the nose up while maintaining a healthy distance from the vertical walls of the storm. He lost sight of Michael as he cranked the Gulfstream around. His eyes were riveted on the instruments in front of him. They were plummeting through 13,000 feet. Donovan held his breath as he continued the turn. If he'd planned this correctly, they'd level out right behind Michael.

"There they are!" Nicolas called out. "Off to the left. We're closing fast."

Donovan gave the *Galileo* a quick glance. They were closer than he'd planned. He raised the nose and slammed the airbrakes shut. "Give me ten degrees of flaps!" Donovan felt the controls respond to the drag. "Now give me twenty degrees."

Nicolas instantly followed Donovan's commands. "They're at twenty. Speed is going through 210 knots."

Donovan added a touch of power as Michael's airplane grew large in their windscreen. "Perfect. Now bring the flaps back up to ten degrees."

"Done," Nicolas replied. "Look at what's left of their right engine."

Donovan adjusted the speed to match Michael's. He moved in until they were only twenty feet from the other plane. Every nerve fiber in his body was wired into what the *Galileo* was doing.

Formation flying didn't allow for even the slightest mistake. He let his eyes wander first to the right engine. Half the cowling was gone, shredded when the turbine section exploded. White-hot titanium fragments had been flung out of the core in what must have been a huge blast. At least half the engine was missing. A collection of wires and tubes was fluttering in the slipstream.

"Look at the horizontal stabilizer." Frank leaned forward between them. "It looks like Swiss cheese."

Donovan studied where the shrapnel had peppered the airframe on the right side. It looked like the aluminum had been ripped with machine-gun fire. His heart sank as he studied the damage. It was a testament to the sturdy Gulfstream that Michael could even control the wounded airplane.

"What do you think?" Donovan looked over at Frank.

"I think it's a pretty tough airplane," Frank responded, as if he were a million miles away. "Nicolas, hand me my binoculars."

"Michael, you can't see us, but we're here," Donovan transmitted.

"It's about time. What do you see?"

"You were right. There's not much left of your engine. Most of it's gone. There's some damage to the tail, as you suspected. Lord only knows how many turbine wheels burst when the engine went. Frank is still giving it the once over."

Donovan looked over as Frank lowered his binoculars. The engineer shook his head solemnly.

"What does that mean?" Donovan needed to hear the words.

"The horizontal stabilizer is damaged the worst. I'm not sure how it even stayed on the plane. From what I'm looking at, it could break away at any moment."

"So back out through the storm isn't an option?" Donovan's hopes deflated as he asked the question.

"No way," Frank offered, quietly. "They wouldn't last five minutes."

"Damn it!" Donovan used his right hand to pinch the bridge of his nose. "How high could they climb fully stripped?"

"Not high enough, I'm afraid. On one engine, there just isn't enough thrust to get them over the weather we just saw."

Donovan looked at the *Galileo* as it seemed to float just in front of them. He swallowed hard as he thought of all on board. Donovan glanced into the expectant eyes of both Nicolas and Frank. They were waiting for him to say or do something.

"Michael," Donovan finally keyed the microphone. "We need to talk."

CHAPTER THIRTEEN

Lauren had cleaned Randy's wound and bound it as best she could. At least she'd gotten the bleeding to stop. His breathing and heartbeat were both strong and steady. She and Brent had packed some blankets and pillows around him to try to make him comfortable.

"What in the hell happened?" Carl moaned as he tried to free his hands from the tie-wraps that bound him to the console.

"I don't think he's hurt all that bad." Lauren put her hand on Randy's forehead, brushing her fingers lightly on a bump that had formed there. She'd flown with him a dozen times. He seemed like a resilient young man.

"Where are we?" Carl leaned down and looked out the window. "Are we headed home?"

"Guess again," Brent remarked, smartly. "Thanks to you, we're in Helena's eye."

Carl slumped in his seat, a look of resignation coming over his face.

"I need to get back to the cockpit. Michael wanted us to check for fuel leaks. Then maybe we should clear an aisle. Get all this mess off to one side."

"You got it," Brent replied quickly.

"Everything back here is dead. Does the cockpit have power?" Brent asked cautiously.

"The cockpit is fine. Michael told me when the airplane is down to one generator we don't have any power to the cabin."

"Makes sense."

"Check on him every so often." Lauren pulled a blanket up over Randy's shoulder. She stood and looked at her blood-covered hands, then wiped them on her pants. "I'll be back in a minute."

Carefully, Lauren threaded her way back up to the front of the plane. She found herself hoping that Michael had heard from Donovan. Lauren glanced at her watch. They were down to a little over four hours possible flight time. She knew at some point she needed to share what she knew with Michael. Lauren hated the thought, and tried to put herself in their position. Would she want to know? Would it crush everyone's will to survive, would they deflate and crumble under the certain knowledge that they were all going to die?

Lauren stopped under the weight of her thoughts and tried to collect herself. She clenched her fists, angry at being the only one on board who knew what was to come. Her anger turned to fear as she thought of Abigail. For all she knew, her daughter and mother were still at the Newark airport, virtually ground-zero for Helena's fury. She briefly wondered if they'd halt the bombing with them trapped in the eye. Then she thought of the cataclysmic damage Helena would inflict—and knew the answer was no. Five people didn't warrant the loss of tens of thousands; the White House would reach the same conclusion. She took a few deep breaths to calm herself, then slipped into the cockpit.

"I'm glad you're back." Michael turned as she entered. His eyes grew wide at the sight of blood. "Are you all right?"

"I'm fine." Lauren maneuvered herself into the copilot's seat. "It's not mine. It's Randy's. I managed to bandage his wound. But he took a blow to the head. He might be out for a while."

Michael nodded, grimly. "How about the others?"

"They're as good as can be expected. Carl has been immobilized and Brent is checking for fuel leaks." Lauren looked out at the wall of weather surrounding them. The Gulfstream was in a shallow bank to the left.

"I know. It's pretty weird, isn't it?" Michael motioned to the eye wall. "We're just going in a circle, like a mouse trapped in a bucket."

Lauren was about to answer when Michael held up a finger, then reached over and put the VHF radio on speaker. Donovan's voice filled the cockpit. "Michael. We need to talk."

"I'm all ears," Michael replied.

"They're here?" Lauren felt a rush of warmth at the sound of Donovan's voice.

Michael nodded, "He's right behind us. We're about to learn what our options are."

"I've got bad news, buddy," Donovan started, then hesitated. "We all agree you can't risk going back into the hurricane. Your tail section is pretty chewed up. Frank doesn't know how it's worked this long. So go easy on the thing."

"And the good news is.....?" Michael gave Lauren a grim look as he waited for Donovan's response.

"The good news is we still have lots of time. We don't see any fuel leaking, so you're in good shape there."

Lauren looked at her watch. An empty hollow formed in the pit of her stomach. She fought the urge to be sick.

"I think the best bet for now is to get a Coast Guard plane out here, or even the Navy. I'm thinking they could drop an inflatable boat of some kind. At least it would be more seaworthy than the rafts on the Gulfstream. You can stay safely in the eye until a ship can get out here to pick you up."

Lauren tried to find her voice but couldn't. She reached out for Michael's hand.

"What is it?" Michael said as he saw her distraught expression.

"I..." Lauren choked on her words. "I need to tell you both something."

"Donovan, hang on for a second," Michael said, quickly, then took her hand. "Lauren. What's going on?"

Lauren fumbled with the microphone as she brought it to her mouth.

"Donovan?" Lauren said in a hushed voice. "Michael... I need to share something with you both. Before we all get too carried away here."

"What's going on?" Donovan's alarmed voice poured through the speaker.

"In..." she nervously glanced at her watch again, "in about four hours, the Air Force is going to detonate a hydrogen bomb in Helena's eye."

Lauren saw the crush of defeat as her words registered with Michael. He closed his eyes and put his head back, the color draining from his face.

"They're what?!" Donovan said, incredulously. "You can't be serious. Who in the hell dreamed up something like that?"

"I did," Lauren whispered, "A long time ago." She was overwhelmed with guilt.

"You've known all along?" Michael whispered.

"Yes. This mission is designed to give the B-1 bomber the most accurate targeting information."

"Lauren...Michael. Someone say something." Donovan's voice was frantic. "Who do I need to reach to get them to call this off?"

Lauren sniffed and felt the burn of tears in her eyes. "Donovan, they won't. This hurricane is going to hit New York City with unimaginable power. Tens of thousands of people will die. The devastation is off the economic scale. They won't stop their plan for us."

"We'll see about that," Donovan said, defiantly.

"So pretty much, we're toast." Michael released her hand. "Even if we ditch and get out of this thing. Nothing can save us from the blast."

Lauren shook her head.

"Donovan," Michael pushed the transmit button. "I don't know about you. But I'm for flying this damn thing back out the way we came. I'd rather risk that than sit here waiting to be vaporized."

"Stand by, Michael. Frank and I are talking about it."

"Talk all you want. But I'm not going to wait here."

"Just hang on a minute," Donovan urged. "There might be other options."

"Like what?" Michael replied.

"Michael," Donovan's voice intruded. "Are you still linked up with DIA headquarters on the satellite phone?"

"No. We lost them as we descended. There's too much storm interference."

"Okay. Ours isn't working either. I want you to stay put for now. I need to talk to some people. All I want is for you to stay right here. Promise me you won't try to fly out of the storm by yourself."

"I'll wait for a little while," Michael replied. "What are you going to do?"

"One of several things. I don't have time to explain it all right now. We need to get back on top and make some calls. But for now I need you hang in there, buddy."

"We will."

"And Lauren..." Donovan's voice broke as he spoke.

"Yes."

"I'm sorry about this morning. I was wrong. Perhaps I've been wrong about a great many things. When we get home, I'd like it if we could sit down and talk. There are things to be said. Would that be all right with you?"

"I'd like that." A tear rolled down her cheek.

"It's a date then. We're out of here." Donovan paused. "And Michael...if it comes down to your trying to fly your way out of the hurricane, you won't have to do it alone. I'll come back and lead the way."

Lauren looked out the side window, and for the first time saw the other Gulfstream. It was a beautiful sight. The sleek jet was picking up speed as it passed them only fifty feet away. In the pilot's seat, she could just make out the silhouette of Donovan as he waved. She waved back and wondered if he could see her. She and Michael sat silently and watched as Donovan quickly climbed away from them. Lauren thought of Abigail. She knew in her heart that before it was too late, she'd have to tell Donovan about his daughter. He could very well end up being her only living parent.

"Dr. McKenna. Did you see the other plane?" Brent shouted from the passageway behind her. "Are they here to help us?"

"Do they know?" Michael asked at the sound of Brent's voice.

"No, not yet." Lauren shook her head. "I guess it's time, though."

Michael nodded, "I'll wait up here for you."

"They're leaving!" Brent stuck his head into the cockpit. "What's going on?"

"I'm coming back there." Lauren looked up into his young face as she slid out of the seat. "There are some things you need to know."

Donovan gripped the controls of the Gulfstream as they spiraled up through the eye of the hurricane. The cockpit had been deathly silent since Lauren's emotional disclosure. Donovan's body felt leaden and his limbs seemed unattached to his body. Inside, he was reeling between anger and terror. He'd heard of plans back in the 60s to try to dissipate a hurricane with an atomic bomb, but the idea had been shelved. What did Lauren mean it was her idea? How could this be happening? He set his jaw and kept the airplane climbing toward the circle of blue sky above them.

"If you come back and help them fly out of the hurricane," Nicolas looked at Donovan, "count me in."

"I appreciate that." Donovan saw the determination on his copilot's face. "I'm hoping it won't come to that, but if it does, we'll go together."

"What's our next plan of attack?" Frank asked.

"Get them to delay or cancel the bomb drop," Donovan said, matter of factly. "We can't let them do it...It's crazy, as well as irresponsible. Hurricanes are a part of nature. They're meant to exist."

"I'm with you, Skipper," Frank agreed. "I wonder what would happen if we leaked this to the press. What would the public outcry be?"

"I'm loving this!" Nicolas said, enthusiastically. "We've even got a reporter in the back."

"We can't," Donovan countered. "It goes against Eco-Watch's confidentiality policy. I won't go there ...yet."

The upper reaches of Helena were just above them. The cockpit began to grow lighter as they thundered higher into the morning sky. Donovan put the Gulfstream into a sharp turn to the west. They just cleared the edge of the clouds as they soared clear of the hurricane.

"Nicolas. You have the plane. Get us a clearance to orbit here for now. I'm going to the back. Frank. Get on the phone to everyone you know at the Gulfstream factory. Brainstorm with their engineers, dissect every possible scenario—I don't care how far-fetched it might be."

Donovan pulled himself out of the seat. Nicolas was instantly on the radio to New York Center. Frank was furiously dialing the phone. Confident that his crew would accomplish what he wanted, Donovan hurried to the cabin.

"Why are we leaving? What's going on?" Erin began the second Donovan was within earshot.

"Just sit there and listen. You'll hear everything you need to know." Donovan sat in the seat and began to dial. It felt like an eternity as the signal went through.

"Peggy. It's Donovan. Is William there yet?"

"Yes. Stand by. He's going to your office. Are Michael and Randy okay?"

"Randy's hurt, but Michael's fine." Donovan debated about whether or not to have Peggy call their wives. It would be easy for Eco-Watch to send a car to bring them to the facility. He thought of the sealed file that contained all the procedures in case of an accident. It covered the spectrum, from dealing with the press, to having clergy and support counselors standing by for the families. The thought made Donovan shudder. It was still too early to press that button.

"Mr. VanGelder is ready now," Peggy said. "Let me know if I can do anything at all."

"Thanks, Peggy. I will." Donovan waited as the call was transferred. If William had gone to his office then there must be new developments at his end.

William picked up the phone. "Donovan, I've hit a dead end with both the Navy and the Coast Guard. All I'm getting is the run-around. It's the damndest thing."

"I know why." Donovan eyed Erin, who was hanging on to his every word. "I just found out from Lauren. Their plan is to detonate a nuclear weapon in Helena's eye."

"They're going to do what?"

"You heard me."

Erin's hand shot to her mouth, her eyes filling with dismay.

"In less than four hours a B-1 bomber is going to drop the thing to try to dissipate the hurricane. It's why you're not finding any rescue ships. Everything is probably being ordered to stay in port."

"Those sons of bitches!" William said, angrily. "I can't believe the President didn't tell me anything about this."

"We need them either to delay or to cancel this thing. Michael's airplane is damaged. I don't think he'll survive if we try to fly him through the hurricane. Can you talk to the President again? See what our options are?"

"You're damn right I will!" William thundered. "I'll call you back as soon as I can."

"Let me call you," Donovan explained. "I'm in the back of the plane with Erin. I don't want Nicolas or Frank to hear our conversation. If we have to...I'm willing to try to buy our way out of this one."

"What are you getting at?"

Donovan's eyes met Erin's. "In a few days, the world is going to know I'm Robert Huntington. The game's up. If I have to spend my money openly to save these people, then so be it. Get the President to postpone the bomb. We can buy a ship and hire a crew to go save them. Whatever it takes...I don't care at this point."

"Let me talk to the White House. Call me back in ten minutes."

"Will do." Donovan ended the call. He was still staring at Erin. "You getting all this—for your exclusive?"

Erin sat motionless.

Donovan swiveled in his seat and pulled a piece of paper from one of his zippered pockets. It was the sheet Steven had given him. He found the phone link for DIA operations and pounded out the numbers.

"This is Donovan Nash. I want to talk with Reynolds!" Donovan rubbed his eyes, thinking as he waited.

"Reynolds here."

"I want you to listen carefully." Donovan spoke in a hushed voice, but it was filled with anger. "I know about the bomb. If you drop that thing you'll kill five people—Dr. McKenna included."

"I'm sorry, Mr. Nash. I've already tried to stop it. The answer is no. When the eye reaches the 250-mile point...they're going to detonate it."

Donovan's insides twisted at Reynolds' words. "Is that all you have to say for yourself?"

"If I could stop it, I would." Reynolds shifted his tack. "There's something else I need to tell you."

"What NOW?" Donovan raised his voice out of frustration.

"We know now that Carl Simmons is dirty. He's the man we've been trying to find. The fact that he was caught trying to reprogram *Jonah* is proof of his guilt. But we need to know more."

"After all the time you spent chasing after me?"

"Mr. Nash, I'm not through explaining this to you. The more information we could get from him before...well before they—"

"You know what?" Donovan interrupted, trying to keep his temper in check. "I'm through listening to you. My focus is on saving lives, not on interrogating your spy. If this is so urgent, use it to call off the bomb."

"I can't reiterate how important his information might be to the safety—"

Donovan pressed the button to disconnect the call. He'd heard enough from Reynolds. In one swift motion he dialed the direct line to his office. With any luck, William had already spoken to the President.

"Yes?" William answered on the first ring.

"What have you got?" Donovan tried to stay hopeful as he waited for the reply.

"Write down this number," William said quickly. "It's the direct line to the Chairman of the Joint Chiefs of Staff. He's in the war room at the White House waiting for your call. It's the best the President could do. You'll have the full cooperation of the entire military to find a solution. But the bomb is going to be dropped on schedule. Nothing will change that."

Donovan slumped as the words soaked in. "We're heading back to Dulles. If we can't figure out an alternative, I'm going to drop Erin and Frank off. Then Nicolas and I will fly back out and try to lead Michael through the storm. It's our last resort. Tell Peggy to have everyone ready for a quick turn."

"I'll tell them."

"See you in less than an hour." Donovan disconnected the call and turned to Erin. "Go up front and tell Nicolas to get us to Dulles as fast as he can."

Erin jumped up from her seat and ran forward. Donovan knew he could have used the intercom, but he needed a few moments alone to collect himself. He was running out of time and ideas. Lauren, Michael, and the others were poised to pay the ultimate price for his inability to find a solution. He tried to get a grip on his emotions and steel himself for the next call. He gathered all of his inner strength to fight off the images of his parents and Meredith—people in his life he hadn't been able to save. He felt the Gulfstream make a hard turn and the whine of the accelerating engines filled his ears. It was

Nicolas heading them home. Donovan dialed the number William had given him.

"Colonel Adams," came the reply as the phone was picked up.

"This is Donovan Nash."

"One moment, sir."

"Captain Nash. This is General Edward Porter. We've been briefed. This is a secure line so we can speak freely."

"Thank you, General." Donovan noticed that he was being addressed by his civilian rank as an aircraft commander.

"Now. What can we do for you?" Porter said sternly.

"How far from the blast does my airplane need to be to survive the explosion?"

"Hard to say, Captain. We've never detonated a device of this size. But to be on the safe side, I'd recommend at least seventy-five miles. I understand the aircraft has damage to the flight controls. Do you think they can make it out of the eye in their present condition?"

"I don't know. But without any other options, it's our only chance."

"I'm looking at a report we received from NOAA. Yesterday, one of their P-3s suffered structural damage in the hurricane."

"I already know about that," Donovan replied. "What if you dispatched one of your jets...a fighter. They're stressed for that kind of punishment.

Could we use one or two F-15s to try to find a soft spot in the storm? At least big enough for them to escape the blast area?"

"That's a thought, Captain. General Erickson of the Air Force is with me. He just dialed Andrews Air Force base. We'll have an answer momentarily."

Donovan was buoyed by the exchange. It was a long shot, but that's all they seemed to have left. "General, fuel on the Gulfstream might be an issue here. If we get them away from the blast area, they might still have to ditch. How close are your ships?"

"That's a problem, I'm afraid. All of our submerged and surface assets have been ordered away from the area. Our best bet would be to launch a helicopter to attempt a rescue. That is, of course, if we could get them a survivable distance from the blast."

Donovan's body jerked as if he'd been shocked. In an instant he began to formulate the first fragments of a plan.

"General! Did you say submerged assets...as in submarine?" He tried to grasp each piece of the puzzle and place it in the proper sequence. His adrenaline began to pump furiously as each essential element fell into place.

"Yes. But the nearest one is hundreds of miles away."

"Listen carefully, General." Donovan saw Erin emerge from the cockpit. He covered the phone with his hand. "Erin! Change of plans. Have Nicolas head us toward Norfolk, Virginia! And tell Michael to stay put!"

"Captain?" General Porter queried.

"Sorry about that, General." Donovan collected his thoughts, trying to get everything in order. "Okay. First, forget about the F-15s. Here's what I want. And, needless to say—I'm going to need all of this in a hurry."

CHAPTER FOURTEEN

I can't believe they'd even consider such a thing!" Brent jumped to his feet.

"I know. I had the same reaction when Calvin first told me." Lauren wished he would calm down. "Brent. It's not over yet. They're working on a way to get us to safety."

Carl shook his head in disbelief. "In case you haven't noticed, this airplane is full of holes. If we could fly out of here, why haven't we? We're trapped! All of us are going to be killed like so many expendable lab rats!"

"That's enough!" Lauren shouted, her own panic beginning to rise. She was thankful that Brent had used more than one tie-wrap to secure Carl to the console. "The best people in the world are working on our problem."

"How much time do we have?" Brent asked calmly.

Lauren looked at her watch. "Three hours and forty minutes or so. Depends on Helena. The minimum distance they'll let her get from land is 250 miles."

"Oh, Christ!" Carl shook his head as he looked vacantly up at the ceiling. "The hurricane was speeding up last time we looked. And everything back here is dead! We won't even know it's time until we're vaporized!"

"That's not true," Lauren countered.

"Carl, why don't you shut up," Brent warned.

Carl sat motionless, his chest heaving. His eyes darted around the cabin, then he leveled a murderous gaze at Brent. "You don't get it, do you? Everyone's going to die!"

"But we're not dead yet," Lauren said. "Now please calm down."

"I don't mean just us," Carl's voice dropped noticeably. "I mean everyone...my entire family. They're going to kill my wife and children like they killed Kenneth."

"What?" Lauren spun and faced Carl.

"It's why I shut down *Jonah.* I had to conserve all the power so it would stay aloft until it was over land. They want the hardware."

"Who are they?" Brent asked.

"I don't know. It was Kenneth who was first contacted. According to him, it was a simple case of corporate espionage. He said an aerospace company wanted to get a jump on their competitors. They were willing to pay handsomely for certain information. No one was supposed to die. I swear I'm not a traitor."

"What about Donovan Nash? How is he involved?" Brent urged Carl to keep talking.

"He's not. We were going to let him be the focus of any internal investigation. He was already a suspect so it worked perfectly. Besides, Kenneth hated him for what he did to Lauren."

"What!" Lauren was stung by his words.

"Kenneth leaked some documents to a reporter to try to get back at Nash for everything he'd done to you."

"What did Kenneth think Donovan had done?" Lauren asked.

"He said he thought Donovan was Abigail's father. That he'd left you to fend for yourself. Kenneth was furious and wanted to get back at him."

On impulse, Lauren leaned in and whispered. "I hope you realize what you've done. You've killed three people already, and who knows how many more people are going to suffer."

Carl turned away and lowered his chin to his chest. "Please protect my family." Tears rolled from his red eyes.

"That might be problematic," Brent replied. "But the only way we'd even try would be in return for your complete cooperation—if we survive."

Carl nodded, weakly.

Brent turned to Lauren. "Is there any way we can talk with DIA headquarters?"

Lauren looked around them. "With all of the damage to the airplane, I'm not sure it would be wise to power up any of the systems."

Brent lowered his head and exhaled in agreement. "I just thought we could pull some data from the computers, maybe even re-task *Jonah*. The least we could do is let Reynolds know about the threat to Carl's family. It might help us catch the people we're looking for."

"As far as I'm concerned, Carl isn't very far up my list of priorities." Lauren was furious. "He's responsible for nearly killing me in Bermuda! For that matter, he may well kill us all."

"I understand," Brent replied. "But this is important."

In the rear of the plane, Lauren thought she saw some movement. She snapped her head around and was flooded with relief. It was Randy, trying to raise himself up off the floor.

"Oh my God. Randy, you're awake." Lauren hurried to help. Brent was right behind her.

"Take it easy." Lauren crouched next to him. "Go slow."

"What happened?" Randy's voice was thick and groggy.

"You took a nasty little spill." Lauren reached out for him as he tried to get to his feet. Together they stood, Randy swaying slightly and reaching out for the bulkhead.

"Is Michael all right?" Randy slurred his words slightly. His eyes blinked hard as he tried to focus.

"Help me get him to that seat." Lauren moved aside and let Brent reach in. Together, they carefully guided Randy to the nearest vacant science station. They eased him down, careful to not let his injured back hit anything. A mask of sweat and pain glistened on Randy's face.

"Oh, man," Randy gasped, "my shoulder is killing me."

"You were bleeding. It was a puncture wound; I think something from the explosion got you." Lauren stood with her hand on his shoulder, not sure he was quite ready to sit unassisted.

Randy winced as he moved. "I think I need to put my head down."

Lauren pulled a blanket off the floor and wrapped it around him. "You rest. Michael is fine for now." She gave Brent a look of concern. "Can you stay with him? I'm going back to the cockpit. Let me know if anything changes. I'll do the same."

Lauren turned to make her way up front to the cockpit. After the emotional turmoil she'd just experienced, the flight deck seemed like an oasis of calm in their own miniature storm.

"How'd it go?" Michael turned as she sat down in the copilot's seat.

"About as well as could be expected." Lauren brushed a strand of hair away from her face. "Randy's awake. He's not in great shape, but at least he's alive."

"Is he good enough to come back up here and help me?"

Lauren shook her head. "Not right now."

"I do want to apologize for my behavior earlier—back at the hangar," Michael began. He lowered his eyes as he spoke. "I was out of line. Donovan is my best friend, but I shouldn't have said the things I did...I'm sorry."

Lauren was both shocked and touched. The last thing she'd expected was a heartfelt apology.

"I'm old enough to know every story has two sides. I'm afraid I lost my perspective back there."

"Thank you, Michael."

"He was glad to see you the other day." Michael shifted in his seat. "He was caught a little off guard, but he was happy."

"If you say so," Lauren said before she could stop her response. She silently berated herself. Here was an opportunity to get into Donovan's mind and she'd come off as being disinterested.

"I'm serious," Michael reiterated. "I don't know if it changes anything, but he's never stopped thinking about you."

"He saved my life in Bermuda. Of all the people in the world to come to my rescue..." Lauren let her words trail off quietly.

Michael smiled, "You should have seen him blow out of the plane when he heard it was you who was missing. He was a man possessed."

Lauren processed what Michael had said. Had Donovan really charged to her rescue?

"I was thinking," Michael paused as he scanned the instruments. "This is just me talking. But from the outside, it seems as if you two got lost somehow. And for whatever reason, you can't find your way back to each other. I saw both of you on Saturday. From my experience, there can't be that much tension without feelings, and I'm willing to bet the feelings aren't all bad. Are they?"

Lauren wondered if they were really just Michael's words. How much did he really know? A million questions flew through her mind. Was Donovan separated? Did Michael know anything about the emotional exchange she'd had with Donovan this morning?

"I don't really think Donovan cares one way or another." Lauren let her words hang, not sure what she wanted Michael to say in response.

"I've said enough." Michael shifted in his seat. "You know, I've been sitting up here watching all of this." He spread his hand toward the boiling wall of dark clouds that surrounded them.

"What about it?"

"We're just going around in a big circle, but each time we head north, the radar shows what looks like a weak spot in the eye."

"Really?" Lauren's brow creased. She wondered what Michael was thinking or why he suddenly changed the subject.

"There's a part of me that says we try to get ourselves out of here on our own. I know Donovan told us to sit tight, but...I don't think I really want him to come back here and try to lead the way. It could be fatal for him, too, and that's the last thing I want."

Lauren pondered what Michael had said. She, too, had heard Donovan's defiant words. Did he really mean what he'd said about putting his own life at risk to help them? It only took her a moment to realize that's exactly what he would do. If something happened to both planes, in one terrible moment Abigail would be an orphan.

"What are you thinking?" Michael leaned forward.

Lauren turned to face him, her eyes locked with his. "I'm thinking you're right. But I'm also thinking we have to wait. We still have some time to work with."

Michael swallowed and ran his hand back through his hair. "How far do you think we have to be from the eye to survive the blast?"

"I was thinking about that, too," Lauren replied. "Maybe a hundred miles?"

Michael did the math in his head. "At T-minus forty-five minutes, we're going to go for it. The hard part will be convincing Donovan to leave us alone."

"I think I can convince him."

"How? He's as stubborn as they come."

"I'll tell him our daughter needs at least one living parent."

Michael looked as if he'd just been slapped. "Your what?"

"Donovan has a little girl. Her name is Abigail."

"How? When..?" Michael sputtered.

"Donovan and I had gone our separate ways when I discovered I was pregnant." Lauren held Michael's eyes with her own. "Oh, Michael, she's the most beautiful thing you've ever seen."

"Why didn't you tell him?"

"I wanted to, but my decision to break up with him was based on a lot of factors. First and foremost was the fact that he's married. I was crushed, angry that he'd lied. You know him better than I do. There's a part of Donovan Nash that no one will ever get close to, a distance I could never penetrate. The last thing I wanted was an unwilling husband."

"What do you mean, married? Donovan's never been married," Michael said, flatly. "He loved you. He was devastated after you left. He might be guilty of maintaining some distance, but that's just him."

"Michael. I'm not some flighty girl who dreamed it up. I saw the proof. I heard a message on his machine. I can still remember her name ...it was Elizabeth. I saw them together, and when I confronted him, he said nothing—not one word to defend himself. He left me no choice. It's when I knew it was time to leave."

Michael frowned and shook his head. "There's got to be another explanation. If you had seen him afterward, you'd believe me."

"It doesn't matter anymore." Lauren's words were clouded with doubt at Michael's insistence of Donovan's innocence.

Michael lowered his head. "I think it matters a great deal."

"I don't know if I agree. But considering everything that has happened, Donovan should know he has a daughter. He grew up an orphan. I'm hoping the last thing he'd want is for his daughter to grow up that way also."

"You know about his parents?"

"I know there was a boating accident. I just assumed it was when they died. He never explained much, but he used to wake up with horrible nightmares. Donovan survived, but he was adrift for days after their boat was sunk in a storm. Oh, God, it must have been awful. He was just a boy."

"I never knew all the details," Michael said, "Only that his parents died when he was young."

"Enough of this talk." Lauren sniffed and straightened in her seat. "I've already told you far too much."

"I'm glad you did."

"There's one other thing." Lauren looked wistfully out the window of the airplane. "Abigail is with my mother. They were supposed to travel to Chicago, but it got all fouled up. The last I heard they were stranded in Newark. If this hurricane comes ashore, they'll be directly in Helena's path."

"We'll let Donovan know. Through Eco-Watch, or even William, they'll be safe," Michael said, quickly. "Trust me. They'll move heaven and earth to make sure they're away from the coast."

"I hope so." Lauren brushed away a tear that had formed.

Michael studied the instruments. He punched several buttons on the FMS. "How long do we have?"

"It's just a guess at this point," Lauren said as she looked at her watch. "Three hours."

Eco-Watch 02. This is Navy Norfolk. You're in sight and cleared to land on runway two-seven. Wind is 340 degrees at fifteen knots. Exit the runway to the left. There's a vehicle standing by to lead you to the ramp."

"We copy," Nicolas transmitted. "Cleared to land."

Donovan could see the sprawling Naval facility straight ahead. He'd flown the Gulfstream as fast as he'd dared. They were minutes from touchdown.

"Ask them if the Air Force plane has arrived yet." Donovan's eyes swept the ramp.

"Uh. Navy tower. This is Eco-Watch 02. Has the Air Force plane made it here yet?"

"That's affirmative. They landed five minutes ago. You'll be directed to their position once you're on the ground."

Donovan set the *da Vinci* down hard. He braked heavily and deployed the thrust-reversers. With little fanfare, the jet quickly came to a stop. Off to his left, he saw a Navy vehicle waiting for them, its yellow lights ablaze.

Donovan smoothly guided the Gulfstream off the runway and fell in behind the Jeep. As they rounded a corner of the taxiway, Donovan spotted the Air Force plane. The Boeing C-17 Globemaster III sat next to a large hangar. Under its huge tail, the rear cargo doors were open. As he swung the *da Vinci* around to park it clear of the C-17, he thought the giant cargo plane was the prettiest thing he'd ever seen. Four powerful engines hung from its high-wing design. Behind the C-17 sat a wheeled mechanical loader. The entire airplane was abuzz with activity.

"That's one big airplane," Nicolas remarked.

"Let's hope it's big enough." Donovan shut down both engines and set the brake. Without hesitation, he unbuckled his harness and headed for the door. Frank was already up out of the jump seat and lowering the steps to the ground. He and Frank exchanged determined looks as the airstair descended the last few feet. He and Nicolas were going to stay with the Gulfstream and handle any communication from Eco-Watch or the White House. Donovan had instructed them to keep Erin on the plane and off the phone. As soon as the stairs touched the ground Donovan was off and running.

"Captain Nash?" An airman wearing an olive drab flight suit jogged from the C-17 to meet him. "I'm Sergeant Taylor. We just got here; they told us you'd explain everything once you arrived."

Donovan reached out and eagerly shook the man's hand. "You're the loadmaster, I take it?" Sergeant Taylor looked to be in his mid-thirties. With piercing dark eyes and a rigid posture, Donovan got the immediate impression that this man took his job seriously. They fell in side by side and hurried toward the C-17.

"Yes, sir. You tell me what we're hauling, and I'm the one who makes it happen," Taylor said curtly. "We were headed to our base in Charleston when the order went out to divert here. Word has it, it came from the very top."

"Where's the rest of your crew?" Donovan looked around; he only wanted to explain everything once. He couldn't get over the feeling that the C-17 kept growing the closer he got. The aircraft was immense and it looked to Donovan like you could play basketball in the cargo hold. Off to his right, a fuel truck pulled up and several men began to reel out the hoses.

"They're still inside the aircraft. Right now I need to know how heavy is this cargo? How far we going? We need to figure out how much gas to pump." Taylor pointed at the fuel truck.

Donovan pulled out a sheet of paper and handed it to Taylor. On it were the pertinent weights and dimensions. "Here's the breakdown...will it fit?" Peggy had pulled a file and transmitted everything to him as they'd sped toward Norfolk.

Taylor studied the figures. "Yeah, it'll fit. Odd sizes are our specialty—what is it?"

"Let's find the aircraft commander. I can brief everyone at the same time." Donovan put his hand on Taylor's shoulder. "We need to get this thing back in the air ten minutes ago."

"It's how I always work." Taylor waved the paper in the air. "Now, tell me—where's my cargo?"

"It's coming. You can't miss it. It's being ferried here by helicopter." Donovan followed as Taylor led him up the main steps into the C-17. They went around a bulkhead, then climbed fifteen feet up a narrow ladder to the lofty flight deck. From this perspective, Donovan looked down, amazed again at how big the C-17 was inside. It would easily hold the cargo that was on its way. Donovan went forward to the cockpit, which, like everything else on the C-17, was three times larger than the Gulfstream's.

"Skipper," Taylor called out. "This is Captain Nash."

"Nash. I'm Lieutenant Commander Hays; this is Lieutenant Jacobs. What in the hell is going on?"

Donovan nodded at the two men; they were still seated at their positions. From the guarded expression on Hays' face, Donovan feared this mission might be a tough sell.

"I'll give you the short version. What you're about to hear is top secret, so you'll repeat it to no one." Donovan knew he had everyone's attention. "I have a crippled Gulfstream out there. It's trapped in the eye of the hurricane. In less than three hours, a B-1 bomber is going to nuke Helena. Our job is to get there and save my people before that happens."

Hays remained silent. He looked at Donovan, then around the cockpit at the rest of his crew.

"I've already given Sgt. Taylor the dimensions of the cargo we're going to drop," Donovan continued. "He assures me it'll fit."

"He always says that," Hays said without a trace of humor. He looked Donovan squarely in the eye. "What is this cargo?"

"It's a submarine. A small research sub from one of Eco-Watch's ships. It's being brought here by helicopter."

"A submarine?" Taylor once again looked at the sheet that Donovan had given him, and put his other hand to his forehead. "You're kidding. I've never heard of anyone doing that—ever."

"Just tell me you're the man to do it," Donovan said, quietly. "Those people don't have any other option."

"Skipper...?" Taylor let the words hang.

"Can you do it, Sergeant?" Hays asked. "Is what Captain Nash has in mind possible?"

Taylor looked up at the ceiling as he did his mental calculations. "This thing not only needs to soft land in the ocean, but I gather you want to be able to maneuver as soon as you're in the water."

"That's the plan." Donovan nodded.

"That's going to make rigging the pallet a little tricky. Do you have any idea how many chutes it's going to take? This 'little' submarine of yours weighs almost 25,000 pounds. It's going to take a rig of eight G-11 chutes. They're 100 feet in diameter, which in itself is a complicated task. Once you touch down, there's going to be a jungle of lines in the water. That's in addition to the webbing I'll have to rig to the pallet."

"If that's what we need, then ask the Navy." Donovan gestured to the small army of men on the ground. "They've been ordered to cooperate, so anything you want is yours."

"Just so you know what you're up against." Taylor was still eyeing Commander Hays. "How much longer until the sub gets here?"

"About three minutes." Donovan pointed out the forward windshield. In the distance, he could see a Sikorsky CH-53 helicopter as it headed toward them. Suspended underneath was a white cylindrical object, the *Atlantic Star.* The submersible had been purchased by Eco-Watch Maritime almost a year earlier. Its mother ship was moored in Norfolk Harbor, undergoing refit. Donovan was looking at the one thing that could save Lauren and the rest of the people on the *Galileo.*

"Good lord almighty," Taylor cried out as he bolted from the flight deck.

Commander Hays turned from the sight of the helicopter and looked up at Donovan. "Okay. Why not? Let's make this happen. How far is it to the eye?"

"One hour. I just came from there." Donovan was flooded with a new surge of adrenaline as Hays began to issue rapid-fire orders to his copilot. He wanted to get out of their way, and quietly stepped toward the cockpit door.

"Before you go," Hays said, evenly. "How high up the chain of command did you have to go to get clearance for this mission?"

"The President," Donovan replied, then swung himself through the door and left the pilots with dismayed expressions on their faces. He used both arms to suspend himself as he slid down the ladder from the cockpit to the main cargo deck. The beating of the Sikorsky's huge main rotor blades began to fill his ears. Donovan jumped to the tarmac and ran to the rear of the C-17. At least twenty men stood by and reacted as Taylor barked orders. A metal pallet had been positioned on the loader, which in turn had been wheeled out onto the open ramp away from the C-17. It only took Donovan a moment to understand what Taylor had in mind. He was going to have the *Atlantic Star* lowered directly on the loader, which could then easily slide inside the rear door of the C-17. The thumping of the blades resonated in his chest as the helicopter came to a hover directly over them. Heavy exhaust from the three powerful turbine engines filled his nose as the rotor wash buffeted him.

"YOU MUST BE NASH!" a man shouted.

Donovan turned and found a young man, arm outstretched. Almost as tall as Donovan, the man's muscles pushed against his tee shirt as if threatening to rip the fabric. Donovan found an open yet chiseled face. The man looked at him with welcoming, friendly eyes, but Donovan immediately sensed something cold and dangerous behind them. The stranger seemed oblivious to the noise from overhead.

"I can't hear you!" Donovan yelled. He shook the offered hand as they both looked up at the hovering Sikorsky. Donovan studied the ungainly submarine. The twenty-two-foot long, white cylinder had two smaller tubes attached near the keel. A row of windows marked the side of the passenger compartment. The section of the hull that housed the main hatch jutted up from the main superstructure. The *Atlantic Star* bristled with various small directional thrusters, as well as a battery of searchlights. In the rear was the single main thruster, larger than the others and shrouded in a metal casing. The entire vessel rested on sturdy iron skids.

Donovan held his breath as the helicopter crew expertly set the *Atlantic Star* down exactly where Taylor wanted. When the signal was given, the cable was released and the Sikorsky clawed upward and climbed away. Where was his sub pilot? Peggy had assured him that a man by the name of Billy Graff had been briefed; he'd volunteered for the mission, but Donovan didn't know him. Peggy had explained he wasn't an Eco-Watch employee, but was fully qualified to pilot the *Atlantic Star.* So engrossed with the process he'd witnessed, Donovan had forgotten about the man standing next to him.

"Mr. Nash. I'm Lieutenant Howard Buckley, U.S. Navy SEAL. Everyone calls me Buck. I understand you might need a little help?"

"Lieutenant Buckley—Buck." Donovan silently thanked General Porter. "You know what it is we're trying to do here?"

"Yes, sir. You're going to drop that piss-ant little sub out the back of this C-17 to try to save some people. Is that right?"

"Something like that. Though I'm not sure it's really a piss-ant little sub."

"Sorry, sir," Buck said. "Last submarine I was on was a Los Angeles class attack boat."

Donovan couldn't help but be struck by the quiet air of confidence the man possessed. "You sure you're interested? I'm kind of making this up as I go."

"It's why I volunteered, sir."

"Why would you do that?" Donovan couldn't help but ask.

"Because General Porter and I are friends. He called personally and asked me if I could lend a hand. As a favor to the President. You're going to need someone with ocean rescue training once the sub is in the water. I've taken the liberty of having some of our specialized equipment sent over. It should be here any second."

"Glad to have you aboard. First order of business is to quit calling me sir. My name is Donovan. And right now we're at the mercy of Sergeant Taylor. He's the loadmaster on this thing. I'm also short one sub pilot."

"Is that him?" Buck pointed toward the *Atlantic Star.*

Donovan turned and saw the top hatch of the sub open. A bearded man with a bald head lifted himself out of the *Atlantic Star.* He was wearing cut-off jeans and a tattered tank top. He wore flip-flops on his feet.

"That must be him." Donovan set off in the direction of the sub.

"Mr. Graff." Donovan waved at the bearded man. Buck stayed close to his side. "I'm Donovan Nash."

"Mr. Nash." Billy Graff let himself down from the sub and dropped to the ground. "Glad we could finally meet. I've heard a lot about you."

Despite his aging beachcomber appearance, Donovan was struck by Graff's intelligent eyes and earnest handshake.

"Is the *Atlantic Star* ready?" Donovan stepped back as the loader began to slowly inch its way toward the ramp that led up into the C-17.

Graff nodded, "Everything's good to go. You're lucky I was around. Another fifteen minutes and I'd have been down at the harbor bar having a beer."

Donovan caught sight of Graff's earring and stopped in his tracks. "I don't want to sound ungrateful for your help, but exactly who are you, Mr. Graff?"

"I work for Submersible Technologies, the company that builds these. I was called out by Eco-Watch to help oversee some modifications. And yes, Peggy, your most efficient assistant, explained what we're doing. I have to tell you I was a little hesitant to volunteer at first."

"Mr. Graff. I'm Howard Buckley. How fast can this thing dive?"

"A maximum performance dive is somewhere close to seventy-five feet per minute," Graff explained. "To a maximum depth of 1,000 feet. On a good day we can make it in less than fifteen minutes."

"How many pounds per square inch can the hull withstand?" Buck probed further.

"If you're asking about the shock wave from a nuclear detonation, we're fine. It's the acoustic shock I'm concerned about," Graff explained. "As you know, sound travels very well underwater, and there's going to be one very loud bang when the thing goes off. I'm a little worried about the acrylic windows and forward observation dome. Sound waves can do funny things."

"How do we avoid that problem?" Buck scratched his chin as he pondered the information.

"If we can get below 600 feet I think the thermocline will deflect much of the acoustic wave. At least in theory."

Donovan pictured the stratified layers of the ocean, knowing the thermocline was a naturally occurring temperature inversion. What Graff explained made sense.

"That'll have to do." Buck nodded as a Navy truck pulled up and stopped next to the C-17. "Excuse me, gentlemen. My equipment has arrived."

"Mr. Graff. What changed your mind...about volunteering?" Donovan kept one eye on the sub pilot, another on the truck that Buck and several other men were starting to unload.

Graff looked both ways, then lowered his voice. "At first I thought the idea was insane. But, if we manage to pull this off, it'll be the best marketing tool I could have ever hoped for. That, and a man named William VanGelder was very persuasive. He offered me two million dollars."

"You help Sergeant Taylor get this thing secured properly in the next ten minutes and I'll add another million."

"Ten minutes it is. But you have to understand one thing. When it's time to dive this sub, the hatch closes. No arguments."

"Fair enough," Donovan nodded in agreement.

"Good. Just so you and I are on the same page." Graff turned and scurried up the ramp to oversee the attention being lavished on the *Atlantic Star.*

Donovan's head was swimming. He'd been on the ground for less than half an hour, and each tick of the clock added another twist to the knot in his stomach. An officer came running up to Donovan.

"The C-17 commander says he's fueled and ready to go. We're just waiting for the word from the loadmaster."

"Thanks." Donovan turned and jogged toward the side of the C-17. Buck had just brought Taylor out from the rear of the plane to look at something. As Donovan approached he could hear Taylor's astonishment.

"You're kidding me!" He gave Buck a look of amazement. "You have these in your inventory?" Taylor knelt down to inspect the crate.

"How much longer?" Donovan called out. His tension had started to build even higher as he began to understand how much was left to do. He couldn't imagine why Taylor was smiling from ear to ear.

"I think our friend here solved our biggest problem." Taylor turned and shouted an order to a group of men standing close. "Uncrate this and carefully move it into the plane. Let's look sharp, men. I'll be right in to help get it positioned."

Donovan watched as the men descended on the wooden box. "What is it?"

"It's called GPADS," Taylor said with enthusiasm. "It stands for Guided Parafoil Delivery

System. It's a single parafoil, over 7,000 square feet of silk. Forget about the cluster of eight G-11s, one of these will do nicely."

"What's the maximum payload?"

"It's been tested up to 35,000 pounds," Buck recited.

"Minimum drop altitude?"

"2,000 feet," Buck stated, evenly.

"Beautiful." Taylor rubbed his hands together as the canister was lifted from the crate. "Okay, men, this way, and be careful!"

"Your doing?" Donovan looked at Buck.

"A little something we've been tinkering with." Buck reached down and gathered up his wetsuit and harness, mask, and flippers. "I'm ready when you are."

"Sergeant Taylor, how much longer till we can roll?" Donovan asked as the heavy GPADS was carried off toward the waiting C-17.

"Give me five minutes to make sure I have everything I need. Once the sub is secured in the cargo compartment we can go. I'll rig the chute and harness when we're airborne. How we doing on time?"

"If we can be in the air in ten minutes." Donovan looked at his watch and did the calculations. "We'll be at the drop zone with about forty minutes to play with."

"That's cutting it pretty close," Buck said, as he envisioned the task at hand.

Donovan's head was beginning to pound from the stress. He knew once they were in motion he'd be fine. But all this organized chaos just added to his stress level.

"She with you?" Buck glanced at Donovan, then motioned behind him.

Donovan turned and found Erin running at full speed across the ramp toward them. He'd told Frank and Nicolas to keep her on the plane. She must have slipped out on her own. In his mind, she was now nothing but a liability.

"Donovan!" Erin gasped as she came to a stop. "General Porter is on the phone. He says it's urgent!"

"Go!" Buck urged. "We can plan the rest of this once we're airborne."

"When I see the main cargo door close, I'll run over and jump on," Donovan yelled over his shoulder as he sprinted toward the *da Vinci.*

"Sorry," Frank confessed as Donovan pounded up the stairs, taking them three at a time. "She bolted out of here before we could stop her."

"Don't worry about it. Which phone?" Donovan replied, winded from running.

"In the back."

Donovan covered the distance quickly. He threw himself into the chair and snatched the receiver while keeping one eye on the C-17.

"Nash here."

"Captain Nash. I understand you're a go at that end. How close are you to leaving?"

"In a matter of minutes, I hope."

"Two things. First, the eye is starting to shrink even further. It's now less than eight miles across. As you know, our primary targeting information was going to come from the *Galileo.* Our experts at this end think the device should be detonated at 25,000 feet, but there is some debate on this. I'd sure like to hear Dr. McKenna's opinion. She is, after all, at the scene."

"I think we could relay that information once we're out there." Donovan hated the thought of Lauren directing the bomb on top of herself and the others.

"Good. Is Lieutenant Buckley with you?"

"He's in the C-17. We've just loaded the *Atlantic Star.*"

"Very well. Could you please inform him that one of the scientists on your airplane is a suspected spy. It's Dr. Carl Simmons. It's information he should be made aware of."

"I'll brief him, sir. I've met Dr. Simmons." Across the busy ramp the rear doors of the C-17 began to close. "I have to go, General. Thanks for all your help."

"Godspeed, Captain Nash."

Donovan dropped the phone and headed toward the door of the Gulfstream. He slowed at the expectant faces of Nicolas and Frank.

"Go bring them home." Frank reached out and grasped Donovan's hand. Volumes of unspoken words passed between the two men.

Donovan nodded, deeply touched by the loyalty and friendship of his crew.

"They're moving!" Nicolas pointed out the door as the giant C-17 began to slowly wheel around.

"See you guys later!" Donovan hoped he could keep his promise as he leaped to the ground and ran toward the slowly taxiing cargo plane. As he neared the C-17, a side door opened and Buck stood in the entrance.

Donovan timed his jump perfectly, gripping Buck's waiting hand. He was pulled into the stark interior of the C-17. The instant the door was shut, the C-17 began to taxi faster. Donovan followed Buck's lead and pulled a retractable seat from a bulkhead. The two men quickly strapped themselves in.

"Mind if I ask what General Porter wanted?" Buck casually crossed his legs.

"He wanted to tell me the eye is getting smaller, and so is our window of opportunity."

"What else?" Buck probed. "I doubt he called to tell you something we'll know in short order."

"There's a suspected spy on the *Galileo.* His name is Carl Simmons. You can't miss him. He's a big man, probably close to 300 pounds, so be careful. General Porter wanted you to know about him." The C-17 swung onto the runway. The four big Pratt and Whitney turbofans began to spool up. As Commander Hays released the brakes, Donovan felt the push from a combined 166,000 pounds of thrust. He watched as the *Atlantic Star* sat unmoving in the cavernous belly of the C-17 as the airplane pitched up and clawed its way into the sky.

"Where's everyone else?" Donovan couldn't see Graff or Taylor.

"They're probably up top with the flight crew." Buck pointed behind them. "Your assistant is quite a little fireball. Damn good looking if I say so myself."

"My what?"

"Ms. Walker." Buck smiled.

"She's on the plane?" Donovan shook his head in disgust. He'd had every intention of leaving her stranded in the middle of the Naval base.

"Yeah. She's up with Graff. I've never been on a mission with so many civilians. Especially a looker like her."

"You can have her. She's nothing but a pain in the ass."

Buck grinned, then changed the subject. "I've been thinking about the best way to get your people in the sub once everyone's in the water."

"I'm listening." Donovan was miffed at Erin's presence on the C-17.

"We have the Gulfstream ditch at the far northwestern quadrant of the eye." Buck used his hands to illustrate. "Once we know there are survivors, we'll drop the submarine in the middle of the eye. By the time they drift to where we are, I should be ready to retrieve them."

"I saw some of your equipment. Were those line guns?"

Buck nodded. "Once I free the sub of the chute and harness, I'm going to fire a pattern on both sides of the sub. The explosive charges will shoot a rescue line out to 300 feet. I've got three of them. As the survivors drift past, they should intersect one or more of the lines."

"Sounds like a good plan." Donovan was grateful for Buck's matter-of-fact approach. The SEAL left no doubt he could accomplish what he'd just outlined.

"Do you think your people will be in rafts, or in the water?"

"I'm guessing rafts." Donovan pictured the two inflatable life rafts on board the Gulfstream. "That would make it easier, wouldn't it?"

"Affirmative. Spotting a raft in sixty-foot seas is easier than trying to find a person's head."

Donovan nodded, then squirmed uncomfortably at the thought of sixty-foot waves.

Buck cocked his head. "You don't like the water?"

Donovan shook his head before he could stop himself. Admitting to his fear was the last thing he'd wanted to do.

"That's a bitch," Buck said sympathetically. "Did something happen?"

"Yeah," Donovan said wistfully. "Something happened."

"Good thing I'm here then," Buck continued. "My diver's mask is outfitted with a two-way radio. I'll be able to communicate with you in the plane. Depending on how much time we have to work with, I'd like it if you could relay to me their exact positions in relation to the sub. It'll help me retrieve them quicker."

"You ever do anything like this before?" Donovan asked, not sure if he wanted to hear the answer.

"There's nothing a Navy SEAL can't do, sir." Buck unbuckled his seat belt. "The air is pretty smooth. I'm going to go get my equipment ready. I'm sure Sergeant Taylor is going to need my help to rig the sub."

Donovan released his straps as well. "I'm going to the cockpit. I need to brief Commander Hays on what to expect once we get to the eye."

As Donovan turned to go, Taylor, Graff, and Erin were coming down from the cockpit. Donovan stopped as they approached.

"Commander Hays says we've got a hell of a tailwind. We'll be there in less than an hour."

Donovan nodded at Taylor's update, then looked directly at Erin. She averted her eyes. Donovan gently gripped her upper arm as she tried to move past him.

"Let go of me!" she snapped, but her defiance vanished under Donovan's withering glare.

"You've got a lot of nerve to come on this flight," Donovan's tone was quiet, yet forceful. "If I'd wanted you here I'd have invited you."

"Look," Erin's tone softened. "This is the story of the decade. I had to be here. This is what I've dreamed about since my first day as a journalist. Plus, I can help. Sergeant Taylor said he could use me to help get the submarine ready. Mr. Graff agreed."

"I thought you had reservations about my single-minded rescue mission. That I'm only doing this for Lauren?"

Erin lowered her eyes. "I'm sorry about what I said earlier. I was wrong. I've learned a great deal about you in the last few hours. You've got to understand that for the last six months I've had a picture of you in my mind. I had you pegged as a traitor, a manipulator, someone who would sell classified data for money. I'm still trying to readjust my point of reference. I'm truly sorry."

Donovan let go of Erin's arm. He saw the honesty in her eyes, and for the first time since he met her, he felt as if she were telling him the truth.

"Go then," Donovan said. "I hope your story does justice to everything these men are trying to do."

"Trust me. It will." Erin took several paces then stopped. "I still don't quite know what to make of you."

Donovan turned and climbed the steps up to the flight deck. Erin's attitude shift bothered him. Earlier, she'd ignored his words. Now she seemed eager to embrace them. Was she telling him what he wanted to hear, or did she have another agenda?

He buried his misgivings at her being on board the second he entered the cockpit. Out of the front of the plane, he could see the familiar white clouds that marked Helena.

Donovan leaned down between the two pilots. His practiced eye swept the panel of the modern jet. He could see they were about to level at 45,000 feet, their speed building.

"Captain Nash," Hays said, leaning back. "How we doing on time?"

"We still have a workable window," Donovan replied. "I didn't know a C-17 could get to 45,000 feet."

"It can today," Hays replied, dryly.

"I'm told the eye is starting to contract." Donovan knew that Hays was doing whatever it took to get the job done. "Last report gave it a diameter of only eight miles."

Hays lovingly patted the glare shield. "She's big, but she's pretty damn maneuverable."

"The Gulfstream will be listening on VHF, 129.72. The sooner I can talk to them the better. Their call sign is Eco-Watch 01."

Hays nodded as Jacobs dialed in the frequency. "Done. Anything else I can do for you?"

"Fly fast."

CHAPTER FIFTEEN

"Is it my imagination," Michael craned his neck to look out the window, "or is the eye shrinking?"

"I was thinking the same thing." Lauren looked at the same cylinder of thunderstorms that towered above them. "This hurricane has rewritten the books. There's no telling what she's capable of doing. But I think you're right."

"How's our time?" Michael asked, well aware of each passing second.

"We've got an hour and fifteen minutes before the B-1 bomber gets here." Lauren looked at her watch. "Or, thirty minutes before we try to pick our way out of the storm on our own."

"Seems like a long time," Michael said, wearily.

Lauren could see the strain on Michael's face. His usually vibrant eyes had dulled from the pressure. His sarcasm had vanished long ago.

"I have this bad feeling," Michael offered, "That something's gone wrong for Donovan. I would have thought he'd have been back by now."

"Maybe it's a good thing he's not." Lauren regretted her words the second she said them. "I mean that in a good way. We won't have to convince him to leave us alone."

"I know." Michael tried to smile. "But you have some things to tell him. Things he needs to hear."

"How do you think he'll react?" Lauren lowered her head.

"Underneath it all, he'll be thrilled. He's always loved children. You should see him when we're out on trips. He's the first one to stop what he's doing, and give some child a tour of the airplane. You can see in his eyes how much he loves them."

Lauren bit her lip at the image Michael had painted. "You really think so? I've bounced back and forth, from imagining the best to the worst."

"Eco-Watch 01. This is Reach 410. How do you read?"

"Who's that?" Lauren looked at Michael as the strange voice sounded over the speaker.

"I don't know. It's the call sign the Air Force uses for cargo flights." Michael quickly went for the microphone. "Reach 410. This is Eco-watch 01. We read you."

"Good to hear your voice, Captain. Stand by."

"What are they doing here?" A surge of hope swept through Lauren's tired body.

"Michael. It's Donovan. How you doing, buddy? You haven't given up on me, have you?"

"Where are you?"

"I'm in an Air Force C-17. We'll be there in twenty minutes. Things are going to happen fast once we arrive." Donovan paused. "Is Lauren still with you?"

"I'm here." Lauren had slipped on her headset at the first sound of Donovan's voice.

"Okay. Lauren, I'm told they're planning to explode the bomb at 25,000 feet, but they want your opinion. Seems there's some disagreement about this."

"I've been thinking about that, too. Tell them it needs to be much lower...more like 5,000 feet. Helena's energy needs to be forced up into the stratosphere, not compressed against the ocean."

"I'll tell them." Donovan replied.

"So they're not going to call this off?" Michael asked.

"No. But here's what's going to happen. Michael, you're going to get into position to ditch as soon as we arrive. Frank talked to his people and the only addition to the emergency procedures manual is to open at least one of the over-wing exits before you touch down. It will ensure an exit."

"Wait a second!" Michael sat up straight. "We're not going to fly out of this storm? You want us to ditch? How is that going to save us?"

"Because seconds after you're in the water, we're going to drop a submarine out of the back of this plane. You'll be out of the storm, buddy, a thousand feet below the surface."

"Holy mother of God!" Michael replied, awe-struck. "You've got to be kidding."

"Nope. I've got one of our subs, the *Atlantic Star.* She's all buckled up ready to go. All you need to do is ditch, then get out of the plane into the rafts. We'll do the rest."

"Are you sure this is the only way?" Michael gave Lauren a concerned look. "You make ditching this airplane sound easy. Have you noticed the waves down there lately?"

"It'll work. Trust me on this one, Michael. Frank says it's very predictable. The airplane will hit twice, then spin ninety degrees as you come to a stop. You'll have plenty of time to get out into the rafts."

Michael rubbed his tired eyes as he processed the information, then looked down at the rolling ocean below.

"If anyone can do this, it's you." Donovan urged. "There's not another pilot alive I'd rather have in the left seat doing this."

"It's that alive thing that's got me worried." Michael took a slow measured breath. "Okay. If this is what we need to do...let's do it."

"When we get there we'll go over everything one more time."

"I copy," Michael replied. "I'm going to descend and get an up-close look at the waves. I need to figure out the best way to set us down."

"Lauren, is Randy able to swim? Do you think he'll be able to get out of the plane on his own?"

"He's awake. He'll need some help, though."

"Okay, Michael will explain everything that needs to happen. But hurry. We don't have much of a window. And like I said, once we arrive, this is all going to happen very fast."

"I need you to relay a message to Calvin Reynolds." Lauren thought of what Brent had suggested earlier. "Carl confessed to trying to steal information from the DIA. He also said his family is at risk. Calvin will know what to do."

"I'll tell him."

"Donovan...Lauren has something to say to you." Michael gave her a sideways glance as he transmitted.

"No!" Lauren shook her head. "Not now."

"What is it?" Donovan asked.

"Nothing. We've got a lot of work to do," Lauren said sternly.

Michael leaned closer. "This is the time Lauren. He needs to know. There's no guarantee this is going to work. I'm serious. Despite Donovan's pep talk, we might not survive the ditching."

"Lauren?" Donovan questioned.

"Go on." Michael urged.

Lauren nodded; butterflies fluttered in her abdomen. She took a breath and sighed heavily.

"This is never how I pictured saying this," Lauren said, her voice wavering on the edge of tears. "I hope you can forgive me."

"I'm listening," Donovan urged.

"If something happens..." Lauren choked as she tried to talk. "If something happens to me, you have to promise you'll take care of our daughter. She's with my mother...Her name is Abigail."

Lauren broke the connection and sobbed into her hands. She felt Michael's hand on her shoulder. The only sounds in the cockpit came from the hum of the *Galileo.* The silence from the radio was deafening.

Michael was about to key the microphone when Donovan's voice came across the miles.

"I promise," came Donovan's emotion-filled reply. "I can't believe...When did you...I wish you'd have told me."

"Lauren told me earlier," Michael continued. "I thought you should know. Sorry to force the issue, but I thought it was important. The other thing is, at last report, Abigail and Lauren's mother were stranded at the Newark airport. Hopefully they're gone by now...but they need to be out of there."

"Lauren. Thank you for telling me. We'll see her later. Together," Donovan said, his voice stronger. "I promise you I'll make sure they're safe."

"Really?" Lauren sniffed, her eyes filling with tears and her body shuddering under the emotions she felt.

"I'm thrilled, Lauren. I really am."

Lauren tried to wipe her eyes. A reluctant smile came to her face as she silently thanked Michael.

"Michael." Donovan spoke to his friend. "I have to get to the back and make sure everything is ready when we arrive. You need to do the same. We're going to want you to ditch as close to the northwestern quadrant of the eye as you can. It'll buy us some time."

"I understand."

"You'll hear from us again as we enter the eye. Take care of Lauren for me."

"You can count on it."

Thanks, guys." As Donovan handed the microphone back to Hays, he ignored the questioning looks on the pilots' faces. "I'm headed down below."

"After the drop," Hays said before Donovan left, "we're going to have to hightail it out of here."

"Will you be in contact with the B-1?"

Hays shook his head. "No, not directly, but there's an AWACS aircraft moving into position about 200 miles from here. They're going to monitor the explosion. They're working the B-1. We'll forward the information from Dr. McKenna through them."

"Perfect. I'll be back." Donovan hurried out of the cockpit. The news that he had a daughter filled him with both joy and dread. If he couldn't protect Meredith, how could he hope to protect his daughter—especially as he was about to once again become Robert Huntington? Donovan carefully gathered his fragmented emotions and tried to redirect them into purpose.

With a new determination, he raced to join the others in back. The *Atlantic Star* was still strapped tightly to the cargo floor. Nylon webbing was now pulled tightly around the gleaming white pressure vessel. As he rounded the cylindrical hull, he found the others. They were all staring at him.

"What? Is there a problem?"

"We heard," Erin spoke first. "Buck was testing his radio. We heard what was said from the Eco-Watch plane."

"Forget about it." Donovan wanted everyone focused on the coming job. "It'll be fine; nothing's changed. Now explain to me exactly how this is going to be a soft landing."

"I was just about to explain what I've done." Taylor tested one of the wire-taut restraining straps with his gloved hand. "The webbing will distribute the stress of the chute opening all along the vessel's superstructure. Mr. Graff has assured me the hull can easily withstand the strain."

"What about getting rid of all this mess once they're in the water?" Donovan followed Taylor to the rear of the submarine.

"That's the beauty of my design." Taylor strutted to a different section of the sub. "I've rigged the webbing to the pallet. It all gathers on top and connects in two places. Here at the bow, and again at the stern. All Buck has to do is cut the lines, and the weight of the pallet should pull everything under the water. We're counting that the chute will fall off to one side when it deflates. This should eliminate any of the parasail's lines fowling the sub."

"Brilliant." Donovan turned to Buck, who had donned a wetsuit and harness. His mask was propped up on his forehead; his flippers lay next to him. "How does all of this set with you?"

"I'm good to go. My only concern is an accurate drop in relation to the people in the water."

"You leave that to me." Taylor patted the side of the C-17. "With this plane and the GPADS system—I could park this sub in your garage from eight miles up."

"Where's Graff?" Donovan looked around.

"He's in the sub," Erin offered. "He's running pre-dive checklists."

"Okay, then." Donovan glanced at his watch. "So once we know they're in the water, we open the rear door, cut these straps holding the sub to the floor, and away you go?"

"Something like that," Taylor replied. "Once we're in position, I'll cut all but two restraints. It'll make the last little bit go smoother."

"How do you get the sub out the door?" Erin asked.

"Right here," Taylor pointed. "Three twenty-eight-foot extraction chutes. We open them up and they deploy in the air behind the C-17. The drag pulls the sub out on the rollers. It's a set of physics that won't be denied."

Donovan heard the sound of a chime at the same instant the roar from the four engines began to subside. He knew Hays must be slowing for their descent into the eye.

"Show time," Donovan said. He wanted to say something specific to Buck, but words to express his gratitude and hope wouldn't come. He looked on as the SEAL slipped a flotation device over his head and cinched up the straps.

"Buck. Good luck down there." Donovan tried to be encouraging, but both men knew the extreme nature of the job.

Buck checked his range of motion with the life preserver secured. "SEALs don't need luck—we make our own. Don't worry. I'll do everything I can to get them all in the sub safely."

"Thanks."

Buck pulled a sheathed knife from his duffel bag. He inspected the blade in the light. "Make sure your man down there knows what to do. If the ditching somehow goes wrong—there's no use dropping the sub. It's all on him right now. He does his part, I'll do mine."

"Is there any way I can talk to the *Galileo* from here?" Donovan asked.

"Yeah, sure." Buck handed Donovan a small hand-held VHF radio. "It should be fully charged; the frequency is already set. It's how we accidentally heard the earlier exchange you had with your lady friend."

Donovan switched on the volume and adjusted the squelch. "Michael, you ready?"

"Almost." Michael's reply was almost instantaneous, though the signal was scratchy. "I'm as close to the eye wall as I can get."

"We just came over the top and have started our descent. Say your altitude." Donovan paused. "Captain Hays. Are you on the frequency, too?"

"We're right here," Hays replied from the cockpit.

"Good. Michael, I'm sorry. Say your altitude again?"

"We're down to 500 feet. I've been looking at the waves."

"And?" Donovan had only a vague idea of what the surface conditions might be.

"They're huge, but without any wind, they're mostly flat on top. They're big enough to set the Gulfstream down on the backside of a swell. They're rolling at a long enough interval that we should have a fairly smooth time of it for at least twenty seconds after we touch down."

Donovan nodded. Michael had everything under control. "Is everyone in back ready to go?"

"As far as I know. We've already pulled one of the emergency hatches and both emergency rafts have been readied."

"I understand. Is Lauren going to be in front, or in the back when you ditch?"

"She's going to be up here with me. Randy is still out of it and I'm going to need some help."

"Mr. Nash, I think you should join us on the flight deck," Hays transmitted. "We can see the Gulfstream and I've just been given word the B-1 bomber is fifty-one minutes out. We need to start."

"I copy," Michael replied. "I'm starting down."

"Once I free these straps we're going to open the doors." Taylor explained as he stepped away from one he'd just released. "Ms. Walker, you'd better go with Mr. Nash to the cockpit."

"Go!" Buck urged.

Donovan ran past the sub and headed for the cockpit. Erin followed close behind. Donovan climbed the ladder and burst onto the flight deck. They were getting lower. A quick glance at the altimeter told him they were leaving 5,000 feet.

"Where are they?" Donovan moved behind Hays. He felt Erin squeeze in to get a look also.

"Eleven o'clock low," Jacobs said, pointing. "They're in a left turn."

"Michael. We see you." Donovan was momentarily stunned by the sight of the white Gulfstream against the giant blue-green waves. Not half a mile away sat the swirling, spinning edge of the hurricane. "We're getting into position. Are you ready?"

"We're ready," Lauren answered. "Michael says we're starting now. I love you, Donovan."

Donovan felt a longing at the sound of her words. He couldn't imagine what must be running through her mind.

"We're slowing to 150 knots," Hays said. "That's the speed we need to drop the sub. The rear door is open and Taylor says we're good to go. Everyone keep an eye out for the rafts once they're down."

Donovan keyed his microphone. "I love you, too." He stood mesmerized as the Gulfstream settled lower and lower toward the ocean. A massive wave built beneath Michael's plane. Donovan's body tensed as it appeared the surging water would swat the *Galileo* from the sky. At the last second, the Gulfstream nosed higher and, in a blur of metal impacting water, the airplane vanished in an explosion of white spray.

"They're down!" Hays shouted.

Donovan couldn't breathe. As if in slow motion, the Gulfstream emerged from the eruption of water and staggered along just inches above the ocean. It slowed and settled once again into the back of the wave, finally enveloped by a plume of water. Donovan could just make out the tail of the *Galileo* as it whipped around violently, then stopped. Though it looked horrible from above, Donovan knew Michael had just done a brilliant job.

"LOOK OUT!" Erin screamed beside him.

"Oh, God!" Hays slammed all four throttles to the stops.

Donovan looked up. Directly in front of them was *Jonah.* All eyes had been glued to the surface of the water. Somehow, he'd forgotten about the one aerial hazard that existed. Donovan's fingers dug into the seat back as the C-17 responded and accelerated. Hays fought the massive forces working on his airplane. The balloon raced closer and filled the windshield. Erin screamed once more and wrapped her arms around Donovan.

"Hang on," Hays yelled. He abruptly yanked the controls and the C-17 pitched up into a violent climb toward the circle of blue sky above.

Donovan fought the G-forces and waited for the impact, the engines howling in his ears. *Jonah* flashed past them on the left and was gone. Holding tight, Donovan came off the floor as Hays tried to regain control from the evasive maneuver. In an instant of recognition, Donovan saw they were headed into the eye wall. Nothing Hays could do could keep them from entering the full fury of Helena.

Donovan felt Erin's grip on him loosen. In horror, he looked down as she was pulled toward the precipice that led to the cargo floor below. In one swift motion, he tried to grab her as she broke free—his fingers finding hers. Her terrified eyes told him that he didn't have a firm grip; she was slipping from his grasp. Donovan catapulted himself toward her, sliding an arm around Erin just before she vanished over the ledge. With his free hand he made a desperate stab to reach the railing. Erin screamed as Donovan managed to hook his free arm around the cold steel. The C-17 banked hard; Erin teetered over the drop-off.

Donovan strained as she kicked her legs in space, trying to get a foothold. With a desperate surge of energy, Donovan pulled her from the ledge and gathered her in his arms. He locked his arm around the railing and held her tightly as the C-17 staggered through the sky and penetrated Helena's eye wall.

CHAPTER SIXTEEN

Lauren screamed as the Gulfstream slammed into the dark swell, whipping her body around and throwing it heavily against her harness, the water impacting the windshield and cascading with a deafening roar.

"Michael!" She looked over, horrified to see him slumped in his seat, a smear of blood running from his nose. She threw off her harness and reached out to him. He'd made her assume the crash position and she'd held on tight as they hit the water. But Michael had no such luxury... she was sure his head had been flung forward by the furious deceleration. He moaned as she tilted his head toward her.

"Michael! Wake up!" she pleaded. "We've got to get out of here!"

"What?" Michael gurgled. "Where are..."

"We're in the water." Lauren braced herself as the Gulfstream tilted and was swept down the side of a wave. She heard the ominous sound of creaking metal. "Please Michael...please get up!"

Michael raised one hand and felt his face. He winced at the pain.

Out the windshield, Lauren could see another wave bearing down on them. She didn't have any idea how long the Gulfstream would stay afloat. Michael hadn't thought it would last very long. She held on tight as the helpless airplane was lifted by the water and crashed hard to one side. A wash of seawater pushed into the cockpit and sloshed above her ankles. Lauren scooped up two handfuls and flung the salty water in Michael's face.

"Oh, Christ!" Michael cried out in pain, and cupped his face in his hands.

"I'm sorry, Michael." Lauren released his seat belt and tried to hold him upright. She hooked her arm under his and began pulling him toward their only escape from the sinking plane.

"I'm up." Michael fought his vertigo as he came to his feet. He lurched to the side as another wave slammed into the plane.

"We don't have much time." Lauren pointed out the window at the rolling ocean. "They're bigger and coming at quicker intervals than I expected."

Michael bent down to see what Lauren was pointing at. He recoiled from both the pain and the mountain of water bearing down on them.

"Go! I'm right behind you!"

With Michael following, she hurried to the cabin. The tremendous force of the ditching was even more evident in back. They'd stowed all the loose equipment they could find, but the cabin was still a disaster. Everything had been catapulted forward; wires and sections of upholstery floated in the green water. Papers and pieces of insulation were strewn everywhere.

"Help us!" Brent cried out, struggling to lift Randy to his feet.

Carl was still seated but nearly doubled over, cradling his left arm, his expression showing his great pain.

"Get the rafts out!" Michael yelled.

Brent nodded and threw the first one out the open emergency exit. He pulled the lanyard and secured the line to the airplane. A foot of water already covered the floor of the Gulfstream.

"Carl," Lauren said, looking down at him. She could see Brent had freed his hands. "How badly are you hurt?"

"I don't know. It's my elbow. I was thrown against the console." He squeezed his eyes shut.

"Help me get him out!" Brent yelled, an unconscious Randy engulfed in his bear hug.

"I'll get the other exit!" Michael gathered his momentum and made it to the opposite side of the plane and yanked on the handle.

Lauren had just reached out for Randy when a solid column of water poured in through the emergency exit, sweeping both Michael and Brent from their feet. They vanished under the onslaught. Outside, the ocean roared as the next wave gathered itself.

Gasping for air, Michael and Brent pulled themselves up from the aisle and fought their way forward. The Gulfstream began to tilt from all the water it was taking on.

Lauren pushed Randy toward the exit. Michael was quickly at her side, grabbing the yellow bundle at her feet and lifting it up and out the window. He secured a line and pulled the automatic inflation cord. Instantly, the second raft expanded and took shape.

"Your vest!" Michael yelled, reaching out and pulling the lanyard that would inflate her personal flotation device. "Now go!"

"Randy first!" Lauren stepped out of the way. Brent lurched heavily against the side of the plane as another wave pummeled them. Michael inflated his own vest and tumbled head-first out the exit. She watched anxiously as he steadied himself on the wing. He reached back in the opening as Brent eased Randy out. Within seconds, Michael had the injured copilot in the raft. Lauren looked down. The water was now up over her knees.

"Now you!" Michael reached for her.

"No!" Lauren shook her head. She wanted Brent to go next, then Carl.

"Brent!" She turned to him. "The other side. Get Carl to the raft!"

Brent nodded and waded through the water. With great effort he pushed Carl toward the opening.

"What about you!" Brent stood his ground, a look of bewilderment flashing across his wide face.

"Brent, you get out and help Carl." Lauren instructed. "I'll push from in here."

"I'm not sure I'm going to fit." Carl measured his girth against the exit.

"You'll make it. Now go!" Lauren said, angrily. The *Galileo* began tipping on its side. "Don't inflate your vest until you're through the opening. It'll give you more room."

Carl nodded and swallowed hard. He turned and with two powerful steps lunged at the opening toward where Brent waited. Lauren followed and pushed with all her might. A wave crashed down over the top of the jet and Lauren lost her balance...she went down hard, her jaw glancing off the side of a table. Lauren struggled to her feet. The bitter taste of blood filled her mouth. The exit was clear; Carl had made it out. With water pouring in from both exits, she struggled waist deep, pushing her way to the exit. From outside, Michael called her name. Lauren reached out and tried to steady herself. The floor under her feet tilted further as the airplane began to heel over. Visions of Bermuda flashed through her mind. Was Helena going to finish the job she'd started?

She used her legs to push toward the roof of the plane. Her face broke out into a narrow sliver of air and she gasped for oxygen. Thankfully, her vest held her in the small confines of life-giving air. In the growing darkness of the water-filled plane, she saw a shaft of light below. She took one deep breath and dove for the exit, only to be pulled back up by her flotation device. She only had time for one more breath as the water reached the ceiling.

Under water, she ripped off her vest and left it behind, clawing for the fading square of light. Her lungs screamed for air as she pulled herself one hand at a time through the emergency exit. Her ears popped as she was sucked under by the sinking plane.

With one last furious push, Lauren cleared the opening. Disoriented, she opened her eyes, not sure which way was up. She released some of her precious air and watched as the bubbles rose. With the last of her oxygen, she kicked toward the surface. Her body was going numb as she pulled against the water for all she was worth. In a moment of pain and relief she burst to the surface.

"LAUREN!" She heard screams as she took in one painful breath after another and treaded water as she struggled to get her bearings. Next to her, the graceful tail of the *Galileo* slipped below the waves.

"Over here!" Brent called out

Lauren pivoted in the water. A yellow raft was swept up the side of a tremendous wave. Brent steadied himself and threw a line in her direction. With what felt like the last of her energy, she swam to the nylon rope that floated in the water. She gripped the ring with one hand and held on tightly. She felt as if her arm was being jerked from its socket as the line grew taut. The raft vanished as it slid down the other side of the swell. The rope cut through the water like a whip and pulled her beneath the surface. Seawater filled her ears and shot up her nose, but Lauren managed to keep her grip. Painfully, she endured the rhythmic pull on the line as Brent drew her closer. She'd hoped to be in the raft with Michael, but he was nowhere to be seen.

Once again, Lauren broke to the surface, but this time she felt someone reach out and grab her. She was pulled over the soft sides of the inflatable raft and lay gasping on her back. The sound of waves and thunder assaulted her ears.

"I've got you!" Brent shouted, triumphantly.

Lauren opened her eyes. She could see the constricting cylinder that was Helena's eye. All around them the rotating clouds erupted with sharp peels of thunder. Lightning danced in the greenish-black caldron. The wind screamed with an energy Lauren had only imagined.

"Oh, thank God!" Brent sat back, exhausted. "I thought I'd lost you."

"Where's Michael? Is he all right?" Lauren coughed and choked as she tried to speak. Carl was on his side, his fleshy face a mask of shock and disorientation.

"They're in the other raft. But we lost sight of them." Brent collapsed against the side of the raft. He was breathing heavily. "Where's the other airplane?"

Lauren scanned the sky above them, but all she saw was *Jonah*. "Where are you, Donovan?" she whispered to herself.

As if responding to her silent plea, the C-17 erupted from the wall of the hurricane. In a flash of gray aluminum, it swept over them, the whine from its engines blotting out the ghostly, inhumane roar from the storm.

Erin moaned and wiped at the blood coming from her forehead. "Are we still flying?"

With the worst of the turbulence past, Donovan released her and sprang up from the floor. Commander Hays had managed to fly them out of the storm. The C-17 was down low over the water. Donovan silently urged the plane to climb.

"Come on....nice and easy," Hays said out loud, his hands pulling back on both the throttles and the controls.

Donovan rejoiced as the C-17 began a powerful climb away from the ocean. He leaned forward to see if he could find the Gulfstream, but all he could see was empty water.

"Where are they?" Donovan desperately tried to look out the opposite window. "Anyone see them?"

"I'm bringing it around! Somebody keep an eye out for that Goddamned balloon!" Hays clenched his teeth and banked the C-17 in a tight turn. "We saw them hit. We know they're down!"

"There!" Jacobs shouted. "I see something!"

"Hang on." Hays brought the airplane around in the direction Jacobs had pointed. "Where? I don't see anything."

"I've got them." Donovan spotted the two yellow rafts in the pitching ocean straight ahead. Both rafts were riding the crests and valleys of each giant wave.

"I'm climbing up to the drop altitude." Hays rocked his wings back and forth as they passed over the survivors. He made a wide circle to get into position.

Donovan helped Erin to her feet. She'd taken the worst of the beating when they punched into Helena's wall. As hard as he'd tried to hold her, the massive up and down drafts had been overpowering.

"We've got a problem." Hays turned around and faced Donovan, his face white and drawn from the stress of the last few minutes. "Taylor needs help. There's a problem with the sub."

"Oh, no," Donovan said with a hushed voice. He catapulted himself down the steps to the cargo bay. The instant he saw the sub, his shoulders slumped. Instead of being in the center of the cargo space, it had skidded to one side from the severe turbulence. The aft cargo doors were open; the wind inside the compartment created a continuous low howl.

"Over here!" Taylor yelled and waved from where the *Atlantic Star* had impacted the side of the plane.

"Hurry!" Graff was out of the submarine. He stood next to Taylor.

Donovan scanned the sub for any immediate signs of damage. He knew Hays would leave inside of ten minutes—whether they'd dropped the sub or not.

Using the sub as a handhold to steady himself, Donovan slid around the stern and was met with a grisly sight. Pinned between the sub and the curved wall of the C-17 lay Buck. Donovan recoiled. He couldn't imagine that the SEAL was still alive.

"He's hurt bad," Taylor yelled, as Donovan quickly knelt beside them. "He was going for the straps. He tried to stop the sub from fishtailing in the turbulence."

Donovan swallowed hard as he saw Buck's misshapen shoulder and collarbone. The hull of the sub was pressed hard against his chest. Buck was still conscious. The SEAL slowly reached up with his good hand and gripped Donovan's arm with an iron grip. Donovan leaned down and put his ear next to Buck's mouth.

"You can do it. Get this sub in the water," He gurgled.

Donovan pulled off Buck's dive mask. The SEAL's face was a sheen of sweat and agony. Without hesitation, Donovan fumbled for the radio in his pocket.

"Hays. I want you to bank this thing thirty degrees to the right. Hold it there. We have to get the sub away from the wall!" Donovan slid his arm until he had Buck's hand in his. "Get ready. This thing is going to be off of you in a second."

Donovan felt Buck squeeze his hand as the C-17 began to heel over.

"I'll tell you when to stop!" Donovan yelled into the radio. He braced himself, ready to catch Buck before he fell. He felt the forces pull on his body as the floor canted. He used his shoulder to try to push the sub away.

"It's moving..." Taylor warned; he, too, trying to push the sub.

With a shriek, the pallet holding the *Atlantic Star* began to slide away from the wall. Donovan supported Buck with his body and put the radio to his lips.

"Level off now!" Donovan yelled as the pallet scraped and pivoted across the floor of the jet. With all of his strength, he slowly lowered Buck to the floor. The SEAL's eyes were narrow slits as he fought the pain. He reached out and clutched Donovan's arm.

"She needs you. They all need you," Buck gasped, then lost his fight to remain conscious.

"Oh my God." Erin appeared at Donovan's side. She was holding her hand to the slash on her face. "Is he dead?"

"I don't think so, but he will be if we wait around here any longer." Donovan looked behind him. Taylor crouched down, looking at the bottom of the submarine.

Donovan stared at Graff. "Can it still go?"

"Yes!" Graff yelled. "That part of the sub is almost indestructible."

Donovan's palms grew wet as he pulled himself up. The floor of the C-17 seemed to be swaying beneath him. He tried to ignore the warning bells sounding in his brain. He felt sick. He knew what the waves were doing in the ocean below them. In a flash, he saw his mother's hand as it slipped beneath the waves, heard her cries for help. Donovan looked down. He had a death-grip on the side of the sub. If he went into the water, Donovan knew the sea would kill him. If he didn't, Lauren and Michael would die. He thought about what he'd told Erin—how terrible it was to survive. There was really no choice. He was dead either way. With trembling hands, he bent over and picked up Buck's diving mask, then slid the knife from the sheath strapped to his leg. He looked into the expectant eyes of the others.

"Is the rest of Buck's stuff in the sub?" Donovan asked. The inside of his mouth felt like cotton. The shrill whistle in his head wouldn't stop. He turned to find Erin.

Donovan leaned close to make sure she heard every word. "You have to find William VanGelder. Tell him about my daughter. He has to get her and Lauren's mother somewhere safe. If Lauren and I don't make it, please let him get to Abigail before you publish the story. He'll know what to do. It's the last favor I'll ask of you."

Erin nodded and lowered her head at the gravity of Donovan's request.

"What are we doing?" Graff shouted.

"We're going!" Donovan said as he followed Graff up the welded steps that led to the small hatch.

"Get strapped in tight!" Taylor yelled. "I'll give you sixty seconds, then you're gone!"

As Donovan lowered his frame through the narrow tube, he couldn't help but imagine that he was climbing into his own coffin. Graff climbed in after him and secured the hatch. The outside noise vanished and the interior of the sub became eerily quiet.

"Sit there," Graff pointed. "And give me that before you kill someone!" Graff barked and pulled the razor sharp knife from Donovan's hand. The submarine pilot tossed him a life jacket.

Donovan slipped the vest on and quickly strapped himself into the hard metal seat. Inside, the sub was a maze of tubes and junction boxes. Graff sat behind a control panel not unlike an airplane's, but Donovan didn't recognize any of the instruments. The interior of the sub smelled of mildew and human sweat. Donovan had no idea what to expect as he braced himself with both hands. All he could picture were the giant waves below.

"Get ready!" Graff yelled as two clangs resonated through the hull. It was Taylor's signal they were going to drop. As Graff began to flip switches at his console, he grumbled under his breath. "I may be crazy, but at least I'm going to die a rich man."

Without warning, the sub lurched. The wall of the C-17 flashed past and was replaced by nothingness. Donovan felt like he was tumbling. Assaulted by vertigo, his stomach tightened even further. Through a small porthole, Donovan caught the image of the C-17, far above. A crack echoed through the small interior of the *Atlantic Star* as the chute deployed. Donovan was pressed hard into his seat as they decelerated. In silence, they were now drifting downward to the raging sea below.

"Holy shit!" Graff cried out as the main canopy swelled and opened. "It worked!"

Suspended from the parafoil, Donovan's disorientation passed. They twisted and turned as they floated closer to the ocean. In the tiny cockpit, Graff was busy powering up the *Atlantic Star*. Off to Donovan's side lay Buck's equipment. Three rifle-lines were carefully secured with elastic cords, as were his flippers. The only thing Donovan didn't have was the harness. A quick search revealed the rope Buck had intended to use to tie himself to the sub.

"We're almost there." Graff turned in his seat. "I can see both rafts. You're going to have to work fast. Do you remember which lines to cut first?"

Donovan nodded. His fear was dulled by the mention of the rafts and he closed his eyes, focusing on saving the survivors. He told himself that no matter what happened, he had to save them. Then the sea could do whatever it wanted with him.

"Fifty feet," Graff called out. "We're going to hit on top of a wave, so don't open the hatch until I tell you to."

Out the small round porthole, the ocean drew closer. Donovan held his breath until his lungs protested. He couldn't swallow; his throat had closed off. Every muscle in his body was tense. The first impact rocked the sub; the second one heeled them over. The water buffeted them as they slammed into the sea. With unblinking eyes, Donovan watched in horror as they plunged beneath the surface of the water. Donovan couldn't have been more terrified than if he'd just parachuted directly into hell itself.

"We're back on top!" Graff yelled, handing him Buck's knife. "Get those lines cut as fast as you can!"

Donovan bolted past Graff and spun the small wheel at the top of the conning tower. He swung it open and stuck his head out into the fresh salt air.

Above and behind him, the huge parafoil was losing its lift, folding up on itself as it crumpled into the water. Donovan climbed out, sickened by the sight of a mountain of water rising toward him. He turned his head and held on, terrified at the realization that he wasn't tied to the sub. As the monstrous wave approached, Donovan froze as the *Atlantic Star* rode up the side, balanced itself precariously at the top, then washed down the backside with dizzying speed.

"Cut the lines!" Graff screamed from below.

Donovan knew he had only seconds before another wave came. He forced his eyes from the deadly ocean and with two quick slices of the knife freed the submarine from its harness. First the webbing, then the parachute, was pulled down into the dark water. Keeping his eyes fixed on the white metal, Donovan lowered himself back into the submarine.

"Good job." Graff had both hands on the controls. "Get yourself tied to the sub!"

Donovan gasped an acknowledgment. He grabbed the rope. Quickly, he tied one end around the waist of his flight suit. The other he wrapped around the welded base of the chair. His next move was toward the mask. He pulled it around his head, tested the seal, then slid it up on his forehead. Caught in his own worst nightmare, Donovan felt them rise and fall with the next wave. Water poured in from the open hatch. With sheer determination, he yanked the first rifle line from the wall.

"I'm turning us around." Graff leaned to his left as he used the thruster controls to maneuver the submarine. "Both rafts should be to our left now."

Donovan nodded. He pulled the mask over his face and lifted himself up out of the sub once more. His stomach lurched as they reached the top of another wave. From his position atop the giant swell, he spotted the rafts. Graff was wrong. One was a hundred yards to the left, the other, half that distance to his right. They were going to pass directly between the two. Behind him an explosion of thunder ripped through the air. Donovan ducked and turned. For the first time he was aware of the eye wall. It roared and rumbled as it grew closer, angry clouds spiraling and twisting upward. High above him, the C-17 was a tiny speck as it climbed out of the storm.

Donovan braced himself and raised the rifle to his shoulder. He adjusted the angle as best he could and pulled the trigger. The gun lurched in his hand; the spool beneath the barrel whistled as the charge snaked the line out from the sub in a high graceful arc.

"Tie that line off and give me another gun!" Donovan yelled inside the hatch as he shoved the spent rifle inside. Moments later, he felt Graff push the second gun into his hand. He checked the safety and twisted around to fire it the other direction. Just as he was about to pull the trigger, the sub crashed into the valley between waves—the gun was flung from Donovan's hand. It clattered against the hull as he stretched to catch it. His fingertips brushed the metal just as it bounced and vanished in the ocean.

Terrified and on the edge of panic, Donovan lurched forward, clenched his fists, and fought for control. Memories of a fourteen-year-old Robert Huntington flooded his mind.

"I need the last gun!" Donovan yelled. This time he gripped it tightly and fired it into the sky. The sub rose as the line shot out away from him. It was perfect, floating over the water and settling just in front of the raft. Michael reached out and grabbed the line.

As Michael kept pulling, Donovan knew that the other raft—the one he prayed Lauren was in—should be approaching the line. He waited until they crested a wave and turned. To his immense relief they had found the line and were drawing themselves closer. Donovan's relief was short-lived. Someone was pulling the raft toward the sub—but he was the only person visible.

"I need help! I have an injured man." Michael called out as he neared the submarine.

Donovan spun and pulled Michael the last ten feet. Randy was lying in the bottom of the raft, the water mixed with blood. He tied off the line and reached down to help. Wearing a mask and vest, Donovan knew Michael hadn't recognized him.

"I'll take his legs!" Michael jumped into position. "Lift!"

Donovan and Michael both strained. They managed to maneuver the dead weight up on top of the sub, then held Randy tightly as they raced down the back of a wave. Graff pulled Randy's legs inside as Donovan lowered the injured pilot into the sub.

"Oh, Christ." Michael lay exhausted on the cold metal of the sub.

Donovan removed his diving mask; it had become partially fogged from the exertion. He looked into the battered face of his longtime friend, then grabbed the remaining line.

"Donovan?" Michael struggled to his feet, wiping the water from his eyes.

"I'll explain later."

"How in the hell?" Michael shook his head in dismay and together they began to pull the others closer.

Donovan formed the words he was almost too afraid to ask. "Did Lauren make it out of the plane?"

"Yes," Michael answered. "She made it...We all did."

Graff stuck his head out of the sub. "I just got a final transmission from the C-17. The B-1 is nineteen minutes out. We've got to hurry! In nine minutes—I'm shutting this hatch and diving. I don't care which side you're on!"

"We'll make it. They're close!" Donovan shouted. He turned and could finally see two men in the raft. Simmons had raised his bulk, and without warning, lunged at the smaller man. In an instant the raft was swept upside down. A sick feeling came over Donovan. Lauren was nowhere to be seen.

"Where is she?" Donovan cried out.

When another wall of water separated them, Donovan and Michael felt the line tighten as tons of ocean pressed on the rope, threatening to rip it from their hands. As they held on and waited, Donovan strained to once again catch sight of Lauren. The sub lifted and they were swept up and over the top. Donovan watched as the two men tried to cling to the overturned raft.

"Over there!" Michael pointed, "What's that?"

Donovan turned to look at what Michael had seen. Twenty yards from the raft, arms thrashed in the water. He caught sight of auburn hair...it was Lauren. In the same horrible instant, Donovan saw she wasn't wearing a life jacket.

"She's in the water!" Donovan cried out to Michael. He heard the panic in his own voice.

"I'm going after her." Donovan pulled his mask down over his face. "Pull me in when I reach her."

Donovan hovered over the water. The reality of diving into the treacherous ocean felt far more terrifying than being on the submarine. The turbid water seemed to reach up for him... almost daring him. His knees threatened to lock. Donovan thought of Buck, and gathered strength from the SEAL's quiet determination. With every fiber of his being screaming in protest, Donovan thrust himself headfirst into the foaming water.

His body stiffened as his life jacket propelled him back to the surface. He put one arm over the other and began to kick. Each time he was swept in the upsurge, he stopped and tried to spot Lauren. Flung downward, he swam harder, needing desperately to make it to the pinnacle of the next wave.

Donovan hesitated; he'd lost his bearings. A wave spun him sideways, but he managed to right himself. To his left, a faint cry for help penetrated the storm. He ripped his mask away from his face. He heard it again and twisted around in the water. He saw Lauren just as she disappeared behind a mountain of water. He waited. If he judged this right, she'd be within his grasp as the next wave passed.

Donovan turned quickly and tried to spot the sub, but it was too low in the water. He spun around, kicking to keep himself in position. He treaded water, not knowing which way he was going to have to swim to reach her. The pressure grew behind his temples as he rode through the next swell. His terror grew as he scanned the empty ocean.

"Lauren!" he screamed.

"Here. I'm here!"

Donovan turned in the water at the fading sound of her voice. Ten feet away he saw a hand as it floundered. Without hesitating, Donovan swam to where he'd last seen her. In one swift motion he shed his life jacket and dove beneath the waves. In the silent, murky world beneath the surface he saw her struggling, trying in vain to reach the surface. In seconds he had his arms around her. He kicked as hard as he could for the surface. They broke free and Donovan held her tightly.

Donovan's life jacket had floated out of reach. He rolled over on his back, making sure Lauren was face up on his chest. After several seconds of furious kicking, Donovan reached out and grabbed the precious orange vest. He put his arm through it and relished the floatation it provided.

"You're safe," he whispered into Lauren's ear. He raised an arm and waited for Michael to start pulling them toward the sub. His internal clock told him they still had enough time.

Lauren choked and flailed her arms weakly.

"Lauren. Can you hear me?" Donovan rolled her over to get at least one of her arms into the vest. He looked into her exhausted face. Her eyes were still closed. He pulled her close and kissed her lips lightly. He pulled back as she wearily opened her eyes and looked at him. No words were needed as she wrapped her arms fiercely around him.

They were still locked in a silent embrace when Donovan felt the tug of the rope around his waist.

"Can you kick?" Donovan asked as they moved slowly through the water.

"I'll try," Lauren said breathlessly, then her eyes flew open, and she turned to face Donovan. "How can you be here...in the water?"

"Because you're here." Donovan continued to kick. He caught a glimpse of the sub. They were still a long way away.

"He pushed me," Lauren blurted as if suddenly remembering. "Carl went crazy. He shoved me out of the raft!"

"I'll deal with him later," Donovan vowed. "Kick harder!"

Lauren nodded and tried to do what Donovan asked.

Assured that Lauren had a good grip on him, Donovan reached out and began to pull on the rope with both hands. With he and Lauren both kicking, he put one hand over the other in a painful process to go faster.

"How much farther?" Lauren gasped.

"Don't give up...keep going." Donovan knew he was reaching his limit. He swallowed a mouthful of water, the salty froth burning his throat. He felt for the rope and discovered some slack. He pulled harder and the line slipped easily through the water. He turned to Lauren, his face a mixture of shock and fear.

"What is it?"

"The line..." His anguished voice was filled with disbelief. "We're not connected anymore."

"Oh, no!" Lauren dug her hands into his back. "Donovan...They're leaving without us."

Across the waves, on the tiny deck of the *Atlantic Star,* Michael was struggling with Carl. Donovan watched as Simmons threatened to pull Michael into the ocean. The huge man had a death grip on Michael's leg as he tried in vain to pull his bulk up onto the sub. Brent was now on the deck and had joined in the efforts to free Michael.

Donovan silently urged them to start pulling him and Lauren toward the *Atlantic Star.* A second later Graff appeared in the hatchway. He joined the fray and locked his arms around Michael just before the pilot was pulled into the water. Simmons lost his grip on Michael and locked his huge hand around Graff's leg. The submariner tried in vain to twist away. A second later, a single shot rang out across the waves as Brent ended the conflict. Carl's lifeless body rolled over and drifted silently from the sub.

"Oh my God." Lauren gripped Donovan even tighter. "Brent killed him!"

Graff reached up from the main hatch and helped Brent subdue a now frantic Michael. With one last effort, Michael tried to free himself to grab the rope connected to Donovan and Lauren. But Brent and Graff forced Michael down into the sub, then climbed inside. Above the roar of the storm, Donovan heard the sharp metallic clang of the hatch as it swung shut. The next wave blocked his view, but Donovan knew they'd run out of time. As promised, Graff was submerging.

Lauren sobbed into Donovan's shoulder. "You were never supposed to be here. Oh God, Donovan. We're both going to die."

Donovan held her tightly as they rode up the next swell. The sub was gone. They'd started their dive, and Lauren's body shuddered in his arms. There weren't any words to refute her statement. They were going to die.

"I'm so sorry." Lauren buried her face in his shoulder. "I wanted Abigail to know her father. I'm so sorry."

Donovan heard Helena's terrifying shriek as the vertical mass of the eye wall grew closer. The roar of the thunder was almost non-stop. In the rolling black clouds tentacles of lightning spread out in the spiraling storm. Donovan closed his eyes and gave in to the storm; there was no use in trying to swim away from the inevitable. He drifted back to when he was fourteen—the typhoon that had killed his parents had for some reason spared him. Now Mother Nature had come full circle. After all these years, she'd finally caught him back in the water. For Lauren's sake he hoped the end was quick. He prayed she'd go first. He knew all about drifting alone in the ocean, and if she could be spared that agony, even for a few minutes, he could die easier.

"I do love you," Lauren whispered into his ear. She, too, eyed the crushing wall of weather. She wondered if they would die from the wrath of Helena, or in the single instant when the sky grew brighter than the sun. "I love you so much."

Donovan felt the warmth of tears flood his eyes. He'd stopped swimming. They were bobbing in the ocean, the single life jacket wrapped around them. A strange peace came over him. Erin could write her story; it wouldn't matter now. He knew William would act decisively. Abigail would be well cared for.

Lauren lifted her head and put her cheek on Donovan's. "Her last name is Nash. I did give her that," Lauren confessed. "Abigail Nash."

Donovan pulled back to gaze into Lauren's eyes. "Her last name is Huntington. Abigail Huntington. My real name is Robert."

Lauren's brow creased as she looked into his face. She'd heard the words but they didn't make sense.

"Donovan, what are you saying?"

"A long time ago I left one life for another. My family name is Huntington."

Confusion filled Lauren's lovely face.

"She'll be well taken care of."

"Oh, Donovan. No." Lauren's eyes grew wide as she finally connected the names. "Costa Rica ...Meredith Barnes...Oh my God!"

Donovan nodded.

"Who is Elizabeth?"

"Elizabeth was my mother. I finally had her remains brought to Virginia, to a house I own out in the country. The woman you saw me with was William's niece. He raised me after my parents were killed. I'm so sorry."

"Why couldn't you tell me?" Lauren slumped at the revelation. "I thought you were married. I left you and you could have easily stopped me. Why?"

The first breath of a breeze brushed against Donovan's face. High above them the eye wall relentlessly drew closer.

"To protect you." Donovan watched as Lauren also felt the wind. She turned to look up as Helena bore down on them. "After Meredith was murdered, I fled the media...and my life. I became Donovan Nash. I never told you, because I always feared the same thing could happen all over again. It's a secret I've never told anyone."

"Oh, Donovan," Lauren held him tighter. "I'm so sorry I doubted you."

Donovan closed his eyes and breathed her in, as the precious seconds of his remaining life ticked away in his head. Rain began falling from the sky. The first drops hit his face. Without warning, Lauren suddenly stiffened in his arms.

"Donovan, look out!" Lauren screamed.

Donovan twisted to look as a huge black object erupted from the ocean behind them. A giant black cylinder breached the surface and crashed heavily into a huge wave. Spray exploded into the air and the object momentarily vanished. Slowly, a conning tower materialized from the geyser of water. Donovan held his breath as the massive black object swayed and righted itself under the onslaught of the hurricane. In seconds, hatches flew open, and men came bursting out onto the deck, searching the water. In the fading light of the approaching storm, the Cyrillic markings on the submarine were clearly visible.

"Swim, Lauren. Swim!" Donovan yelled and began to kick with all his might toward the Russian submarine. He felt his own efforts matched by Lauren as together they struggled against the wind and rain. The eye wall was nearly upon them. Helena's fury peppered Donovan's face with the sting of wind-driven rain; it felt like buckshot on his exposed skin.

"Here! We're here!" Donovan's screams were joined with Lauren's.

He feared their cries were being swept away by the steadily rising wind. In the noise and chaos of the hurricane, Donovan pulled the orange life vest from Lauren. He kicked to keep them both afloat as he waved the brightly colored material in the air. They were going under when something solid stung his neck. With all his strength, he grabbed the line and looped the rope first around his hand, then Lauren. In seconds, they were being propelled through the water. Donovan held Lauren as they were pulled to the surface, gasping for air. Moments later, strong hands clutched them, hauling them up onto the ice-cold metal deck.

Donovan looked gratefully into the anxious faces of the sailors. The men shouted orders in Russian...lines were discarded into the heaving water. There was no time to retrieve them. Heavy wool blankets were thrown around him and Lauren, and they were whisked off toward an open hatch. Donovan reached for Lauren's hand as they collapsed against a heavy iron bulkhead and sank to the solid floor of the submarine. The sailors quickly battened down the opening and helped them to their feet.

"This way, quickly," one of the sailors said in heavily accented English. "We are going to dive now."

Donovan shook his head in disbelief. His saw his own expression of shock and profound relief mirrored on Lauren's face.

"This way," the sailor urged, ushering them into a larger room.

Equipment panels lined both walls. A myriad of lights glowed in the semi-dark room. Donovan knew by the periscope that they'd been brought to the control room.

"Captain Nash. Dr. McKenna. I am Captain Viktor Zirnov. Welcome aboard the submarine *Voronesh*." The short tank of a man called their names in perfect English. He nodded at them, then turned and issued a series of orders in Russian. He spun and stared at a panel. An instant later, several lights flashed from red to green and Zirnov shouted the order to dive.

"You may want to brace yourselves." Zirnov turned to face Donovan and Lauren, as he himself reached out and held on to a handle.

Donovan leaned over and kissed Lauren's forehead as the floor of the submarine began to tilt under their feet. The force of gravity caused him to grip the pipe harder. He caught Zirnov's eye.

"I take it you know about the bomb?" Donovan asked.

Zirnov nodded, then looked over at a large chronograph. "We still have four minutes."

"There's another sub," Donovan explained. "It has to be at least 600 feet deep to survive the explosion. Do you know where it is?"

"Yes. We have it on sonar." Zirnov quickly spoke in Russian to two men seated at the sonar station. They replied to Zirnov's words.

"They are not capable of diving as fast as we are," Zirnov translated. "They will only be at 400 feet when the bomb goes off."

"Oh, no," Lauren gasped. Several of the crew glanced at the captain with concerned expressions on their young faces. She looked at Donovan.

"What was their concern?" Zirnov asked. "Their hull should be able to resist the pressure wave from the detonation."

"It wasn't that." Donovan thought back to Graff's explanation. "It was the acoustic shock. The designer was worried that the acrylic windows might not react well to the sound waves transmitted through the water. He thought that by diving below 600 feet, they could take advantage of the thermocline..."

"...which might deflect most of the sound waves." Lauren finished his sentence.

Lauren turned to Zirnov. "I'm assuming this vessel is shock hardened. Would it be possible to position this sub on top of the other one? Would your hull work to shield the *Atlantic Star* from the acoustic shock?"

Zirnov immediately barked a string of orders to his crew. The control room was a flurry of activity. The sloping deck under Donovan's feet twisted to the right.

"Clever woman." Zirnov gave Lauren a wry smile. "Your reputation is well-deserved."

"How did you know we were out there?" Donovan couldn't stand the mystery any longer. "How could you have known any of this?"

"On the contrary, Captain Nash. Our two governments have been in contact since this plan was revealed to us. My government is in full support of trying to destroy this hurricane."

"But..." Donovan didn't know what to say. "How did you know we were in the water? Why did you risk surfacing?"

"One moment, Captain Nash." Zirnov walked over and peered over the shoulder of the sonar operator. Without looking up, he issued another series of commands. The deck of the *Voronesh* began to level. Zirnov looked up at the clock, a worried expression flashing across his face.

"Can we get there in time?" Donovan asked, quietly.

Zirnov frowned at Donovan, then issued another series of orders. In the confines of the control room, crewmen spoke back and forth with what sounded like a growing urgency.

"Oh, Donovan." Lauren squeezed him, as she too waited.

"It's going to be close." Zirnov turned to them after listening to his sonar operator give bearing and distance.

Donovan had no idea where they were in relation to the tiny sub, or how long until the bomb went off above them. He silently urged the men around him to somehow get there in time.

Zirnov asked for a report. Beside him, his second-in-command began to count down from ten. Zirnov looked at Donovan and translated the numbers to English. The two sailors at the sonar station removed their headsets and placed their hands over their ears, as did the rest of the crew.

Not knowing what to expect, Donovan and Lauren followed suit. The main lights flickered briefly and the control room was bathed in an eerie red glow. Each person stood silent and looked upward in the direction of the explosion. Moments later, the submarine shuddered. It sounded as if a giant sledgehammer had struck the hull. Donovan winced. Even with his ears covered, the deafening metallic sound resonated sharply through the confined quarters. The overhead lights came back on and Zirnov looked up from the screen, a wary expression on his face.

"The other sub?" Donovan questioned.

Zirnov looked at the men seated at the sonar station. They were putting their earphones back on and adjusting their equipment. One turned and spoke to Zirnov.

"Still making a lot of noise in the water. Their signature is as it was before," Zirnov announced, triumphantly. "I believe we were in time."

Donovan and Lauren hugged and kissed in front of Zirnov and the others.

"I believe you asked me a question." Zirnov walked over to where Donovan and Lauren stood. He turned and addressed his crew in Russian, then turned to them both. "Allow me to shake the hand of the hero who saved our submarine comrades in the Arctic. We as a group owe you our profound thanks."

Donovan warmly shook Zirnov's outstretched hand. He saw a genuine look of gratitude in the captain's eyes. The sailors in the control room all voiced a unanimous agreement and issued a respectful salute.

"I still don't understand how you knew we were in the water."

"We had just arrived when we intercepted a desperate radio call from the other submarine. Someone was pleading with your B-1 bomber to give them time to retrieve you. Their calls went unheeded. I doubt very much their transmissions penetrated the storm. When I learned it was you in the water, I made the decision to surface."

Donovan leaned back against the wall. "It must have been Michael on the radio before they dove. But why were you even in the area? Surely you were ordered away along with our submarines."

"This is an Oscar-class, nuclear-powered missile submarine," Zirnov said, proudly. "We operate independently. Not even our government knows exactly where we are at any given moment. We received an urgent flash message about the damaged airplane and the planned rescue attempt. I believe someone by the name of William VanGelder contacted our embassy in Washington. They in turn contacted Moscow. My superiors suggested we try to assist. They had no idea if we could arrive in time, so nothing was said to your government."

Donovan nodded as the pieces of the puzzle fell into place.

"I'm glad we could be of service," Zirnov remarked, casually. "Now. Let's get you some dry clothes. We have a cabin you can use while you're with us."

"Captain, thank you for everything." Lauren hesitated; her brain was in overdrive. "Is there any way we could observe the effects the bomb is having on the hurricane?"

Zirnov rubbed his chin as he pondered the request. He looked at Lauren, then Donovan. "It is possible. But I am afraid I cannot allow you to observe the process; it is highly classified. But I could perhaps allow you to study pictures from our satellite...would that suffice?"

"That would be very gracious of you," Lauren said, warmly. "There's some legitimate concern that the experiment might not work. I'd be grateful for any information you could pass on."

"I will see what I can do. Now. Allow us to show you some of our Russian hospitality." Zirnov turned to one of the other officers and spoke briefly in Russian.

The officer nodded and casually saluted.

"My man will show you to your quarters. I believe there should be some dry clothes waiting for you there."

"Thank you, Captain." Donovan put his hand in Lauren's and followed the sailor down the narrow passageway. They traversed through two different compartments, the Russian sailors openly eyeing Lauren.

They stopped, and their escort pushed open a door. He gestured for them to enter. Donovan ducked through the opening, and with Lauren behind him, walked into the tiny cabin. It was stark yet functional—a single bunk folded out from the wall. There was a small desk with a reading light. A narrow locker reached from floor to ceiling. A pile of dry clothes and towels had already been set on the bed. Their escort saluted, then backed out of the room. They both heard the distinctive sound of a lock being thrown into place.

"I guess we know how far their hospitality extends." Donovan tested the door. It wouldn't budge. He turned and his eyes met Lauren's—the swell of her breasts accentuated by her rhythmic breathing. He moved closer and they embraced, kissing slowly at first.

"I can't stand not knowing," Lauren said, bringing her hands up to her face. "I have to know if it worked. I was just guessing about the targeting information. Oh, Donovan, what happens if it didn't work? What about Abigail?"

"She's safe." Donovan held her in his arms, this time to comfort her. "William will see to it."

A gentle knock sounded at the door. They heard Zirnov call out for them. Donovan went to the door and found it had been unlocked.

"Captain," Zirnov greeted him. "I think Dr. McKenna might be interested in these."

"Thank you." Donovan smiled and took the folder from Zirnov's hand.

"One last thing," Zirnov added. "We'll be underway soon and we won't surface for quite some time. So you're free to get some rest. I have a man stationed outside your door. Let him know if you need anything."

"We will," Donovan said and held the folder up. "Thank you again."

Donovan closed the door and waited for the click of the lock. Lauren came up from behind him and anxiously snatched the folder from his hands.

"I can't believe they got these so fast." Lauren sat down at the desk. She motioned for Donovan to come stand next to her.

"How'd they get them at all?" Donovan moved behind her, his fingers finding her shoulders.

"It's easy," Lauren explained as she opened the folder. "They float an antenna to the surface. From there, they can easily access their satellite system."

Donovan leaned closer as Lauren held up the first picture.

"Oh my God!" Lauren studied the first of the black and white satellite images. "Look at this. The resolution is amazing. They've blacked out some of the data. I'm guessing these are position and telemetry notations."

"Turn to the next one," Donovan urged.

"This is incredible!" Lauren nearly shouted out. "Look, you can see the eye right before the explosion. This small dot is the B-1; it's east of the eye so the bomb has already been released. In the next shot you can see the detonation. The pressure dome has risen above the eye wall, and the shock wave is stretched out in a concentric ring through the storm."

Donovan followed along as she explained each of the series of satellite photos. He could clearly see the vacuum left behind as the tremendous mushroom cloud roared into the stratosphere. That they were beneath the epicenter of the blast and survived seemed somehow impossible.

"Look at this one!" Lauren's excitement was building. "The eye wall is gone, as well as all of the significant weather surrounding it. I can't tell exactly how far from the eye the blast reached, but the bulk of the storm is gone—vaporized!"

Donovan took the last photo from her. A round chimney of water and other remnants from the explosion reached up from the surface and hung high in the atmosphere. The area around the blast was scrubbed clean of any clouds whatsoever. Helena had been gutted. All that remained of the most powerful hurricane in history was now only a few hundred miles of scattered showers.

"It worked!" Lauren shook her head in quiet amazement. "It really did work!"

"I'm so proud of you." Donovan leaned down and kissed her neck. "You're amazing."

"How long did the captain say we had?"

"Quite some time, was all he said." Donovan casually wondered how many American citizens had made love aboard a Russian submarine.

"Any idea where we're headed?"

"I didn't even ask."

CHAPTER SEVENTEEN

Donovan ducked through the hatch and stepped out into the bright sunlight. Lauren held his hand and followed him out into the fresh sea air. The deck of the submarine was steady in the slight ocean swell. Off the port bow sat the U.S. Coast Guard cutter, *Gallatin*. The rakish white vessel bore the Coast Guard's familiar red stripe on its forward hull. The American flag fluttered high above the pristine superstructure. Nearing the submarine was a small boat from the cutter.

He and Lauren both wore freshly laundered clothes, courtesy of the Russian crew. Donovan didn't know if he'd ever inhaled sweeter air. Somewhere in the distance, an Eco-Watch ship was steaming to recover Graff and the *Atlantic Star*.

The feisty submarine builder had earned his three million dollars.

"It's been a pleasure to have you on board, Captain Nash." Zirnov extended his hand. "And you, too, Dr. McKenna."

"Thank you so much." Lauren moved in and gave Zirnov a kiss on the cheek. "You saved our lives and for that we'll be forever grateful."

"I only returned a favor." Zirnov smiled. "Good luck and a long life to both of you."

Donovan reflected on the twenty-four hours that they'd been submerged. In that time, he and Lauren had come to enjoy Zirnov a great deal. The Russian was an intelligent and compassionate man. He hoped they'd meet again one day.

"Permission to come alongside!" a Coast Guard seaman called from the boat.

"Granted," Zirnov replied as he watched his men catch the bow line and secure the boat against the black hull of his submarine. Donovan steadied Lauren as she stepped down into the waiting arms of the Coast Guard crew. He followed once she was aboard.

"Welcome aboard, Mr. Nash, Dr. McKenna." The lead sailor smiled as a Russian seaman tossed him the mooring line. "I've got to say, this is a first for me."

"A few firsts for us, too." Donovan glanced at Lauren to see if she would get his double meaning.

"The helicopter went to pick up the remainder of your crew. They should be back soon."

Donovan turned and waved at Zirnov. His men were clearing the decks as they prepared the submarine to dive back into the depths of the ocean.

"He couldn't have been any nicer." Lauren waved also.

"I'm going to miss this life," Donovan said, wistfully. At some point over the last twenty-four hours, laying spent in the small bunk, he'd finally explained to Lauren about his past. He told her about the exposé that Erin was going to write. They'd talked briefly about where they might go…where he, Lauren, and Abigail could be safe.

"I know you will." Lauren wrapped her arms around him. "It'll be all right…somehow."

Donovan watched as they maneuvered up close to the Coast Guard cutter. The crew expertly pulled the small boat under two davits. The boat was secured and they were quickly hoisted up out of the water. Moments later, he and Lauren had their feet firmly on the deck of the ship.

"I'm Captain Gregory Scott. Welcome aboard the *Gallatin.* Do you require any medical assistance? Can I get you anything?"

Donovan shook the captain's hand and started to introduce himself and Lauren.

"No introductions necessary," Captain Scott replied. "Your reputations have preceded you. It's an honor to have you both aboard."

"There they go." Lauren pointed at the Russian submarine as it silently slipped beneath the water.

"They came out of nowhere and they left the same way." Donovan marveled as within seconds all trace of Zirnov and the *Voronesh* disappeared.

"I have strict orders to connect you with DIA headquarters as soon as you set foot on the ship." Captain Scott gestured for them to come with him. "This way, please."

Donovan and Lauren followed Captain Scott as he led them into the radio room. A seaman on duty connected them via satellite link to Washington. Within moments, Calvin Reynolds was on the line.

"Lauren. I'm so relieved you're safe. Are you okay?"

"Yes, sir," Lauren replied. "Donovan and I are both fine."

"I think you'll be happy to hear we recovered your computer in Bermuda." Calvin continued. "We have a suspect in custody and we feel confident we'll make more arrests in the coming days."

"Who was it?" Lauren felt relieved that the people responsible had been caught.

"The individuals will probably turn out to be just the tip of the iceberg," Calvin replied, "but we feel the trail will lead us back to our usual enemies in the Middle East."

"You do know that Carl is dead?"

"Yes, I was able to get a brief report from Brent aboard the *Atlantic Star*."

"What about Abigail? Did you find her?"

"She and your mother aren't in Newark. We're still looking."

Lauren looked up at Donovan. "I told her to get out of Newark, so who knows where they might be?"

"We'll find them," Donovan reassured her.

"I can't thank you enough, Mr. Nash," Calvin said. "What you accomplished was nothing short of a miracle. We at DIA will forever be in your debt."

"Sir." A crewman stuck his head in the door. "The helicopter is in range."

"Thank you," Captain Scott replied.

"Calvin, we have to go," Lauren said. "The others are about to arrive."

"Very well."

Lauren said goodbye, then the three of them climbed on deck to greet the incoming chopper.

In the distance, Donovan heard the unmistakable sound of a helicopter as it neared the ship. He scanned the horizon until he found the dark speck in the sky.

"Come with me. We'll meet them on the fantail when they land. We'll have to refuel the chopper before you can take off for Washington. But it doesn't take long."

The sound of the Coast Guard helicopter grew quickly as the sleek red and white HH-65 Dolphin swung around to set up for a landing.

"This way." Captain Scott raised his voice against the noise of the beating rotor. He led the two civilians aft to the helicopter deck.

"They don't know we survived, do they?" Donovan positioned himself and Lauren behind several armed men as the Dolphin hovered in close to the deck.

"They've been told nothing." Scott pulled his hat low as the rush of air from the helicopter swirled around them.

Donovan waited patiently as the Dolphin settled. Two seamen rushed out and lashed the landing gear to the deck. The whine from its two turbine engines began to wind down as the first person leaped from the helicopter. Dressed in a bright orange jumpsuit, Donovan knew it was a crewman from the Dolphin. The next out the door was Brent, followed by Michael.

Donovan and Lauren slid out from behind Captain Scott and walked toward the helicopter.

"Donovan?" Michael looked at his friend, then at Lauren. He stepped closer, as if he needed to get a better look at people he thought were dead.

"Michael." Lauren wrapped her arms around the shocked pilot.

"I thought you were—" Michael whispered. He was on the verge of tears. "I tried to make them wait but they wouldn't."

"We know." Lauren pulled away. "Your radio calls saved us."

"What?" Michael shook his head, his eyes narrowed as he tried to understand.

"A Russian submarine surfaced and rescued us," Donovan explained as he affectionately gripped the back of Michael's neck. "They heard your calls and knew we were in the water."

"Let me get this straight. You make me get on that dinky little sub with no bathroom, and you two get on a full-sized nuclear submarine? Don't tell me you had a shower and a hot meal, too."

"Something like that." Donovan smiled.

Brent finally found his voice. "I can't believe you're here. I'm so sorry I didn't protect you from Carl. I had no idea he'd erupt like that in the raft. I think when he realized he'd never make it into the submarine he completely panicked. Graff was going to dive. I did what I had to do...or he would have killed us all."

"We saw it all," Lauren replied. "You did the right thing."

"Randy." Donovan leaned into the helicopter and put his hand on the injured pilot's arm. "How are you?"

"I'm okay," he replied with a clenched jaw. "Though between airplanes, submarines, boats, and helicopters...I'm a little worn out."

"I think we all deserve a nice long rest," Donovan announced.

"Time off with pay?" Michael grinned, then motioned toward Lauren. "So...you two finally get it figured out?"

"Yes." Lauren smiled up at Donovan. "In fact, isn't there something you wanted to ask Michael?"

Donovan ceremoniously cleared his throat. "So, Michael. I was wondering...would you be the best man at my wedding?"

"Of course." Michael gave them both a wide smile. "Unless it interferes with my paid leave."

"I hate to break this up, but the helicopter is fueled and ready to go," Captain Scott interrupted.

"Randy," Donovan asked, "You got enough in you for one more helicopter ride?"

"Where to now?" Randy rolled his tired eyes.

"How about home?" Donovan was relieved to see Randy nod his approval.

"Yes, sir. Home sounds good."

EPILOGUE

Donovan breathed a silent sigh of relief as the Eco-Watch facility came into view. The Coast Guard pilot touched down gently on the concrete ramp. Donovan felt like he'd been gone for a very long time. Michael jumped out and ran across the ramp toward Susan. Their embrace warmed Donovan's heart. Frank and others were quickly there to assist Randy into the waiting ambulance.

Brent had said his good-byes in the helicopter and quickly dashed off to a waiting car sent by the DIA.

"You son of a gun!" Frank grinned and slapped Donovan on the shoulder. "You pulled it off."

Donovan returned the smile, then caught sight of William walking toward the helicopter. He knew there would never be words to thank his old friend for all he'd done. Donovan followed Lauren out of the chopper. He stopped and stretched his frame from the two-and-a-half hour flight.

"Welcome back, son." William reached out his hand.

"It's good to be home." Donovan returned the handshake.

"You remember Lauren?" Donovan pulled away from William and put his arm around her shoulders.

"Of course," William said, smiling.

"Hello, William," Lauren kissed the aging statesman on the cheek. "Donovan told me a great deal about you in the last few hours."

"All lies, I'm sure."

"Who in the hell do you know in the Russian government?" Donovan asked with great amazement. "You never cease to astound me."

"I think I called in every favor I had. After all the dust settles, I'll be working for free for the next ten years."

"Any word on the C-17 crew? There was an injured man; he's a Navy SEAL." Donovan voiced his concern about Buck and the others as they moved away from the helicopter.

"The crew is fine, and Lieutenant Buckley will live," William explained. "He suffered a broken collarbone, some fractured ribs, and a punctured lung. He's in a Navy Hospital in Norfolk."

"Where's Erin?" Donovan whispered. He had no idea what havoc she might have brought down on him since he'd left her.

"Donovan Nash! You rascal you!"

Donovan turned as Susan ran over and threw her arms around him. He saw Michael hold out his hands as if he were helpless to stop her.

"You two," she whispered as she hugged him. "When are you guys going to quit doing this to me?"

"Probably never," Donovan lied. He knew his days at Eco-Watch were over.

"You're probably right." Susan pulled away, then turned toward Lauren. "I'm Susan. Michael just told me. I'm so happy for you two."

"Thank you," Lauren said. "I never thought I'd get a marriage proposal on a Russian submarine."

"Take it where you can get it," Susan laughed, then reached for and held Michael's hand tightly. "I hate to hug and run, but I'm taking my husband home. He won't be in for a few days?"

"Make it a week," Donovan laughed. "He sank his airplane, and we're not sure we're going to let him fly the only one we have left."

Michael shrugged as Susan led him away. "I was just following orders."

Donovan, Lauren, and William walked toward the hangar. Donovan felt a little sad at the thought of the *Galileo* resting on the bottom of the ocean. One by one, the employees on duty came by and shook his hand and offered words of congratulation. He received a huge hug from Peggy, who he thought was going to burst into tears.

Donovan looked around and finally asked. "Where's the other airplane?"

"They called just before you landed." Peggy dabbed at her moist eyes. "The *da Vinci* will be on the ramp any minute now."

"There was a trip," William added. "Government business."

No sooner had William spoken than the high-pitched whine of a Gulfstream invaded Donovan's ears. The lone remaining Eco-Watch jet rounded the corner and taxied onto the ramp. It gave the departing Coast Guard helicopter a wide berth and rolled to a stop in front of the open hangar. The door swung down and Nicolas stepped aside to let out a passenger.

With an empty feeling in the pit of his stomach, Donovan saw Erin Walker start down the stairs. She smiled and waved as she saw the three of them. Donovan didn't return the greeting. A moment later, another person materialized in the doorway of the Gulfstream. Donovan was stunned as he recognized Lauren's mother, and in her arms was a little girl. Abigail was dressed in a pink dress, with a matching headband. Donovan's vision clouded as he laid eyes on his daughter for the first time.

"Hello, Donovan." Erin stood to one side so as not to block his view. "I brought you a present. Well, actually it was William who made it happen...but I managed to find them. Lauren's mother is a resourceful woman. She had taken Abigail from Newark to La Guardia. From there, they managed to get on a flight to Buffalo. It's where I found them."

"How did you...?" Donovan stumbled over his words. "I can't..."

"I'm an investigative reporter." Erin held out her hands. "It's what I do."

Lauren rushed to the foot of the stairs, hugged her mother, then took Abigail in her arms, smothering her with tiny kisses.

Donovan quickly went to Lauren's side.

"Look who I have here," Lauren cooed.

Donovan could plainly see how much Abigail resembled him. It was as if she'd stolen her looks from his own baby pictures. He reached out, hoping Lauren would let him hold his daughter. Without hesitation, Lauren gently placed Abigail in his arms. Donovan's throat constricted as he marveled at every small detail: her large blue eyes, her tiny hands and flawless skin. He breathed in the smell of her as he cradled her in his arms.

"She's perfect." Donovan looked up into Lauren's radiant face.

Without warning, Abigail started to fuss. Lauren instinctively reached out, but Donovan held his daughter protectively. He kissed her on the cheek and Abigail quieted almost immediately.

"Take your family home. You deserve a break." William looked in the direction of Lauren's mother. "Besides, you've lost your baby-sitter. Lauren's mother and I are going out to dinner."

Donovan shook his head. "There's so much to do right now."

"Not really. With Erin's help, the press has been dealt with. Your name won't be mentioned. She and I decided we'd let the military have the spotlight on this one. We'll call it our return favor to the President. I've already spoken with the insurance company, and they've agreed to replace the *Galileo.* But we can talk about all of that next week." William lowered his voice. "I've had my staff out at your country house. It's been cleaned, stocked with food, and I also took the liberty of having everything Abigail might need sent out and set up. I thought the three of you might like to get away...have a little privacy."

"Thank you." Lauren slipped her arm inside Donovan's. "Shall we then?"

"I guess it's settled. We'll be on our way." Donovan looked down at his daughter, then up at Lauren. "We do have some lost time to make up for."

"Donovan..." Erin motioned him aside. She waited until she had his full attention. She kept her voice low so as not to be overheard. "As promised, you gave me the front page story of the decade. The destruction of hurricane Helena is all anyone can talk about. I was there; I saw the explosion from the C-17. I'll never be able to thank you for that...except to promise you something."

"What's that?"

"You know that other story I was working on. The one about someone named Huntington. It turned into a dead end."

"Are you saying what I think you're saying?"

"The story will never see the light of day. I promise. And please, keep doing what you do best—don't ever leave Eco-Watch. I've said enough. Now go take care of your family."

Donovan looked over his shoulder at Lauren, then down at his daughter. "That I will."